MW00617873

But if you bite and devour one another,
take care lest you be consumed by one another.
–*Galatians* 5:15 (*NASB*)

I feign that devils can, in a spiritual sense, eat one another; and us.
Even in human life we have seen the passion to dominate, almost to
digest, one's fellow; to make his whole intellectual and emotional life
merely an extension of one's own—
–C.S. Lewis in Preface to *The Screwtape Letters*

For of all sad words of tongue or pen,
The saddest are these: "It might have been!"
– from "Maud Muller" by John Greenleaf Whittier

Condensed from the logbooks of Dr. Chase Callaway

Presented originally as a 5,450-page manuscript (plus supplementary material) to: Dr. Ray Divine – Director, Stereotactic Psychosurgical Unit, Matherville State Mental Hospital

CANNIBAL CLUB

For Debbie (& Bubba)
BFF
Ann Hollingsworth
a.k.a. John Alberto

Introduction by the Editor

Considerable backstory to *Cannibal Club* was revealed in *Nutshell* concerning the strange case of Dr. Chase Callaway and the equally bizarre case of Ivy Pettibone. As the primary architect in the assemblage of *Nutshell,* my role was mostly to gather twigs from several authors to create a facsimile of omniscience. Not so in *Cannibal Club* where I bestow the role of primary author to Chase Callaway, leaving myself as the "carving" editor whose task is primarily to slice away the fat, leaving the meat intact. Since more than 90% of Dr. Callaway's manuscript is, indeed, excessively overweight (longhand, typed or dictated), entire chapters and sections have been summarized or deleted, while sometimes leaving tracks in the sand as "Editor's note."

In a sense, this book could be considered epistolary, that is, composed of letters and documents; however, it is better described as a single, long petition. Supporting documents were excluded to meet the goal of brevity, though these are available upon request. Importantly, the epistolary feature focuses on actions, conversations, and ruminations, leaving the story somewhat barren when it comes to descriptive passages aimed at the reader's need to visualize the ambience.

But to jog the memory of *Nutshell* readers for characters brought forward, the Editor offers this listing:

Chase Callaway: 6'2" point guard in high school (2nd string in college), heavy lidded eyes spaced a little too far apart, thick shock of near-blonde hair, plus a wide and inviting smile. Completed surgical residency at Far West Texas University College of Medicine.

Wesley Callaway: 6'6" forward (a living legend in basketball at Far West in the 1930s). Chase's father. Retired physician.

Sukie Spurlock: Silver hair, caramel skin, one-quarter Comanche, three-fourths African American. Long-term employee and family friend of the Callaways.

Porter Piscotel: hawkish stare with slit-like eyes beneath a hooded brow. Premature thinning of pitch-black hair while in medical school (same class as Chase Callaway). What remains of the coiffure now is a horseshoe rim kept black with hair coloring.

C.C. Chastain: self-described Hobbit. Songwriter. Physician.

Ivy Pettibone: diminutive resident of the asylum with unintelligible speech, though without a recognizable psychiatric disturbance. Middle-aged and graying. Elfin face, ears out, close-set eyes, bowl haircut with cowlick, fused fingers (corrected surgically), club foot with severe limp, and her most unique feature – huge sublingual salivary glands rendering Ivy able to harness a steady stream of acidic saliva used as a defense weapon.... or, to spell out one word on absorbent paper, that is, the only word she can write: "God."

Backstory helps immensely in *Cannibal Club*, though it is not mandatory. In *Nutshell*, the reader walked in the shoes of Chase Callaway over multiple pathways in the medical education process, witnessing his insistence on excellence in the professional sense, while trending toward self-destruction privately. Readers might have already noted that this "emotional acupuncture" worked well to create pain in one spot while relieving greater pain in another. Growing further and further from the religious ideals of his youth, Chase still clung to magical thinking with metaphysical underpinnings, absolving himself of some measure of responsibility for his personal decline. Indeed, his growing belief that he was the 13th generation of a 13-generation curse began to affect him in all matters, with random coincidences donning a fatalistic cloak.

Dr. Chase Callaway was accompanied in the first phase of his journey by the strange case of Ivy Pettibone, institutionalized decades earlier at a mental hospital, based on multiple birth defects and her odd speech pattern. The connection between Chase and Ivy grew strong, revolving around the quest to repair the birth defects involving her hands, as well as using those hands to create music on the piano. Gradually, Chase realized that Ivy was apparently misdiagnosed as schizophrenic years earlier due to a lack of understanding by the psychiatrists regarding her special language. Ivy's backstory was told from revelations provided by Chase's grandfather, "Doc" Callaway, who delivered baby Ivy four decades earlier, prior to his colorful conversion to Christianity and full-time ministry. Ivy's role as Chase's figurative guardian angel eventually raised the question (for some) as to whether or not she might truly be a heavenly force.

At the conclusion of *Nutshell,* Chase Callaway was shaking the west Texas dirt from his boots and heading to California, leaving behind irate parents, frustrated friends, and his stunned, estranged wife. His geographical therapy was not for the purpose of practicing medicine, however. Rather, he was obsessed with resurrecting a career in songwriting that he believed had been taken from him through the plagiarism of a song he co-wrote with medical school buddy, C. C. Chastain. The stolen song became a mega-hit for the pirates, launching their careers. Chase could not shake the fact that someone else was living the life that would have been his (and C.C.'s) had it not been for the 13-generation curse.

Chapter 2 in *Nutshell* provided details from the genealogical research done by Chase's grandfather, Zebulon Callaway, with the technical help of Sukie Spurlock. Zebulon, too, came to believe that the 13-generation curse was real, based on recurring themes dating back to the 1600s. If so, his grandson would suffer through the 13th and final phase. Although it is simplistic to posit the origin of Chase Callaway's religious conflict as the product of his grandfather's altar calls, involving a youthful Chase as a staged "catalyst" at tent revivals, it remains a point to consider. Although Zebulon Callaway passed away before the events in *Cannibal Club*, his influence on Chase will persist to the end.

Chase Callaway's last conversation in Texas was an exchange with Sukie Spurlock, the Callaway's housekeeper, later a nurse, who helped raise Chase from childhood. Sukie's influence on Chase ran deep, and her parting words as he left for southern California were cautionary. She reminded him that, yes, he'd been born with a golden key that could open many doors, including the one to Paradise. "Yet, it's the same key that unlocks the Gates of Perdition."

And so it began.

1
PARABOLIC GENESIS

I have come to believe that all mental illness – including my own – is abstract and luscious, wrongly confined by the certitude of taxonomists who, more like taxidermists, stuff the dead with rubble. My condition, though crippling, is also the creative mother to the most profound developments in science.

Freud, a master of the neologism-taxonomy game, would have saddled me with "epistemophilia," an abnormal preoccupation with knowledge. Sadly, this word is all but lost today, missing even from dictionaries with the broadest of spines. Yet, Freud would have been wrong, for my obsession is not the arid collection of meaningless facts – it is the fusion of facts heretofore considered unrelated. You will steer closer to truth if you consider this as "creativity," but I prefer the archaic term "Newtonian synthesis." Ah, to harvest the grain of the autodidact.

Renaissance Man? Today, a washed-out phrase to denote a gourmand/oenophile who dabbles in watercolor, plays the cello, climbs mountains (or man-made rock walls), discusses books he plans to read, and does his own taxes. In its original context, though, it meant borrowing from the arts and the sciences to cross-pollinate, forging innovative technologies and new beauty. It meant the merger of science and creativity or, in today's parlance, "the right brain and the left brain," a process little understood by the half-brained who excel only in heartless taxonomy.

Of the various liberal arts in the palette from which one creates new color, my illness drew me into the ancient quadrivium – arithmetic, geometry, astronomy, and music – all recognizable as different faces of mathematics. Indeed, Johannes Kepler wrote music that was mathematically in harmony to the elliptical planetary orbits he described. So, like Pythagoras and those from whom he drew, I have grown to believe that all science, including biology and medicine, must be boiled down to well-cooked mathematics to confirm what is true and what is not. Of course, this has nothing to do with happiness or purported "mental health." Converting observations to mathematics merely separates truth from bias, an exercise that leads to wise anguish, not mindless joy.

That said, I cannot attest to the truth of this log, for it is the failure of numbers to explain all that has happened, which drove me into the current nest of my torment, where resides a covey of insatiable wants and musts. This log is the way I see it. Others would sharply disagree. Others would claim no absolutes at all when it comes to truth.

Like the man who spends fifty years until death building a miniature city out of pebbles found on his forty acres, my obsession has lifted me far away from cluttered civilization to cluttered minutiae. It is on this issue that I concur with a diagnosis of a madness of sorts, but madness more useful than the oblivious man who toils his life away in pebbled desperation.

You might think such grand obsessions are simply diversions of white noise to drown out the coming sound of death. Even in my youth, I theorized that philosophy was nothing more than thanatology wearing a fake moustache and goatee. Yet, no longer fearing death, even welcoming its lure, I am still at a loss to explain what happened – and why.

But you, as a neuro-interventionalist reading this petition, will want simple explanations packaged in the fewest number of vinegar-soaked diagnoses that fit into the straight-jacketed billing system. So, to comprehend my plea that cowers behind the words, I must start at the beginning, when I first knew myself to be different from others, albeit the same as some, equally pickled.

Even in my youth, as frivolous as it seems now, while trying to excel at my father's sport – basketball – my mind was in a different place. My parents thought me obsessed as they observed their son shooting baskets late into the night. Indeed, I was. I was obsessed with discovering the "perfect geometry" that would maximize a sphere going through a hoop, according to the laws of trajectory. My studies took me to the public library in Matherville where I traced the study of trajectory back to the science of wartime gunnery. After cannons were developed, it was the mathematicians who were summoned to calculate the correct elevation of the weapon to achieve the desired distance. Whereas Tartaglia was the father of this new science of gunnery, it was Galileo who demonstrated the parabolic path of projectiles.

In my 12-year-old mind, this was the key to overcoming the torture invented by Mr. Naismith – the perfect arc, allowing the greatest probability that the sphere would pass through the hoop. The sphere would "see" the hoop as an ellipse that changes shape continuously during its trajectory. Thus, the rounder the hoop (as perceived by the ball) the better, and therefore, my conclusion that a higher arc was key for scoring, even though the 45-degree angle, as per Galileo, was the key to distance. The whole idea was a miserable failure, forgetting the impact of the rim and the backboard. I was never the player my father was, a man completely ignorant of Tartaglia's contributions to trajectory. My B-plus skills in the sport shined more brightly due to my father's name, and though I made the team in college, I sat at the lonely end of the bench.

Today, as I write this log in contemplation of offering my help to forge a new trajectory in neuroscience, I see the extremes of my early tendencies that now threaten to paralyze. For instance, I'm writing in pencil, long hand, in a college-ruled notebook. This might seem ordinary and outdated. Yet, far from it to my mind's eye. I see the yellow color of my pencil as the Chinese expression of royalty and respect, knowing that the pencil manufacturers of the last century were communicating to their legions that the best graphite in the world came from China. Yet, inferior graphite could be bound with clay, as Thoreau introduced in his family's pencil factory. Too, I traipse back to the years of the lead stylus, on to the mysteries of papyrus, a lost art, then to the path forged by Tsai Lun in turning useless cellulose into paper a thousand years before such litter appeared in Europe. (*Editor's note: 6 pages are deleted here on papermaking and printing.*) Finally, I must force myself to see the words as words, for my visual cortex desperately wants to view chunks of graphite spread like caps of black snow on the mountaintops of pulp, as if looking through an electron microscope.

Is this insanity? If so, many of the ancients had my same disease. All of "us" are simply looking closely, perhaps to drown ourselves in the soup of the universe, while we search for its Chef. Both the telescope and the microscope, cousins to the cause, while shunned at the time of their invention as distorting reality, help us take an expanded view. We must remain en garde, though. If we limit our Chef to the role of "God of Mystery and the Unexplained," relying on our polished lenses to inspire awe, then our God will forever be shrinking as mysteries are solved, one by one.

On the heels of catastrophe, people demand explanations. Such musings don't need to be true if they serve to satisfy and heal. I hold a universal key but remain contemplative as to the lock I will choose. Regardless, I offer this log as explanation of my abiding dilemma. I concede "illness" in light of my self-imprisonment and the darkness of liberty. Since the resultant hypergraphia – no, graphomania – of my tangential thoughts reflect my attempts to look closer (micro-), or to look farther (tele-), commanding me to wax excessively, I will not always be able to restrain. *Divertissement*, as Pascal would have said. Diversion. Without diversion, there is no joy. With it, no sadness.

Editor's note: 33 pages are deleted as Dr. Callaway describes how Plato wrote in "Phaedo" about the Pythagoreans and their belief that the body was to be strung like an instrument to a certain pitch. Musical tuning and health drew many comparisons throughout history, and Dr. Callaway's log covers this ad nauseum.

While such miscellany might seem far removed from my tale, consider the early English novel *Tristram Shandy*, wherein author Sterne claims "exact justice" comes through <u>digressions</u> in storytelling. Digression. Diversion. *Divertissement*. Realism was, for Laurence

Sterne, created through omissions and distortions. For me, these techniques will come naturally as part of my illness. Paraphrasing Dostoevsky in "The Dreams of a Ridiculous Man," society may call me a madman now, but that would be a rise in my social position. Oh, how hard it is to be the only man to know the truth. But they won't understand that. No, they won't understand.

2
EXOSKELETONS

I have molted three exoskeletons. Thereby, three tales are shed. Each shell cracked and split, not from inherent weakness, but from the grotesque growth within, forcing a new organism to emerge. This log explains the three transmutations, charitable with words in one sense, frugal in another.

An entire generation of humans has perished since I shook the west Texas dust from my feet for the velvet touch of Pacific sand between my toes. But how foreign "I" becomes when considering metamorphosis. Does the moth flutter about its empty cocoon with a sense of kinship? To me, the Chase Callaway of 1980 might as well be a jellyfish. Or a zero, the non-existent centerpiece of mathematics. So, "I" becomes "he" until "I" can recognize itself.

Chase left Texas with a stain. He had been raised in a swirl of homegrown homilies provided by housekeeper/nurse/mother Sukie Spurlock who reverberated "sayings," foremost of which was, "Always be nicer than you need to be." The original Chase lived by this, without exception. Another: "Make yourself an honest person, and you can be sure there's one less rascal in the world." Chase lived by this as well, at least until the Collapse.

In his youth, he had enthusiastically served two lost populations – senior citizens and ownerless pets – by volunteering at a rest home (archaic understood) and the dog pound (also archaic), not to broadcast his own benevolence on a future resume, but without fanfare, even without admission. He had expanded Sukie's dictum into: "Be nicer than you need to be *and don't boast about it*." This modification came from his reading, at age twelve, a popular novel wherein a physician achieves mystical powers of healing through acts of kindness that are strictly anonymous. In the fictional story, these acts of benevolence were documented in an equally fictional "secret journal," for which the reading public yearned so greatly for it to be true that the author had to invent a sequel about the journal itself.

With light and gentle steps, Chase Callaway walked on clover. His charmed life was protected by the girl who became his wife, Olivia, known to all as Livvy. During Chase's tall and gangly days, Livvy had been the only girl to appreciate ears too large, nose too broad, and eyes too squinty, angling downward at the sides of his face as if melting. But years later, after marriage, those same features, now seasoned, had a more general appeal that took Chase to the precipice. With the self-realization of his gift, Chase let a stranger in. Others followed through the open door. So he left Texas with a stain, made worse by his pitiful claim, which he tried hard to believe, that he and Livvy would reunite once he was settled in California.

But he would never be "settled" in California. The young doctor's first job was a shocking experience. He had joined a satellite office of a large multispecialty group that had recently converted itself into an HMO. The acronym was new to Chase, so he was chagrined to learn that every time he wanted to perform elective surgery, or even to schedule certain tests, he had to appear before a so-called utilization committee composed of fellow physicians to plead his case. As it turned out, of course, these doctors were pioneers in what has since become cliché – less is more – the *less* done on Chase's part meant *more* profits for them.

"These docs are rationing health care!" he protested to his medical school friend C.C. Chastain, now a California baron who lorded over an emergency room empire.

"It's the beginning of the end for medicine," his friend replied. "We've been wasting money for years in medicine, and now the pendulum will swing too far the other way while costs escalate. Chaos is on the way, my friend. But no matter – we're going to be stars someday, so who gives a rip? We'll be out of this mess."

Once, rejection by the despised utilization committee prompted Chase to reflect. His request that a mammogram be performed prior to a breast biopsy was denied. At first, Chase was outraged. He had been taught to order mammograms prior to every operation on the breast. Yet, when asked by the committee to defend his reasoning, he couldn't. This only outraged him further. Mammograms were a new test at the time, and their role was ill-defined. Admittedly, he had never seen one yet. For a palpable lump, he would be removing it no matter what the mammogram showed. Then, if malignant, the only treatment option was mastectomy, again with or without a mammogram. After nine years of medical school plus surgical residency, a Master of Life and Death, he'd never once been taught to challenge authority or to ask "Why?" His surgical education had been all about technique and the preservation of dogma.

Editor's note: Writing almost 20 years later, Dr. Callaway launches a diatribe against the current construct of medical education where schools believe themselves lacking in either art or the science when, in fact, the two must be synthesized as one. 17 pages are deleted.

"Art" is not about bedside manner. It's about filling the cracks of science with mortar born from logic and philosophy, such as distinguishing association versus causation, and errors of *post hoc ergo propter hoc,* or *petitio principii.* It's a rare clinician who can thoroughly dissect a landmark study and "hold nature to the rack" as suggested by Francis Bacon.

Chase's assimilation into the surgical community in the San Fernando Valley was abruptly defined when one of the local surgeons, riding the hospital elevator with Chase, struck up a conversation. "To be fair," said the potential colleague, "you should know, Dr. Callaway, that you'll never be one of us, one of the guys, I mean, working for that HMO."

"What do you mean?" asked Chase, wondering how the surgeon knew his name.

"You've got the uniform all right, blue blazer and tan slacks, but you'll never get in the club. No offense intended, but you sound like you're from the south, which shouldn't matter but it does. Then, you add working for the enemy, an HMO, and frankly, it doesn't matter how good you are. The club is pretty much a closed shop in L.A., and as long as you're helping HMOs destroy medicine, you won't find a friend on staff. Not here at least. You appear to be a likeable guy, and I'm just giving you some sage advice. That's all."

Taken back, Chase was speechless. He recalled the adage from his mentor, Thatcher Nolan Taylor, MD: "If you're good, you can go anywhere." He would need to pull that phrase from its scabbard many times in order to win surgeons over with what he knew to be superlative skills. So, for his formal proctoring (direct observation by the senior surgeons on staff) during his probationary period, he selected the hardest cases possible.

．　　．　　．

A hulking presence stood behind Chase in the operating room, peering over the surgeon's shoulder at the operative field, the patient's neck laid open for exploration. Chase could hear the observer's throat-clearing tic that seemed at first to be a sign of disapproval, timed every 15 seconds. Once Chase realized it to be a nervous habit, unrelated to the operation in progress, he relaxed.

For this proctored surgery, Chase had picked one of the most humbling procedures, potentially, in the discipline of general surgery – the removal of a parathyroid adenoma. Four tiny parathyroids were usually present, hiding behind the thyroid gland, though any one of the four glands could be resting somewhere else in the neck, amidst a complex network of arteries, veins and critical nerves. When one or more of these glands, for whatever reason, transformed into a benign growth, still soft and small, they could wreak havoc, given their delicate role in calcium metabolism. If untreated over a period of years, the adenoma could run amok and drain the host of calcium, leaving the bones to melt and kidney stones to proliferate.

At this time in medical history, there were no reliable options for pre-op localization of the parathyroids. Instead, the standard approach was a potentially perilous search via dissection. Search and destroy. All four glands had to be identified since two, three or four glands might be causing the calcium problem. The procedure could humiliate even a master surgeon where, on occasion, the adenoma could not be found, sometimes resting behind the sternum due to an embryologic fluke.

Chase waltzed around the complex anatomy of the neck, while delivering a brisk discourse to the proctor, adding zest and pride to operative skill. He spoke of parathyroid physiology, embryology, pathology, calcium metabolism, and research strategies to locate pre-operatively which of the four glands might harbor the benign tumor, all while he skated around the neck, identifying three normal parathyroid glands. Then bingo for number four. "There it is, about the size of a pinto bean, not exactly where I would have expected." Chase removed the adenoma. Calcium metabolism would start correcting before the patient emerged from anesthesia.

Afterward, in the doctors' lounge, the senior proctor told Chase, "I realize you could have postponed this patient until after you passed your proctoring. You deserve an A+ for your guts alone, choosing a parathyroid case. Plus, you did an outstanding job. We have gray-haired surgeons on staff who would've struggled with what you just did. I looked at your first two proctored cases, and they weren't a walk in the park either. First, converting a failed Belsey that one of my partners did several years ago into a Nissen fundoplication for acid reflux, then secondly, you took on a large adrenal carcinoma that was a very difficult dissection that— well, I'm going to recommend no further proctoring. We usually proctor five cases, but since I'm the current Chief of Surgery, I'm saying you're done. Of course, the vascular guys are going to look at their privileges separately from general surgery, but welcome to the medical staff and the general surgery department. Now, how can I talk you out of working for that HMO? We have three main surgical groups here, and any one of the three would be interested in discussing a junior position for you after what I've seen."

It was on this day where the joy of medicine reached its zenith, then began a downhill trajectory for Chase, violating the principles of

Tartaglia and Galileo as the descent would continue for an insanely disproportionate 30 years. Three weeks up. Thirty years down.

⋅ ⋅ ⋅

"Dr. Callaway, we are somewhat surprised that you chose to request vascular privileges," said the chairman of the credentials committee, a peripheral vascular surgeon. "First, let me ask this— Was your residency program fully accredited? Where was your training again? Arkansas?"

Chase felt the blood drain to his feet, leaving only enough to flush his cheeks. "Far West Texas University. And yes, it was accredited. Dr. Thatcher Nolan Taylor was my chairman, recently elected vice-chair of the American board."

"Who?"

Chase couldn't believe they'd never heard of T.N.T. He groped for the right words to justify his request for vascular privileges. "I realize my case mix is pretty thin. I've done mostly aortic work and mesocaval shunts, but the principles are the same everywhere in the body."

"Well, the anatomy's not the same everywhere. I don't understand how you can finish an accredited program without having done a single carotid endarterectomy. And no fem-pops? This is remarkable, to say the least. Was there someone in charge of your peripheral vascular training? Did you have a vascular rotation, at least? Frankly, we don't issue new peripheral vascular privileges in California unless a surgeon has done a one-year fellowship, or at least can total up 12 months on a distinct vascular rotation during residency."

Chase felt himself a long, long way from west Texas. "Our program didn't really have a distinct peripheral vascular service. Nor a fellowship. We mixed vascular in with the rest of general surgery. And, well, the surgeon who supervised peripheral vascular, Dr. Dagmar – (Chase waited for a response to the name, but the three surgeons on the committee were blank-faced) – Brick Dagmar, he felt strongly about keeping vascular as part of general, and well, the carotid thing is a long story about a feud with the neurosurgeons, and then, he didn't like fem-pops as the initial approach—"

"You'd better call back home and deliver a strong message to this Dr. Whomever – and that message is that he is strangling his own residents, killing his own program." The committee members exchanged glances of dismay, some shaking their heads no.

Chase was silent.

"We're going to grant you privileges to do one vascular procedure – insertion of subclavian lines. That's a fairly new procedure, and minor as it might be, it can be tricky. Looks like you've done a hundred or so. That's impressive. Those of us who are old dogs in practice never learned the technique, so there'll be plenty of those for you to do."

Subclavian lines? A pain-in-the-ass procedure that you guys don't want to do anyway because it reimburses next to nothing, even though you can kill someone while doing it? So, you want me to be your scut king? To do your dirty work?

But what he really said was: "Thank you." Later, he thought: *There is a profound mismatch between the sales pitch of surgical training and what general surgeons actually do, at least in major cities. And the staff back at Far West are oblivious.*

Then, only two months into his practice with the HMO, word came from the CEO: "We're having cash flow problems. No elective surgery for the next three months at least, possibly as long as six months. Total moratorium. Emergency surgeries only."

The announcement was surrealistic – this wasn't rationing medical care, this was *denying* care. Up to this moment in time, he had never thought about personal income. As a doctor, he would always be comfortable. *Right?* Yet, if he stayed long-term with the HMO, after this first salaried year he would change over to a productivity formula for his income. If a moratorium like this occurred next year, he could find himself in a world of trouble. Unlike other surgical specialties, general surgeons didn't generate office income. Virtually everything came from procedures in the operating room. Thank goodness he'd seen this outrageous moratorium unfold when there was still time to check out options.

For the next six months, he was stuck in a windowless clinic, surgical skills rotting, Master of Toenail-trimming, Zit-popping, and Hemorrhoid-rubber-banding. Too, he began composing what would be his 10-page resignation letter, blasting HMOs and predicting the ruin of American medicine should they succeed.

The benefit came as he considered the fact that with time on his hands, drawing full salary, he could return to music and lyrics, while nesting at Hotel California where dreams could be hatched and launched – the seaside manor of C.C. Chastain, M.D.

3
PHYSICS OF CRYSTALS AND LIQUIDS – UNIFIED EQUATIONS OF STATE

C.C. lived only a half-mile away from Chase, but a world away in terms of comfort. Chase's breadbox apartment, sparsely furnished, kept his overhead to a minimum. One wall was floor-to-ceiling plate glass, a perpetual big screen view of the beach from a 13-story perch where the distant, breaking waves appeared frozen. A mattress-on-a-frame, a used couch, and a cheap rattan breakfast table from an import shop did little to suggest a home.

When the 56 cardboard boxes arrived from Texas, loaded with the books inherited from his grandfather, Chase converted the shipment into a stopgap solution to the stark décor. Sixteen boxes covered with a stadium blanket made a handy coffee table. Eight boxes on each side of his bed formed smart nightstands. Remaining boxes were stacked against the wall opposite the couch and, with planks of unfinished lumber that he'd found near the communal dumpster, Chase designed a TV stand and shelves. No boxes were unpacked, so the volumes breathed softly inside their cardboard shells.

At C.C. Chastain's beachfront villa, however, the salty air was not barricaded by airtight plate glass. Instead, the archetypal aroma of the sea squared every corner of the home, a constant reminder that the water's edge was only steps away, touchable. Music filled the room during waking hours, which sometimes extended through all 24 and beyond, while a subtle percussive backup was the surf playing endless cymbals with the sand.

For Chase, these crashing waves held special allure in the evenings, after curious drifters from the oceanfront walk, lured inside throughout the day by the music, were drawn outside at sunset by the nightly festival. Then, the majestic oak door to the castle was closed, the drawbridge raised. Through open windows, the nurturing surf reached its fingers inside to massage Chase's forehead, freeing him of the woes he'd left behind in Texas.

"No boring people!" C.C. would shout to the insiders as he filled everyone's glass. "Bobby Mondavi is our host tonight." As though reciting a passage from *The Great Gatsby*, C.C. would continue, "I only want interesting people in my house, night and day. People who do interesting things. Celebrities. Celebrities in vivo. Celebrities in vitro. But no *boring* people. That is, except for Chase Callaway, my touchstone. He's allowed in, only because he's a pseudo-celebrity ex officio, now in vitro, maybe de novo, even though most of his lyrics suck and he's the most boring sonuvabitch I know. More Bobby Mondavi for everyone! So says the Hobbit!"

From the nightly revelry came the founding of a fraternal order – Sigma Alpha Oceanfront, where the motto proclaimed: "La mort apres quarante sans celebrite," or "Death after forty without celebrity." Communal chanting of the motto seemed to add to the resolve of the regulars at C.C.'s., and with Mondavi cheering him on, Chase halfway believed they were all serious.

In such environs, revelations are bound to occur, such as Chase's proclamation, "You know, C.C., in medicine, we're simply restoring people to their normal state. Nothing exciting. Nothing particularly unique. Just getting them back to their *normal*. That's why the gratitude of our patients declines over time, especially when the bill arrives. But in music, we heighten the experience of life. Rapture, if you will. We take people to new levels, and the euphoric memory lasts. Gratitude lasts. People put musicians on pedestals for making them feel more wonderful than life itself. *That's* why music is so much more satisfying than medicine."

"Profound, my good Doctor Dipshit. Absolutely profound." C.C. swirled the wine in his glass before continuing. "But speak for yourself. When I save a life in the emergency room, I'm on my own high. I don't give a crap about gratitude from anyone. In fact, I generally don't even like the bastards I save. My highs don't depend on any freakin' pedestals."

C.C. held court from his grand piano, a black behemoth, joined always by its two ever-present sidekicks – a goose-necked microphone and a half-filled bottle of Bobby. A silver-sparkle Ludwig trap set and two Fender Stratocasters with amps rested in the corner of the living room for anyone able.

On the wall adjacent to a stone fireplace, an aspiring artist had painted an undulating musical staff with treble clef and dancing notes. Known as the Wailing Wall, aspiring talent thumbtacked their rejection slips into the plaster. Musicians, novelists, dancers, actors and actresses stuck their broken dreams together by turning despair to folly, mocking their own sadness through public decoration.

Yet, serving as mortar between these bricks of rejection were autographed photos of those who had indeed achieved a celebrated status. In a mere five years in California, C.C. had amassed on his wall more photos signed by stars than most Hollywood restaurants.

In the evenings, as the golden disc of the sun made a sizzling sound in its illusory dip into the ocean, nighttime "regulars" took over the ground floor of the three-story stucco mansion. What Chase found compelling about the post-dusk crowd was not the fact that most were doctors and nurses, but nearly all were aspiring to enter the arts. A gastroenterologist took acting lessons on his days off, a neonatal nurse worked part-time as a lounge singer, a cardiologist drafted unpublished novels – all of them and many more, wallpapering the Wailing Wall.

Chase felt himself among like minds. Back in Texas, he had thought that C.C. and he were the only dual-minded doctors in the world, joining music and medicine. Now, however, he was surrounded by a carnival of characters, all of whom kept Chase amused during his paid vacation from the cash-strapped HMO. After the oak door was secured every evening of every weekend, white crystals appeared for the revelers.

The plastic surgeons, of course, brought their own, but the rest of the crowd sponged off generous donors.

As sophomore medical students taking pharmacology, C.C. and Chase had been taught that this local anesthetic agent was non-addictive, a curious concept that prompted Chase's further study. "I just finished reading Sigmund Freud's *Cocaine Papers*," Chase offered to the crowd one night. "I'll bring it over next time and read some of the passages I've marked. It's amazing."

"What the *hell* are you talking about?" asked a pulmonologist who intended to become an opera singer.

"Oh, about five or six years ago, this guy compiled all of Freud's writings on cocaine. You know, Freud experimented with it to no end. He thought it might be the ultimate psychiatric panacea. For about three years, he wove the white stuff into everything he did. Played a big part of his interpretation of dreams. Like, one of the papers is 'The Dream of the Botanical Monograph' where he—"

"You've gotta line on the table, Chase, waiting for you. Shut up and snort."

How dearly Chase clung to this restorative hope in chemistry because, for him, the white powder served as a nuclear reactor of sorts, beaming clean energy – orange and red and yellow flames that fueled his thoughts, his creativity, his passions, his dreams. He was capable of so much more than he'd ever thought possible. He cranked out lyrics so fast that the riveting words seemed launched by a machine gun, with a slug of Mondavi to flatten both highs and lows. C.C. put the words to music in a matter of minutes, and they'd sing until morning, unfaltering, having achieved the unified equation, the harmonious chemical buzz from scientifically balanced liquid and crystal. Importantly, too, the chemistry turned the 1,200 miles to Matherville into 1,200 light-years, a comfortable chasm.

Yet, despite the duo's validation of talent several years earlier with their country hit (by proxy), stolen and released as "Demizin'," and in spite of Chase's success eons ago as lyricist for the New Bloods, the only thing that C.C. and Chase managed to create was more paper to be hung on the Wailing Wall.

But Chase made friends – that is, like-minded friends who refused to live in a heliocentric universe where medicine was the sun. Instead, these aspiring artists could look between the stone pillars on C.C.'s front porch and see the real sun pretend to disappear into the watery horizon every evening. Yes, these artists were mesmerized by beauty, and always ready to augment the experience through the physiology of music and the magic of physical chemistry, both of which could alter neurotransmitters and reveal a richer world.

Most of the doctors and nurses who frequented C.C.'s endless summers worked at the local hospital in Ciena. In spite of this suburb serving as a celebrity enclave, the hospital had shady origins and a questionable reputation still today. The tuned-in generation of doctors and nurses who belonged to C.C.'s entourage, however, were intent on improving the standard of care at the hospital.

Larry Gruber, MD, was a struggling playwright who still enjoyed the practice of medicine. A good friend of C.C.'s, dating back to high school, Larry had attended medical school at Far West Texas University, graduating a year behind C.C. and Chase. At C.C.'s urging, Larry had opened his internal medicine practice at the Ciena hospital where C.C. held the emergency room contract. Chase barely knew Larry back in Texas, remembering only his comb-over and his large-frame eyeglasses, but they became friends now through Sigma Alpha Oceanfront.

"You wouldn't believe the incredible saga going on right now at Ciena Hospital," said Larry, as he sipped wine on C.C.'s front porch, sitting with Chase. "Vascular surgery is abysmal there, with a kind of madman as the sole member of the department. Pulls strings to keep others out when new surgeons apply. Probably an addict, a recluse, and no one will pull the plug on the guy. The Department of Surgery is full of his old cronies from way back when maybe the guy was semi-normal."

"Amazing. For a place like Ciena? Unbelievable."

"Get this," said Larry. "The guy did three femoral-popliteal bypasses – count 'em, *three* – on the same patient, same leg, over the past few weeks, first using the patient's own vein from the same leg – bad choice – then a vein from the opposite leg, and then an artificial graft. But the leg had been totally dead from the git-go! Then, he takes the patient to the O.R. three more times for debridement, rather than amputation, all while insisting the leg was still alive. He's yelling at the physical therapist to "walk" the patient down the hallway by forcing the bare bones of the lower leg forward with each step. The physical therapist was threatening to turn the surgeon into the medical board for the horror – creating a skeleton leg between the knee and foot, all while denying reality and claiming heroic efforts at limb salvage. Can you imagine his fees on six trips to the O.R? And he's not done yet."

"Do you think the leg was dead when the patient first presented to the E.R.?" asked an incredulous Chase.

"No doubt. The nurses in the E.R. asked me to double-check because they wanted the referral to go to someone who would amputate, avoiding Dr. Nut Job. I couldn't get a Doppler pulse anywhere and the color was ugly. This wasn't an acute embolus, and it wasn't an acute thrombosis on top of chronic disease. Too late for all that conjecture. It was gangrene. Then, Dr. Psycho gets a tip-off from his spy in the E.R, and he pushes his way into the case. He orders arteriograms. No run-off. Zero. Nothing to tie into downstream. One option from the beginning – amputate.

"And to think – I couldn't get vascular privileges at my current hospital in the Valley because of inadequate training that didn't reach the California standard."

"Obviously, there's a double standard," said Larry, wiping perceived powder from his nose.

"I've never heard of anything like this."

"Sorry to say, the quality at Ciena Hospital is still spotty. I'm in a multi-specialty group, though, where everyone is highly credentialed, and I have no qualms about referring to the others in my group. If I get a peripheral vascular case, however, I send them directly to UCLA."

"So, who's doing the general surgery in your group?"

"Funny you should ask. He's the founder of the group, but he's retiring soon. A bit on the senile side, so everyone my age is excited about fresh blood. But I think they're stymied right now, with one faction wanting one guy, another faction wanting another, and a third faction wanting no one in particular allowing each doc to refer on their own. The surgeons they're talking about, however, are ho-hum, and no one seems excited about the options. Trust me, no one is in the same league with you, Chase."

Wheels began to turn in both heads simultaneously.

"Maybe I ought to consider moving my practice to Ciena," Chase said, putting out feelers.

Larry echoed, "Maybe you ought to move your practice to Ciena. Yes. That's it."

"Working for this HMO is giving me the creeps," said Chase. "If they pull a stunt like this next year, I'll be cooked. I'm making payments back in Texas to my wife, not alimony, at least not yet. Plus, I send support to an old family friend, Sukie Spurlock, where I owe a huge debt. With no savings, I can't risk a surgery moratorium."

"Chase, you'd be great at Ciena. The docs aren't going to know anything about you since you didn't train here, of course, but I'm sure we can tap into that legendary status from Texas. If you're serious, let me do some politicking. I've been out of the loop since I didn't have a strong opinion on this retiring surgeon, but as I understand it, there's a fair amount of heat in the smoke-filled rooms. I'll check it out."

"What if your group says 'no? Do you think that I'd have a chance on my own? If surgery is so weak there in Ciena..."

"Not a chance, my friend. Your super-star talent will mean nothing. As crazy as it sounds, the medical staff is a closed shop, and the only way they'll even give you an application is if you're aligned with someone on staff already. The Chief of Staff carries the applications in his briefcase. How about that! He's afraid the secretaries in the office might slip up and give one accidentally to a solo practitioner. But if The Group, as we're called, invites you to join, you'll be on the medical staff immediately, with office space, personnel, and a low-interest loan if you need it."

"Let's go for it," said Chase. They toasted their wine glasses, congratulating each other on their splendid vision.

That night, prematurely celebrating the potential of a real job, a lucrative practice, Chase lost track of his normally well-calibrated crystals and liquids. The Group opportunity was too good to be true – 25 primary care physicians plus sub-specialists, all referring to a single general surgeon! Instant practice. Instant security. Celebrity locale. Things were looking up.

As C.C. banged away at the piano, Chase couldn't get his mind off the chance of a lifetime. Yet, as the hours passed and chemicals swirled, Chase finally called it quits and headed out for his apartment. Although he would probably fall asleep quickly, he wanted get home to "mellow out," surrounded by his grandfather's books, while staring at the night sky through the plate glass wall.

This is the beginning of something great, he believed, *and I'm going to need to get my act together. I think God is opening a door for me, and I'll need to stop the chemicals, I'll need to bring Livvy out here so that we can undergo counseling, and I'll need to get back on track.*

He only had six blocks to drive, reasoning it would be okay since the back streets were empty at this time of night anyway. So, he climbed into his Cutlass and began navigating the narrow roads of the beachside community, his head swimming.

At a traffic light, yellow it seemed, he goosed the accelerator, only to feel a thud and hear a scraping sound. In his rear-view mirror, he saw the headlights of another car sitting sideways in the intersection. He pulled off the road. Once out of his Cutlass, he realized the other car was a whale of a white Cadillac, its bumper drooping.

An elderly couple, dapper in evening attire, stepped out of the Cadillac. The man was tall, grandfatherly, and sported a checkered fedora, while the woman was rotund in a glittery dress, her neck choked by pearls. Below her glitter, two stick-like legs were hobbling precariously on stiletto heels. *I wonder if they're hammered, too. They sure look it.* Almost on cue, the woman began to moan, though the low-speed accident could not have caused any physical harm to anyone.

Her partner comforted her as Chase approached.

Chase offered the first words. "Gosh, I'm sorry, I thought I could make it through the intersection without any trouble. Hardly anyone on this street at this hour."

In fact, he wasn't sure he was at fault. He hadn't seen the light turn red for sure, though he didn't beg the question, aware that his judgment could be limited.

"Looks like your car took it worse than ours," said the elderly man.

Chase hadn't thought about his own car, but when he spotted the gouge from his front fender all the way to the back, a peculiar anger began to swell. His Cutlass was new. This wasn't the old blue Cutlass that he drove for nine years in medical school and residency. The burgundy Cutlass was a present from his dying grandfather, a reward for finishing his surgical residency. With Livvy hanging on to most their "stuff" back in Matherville, this car was, in fact, his only valuable asset and a link to the memory of his grandfather. Chase was furious. At himself.

"Let's exchange information," said Chase, his voice starting to tremble. "I've got insurance that should cover both cars." Admitting fault without certainty, appealing to their apparent decency, Chase hoped they would overlook the fact that he was so snockered he could barely stand up.

Another car slowed as it approached the accident scene. The glittery, rotund woman stopped moaning. Chase looked up from his open wallet where he was in a fumbling search for his insurance information. A junky Ford Fairlane with spray-painted graffiti on the doors came to a stop near the accident scene. Four Latinos stared at him from the car with mask-like complacency when, suddenly, one of them jumped out, ran toward Chase, and grabbed the wallet from his hands.

Without considering other options, with animal reflex, Chase ran after the kid and tackled him from behind. Then, muddled chaos. A fist smashed into his mouth, and he tasted blood. Chase swung back. Riveting pain shot up his elbow. He stood up. Something struck him again, and he felt himself falling backwards into another collision. For some reason, the elderly woman in the stiletto heels was on the ground, screaming and squealing. Then there was the ambulance. He couldn't figure out what the ambulance was for or who had called it. That's all he could remember. His mouth wasn't bleeding anymore. The robbers were gone. His right hand was swollen and purple, but no need for the ambulance. Darkness.

The next day, Sunday, alone in his apartment, the telephone rang to wake him near noon. His right hand was twice normal size, and his knuckles had disappeared. The useless paw couldn't lift the telephone receiver. With his left hand, he answered the phone whereupon a man identified himself as the driver of the Cadillac. With a calm and friendly tone, the man explained that when Chase had fallen backward in the fight, he had knocked the man's wife down, and that she had twisted and broken her ankle. After her ambulance trip to a nearby hospital in Santa Monica, it had taken a surgical procedure to repair the damage. He merely wanted Chase to know.

Chase was grateful that, if this nightmare had to occur, it had happened with such an understanding, pleasant gentleman. Chase sent the woman flowers in the hospital, along with an apology note. Additionally, Chase thanked the Lord for this wake-up call. Clearly, he had lost his way. No matter who might have been at fault initially at the intersection, the truth was, if he had been crystal and liquid-free, the accident would not have happened, and certainly not the fight afterward. Thankfully, Providence had delivered this message loud and clear. *All things work to the good.*

As he looked at the same swollen hand that had once struck a wooden stud, in lieu of his father's jaw six months earlier, he realized how much more this could have damaged him at any other time of his life. Knuckles were broken, he was sure, but it didn't matter. He was not performing surgery right now anyway. What were the odds of that? What were the odds of a surgeon being paid *not* to operate? Well, the odds were infinitesimally small. Clearly, the Lord had telegraphed this opportunity to get his life in order.

It was an odd epiphany, for sure, but Chase swore off alcohol and cocaine and recklessness and wanderlust and plain old lust. It was a day of reckoning. He had learned his lesson. From that day in medical school when he had fled participation in a Bible study to this very moment, his faith had been on a downhill slide. However, the slide would end now. This was a new start. He would contact Livvy and begin the counseling process he had once promised her. He would stop dreaming of lyrics that might rescue him from an enemy unknown. Furthermore, he would make sure that this enemy was not his Creator.

4
IN DARK WOODS

"I can't believe how lucky I was to fall into this." Chase Callaway spoke into the phone while staring at the countless sailboat masts that formed a nautical fence along the ledge of his office window. "Smack dab in the middle of celebrity city. You woulda thought the top surgeons in the country were right here, Frank, but it's just the opposite. I mean the worst guy in our program at Far West would be a star out here."

At the other end of the phone was Franklin Cooper, one of Chase's former junior residents, now a Chief Resident at Far West Texas. The newly successful and celebrated Dr. Callaway had a mission in mind – to lure his old friend, of like mind and skill, to join him next year as a partner. "I can't tell you how much fun it is out here. You really can't even go to the grocery store without seeing someone famous. And they all need doctors, of course. You've gotta come check this out."

"Sounds great, Chase, I knew you'd get some traction once you got out of that HMO situation," Franklin said. "I'm intrigued, for sure."

"I really fell into a gold mine. Being the surgeon for this group, why, it's turned me into the busiest general surgeon at the hospital, like overnight. Of course, it's all just billings right now, but from this first month alone, I'm gonna clear what a resident makes in a year. I can tell already that I'll need a partner. This group provides everything. Really, you need to—"

Larry Gruber, the internist who had sponsored Chase's entry to The Group, burst into Chase's office, his face twisted and squeezed in anguish. "Hang up, Chase."

"What?"

"Hang up." Larry seemed desperate, life or death. Clearly, he needed Chase's help – pronto.

"Look, Franklin, I'll call you back. Something's going on here. Must be an emergency."

Larry Gruber started to sit down, but he couldn't. He paced as he tried to start a sentence, only to choke back each time. Finally, he blurted, "They want you out, Chase. Out of The Group. Now. Out of the office. Out of the city."

Some words are so foreign they simply won't register, no matter how many times they are repeated. No matter how many years go by. Chase blubbered something, trying to catch his breath at the same time. "Are you...what...you've got to be...what are you talking about?"

"You flunked your proctoring. The hospital credentials committee is jerking your temporary privileges. I should have seen it coming. Shoulda seen it. I had no idea what a fight was going on inside The Group as to who the new surgeon would be."

"Flunked my proctoring? This is nuts. Every one of my cases went perfectly well. And that was just the first week. Since then, everything's gone fine, too. Well, gosh, there was that ninety-year-old with perforated tics. She died, of course, but that was expected..."

The gravity of the situation started to settle in, then a veil lifted as Chase recalled how Larry had, early on, called him on the phone, strangely nervous, after each of the proctored cases to check on how things had gone. "Fine, of course," Chase had said. "It was just a routine gallbladder. Why?" Larry's interest at the time had seemed overly cautious. After all, no one flunked proctoring. It was a formality. A tradition. Until now.

Larry continued, "Your proctors, all three of them, flunked you. Our group found out today. The Group thinks it's better to nip this in the bud before something *really* bad happens. We just had a meeting, and—" Larry choked on his words again.

He looked as though he were about to cry. "Chase, I'm sorry. I've done this to you. It's my fault. I had no idea how strongly some of these guys in The Group felt. Dr. White, you know, has a pure obesity practice, and he wanted *his* obesity surgeon – not you. You told him in your interview that you wouldn't be doing bariatric surgery, which pretty well sealed it against you. And when these proctors heard White talking about how he didn't agree with The Group's choice, namely you, I think the slime ball surgeons on staff got together and, well, ganged up on you. You know how people get when there's an open wound and everyone starts sniffing blood. Of course, that dimwit Cramer who proctored you on the gallbladder never even completed a surgical residency, so what the hell does he know? He joined in the crucifixion, I guess, because you were so busy, busier than he was after thirty years of practice. And Monte Schoenheidt, well, turns out he was bucking for your position with The Group, and he—"

"Wait a minute, Larry, this is just too freakin' obvious. There's got to be a way to sort all this out. If something bad had happened in the O.R., or afterward, it would be different, but—"

"Cramer's telling everyone that you took a gallbladder out backwards."

"Backwards? Jesus H., there *is* no backwards. I took it out from the fundus down to cystic duct, which is, by the way, the safest approach. You can take it out either direction. Crazy, though, now that you mention it, do you know what that old fool said to me during surgery? He says, 'Gee, I've never seen it done that way before.' Do you realize how incriminating that is? For *him*, not me. The freakin' idiot never got boards because he never qualified for the exam. He was a G.P. grandfathered in, with only a year of surgical training in some godforsaken country. He fee splits for referrals with every sonuvabitch in Southern California, and he's got the goddam audacity to criticize me?"

Shock surged to anger, and Chase felt his entire body turning rigid, as though preparing for a physical assault. He clinched his fists over and over, ignoring the pain in the knuckles of his right hand, injured in the midnight brawl several months earlier.

"It doesn't matter what the jerks did, Chase. I'm sorry. You're out. The Group already voted. Maybe you oughta just – I don't know – go back to Texas. I'm sure the HMO won't take you back after your hot letter. One thing for sure, these guys aren't going to let you practice in Ciena. The Group runs this part of town, and they'll make it miserable for you if stay in the area, even at another hospital. They don't want the extra competition for the surgeon they'll eventually recruit."

"I'm not going to sit here and take this, Larry. I'm not budging. If I have to, I'll open my own shop, but I'm not gonna let a bunch of lies ruin my career. There wasn't one freakin' thing out of the norm in my proctored cases. And nothing out of the norm since. I'll be damned if I'm gonna let a bunch of half-wits judge me. Do you realize none of these so-called surgeons, these jackass proctors, would make it for one minute in Matherville? They'd all be booted out. I'll take the worst surgeon there over the best here."

"Schoenheidt said that when you converted that Billroth-2 to a Roux-en-Y, it was the worst thing he'd ever seen in the O.R."

"You've got to be kidding! That fucking liar. The abdomen was rock solid with adhesions, and I did that case with so much finesse I impressed myself. I didn't get into the bowel one freakin' time. I'd like to see *anyone* do that. Plus, the patient did beautifully post-op. Her bile reflux symptoms that she'd been living with for ten years disappeared overnight. I was amazed. And you wanna know who did her original B-2 surgery that gave her reflux gastritis in the first place? That lying bastard Schoenheidt!"

"You do realize, don't you, that he was the leading candidate for The Group's new surgeon? I shouldn't have dragged you into it. I didn't have any idea how committed the members were to their own surgeons. I got you voted in by casting you as a tie-breaker."

"A tie-breaker? I'm not leaving this town, Larry, or this hospital. I won't be slandered by a bunch of freakin' incompetents that aren't even in the same league with me. That's the damnedest thing of it all. A backwards-freakin'-gallbladder, I can't believe it. And after the crappy surgery being done in Ciena that I've heard about from you guys, then this hellhole has the nerve to criticize *me*? I'm staying put, and you can rest assured I'll be a thorn in the side of these jerks for the rest of my life."

"You have no idea of the power of The Group, Chase. I mean, they even control office space around here. You might not even be able to set up shop – in a medical building, that is. Where do you think you'll go? These guys have their fingers everywhere."

"Doesn't matter. I'll find a way."

Words played in Chase's head – "You'll never work in this town again" – a phrase borrowed from Hollywood, perhaps the closest he would come to the dream.

Thoughts along the way:

I don't know what I'm going to do. I've got payments to make back in Texas. I'll need to take out a loan. I'm going to be living off one month's billings for a long time. When I told Larry Gruber I was going to stay here anyway, I thought I could work at the hospitals in surrounding suburbs, but it turns out that all the good hospitals have closed medical staffs. Tick-tock, the game is locked. Closed to new doctors, helping to get rid of the doctor glut in southern California. I've never heard of such a thing. Couldn't even get an application. Friends back in Texas don't believe me. Of course, by joining The Group, I got an automatic staff appointment here in Ciena, but those privileges will be jerked before I have time to respond to that ambush proctoring.

"Look, I don't care what you say, Chase. You're up to your neck in shit soup, my friend. Your buddy, Larry Gruber, didn't do you any favors. He promoted you as God's gift to surgery, and then pushed you onto The Group. Some of the guys had their own pick, by the way. I don't know how to judge a surgeon. I'm not in the operating room to see what goes on. We internists have to rely on what we hear from people we trust. And we heard from surgeons we trust that you're below par, maybe even dangerous. Like I said, you're in it up to *here*." The diminutive physician held his flattened palm to his own chin to accent his words. Chase wanted to yank Dr. Steve Emory's arm from his body, then beat him to death with the bloody end.

"I really can't believe this is happening, Steve. I'm going to tell you something now – my Chairman at Texas, Thatcher Nolan Taylor, is one of the foremost surgeons in the country, and he told me when I left Texas that I'd likely be the most successful surgeon that he ever trained. How do you reconcile that? How can you not give me a chance to prove this is all a bunch of garbage?"

"I've heard that you're going around saying this-and-that about Texas, but none of us have even heard of this Thatcher What's-His-Name. None of the *surgeons* have ever heard of him either, my friend. So I'd advise you to quit saying you were trained under one of the top surgeons in the country. It's only making you look worse. Furthermore, we're not terribly impressed by your medical school. I mean, is Far West Texas even accredited? You're up to here, my friend. Up to *here*."

Chase was stunned at the callousness of Dr. Emory. Until this moment, Steve had always been one of the friendliest in The Group, to the point where Chase hoped they might become social friends someday in addition to colleagues. Chase had already performed two successful operations on Steve's patients, and they were both happy and well. Steve had told him personally they had raved about their care. How did Steve flip the switch toward such disdain? And so quickly?

Despite his determination to fight back, Chase felt disconnected, estranged from himself, lost with no right road in sight. In dark woods. He pleaded with God to save him from this tribulation, a black canopy of surrealism that Chase was afraid might be infinite in its reach.

Chase roamed the halls of the hospital, a pathetic specter, hoping to grab a fair and listening ear. There were none. Not in the doctor's lounge where he was a pariah. Not in the cafeteria where he seemed contagious. Not in the parking lot where he waited for hours trying to buttonhole anyone who'd listen, pretending he'd just driven up in his damaged Cutlass. He was untouchable. Rage swelled. In preparing for all the stressors that life has to offer, this was not in the mix. He had no tools available to cope with such a foreign crisis.

Two weeks after his eviction from The Group's office, Chase saw Dr. Schoenheidt climbing out of his Mercedes in the parking lot, one of the proctors who had spread venom. Chase approached him, not knowing if he were going to strangle the slandering scum or merely launch a verbal assault. Or, perhaps he could be civil.

"Monte, that case you proctored me on, the Roux-en-Y on Mrs. Elliott. You know, she did perfectly fine after surgery, and all her symptoms resolved. I'm having some real trouble understanding what you've been saying about how things went in the operating room."

The surgeon hunched his shoulders, squirming, then he craned his neck while his eyes fell to the ground. "I couldn't follow what you were trying to do in the O.R.," he said. "It was, well, the anatomy was, well, yes, there were bad adhesions, I admit, but I didn't think that you, uh—"

"If anything, what I did was rather remarkable, to get through that entire case without a single enterotomy. I didn't nick the bowel once. *Nothing* went badly, considering how horrible the adhesions were."

Chase's quivering voice betrayed his rage, and it seemed that Monte sensed it. The proctoring surgeon had made an error by predicting doom the day of the operation. Now, two weeks later, the patient was home and reporting that she hadn't felt so good in years.

Dr. Schoenheidt said, "Look, I'm going to tell you something you may not know. The Group offered me your position before they gave it to you. You were *second* choice. Ever since old Tompkins went senile, I've built my practice around that group's cases."

"So why didn't you take the position?"

"Because they don't stay loyal to one surgeon like the days when Tompkins was in his prime. They're not a block referral source anymore. Tompkins formed The Group forty years ago, just to generate referrals for himself. But now, internists run The Group, and they refer wherever they want. So, even if I joined that group, with their god-awful monthly overhead fees, twice what I'm paying now, mind you, I wouldn't pick up enough cases to justify it. Plus, that group generates only fifty percent of my income. So, I'm supposed to start paying their extortion fee that they call overhead, yet I don't get enough extra cases to cover it? What's more, if I joined them as an official member, I'd lose my outside referral sources since other docs don't like The Group. It was a lose-lose deal for me."

"But when you told them 'No' you must have known they were going to bring in someone else?"

"Not at all. I thought things would be status quo. No group surgeon. Just a group of primary care docs and several specialists. I didn't know anything about you. Your friend Gruber told me to hurry and make up my mind about joining – gave me a forty-eight-hour deadline, by the way, *forty-eight hours* – but I didn't know what he had up his sleeve. After I declined, he sprung you on The Group at the last minute."

"I'm sorry for that. I had no idea about the politics here. But do you see what's happening to me? I don't deserve this."

The surgeon lifted his eyes from the ground and drove them into Chase: "Look, Callaway, I just bought a brand-new house, and with my caseload plummeting the past month since you've been here, I'm not going to be able to make my payments!"

Chase backed away, sensing danger beyond his imagination.

• • •

"It's a little hard to explain, Livvy, but I'm having to put our counseling on hold for a while. There's the cost of your airline tickets and the counselor and, uh, I've run into some trouble."

"Ohhh?"

Chase tried to explain the bizarre politics in terms of a machine gun nest he'd stumbled onto, the barrel pointed at him, firing relentlessly.

"Maybe the Lord's telling you to come back to Texas, Chase."

"This will follow me the rest of my life if I don't fight it. Don't you see? These people have ruined my reputation in one fell swoop. Nine years of medical training for this? To be bushwhacked by a bunch of no-talent scum my first month in private practice? I couldn't live with myself if I let them beat me."

"Come home, Chase. Those doctors are playing by a different set of rules, don't you see?"

"I can't come home now, Livvy. I'm sorry. I'll get it straightened out. It's so ridiculous it ought to be laughable, if I weren't hanging from the gallows, that is. And, another thing, I know I told you I'd be able to send enough money to cover your expenses above what you're making..."

Editor's note: Omitted here is a 72-page document entitled, "The Five Proctored Cases of Chase Callaway, M.D.," which Chase used for his defense, distributing the document to the leadership at Ciena Hospital, requesting re-instatement of privileges, if only to serve on the general surgery call panel for the emergency room. The five cases are each discussed in detail, presenting the medical facts, the supporting literature, and a detailed accounting of each procedure and all outcomes.

In addition, he procured and copied the stellar reports from his proctoring at the hospital in the San Fernando Valley the summer past when he began work for the HMO. There, one could read viewpoints at the opposite extreme from Ciena Hospital, coming from surgeons who would have much preferred to criticize the "HMO surgeon," yet they rendered nothing but accolades. Then Dr. Callaway took off the gloves, so to speak, offering sideline vignettes and provocative quotes such as: "Look, Callaway, I just bought a brand-new house, and with my caseload plummeting the past month since you've been here, I'm not going to be able to make my payments!"

But the major coup was a letter of recommendation that set minds to wondering if the young Dr. Callaway might have been given a premature burial – not a letter from Dr. Thatcher Nolan Taylor back home in Texas (Chase was too embarrassed to ask), but from one of the most prestigious surgeons in the country, the Chairman of the Department of Surgery at one of Southern California's finest medical schools, the same surgeon who had first encountered Chase four years prior, during the latter's fellowship in pathology where the two had met over the double-headed microscope to diagnose a mucinous breast carcinoma (without a pathologist present). "The Chairman's Word" on any surgical subject was considered divine, and the final page of the document was a letter with these Words: "Dr. Callaway's method of removing the gallbladder from fundus to cystic duct is, in fact, the preferred method. To suggest anything else, or to propose that there is only one way to remove the gallbladder, calls into serious question the credentials and/or motives of the critic."

5
HOMUNCULUS

Over the next few weeks, Chase became a pitiful beggar. He crept from office to office of "non-Group" physicians in Ciena, pleading his case, distributing his 72-page document, imploring the staff physicians on the Credentials Committee and E.R. Call Panel Committee to grant him temporary, limited privileges. Decisions, however, were postponed from month to month.

He solicited office space as well. Nothing available. Even non-group physicians would say, "If you end up getting privileges, then check back with us."

His back-up strategy was to relocate his practice to a nearby city and work his way back into Ciena. Of the countless suburbs in Southern California, however, Ciena was a diamond surrounded by desert. From suburb to suburb, Chase traveled farther and farther from the ocean, with a folded newspaper in his lap, opened always to ads that read: "Medical Office Space For Rent." The available space, however, was either in strip malls where stucco facades cracked and flaked, or in crumbling office buildings landscaped with sickly palms dressed in soot-covered leaves, choking in the smog.

One day, after exhausting the newspaper ads and deciding to forge beyond his original one-hour radius from Ciena, he stumbled on a small hospital dressed in brown and boring brick, one of countless similar hospitals in Los Angeles with a presence generally unknown. He stopped his still-dented Cutlass at the nearby street corner where a coin-operated newspaper rack stood as a lone sentinel, offering perhaps a fresh crop of ads for office space. The hospital's name – Saint Augustine's – was displayed on the building in metal letters, each of which was weeping rust at its supporting bolts. The second 'A' was dangling upside down.

After he parked, he was surprised to feel grit blasting his face and filling his nostrils with the redolence of west Texas. Minimal greenery, no flowers, and no grass, exposed what nature had originally intended for this landscape without irrigation. The wind was odd, though. It wasn't a seaside breeze, of course. Too far inland. And, the Santa Anas weren't blowing. How could a Southern California suburb be so windy and so barren? In this sepia city, Matherville seemed a paradise. He reached in his pocket for change and found a single quarter.

The newspaper rack seemed to chuckle as he dropped the quarter through the slot. The door wouldn't open. He yanked it again. And again. Finally, he cursed it, kicked it, then kicked it again, until it crashed to the concrete, the newspaper rack still snickering while recovering on its side. Anger swarmed as he stomped on its plastic front, opaque with dirt and stain, cracking it open, and with bare hands, he began to rip out its guts to find the ads for office space.

The newspaper was Korean.

•   •   •

The first malpractice action against Chase left him punch-drunk. He remembered the patient well, even though his involvement amounted to less than thirty seconds. In his brief HMO experience, he had been assigned as the surgical triage officer, farming patients to the proper subspecialty, or preferably, not farming patients *anywhere*.

A woman had presented with a rash involving her genitalia, a perfectly symmetrical pattern in the midline. He remembered his instantaneous response: "They've sent you to the wrong specialist. I have no idea what this is. You need a gynecologist." As mandated by the HMO, Chase referred the patient to the HMO's gynecologist who managed in broken English to tell the woman not to worry. A year later, her cancer prompted a radical vulvectomy resulting in "loss of consortium" in addition to the threat of losing her life. All HMO doctors who had seen the patient were included in the lawsuit.

Chase's fury was nearly uncontrollable when he read the date of his involvement – July 17, 1980 – his *third day* in the practice of medicine. Nine years of medical training. Nine years of sacrifice to avoid this very thing. Nine years of studying harder than anyone he knew, nine years of fanatical attention to detail, nine years of careful communication with every patient, nine years of living in fear that someone might sink their claws into his thin skin – and it happened, yes it did, on his third day in practice!

Though alone when he received notice, he screamed and screamed. And screamed some more. What he screamed about was the fact that the patient was now the enemy. In one fell swoop, he considered his hide more vital, more important, more precious, more in need of care, than that of the patient. How could this change in attitude happen so abruptly? Yes, the gynecologist was at fault. Chase was not. He would never have seen the patient at all if it weren't for ridiculous HMO rules that were intended to diminish referrals. And to boot, the legal proceedings would hang over his head for *years*.

Reluctantly, Chase began work (with temporary privileges) as an emergency room doctor for C.C. Chastain, filling in for vacationing docs at various hospitals about five days a month, while he spent the rest of his time trying to save his skin at Ciena Hospital. A few weeks into his new and humbled circumstance, the second malpractice notice arrived – another HMO patient from six months earlier. Only this time, he had probably saved the woman's life.

It was a straightforward operation. The obese patient had a strangulated umbilical hernia, intestines trapped in the sac, potentially lethal. Chase had rushed her to the operating room, resected the dead loop of trapped bowel, and then fixed the hernia. Her recovery went beautifully in Chase's mind, horribly in hers. A small pocket of fluid developed in the incision, a common occurrence in the obese patient, and Chase tapped the fluid off one time with a needle. That was the end of that. No infection. Perfect recovery.

Then the phone calls began. Every few days. The woman complained repeatedly that she had studied wound healing since her medical nightmare, and the fluid that had developed post-op "is not supposed to happen." Yet, if it is anticipated, as she explained to Chase, he should have placed a drain of some sort. Instead, by his drawing off the fluid with a needle, he threatened her with infection. Furthermore, when Chase had pushed on the fluid to detect its presence initially, this action had caused her to develop an inguinal hernia, in addition to the umbilical hernia that Chase had fixed.

Recognizing the parade of red flags, Chase had taken great care to document details from each of the twelve phone conversations, hours on end, as she complained about Chase's care. He had submitted multiple "incident reports" to his former employer at the HMO as a precautionary measure that is routine when patients sound litigious. He also knew that three different law offices had requested her records, and that his documentation was so powerful, all three legal firms *refused* to accept her case. It would have been a great victory for hyper-documentation, indeed, had it not been for lawsuits *in propria persona* (without an attorney). She was going for Chase's jugular.

The enemy. Yes, the patient as the enemy. Within his exoskeleton, Chase could feel his own hideous growth. Squirming, slimy growth that suffocated him in his shell. He could feel a segmented tail forming, tipped by a stinger, and he wiggled within the rigid confines of his shell as the arachnid took shape.

He would have to use the HMO attorneys, for sure, but nothing prohibited him from hiring his own (other than the fact that he was spiraling deeper and deeper into debt).

"C.C., I need the name of the meanest sonuvabitch attorney you know. I'm not putting up with this shit. After I stomp her trickery into the ground, I'm going to countersue for malicious prosecution, and put an end to this crap. I'm not taking it anymore."

In his prior life form, Chase rarely cursed. The words simply didn't seem to form on his lips. Now vile words were springing forth like weeds.

•

"We had a new baby six months ago. A little girl. Angela, we're calling her."

Occasionally, expatriated Texans, or old friends looking for escape, would appear on the doorstep of C.C. Chastain's Hotel California. Often, these surprise appearances were associated with marital discord back home in the Lone Star State. So, when their drop-out classmate, Will Glendenning, appeared at C.C.'s house, it was like old times again.

Eventually, Will circled around to reveal that his attorney-wife, Claudia, was having "post-partum issues," and that he could barely be in the same room with her. Will's joy about the new baby seemed tempered, and it became apparent to C.C. and Chase that their old classmate was here to take refuge. Once again, C.C.'s beachfront home was serving its purpose.

The threesome – Will and C.C. and Chase – resurrected their customary Hearts game, asking C.C.'s current girlfriend to fill in Amy DeHart's shoes as the fourth. Will had been considering several specialties while in med school, including pathology, but his persistent fantasy was to be a writer of detective novels. When Sam Dinwiddie, the Chief Resident in Surgery, belittled Will unmercifully in the O.R., he'd had enough. Or at least, Will used that as his excuse, and he quit med school on the spot.

Since then, he had been working on his Ph.D. in molecular biology, a never-ending process, it seemed. Even though Chase had lived with Will about a year earlier when the Glendenning home had served as Chase's foxhole for the final few months of residency, it seemed that Will had aged disproportionately to fleeting time. His blonde hair was receding a bit at the temples, and his bright blue eyes seemed to have dimmed, now decorated with crow's feet. Then again, Chase considered the possibility that Will hadn't changed at all. Perhaps, his own perception had done the changing.

After several hands of Hearts, Will said, "Okay, I don't get what's going on around here. Something's up. You guys are acting like somebody died or something. I came out here to get cheered up. Everyone back in Texas keeps saying what a great time you guys are having. Shoot, my wife is bonkers, my PhD committee blasted me, and I'm not sure I'm going to get my doctorate this round either. I may have to do my experiments all over again. They say I had a fatal flaw in my study design. But guys – what's going on here?"

Over the course of an hour, Chase and C.C. relayed in bits and pieces what was happening in Chase's life. Will's jaw seemed to drop a little lower with each story.

"And you're working as an E.R. doc? After all your training in surgery? I don't...it just doesn't.... I mean you were such a big shot, Chase. You were the biggest shot I knew. You were the wunderkind. It's inconceivable. I mean it's impossible that you're so...that you've become so..."

"So small?" finished Chase. "Yes, indeed. I'm the incredible shrinking man. Today, the homunculus, tomorrow a zero."

That night, Will Glendenning took a drive by himself and didn't return until the next morning. He had headed south of L.A. to the beachside communities where he claimed to have stumbled upon an all-glass chapel nestled in the woods on a high bluff overlooking the ocean. Will seemed a changed man. He acted serene, not a care in the world (completely foreign for Will), as if he'd had some sort of spiritual experience, an odd thing for a man Chase knew to be a devout atheist. Had Chase's own life become so mortifying that it could prompt a resolute non-believer into plunging from a cliff into a pool of faith? Will wouldn't talk about it, wouldn't explain his disposition, and his reticence made Chase increasingly perturbed at being unable to figure out what had happened during his old friend's mysterious voyage.

When Will left L.A. that day to return to Texas, the irritating afterglow of contentment was still there. Chase and C.C. drove him to the airport, and as Will lifted his luggage out of the trunk of Chase's dented Cutlass, Chase said, "You know that song, 'It Never Rains in Southern California'? Will, do me a favor, old buddy – don't tell the folks back home how you found me."

"I won't," he said. "But I might have found some peace of mind."

Chase didn't want clarification or any details, fearful that his own life had served as shock therapy for his friend.

. . .

"Lord, I don't know if you're still up there or not, or if you even hear me, but I'll do anything. Save me from this. I can't take it anymore. I need a rest." This became Chase's common prayer, spoken incessantly. He considered the fact that his failure to begin the counseling process with Livvy might be a reason for God's silence. Yet, deepening debt, deepening depression and lost hope precluded his thoughts of a reconciliation. He was in survival mode, focused on his next breath.

The third lawsuit hit while the first two were still in progress. Only this time it wasn't malpractice. It was personal liability. In effect, a death warrant. One million dollars and zero cents. The suit had been filed 11 months and 3 weeks after the car accident where his wallet had been stolen and the fight ensued. This timing had allowed Chase almost the full one-year statute of limitations to build assets and insure himself fully. Of course, he'd done neither – no assets and no insurance. The friendly husband in the checkered fedora who had called Chase the morning after his wife's injury had bet on a dying horse.

The plaintiffs were Mr. and Mrs. Sheldon Rose who claimed that Chase, in an obviously intoxicated state, had lost control of his car, veering into the elderly couple, forcing them off the road. Then, the lawsuit described how Dr. Callaway threatened to assault the couple, whereupon he shoved Mrs. Rose to the ground, causing her to fear for her life. There was no mention of the Latino thieves nor the fight that had pushed Chase into the plaintiff, causing her to fall. A broken ankle from the fall prompted a surgical procedure that, once again, placed her life in jeopardy...

It – was – an – accident, he whispered to himself. He felt nothing but the ice in his veins.

Saved for a special purpose, Chase kept one gallon of the "finest bourbon," untouched, presented to him by his mentor, Thatcher N. Taylor, Chief of Surgery at Far West Texas University (along with a signed photograph wishing Chase: "Good luck in California."). The bourbon had been his going away present upon completion of surgical residency, and the predestined reason for holding onto that bottle was now clear.

Lost in this California cauldron of anonymity where he had cut so many ties to former friends and family back in Texas, with no hope of ever returning to his norm, living under a mountain of debt with years of litigation before him, with reputation snatched away permanently without the redeeming power of prayer, and yes, mostly it was the latter – a prayer answered with a crushing blow – Chase realized how his own life and the life of the liquor were intimately linked, both existing to be consumed. In this endless summer of discontent, the bourbon would extend the hand of friendship that would guide him, allow him, to slip quietly into the sea.

He hooked his finger into the glass ring of the bourbon as he stood at the floor-to-ceiling window of his apartment that had once viewed a broad seascape, but had since become a transparent prison gate, locking him from even the tiniest victory. He had come to California to become a big fish in a big pond, but now he was a tiny fish staring through the glass of his aquarium.

Without emotion, he walked out of his apartment and, forsaking the elevator, hauled the jug of bourbon down 13 stories and across the street to water's edge where a cool mist hung. The taste of straight liquor was usually repugnant, but tonight it seemed like tap water. In the chilly night air of the beach, he felt peculiar warmth – no, not warmth, but room temperature that seemed like warmth – along with the equanimity that comes through understanding that all troubles are eventually finite. There was no connection to Texas, no feeling for his family, no memory of marriage, no love in his heart. No chains of regret, no remorse. He was perfectly gray and completely transparent, a zero.

He took off his shoes, and let the sea foam tickle his feet. He chuckled at the joke of life, and the joke on him. He chugged. After a while, he could barely stand up. Relief was only minutes away. He was at peace like he hadn't felt in years. He looked at his gallon jug, the fond farewell from Texas, holding it up to moonlight, where he saw that he was nearly halfway done. The distorted moon, as seen through the glass bottle above the waves of whiskey, appeared as a demonic eye, peering, non-blinking, waiting its turn.

He tilted the bottle nearly 90-degrees where the neck of glass formed a rudimentary prism and split the moon into two yellow eyes that seemed to burn holes into his brain. In reflex, he pushed the bottle away from his own eyes, as far as his arm could reach, but the two yellow eyes of the moon became six, arranged as three pairs, hovering in front of him, three goblins in one, a three-headed devil, mocking him in triumph.

Something stirred inside. Then it began to erupt. Fury? Ferocity? A flash memory of his grandfather's encounter with a three-headed monster? Whatever it was, it was shockingly quick. Instead of the liquor-induced tranquility he had been romancing, an equal and opposite chemical reaction detonated. It was more than mere explosion. It was unrestrained passion. *All human minds harbor monsters in the darkest of caves*, he thought. Most of these fiends sleep, thankfully, during the lifetime of the host. But what does it take to awaken them from slumber? To provide freedom? Protection? Armor? Now he knew. Head-to-head combat, a war with unseen forces, a duel to the finish.

He screamed, "No-o-o-o!" and threw the jug of remaining poison into the sea.

The exoskeleton split, and a hideous scorpion burst forth.

As I write now, the mist lifts just enough that I am able to recognize, by distorted moonlight, the distant shape of Chase Callaway.

6
HORROR SMOKES

Over the course of the next five years, Chase Callaway emerged as the youngest Chief of Surgery in the history of Ciena Hospital. Had I postulated this outcome a few pages ago, you would have thought it impossible. Yet, this is truth. And truth should be embraced now because it could grow hazy further into this narrative where madness distorts, much like the moon viewed through a bottle of bourbon.

Rather than squander words on the resurrection of Chase Callaway, brevity of sorts will supervene. After all, it is far more captivating to watch dominoes fall than it is to set them upright one by one, each in perfect position, ready to fall again.

C.C. Chastain advised Chase to "lay low" for a while, and to continue working as an emergency room physician at one of Southern California's prestigious hospitals. Palmetto General, located 20 minutes from Ciena, had recently become a certified Trauma Center, one of 15 in Los Angeles, as part of a wave of enthusiasm to improve survival statistics, based on the reverential belief in the "golden hour" of transport and intervention for accident victims. This is where Chase's fortune turned, even though the emergency room staff was a distinct entity from the trauma team. Yes, both services were housed in the same square footage, but the two departments did not cross the invisible line.

One night when Chase was on duty for the "non-trauma" E.R., a gunshot victim nearing death arrived via ambulance at the trauma center's front door. Chase had no obligation to help. It was the in-house general surgeon who would be in charge.

"Blood pressure's sixty and falling, fluids wide open, get blood quick," shouted the EMTs as the automatic doors retracted and the entourage raced inside. A single bullet had pierced the upper abdomen of the young man, a Latino teenager. Someone yelled, "Where's Dr. Singleton?"

Chase crept closer to the trauma zone where nurses and EMTs were swarming. Dr. Singleton was notoriously slow, even with advance notice. "I called him at the nunnery ten minutes ago. Where is he, dammit?"

Palmetto General was a Catholic hospital, and the vacated second floor of the nearby nunnery served as the sleeping quarters for the surgeon on trauma call who was required by regulation to spend the full shift "in-house." The walk across the parking lot took only three minutes, so Dr. Singleton should have been present by now.

The victim was nearly unconscious. "What's his pressure?" Chase asked, peeking over the shoulder of an EMT as he watched the patient's eyes start to roll back into his head. "Down to forty, but I can barely hear it," said one of the nurses, "We're going to lose him. Pour in the fluids. Give the blood. Where the hell is Dr. Singleton?"

Chase pushed his way to the bedside. "Someone get me a thoracotomy tray," he said with such calm that the nurses thought he was joking.

"We don't do that here," said the charge nurse once she realized Chase was an employee, a doctor. And – that he was serious. "Who are you, anyway?"

"Dr. Callaway." Then he added before she could interrogate further, "This is a trauma center, but you don't *do that*?"

The nurse had a piercing, critical eye, but Chase stared back and repeated his request for the thoracotomy tray. "We only have a few seconds. Someone – move – fast. Get that O-negative blood pouring in at top speed, then type-specific as soon as it's ready."

Chase turned to the victim and asked the boy to respond. Perhaps there was a faint moan, but the surgeon knew the patient was only seconds away from full cardiac arrest, irreversible if still bleeding. Chase pressed firmly with his knuckles on the boy's sternum to elicit pain. No response. The thoracotomy tray arrived, and Chase propped open the boy's eyelid and spoke: "When I see you again, it'll be in the Recovery Room or in Heaven…"

"I can't get a blood pressure anymore," a nurse yelled.

"…or in Hell," Chase added.

With a long sweeping motion as if conducting a symphony, Chase sliced open the man's chest, an 8-inch gash located where we envision the piercing lance in the side of Jesus, apropos in that the victim's name was Jesus. "I don't know if you're feeling this or not, but if so, I'm sorry" – then Chase reached inside the thorax and cross-clamped the aorta just above the diaphragm. "Note the cross-clamp time, someone." With proximal control to the injury, blood loss was curtailed downstream, while the intravenous fluids and blood were able to raise the pressure back to 75 systolic.

Yet, the clamp would need removal within 20 minutes, lest the spinal cord or critical organs like the kidneys be deprived of mandatory blood flow. While cross-clamping created great theater in the E.R., in contrast, identifying the source of hemorrhage, then controlling it in a brief time was usually impossible. Even if the patient survived, they could be in a wheelchair or on dialysis, or both, for the rest of their lives. So, the condescending "we don't do that here" from the E.R. nurse was, in fact, entirely justified.

Dr. Singleton finally arrived on the scene, shocked to see the silver finger loops of a Satinsky clamp sticking out of a gaping hole in the victim's chest, sterile green towels covering everything except the clamp that bobbed up and down with each heartbeat. Singleton could barely keep up with the gurney en route to the O.R., with Chase steering the patient and the entourage.

Once Dr. Singleton figured out what was going on, he asked Chase to assist even though Chase had no surgical privileges at the hospital. Dr. Singleton was a gentleman-surgeon, a few years away from retirement and many years away from treating the critically injured. Indeed, he admitted to Chase that he had only signed up for trauma call to augment his income in support of his fly-fishing habit tagged to international travel. After all, some tours of duty on call for trauma allowed a full eight hours of sleep in the nunnery. "Nothing like making money while you sleep," said Singleton. "You go right ahead and do what needs to be done here."

The assistant (Chase) took charge in the O.R, repairing the difficult injuries to the liver, portal vein, hepatic artery, and to top it off in its single trajectory, a partial tear in the inferior vena cava. Importantly, the aortic cross-clamp was removed after 17.5 minutes, while direct pressure on the bleeding sites inside the abdomen was performed, an impossible task outside of the operating room setting. Direct pressure was replaced by hemostatic clamps and other maneuvers, allowing each injury to be permanently repaired.

With blood pressure stabilized, the next four hours in the O.R. allowed Chase ample time to explain his unusual introduction to California medicine to Dr. Singleton.

As Chase had foretold in the E.R., the next time he saw the victim, Jesus Maldonado, the young man was alive and well in the Recovery Room, with the crossroads of Heaven or Hell postponed. Three weeks later, at the time of discharge in good health, the kid was found to have no recollection of his chest-cracking encounter with Dr. Callaway in the E.R.

Word spread of the successful E.R. thoracotomy, a procedure that rarely saves lives (0-5% chance in the published literature), generating a paradoxical axiom: "If you think you've saved a life with an emergency thoracotomy, then you didn't need to do it." Witnesses to the Maldonado save, however, were in universal agreement that the axiom did not apply here.

When the general surgeons on the trauma panel learned that Chase was a board-certified surgeon, plus a newly certified trauma instructor (at C.C. Chastain's request), they arranged for Chase to have "limited privileges," allowing him to take trauma call as well as performing related surgeries. This fell short of full surgical privileges that included the easy daytime work, but it was a major step forward. As time passed, the general surgeons watched Chase flourish, not only in trauma care, but also in organizational and diplomatic matters as well. Within a few months, he was named Director of the Palmetto General Hospital Trauma Center.

This title was a coup of sorts in that Palmetto had been one of the hospitals with a closed medical staff – unwilling to give Chase an application for hospital privileges one year earlier.

Only a single problem stood in the way of an illustrious career as a trauma surgeon. Chase abhorred trauma. Sure, he loved the excitement. He loved the blood. Too, he loved the actual surgical procedures. He also loved his perceived immunity from this "disease" so that he could distance himself. However, trauma usually did its grim reaping at night. Sleep interruption and its evil twin, sleep deprivation, had been a popular tool throughout the years for shock therapy, for torture, and – for training surgical residents. For Chase, the difference between deprivation and torture was negligible. Sleep deprivation altered his personality. For the worse.

Missed meals, missed Holidays, and contracting common colds that lasted for uncommon months due to poor immunity – all these were nothing compared to the change in his priorities, his values, his attitude, his character.

In the months that followed, the senior surgeons taking trauma call grew tired of meeting the requirements and the physical demands of a certified Trauma Center, whereupon they began to surrender their 24-hour rotations to the fresh young surgeon who was new on staff. The resulting assault on Chase's sleep far surpassed any such anguish during his surgical residency. To make matters worse, there were no residents, interns, or students to help at this private hospital with Level 2 trauma status. He was an army of one.

When the call came from Dr. Ted Zink, Chairman of the Board of Directors at Palmetto General Hospital, Chase was both perplexed and curious. What did the "top dog" at the hospital want with him? Was his career in jeopardy once again – for no reason at all?

The two met the next day in Dr. Zink's office, with Chase seated across from the surgeon, separated by an ornate cherry desk cluttered with papers. Against the far wall, Chase could see the standard array of diplomas, but with the print too small to read. He could make out "Johns Hopkins" on one of the certificates, however.

"I've been following your career ever since your…uh…troubles over at the Ciena Hospital," said Dr. Zink, a tan, wiry man with a prominent forehead exposed by receding gray hair. He looked 60-plus, but he spoke and gestured with youth.

Chase was dumbfounded. Palmetto was three suburbs away from Ciena. How had Dr. Zink learned of Chase's nightmare there?

"I grew up in Ciena. Right there on the beach. Three-story house. Dark green with white trim. It's no longer there. I came from a big family. Strong Catholics. Sailed a lot. Still do. Surfed a lot, once upon a time. Believe it or not, I hunted ducks right where the marina is today. That's before they drained the swamp to create all that lovely real estate. And wouldn't you know, after that dry land emerged, a group of doctors decided to put a hospital smack dab where I'd done my duck hunting as a boy."

Chase nodded when appropriate, but he did not enter the one-man conversation.

Zink continued, "Let me get right to the point. We want to expand the Palmetto hospital, but as you may or may not know, we're not allowed by California law to add any new hospital beds. Therefore, we're planning a buy-out of the Ciena Hospital. They're on that prime real estate, and we'll simply merge their name with ours, Palmetto-Ciena. I know it doesn't sound very Catholic, but everyone knows and respects the Palmetto name. That Ciena hospital doesn't have the greatest of reputations, as you apparently found out the hard way. Anyway, in the process of due diligence, working toward a purchase offer, I reviewed the records of the medical staff and the medical executive committee at Ciena. That's where I came across your rather colorful entry into private practice. I was especially intrigued by the total mismatch between your credentials and the Ciena proctoring. Looks like you wrote an entire book trying to claw your way onto staff there."

"I never did make it back on staff," Chase said.

"I saw that your first proctoring in the Valley was superb. Did you consider going back out there when things went south at Ciena?"

"Yes, but my privileges there were based on employment by the HMO, and when I checked with the private practice surgeons I knew there, someone had alerted them to the problems at Ciena. Let's just say the open arms were gone. In fact, I couldn't get an interview. It's very hard for a doctor to wash out stains in their reputation, even when the stains are undeserved."

"Well, regardless, our surgeons here at Palmetto testify to your trauma skills, plus some nice tricks in the O.R. that have really impressed what is generally a sour bunch of old men. Not many young surgeons on staff here since the shop has been closed for a while. However, the stories about you from my colleagues here match up with what I'd expect after reading your recommendations from Texas. Those comments during your training are not merely good, they're superlative."

Then Dr. Zink quizzed him about personal goals and his family life. Chase struggled to explain his marital status, but Zink sensed the hesitation and took over the conversation once again. The older surgeon explained how the last of his children had recently announced plans to attend law school. It was a clean sweep. Not one of his six daughters had chosen a career in medicine. On the spot, Chase Callaway became child number seven, a son, as Zink asked Chase if he'd like to join him in the practice of surgery. (At this point, the two men had never been in the operating room together.)

"Yes. I'd like that very much," said Chase, restraining the temptation to whoop and holler and run around in circles.

With a single phone call to the Palmetto medical staff office, Dr. Zink secured Chase's position with full surgical privileges, something Chase had been unable to do on his own after two years in California.

Then Dr. Zink placed another phone call to a doctor-turned-real estate magnate: "Jim, I'm looking to open a second office in Ciena. A place to put my new partner. Yes, I know, after thirty years in solo practice, it seems odd to take on a partner. Well, Palmetto's going to make a bid on the hospital in Ciena, and my partner and I would like a space in that new office building you did near the marina. I'm going to stay mostly here at Palmetto, but I'm going to plant my new partner there at Ciena."

In the span of 15 minutes, Chase went from being a struggling outcast to junior partner of a prestigious physician, in a practice with built-in referrals. And – his primary office would be in the city from which he'd been banished. "You'll never work in this town again" didn't stick.

A few months later, Ciena Hospital was purchased and renamed Palmetto-Ciena, as Dr. Zink had described. Chase discarded his rags and went to work.

Dr. Zink subsequently revealed how he, 20 years earlier, had been asked to serve as the organizer of the medical staff at the new hospital in Ciena, giving it a measure of credibility that would match its celebrity-rich location. However, when Dr. Zink had seen the list of scoundrels being proposed for the medical staff, he had crossed off more than a third of the names. The principal physician-founder of the Ciena hospital responded: "Listen to me, Ted, these doctors you plan to exclude from staff, why, you're eliminating most of our investors." Dr. Zink was promptly dismissed from his (volunteer) duties at Ciena, a sore point to this day, given the sentimental attachment Zink had to that particular property where he had hunted as a boy. Now, Dr. Zink was returning on his white horse to the land of ducks, accompanied by his eager squire.

Dr. Zink's junior partner was easily intoxicated by Zink's power and influence. Overnight, Chase had a successful practice laid at his feet. Two unholy years were wiped away in an instant. A gift from Above. *Yes, all things work for the good.*

The physicians at Old Palmetto were eager to open branch offices at the lavish Ciena outpost, but they were cautious, leery of the squatters who'd been there since the shady, early days. Palmetto's original plan in the takeover had been to oust all physicians from the Ciena medical staff, then make them re-apply under Palmetto standards, which included board-certification. However, this intent had jeopardized a smooth purchase of the new hospital, so the idea was dropped and the old guard of Ciena, grandfathered founders, would be allowed to remain.

"Chase, we sure appreciate your blazing the trail down there," said the Palmetto physicians, nearly in unison and frequently, sometimes chuckling. "Let us know when you've straightened things up, and it's safe for us to move. We might even close our Palmetto offices if it works out in Ciena."

It was a clean-up mission that was custom made for Chase whose desire for vengeance had been a mere pilot light compared to the furnace now roaring. After his appointment as Chairman of the Tissue Committee, Chase left no room for error by anyone. His prior tormentors would now answer to him. He covered his own tracks as well, making sure he took every imaginable step for proper care with every patient. His practice of medicine had always been thorough, but now it was obsessive. He couldn't leave himself open for criticism by anyone for anything. Not now, not since the shedding of the exoskeleton. Not if he were going to sting his former enemies at every opportunity from here on. He had gone from rags to rage.

As Chairman of the Tissue Committee, monitoring who takes out what from the human body and why, Dr. Zink's junior partner plunged his stinger into his former surgery proctors with relish. He scrutinized their every complication, every normal organ removed, every surgery that might have been unnecessary – everything. He even exposed a fee-splitting scheme that led to formal censorship of anyone who had ever looked at Chase in the wrong way. As he walked the halls of Palmetto-Ciena, he could hear a popular song playing as a theme in his head: "Another One Bites the Dust."

When the carnage was over, five judicial reviews had been held, each with a judge, court reporter, and a jury of peers. Hospital privileges were either limited or removed for all five surgeons. When the Joint Commission on Accreditation of Hospitals performed their review, they were stunned. "We have *never* seen such exemplary self-policing in medicine...*ever*!" Meanwhile, the music played, "Ain't no sound but the sound of his feet, machine guns ready to go."

Then, after four years of anger, angst and depositions, Chase was freed from his personal malpractice accusations as well, that is, from the people formerly known as patients. The woman with vulvar carcinoma stood up and hugged Chase, interrupting his deposition, the moment he testified about her original findings and recounted word-for-word his conversation with the gynecologist, confirming her story perfectly. The unfortunate woman proclaimed, during her hug, "I want this doctor dropped from the lawsuit immediately," but Chase knew something inside him had changed. The exoskeleton was gone. He felt disgust at her touch, not relief. The doctor-patient relationship had been redefined, forever, from an incident occurring on his third *day* in practice. Yes, he'd been dropped from the lawsuit, but the stain on his record was permanent.

As for the second lawsuit following repair of an umbilical hernia and fluid formation, when the judge read the brief, he tossed out the case. The plaintiff, in charge of her own prosecution, had to be restrained and physically dragged from the courtroom. She screamed, "You're all in this together. I'm going to write a book and expose all of you!" A month later, Chase received notice in the mail announcing that the woman had filed for bankruptcy. She had never paid one penny of her bill. Another life saved.

Then a miracle happened. Sheldon Rose, the dapper old man who longed for one million of Chase's non-existent dollars, made national headlines, along with his stiletto-heeled wife. When the call came from his attorney, Chase was alone in his apartment.

His attorney said, "Chase, turn on your TV. Quick. No, you've already missed it. But you'll see it in the paper tomorrow. Sheldon Rose and his wife are in jail. They were caught trying to swindle Ronald and Nancy Reagan on a real estate deal in Pacific Palisades. What gumption! What gall! Trying to con a sitting president. They're flim-flam artists. Successful ones at that. Police have the goods on them dating back for the past twenty years in seven different states, building the case against them over time. The Roses have spent their entire lives bilking innocent people out of millions, but they were always small potatoes, staying ahead of the law, until they got caught on this deal with the president. Since they're both in their late 70s, neither one is going to see sunlight again outside of prison walls.

"Thank you, Murray," Chase said with a forced calm. After hanging up the phone, however, he yelled "thank-you" over and over, as loud as he could, his eyes aimed at the ceiling, then he threw a fit worthy of a full-blown visitation by the Holy Ghost. "I'll never touch a drop of alcohol again," he said to the empty room, loud enough for God to hear. "Or cocaine."

Later, he became the awkward informant to the police detectives on the case, having to admit his own inebriation the night of the accident, while confirming that he was not directly at fault. One trick of Ma and Pa Rose was to travel the streets at night in their Cadillac, forcing accidents at traffic signals in low-speed areas. In Chase's case, they hit pay dirt when the Latino carload appeared, and in the struggle with Chase, pushed him into the stiletto-heeled wife, whereupon she fell and broke her ankle. When the trial of the Roses was over, their racket ended with both husband and wife sentenced to jail for their attempted trickery of Ronald and Nancy. The lawsuit against Chase was history.

But miracles were not always clear-cut in Chase's rise from the ashes. The Group of Ciena physicians apologized to Chase for his premature dismissal as their surgeon. Then, they invited him to become an "associate" member, a new designation since they understood the futility of asking Chase to become a full partner. Chase could see through their ploy that was, in fact, an offer to ingratiate themselves with Dr. Ted Zink, Chase's partner and now head physician for both hospitals as Chairman of the Board of Directors.

Senior partner Zink saw it, too, and objected. "That group has been walking the tightrope of ethics for years. They're very good docs, all right, but they don't take a step without an army of attorneys making sure everything they do hovers barely on the upside of legal."

But Chase argued his point: "I could get enough referrals from this group that I'll be able to stop the trauma and E.R. work. After all these years, I think – no – I *need* to get some sleep." Chase wondered if Dr. Zink could hear what he was really saying, which was: I want to go back to being the person I used to be.

When Chase shook hands with the president of The Group, becoming an "associate" of the very crew that had nearly destroyed him, he felt he was shaking hands with the Devil himself. As their grips released, Dr. "Beelzebub" said, "Well, you might as well start off big. I've got a patient in the hospital now I'd like you to see. I'm thinking she needs a colon resection for intractable diverticulitis. She's the mother of those boys in the music group, The Pipelines. I've been their family doctor since the boys were little when I was starting out with a practice in Hawthorne."

Chase couldn't believe it. The Pipelines had been his teen-age heroes. Their surf music had redefined rock. He had tried to mimic their style in his own work as lyricist for the New Bloods.

During her ten days recovering post-op in the hospital, the Pipeline's mother – their original keyboard player during the "early garage period" – bonded with Chase. During the hour he spent each day talking to her about her sons' decimated lives, served ill by celebrity, he scoured the post-operative details, checking and re-checking every lab result, every temperature recording, and so forth, to best assure she was going to recover without incident. Plus, he met with the Pipeline members (almost forgetting that *he* was the doctor, and *he* was in charge), their wives and ex-wives, their famous friends, the children of their friends, and the celebrity friends of friends. Chase had arrived. On her discharge day, Mama Pipeline, who had confessed to Chase her failure as a mother, said to him, "I bet your mother is so very proud of you." Chase thought to himself: *No, she is not.*

The Group, of which Chase was now an associate member, generated a constant stream of the rich and famous – Chase would have his hands inside their bellies one day, and they would be accepting a Grammy or an Emmy or, in one case, an Oscar, the next. There were fund-raising events held at the movie studios, galas on yachts, and when Chase moved up the ladder to become the new Chief of Surgery at Palmetto-Ciena, his photo appeared in *Beverly Hills People*.

The glitz and the glory of such delicious revenge should indicate an earthly form of Heaven, by all surface accounts. Chase was in line to become the next Chief of Staff at Palmetto-Ciena, yet he had a nagging sense he would be forever alone at the top. For there was an undercurrent – an ugly, vile river that flowed through it all.

The headwaters came from Vivian. Vivian was a red-headed beauty, long-waisted and even-tempered, with whom Chase worked only one time back in his E.R. days at Palmetto General. On their shift together, her mischievous green eyes roamed over Chase's face and body as she spoke through cool, sensuous lips. She was a "temp" – a registry nurse

– whereas Chase was a disgraced surgeon newly employed in the E.R. at Palmetto.

In remembrance, writing this now, Chase had no strong feelings about her or their one-night stand, more accurately described as their one-hour stand. The sleep-tortured Chase could lose all judgment in personal affairs when fatigue hit full force, as though he had to jettison his integrity to make sure medical judgment stayed afloat. *Concentrate all failure into my personal life,* he thought, *where my record is already broken.*

Chase and Vivian spent their hour together in the trauma call quarters, oddly located on the second floor of the nunnery, its first floor still buzzing with Sisters. Chase often joked that he was one of the few men alive who routinely slept in a nunnery, an arrangement created to meet accreditation as a trauma center where "in-house call" was required. It had not been easy to convince the inspectors that the nunnery was part of the hospital, but a covered walkway finally made the difference as, technically, the two buildings were connected.

Near sunrise, Chase bemoaned the fact that his 24-hour shift was not over at 24 hours. He would now be starting a new 24-hour shift, covering for another vacationing doctor. Vivian was un-rumpling herself in the mirror, but she turned and smiled, explaining to Chase how she managed the long hours. She sat down beside him on the bed and opened her purse.

Two pills. Two magic pills, one color-coded for energy, the other coded for sleep.

Chase rationalized the approach. *How is this any different than the military dispensing uppers to its pilots and other critical warriors, along with counteracting sedatives later? Superhuman efforts could not be held in check at the mercy of a clock.*

When Chase swallowed the energy pill, he felt it working instantly, long before the enhancing chemical had time to suffuse his bloodstream. Ten minutes later, he was back at work in the E.R. Chase felt great. Not only was he wide awake, but he also felt "normal." For the first time in years, he felt good. Not high, not euphoric, no cocaine buzz, nothing but the normal he used to know. His long, lost *normal.*

But that same night and well into the next day, and for that matter, many years, he couldn't shake from his memory a young woman, a lunatic he had encountered while working as an aide at the mental institution back in Texas seven years ago. Viola was a paranoid schizophrenic who professed to be an interpreter of tongues, a teller of fortunes. Chase had a single confrontation with the girl who was a patient on his ward for only one night. She had spoken in rhyme, claiming a translation of the gibberish spoken by Ivy Pettibone, Chase's most memorable patient at the asylum. For some reason, perhaps out of its dark and nonsensical madness, he had memorized the paranoid's poem:

"Hickory Tickery start the clock
Boughs will break; locusts flock
Bullets melt in the name of gunnery
Horror smokes after sex in the nunnery."

Crazy Viola had spent one night on the ward, and he never saw her again. So it was with nurse Vivian.

7
RETRACEMENT TO THE PROTOCELL

The story needs telling again, only this time, without varnish. In this promenade redux, one can better appreciate the upward plunge.

With two office locations, two primary hospitals, three secondary hospitals, plus confinement at the trauma center two 24-hour shifts every week, Chase toiled at a clip that dwarfed the residency experience. Plus, he faced considerable debt – not from educational loans, but from minimal income during that first calamitous year, plus legal fees for the Sheldon Rose lawsuit, as well as the support he sent home to Livvy and another bundle to family friend, Sukie Spurlock, to whom he was indebted emotionally. His strategy was simple. As soon as he was debt free, he would resign from the trauma center and assume the more customary labors of a surgeon who performs primarily elective procedures. With his "associate" membership in The Group, Chase figured he would be debt-free within a year.

What if he was, in effect, repeating another year of surgical residency? Chemistry was the charm. It was simply a matter of making sure the same number of atoms were on the left side of the equation to balance those on the right. Being awake, being asleep, was color-coded. Operate on a stab wound at 2:00a.m. with a full schedule the next day and the next night? The answer lay in blue and white microspheres ensconced in a gelatin shell. Then, a six-hour window to sleep? The answer lay in yellow powder compacted into a doughnut tablet with a V-shaped hole in the middle.

Chase became a student, then a disciple, of psychopharmacology. He knew the timing of peak serum levels after absorption, half-lives as a function of metabolism, and side effects (which could be offset with other colors). He studied the effect of the magical V on the limbic system of the brain. He read about the mysteries of brain stimulation with the microspheres that had been designed as diet pills. The fear of addiction was remote. After all, he oozed more will power than anyone he knew. As evidence, he'd abruptly stopped recreational chemicals with a simple wave of the hand. And of course, knowledge was power.

His mastery of pharmacology on the balance beam was never more evident than the day he performed a major liver resection for a primary hepatocellular carcinoma. He had overslept thirty minutes after a minor slip-up on dosage, prompting a counter-adjustment in microspheres. Opening the gelatin seal, he counted out and swallowed 25 tiny spheres to be added to the 80 spheres in one full capsule, all to achieve peak serum levels when his knife made the first cut.

After the complex and tense surgery, Dr. Zink commented to his junior partner, "Chase, I don't know how you managed to do a complicated case like that, making it look so easy. I know a lot of surgeons in practice for twenty years who would have struggled with that procedure, or wouldn't have had the nerve to try it in the first place. Yet, you waltzed in there like you resect livers every day." Chase glowed. Fearing that his minor dosage increase might cause his hands to shake, he had added just the perfect touch – half of a beta-blocker to offset tremor.

As for reconciliation with Livvy, it was now or never. Chase couldn't break from work for any substantial length of time, so the plan had always been to fly his wife to L.A. where they would arrange an intensive course of counseling. It had been nearly three years since their separation, however, and Chase had lived a lifetime of woe in the interim.

While speaking long distance about the counseling plan, he sensed a flat tone in Livvy's voice, prompting this: "I suppose I should ask you,

Livvy, whether or not you even want to pursue counseling. Do you? I'll understand. It's whatever you want."

"Whatever *I* want? My call? That says it all, Chase. It's time. Time for us to split. I know you've had a terrible time out there, but it was my vow to help you in sickness or in health. You shut me out. How could I help you like that? Listen to the words of *Desperado* next time you hear it. It's you."

He fumbled to speak. "I'm sorry. All that's happened out here is beyond my wildest imagination. I had no coping skills for something like this. To survive, I couldn't focus on anything else. Certainly, not complicated relationships. Even now, sometimes I think the only thing that keeps me going is redemption, but I can't tell the difference anymore between redemption and revenge."

"It's so much more than your career, Chase. I completely lost myself in you, and you've lost yourself in an absurd medical nightmare. It's taken me a long time to get to this point, but it's time to quit kidding ourselves."

Like that, it was over.

· · · ·

Then Chase killed someone. Yes, "killed someone" is an exercise in medical hyperbole meant to assuage guilt. It is offered with the intent to evoke the following response in the listener – "You didn't kill the patient. Anyone might have done the same thing." But in this case, Chase killed someone.

Chase was the unanimous choice by all local surgeons to try out a new device that allowed intravenous catheters to be placed into the large subclavian vein beneath the collarbone, with the entire apparatus, including a reservoir, buried beneath the skin – a portal for drug delivery. His record on inserting external lines into the subclavian was both singular and remarkable, not a single collapsed lung after hundreds of insertions. He had studied the local anatomy while in the autopsy lab during his pathology fellowship, and he learned how to judge the position of the large, albeit hidden, vein by analyzing the size and shape of the collarbone. The procedure was risky, yet Medicare reimbursement was a paltry $56, nothing but a glorified IV line as viewed by the U.S. government. Chase was so much in demand for the procedure that doctors simply called in their "lists" to Chase's office, and he would spend hours putting in these lines, nearly every day, to the point that he came to hate the procedure. And now, technology had delivered this "improvement" that implied even greater usage of the subclavian vein and a greater usage of his time.

"I've got to get this monkey off my back," he said to his office manager. "It takes me over an hour in L.A. to drive to whatever hospital, set up, insert the line, then wait for the chest X-ray for another hour to see if there's a pneumo. Then if I need to reposition the line, it's longer. Plus, it's all for a lousy fifty-six dollars from Medicare. A procedure with a theoretical mortality. Fifty-six friggin' dollars. Cardiologists do the same thing, pretty much, when they put in a temporary pacemaker. The risk of pneumothorax and bleeding is identical to my central lines, and they charge $2,000! While I'm getting $56? Half goes to overhead, half of the other half goes back to the government in taxes, and I'm doing a potentially life-threatening procedure for 14 friggin' dollars in pocket change. Somehow, this has got to stop."

Then Chase killed someone.

When the salesman first came into Chase's office, the young go-getter had said, "Everyone in this part of Southern California tells me you're King of the Subclavian. That you've never caused a pneumothorax."

"That's right, but I have to admit, I avoided a sure-thing pneumo by simply not doing the insertion once. Have you ever heard of the country star Jenny Pugh? I was supposed to give her a subclavian for antibiotics. Had no veins. Years ago, someone botched her gallbladder surgery and left her with a common duct stricture that had been repaired about five times but kept recurring. I tried to talk her into letting my old mentor fix it back at Far West Texas. Biliary strictures were his forte, but she wouldn't hear of it. Like most folks, she had the mecca syndrome, so she ended up going to a top-five hospital where they botched her even worse. Anyway, she needed antibiotics, and she told me that, over the years, four different docs had tried to insert subclavian lines – *all four* caused her lungs to collapse. Must have had something to do with her singing and hyperinflated lungs. But I wasn't about to be number five. She said, "Darlin', I'll just tell 'em you tried and couldn't hit the vein. That way, you'll keep your record intact, and I'll keep my lungs just as they are." They gave her the antibiotics intramuscular. So, yes, my record is still perfect. Not a single lung down, not even a partial."

Swelling with ambivalent pride, Chase agreed to be the first to insert the new port device where an outer plastic sheath of considerable diameter – the introducer – was the only real difference to what he had been doing for years. "I've been complaining about subclavians being poorly reimbursed for a long time now. You're adding just enough complexity with this introducer and the subcutaneous pocket for the reservoir that it's close now to being the same risk as a permanent pacemaker insertion. We used to put those pacemakers in as surgery interns, you know. I'll do a few of these ports just to see how it goes, but I'm *not* going to do them routinely until you get a CPT code and decent reimbursement." The salesman replied, "The new CPT should come any time now. No problem. You're going to be a busy man."

For the landmark event, Chase chose a patient in whom he'd resected an aggressive colon cancer that had positive regional lymph nodes. Chemotherapy was advised. The medical oncologist made the request, "He doesn't have any veins, so I'd like you to put in one of those new ports."

Two weeks after the patient's surgery, Chase took the patient to the O.R. for insertion of the new device. Whereas simple subclavian IVs could be done at the bedside, the need to create a pocket for the port's reservoir had moved the procedure to the operating room.

Chase draped out a sterile field near the clavicle. The old method for a temporary subclavian IV was simple – needle in the vein, insert IV line through needle, remove needle, hook it up. Now, however, after slipping the needle in the vein, a guidewire followed and needle removed, leaving the guidewire to dangle outside, with its tip inside. He then threaded a plastic spear with sheath (the introducer) over the guidewire. A fair amount of force was anticipated to push the introducer through the soft tissues into the vein, given its diameter so much larger than a guidewire.

But the spear required more force than Chase expected as he wiggled it through apparent calcifications that had developed in the ligament between first rib and clavicle. He advanced the introducer at his preferred angle, but had to change directions several times because of the calcific obstruction. *I wonder if he broke his clavicle sometime in the past.* All such maneuvers were blind, and Chase was going entirely by his familiarity with the anatomy plus the "feel." Yet the feel was gritty, unnerving. Finally, the spear and its sheath slipped easily into the vein. No more resistance.

Chase pulled out the guidewire and spear, leaving the open sheath in place. With blood rushing out of the pipeline, assuring proper position, Chase slipped the port's catheter through the sheath into place, then removed the breakaway sheath. The risky part was over, and it was now a simple matter of securing the injection reservoir in its pocket beneath the skin.

"Look at this introducer," the scrub nurse said a moment later. She handed the spear to Chase who puzzled over the tip. The thin plastic taper had been split and a tiny hook had formed at the end, much like a tool that a dentist uses to scrape tartar. "Hmmm," he said. "That's odd. Must've happened when I kept running into the calcifications. Patient's doing okay, though. Right?"

"Perfectly stable," said the anesthesiologist.

Dressing applied, surgery over, the patient was lifted to the gurney for transport. "Get the chest X-ray in recovery," Chase said. "I hope I didn't get my first pneumo."

Even though a collapsed lung was usually a minor problem, the shortness of breath frightened patients, and of course, it usually required a needle or a chest tube to re-expand the lung.

A peumothorax, however, would have been a blessing.

"Quick! Recovery room! Your patient is coding," came the panicked nurse as she shouted into the locker room where Chase had started to dictate. "Something must've happened during transport. There was no blood pressure – nothing – first time that the pressure was taken in recovery – nothing. Zero."

"No blood pressure? What are you—" Chase ran to the recovery room where he knew the problem, knew the solution, but it was too late. The vascular system had completely emptied into the chest during the few minutes required for transport. The plastic hook on the introducer had slit the subclavian vein along its entire length, allowing blood to pour into the chest cavity. Transfusion was too late. Chest-cracking was too late. CPR was too late. Chase and his harpoon, not the cancer, had killed the patient.

He described the tragedy to the widow and her family with helpless, pathetic honesty, fully expecting the shoe of malpractice to drop (it never did). He communicated through choking and stuttering, backtracking and justifying, sighing and babbling. Energy drained from every pore as he consoled a grieving family, the additional victims of his hooked spear.

Editor's note: The history of subclavian port placement, up to the present, is deleted here, with Dr. Callaway describing how the procedure was made safer over the years with the addition of fluoroscopic guidance and vascular ultrasound, while the port reservoir shrank in size, all working together to make the procedure routinely safe.

Exhausted, with shoulders hunched, he limped back to his office where he sat motionless for hours, watching the horizontal stripes of sun squeezing through Venetian blinds, creeping across his desktop until the room turned dark. He wouldn't be able to discuss the events with anyone other than his partner, Dr. Zink, and then only to fish for the universal response: "You didn't kill him. Anyone might have done the same thing." Beyond that, the unwritten rule for surgical disasters was: "It's part of the territory. Deal with it."

He couldn't move. He couldn't go on. He couldn't work in a profession where disaster and death lurked everywhere, no matter how minor the procedure. And where such lurking could prompt a stream of malpractice suits, and where such lurking translated to 14 dollars in pocket change, and where such lurking could destroy the physician in addition to the patient.

His thoughts raced erratically – he even calculated that he would need to do 1,000 subclavian vein procedures each and every year to pay his malpractice premium – he envisioned the funeral of his patient where the family would murmur about the murdering doctor at Palmetto-Ciena Hospital – he retraced his steps with the hooked spear countless times as if he could turn back the clock to enjoy his old moniker, King of the Subclavian.

Unable to sustain the pain anymore, he stood up from his desk, flipped on the room lights and trudged to the cabinet of his office pharmacy where, inside, embossed plastic labels on the shelf edges copied the drug cabinet he'd grown up with in his Matherville home – Sinus, Cold, Cough, Allergy, Skin, Heartburn, Sleep, and so forth. He didn't need the color of wakefulness, nor did he need the color of dreams, already regulated so well. He needed unbearable pain to go away. He wanted his "self" back, the self that he'd been before now, before he became a surgeon, before medical school. Regressing to the carefree days of the New Bloods and his music, back to Zanda the Panda forever alone at the top, regressing even further to his childhood fantasy of living beneath the sea as one of Kingsley's water-babies, and finally back to a primordial dot, a protocell awash in an uncaring ocean. He was willing to go anywhere, as long as there was no pain.

White was the key color. Pure, brilliant, sterile, dispassionate white. Opioid white. *Algesis*, Greek for "sensing pain," was roaring for its companion antidote – *Analgesia* – clamoring to become insensate. The color white, once consumed, did its job as advertised – it took away the pain.

But when he scrutinized the plastic label on the shelf beneath the bottle – PAIN – it telegraphed a sense of foreboding so powerful he could barely breathe after fully understanding the message. Pain was not a symptom to be treated – it was a prophecy.

8
NECTAR AND AMBROSIA

As modern archaeology still relies on "floating chronologies," using stratigraphy and seriation, more than absolute dating systems, so, too, this dig through colorful strata dismisses the calendar. The date for the following has been lost, though the moment is etched:

Twelve men seated at a long table, supping. All of them healers, physicians. All are participants in a king-of-the mountain contest, vaunting potions and procedures that have restored celebrity health. The degree of difficulty utilized in the medical intervention plays no role – the king is established by the magnitude of celebrity *(Editor's note: this was pre-HIPAA)*. Hemorrhoidal surgery on an Oscar winner greatly overshadows a successful aortic aneurysm repair on a TV sit-com actor. Chase is one of the twelve.

Th scene now set, a thirteenth physician joins the diners in the cafeteria at Palmetto-Ciena Hospital. Agitated, unable to squeeze a word into the cracks of self-esteem, Dr. Underhill finally blurts, "Have you guys heard? Did anyone read the papers?"

Twelve necks collectively crane at Dr. Underhill as he drags a chair from a nearby table and joins them, sitting next to Chase Callaway. No one responds as they wait for Underhill to explain the interruption.

"It passed the Assembly two days ago, Senate yesterday, signed into law by the governor today. Apparently, no one knew it was happening.

And that includes our illustrious medical association that did absolutely nothing to stop it."

"Calm down, Underhill. What are you talking about?" asks someone.

"Insurance companies, freakin' insurance companies. Now it's legal for them to enter direct negotiations with physicians to establish fees. The HMOs were bad enough. Now, they're going to destroy private practice, too."

Most at the long table resume discourse on the various "plasties" they have performed on the various body parts of miscellaneous notables, dismissing the news with, "All our patients pay cash up front, so it doesn't matter to us." A few disease-treating doctors listen for a while, but they too abandon Dr. Underhill, leaving him in a two-man conversation with Chase Callaway who, in the first nanosecond after the news, envisioned (accurately) the future course of medicine.

Chase understands that, in the la-de-da suburbs of L.A., a world of doctor glut, the insurance companies will force the physicians into competitive bidding, downward, contracting only with those willing to work for the lowest possible reimbursement. Yet doctors were forbidden from the basic right of collective bargaining, with the law calling it "anti-trust." They were powerless. They had been defeated before the battle ever began. Medical societies had failed miserably, local, state, and national. As incomes dropped, groups would coalesce in clever ways to skirt anti-trust laws, but doctors, terminally independent, would be thrown into chaos. Specialties would clash with specialties, all trying to secure larger pieces of the pie. As always, the insurers would secure profits at the expense of both patients and physicians. After this instantaneous flash, Chase describes the future, as he sees it, to Dr. Underhill who responds:

"Christ, Callaway, you seem to be the only one here who gets it. Sorta scary to watch all these fat cats so oblivious to what's happening. Somebody needs to do something. Our leadership failed us." Dr. Underhill, a middle-aged fatherly sort, puts his hand on Chase's shoulder as the former rises and leaves the cafeteria.

As soon as Underhill is out of earshot, someone at the table mutters, "There's always a Chicken Little, isn't there?"

But for Chase, Underhill's words echo: "*Somebody* needs to do something."

Several months later, the major insurer for Southern California met with the Palmetto-Ciena medical staff to explain the new rules. "Here's our fee schedule," they announced. "You can sign up, or you can choose not to sign up. *You* have the power." (The fee schedule was less than half of current reimbursement.) "You'll make up for this proposed reimbursement level by the increased patient volume we'll channel your way."

"My schedule is already full. How the hell can I make it up with more patients?" someone yelled. "How dare you present a fee schedule like that?"

After that, the insurance representative was booed every time he opened his mouth. Doctors shouted, some approaching the podium for direct rebuke. Angry fists rose above the heads of the healers, nearly all of whom were now on their feet, shouting. Physicians began storming out of the room muttering, cursing, growling, with the speaker pleading for them to stay and listen to the future.

Chase was standing next to Dr. Underhill, frozen, unable to join the exodus. Chase said, "The amazing thing is that we still act like we have bargaining power. We've lost, and we've lost big. How could this have happened? All those docs who devote their careers to playing medical politics—they really dropped the ball."

Dr. Underhill replied, "Someone is going to have to lead the charge, a new charge, a new organized front. *Someone*, Chase."

The man at the podium announced, "The sign-up sheet is up here for those who'd like to become providers in our plan."

"We're not providers, damn you," someone hollered. "We're doctors, and don't you forget it." Those who hadn't left yet applauded.

While most doctors continued filing out of the room, a cluster began forming at the sign-up sheet, and the cluster became a line. The individuals in the line stooped over, one by one, to sign their names. It was a "who's who" of the outcasts, the shunned, the charlatans, all in the process of becoming "preferred providers."

Underhill and Callaway looked at each other, eyes widening. "*Someone*, Chase. It appears that medicine is now a profession that when the canary dies, our leaders opt to find more resilient canaries."

"Or, more gullible canaries."

A few months later, a call came from The Group. "Chase, in order to capitalize from this crisis, our group is forming our own IPA. That's an independent practice association. You, with Dr. Zink as your back-up, will be our exclusive providers for general surgery. That means, of course, you can't contract with anyone else."

"But more than a third of my income is from referrals outside The Group."

"We'll try to make that up to you somehow with more business."

"But I'm working as much—"

That day, Chase called the hospital administrator at Palmetto and said, "With this managed care fiasco, I'm going to need to put my name back on the trauma call panel."

In discussions with his partner, Dr. Zink, Chase bemoaned the fact that the honest doctors were being punished for the sins of a few. "It's odd, isn't it? The docs who are the most thorough, spend the most time, offer the greatest skill, now can't charge for their extra service. We're paid the same as the joker that doesn't give a squat, cuts corners, and basically practices crappy medicine. It's not even close to being fair."

"But it's never been fair, even under the old system," replied Dr. Zink. "Those that cut corners usually charged more. There's always been corruption. For instance, once they had a general surgeon at Ciena who operated on imaginary hernias."

"What?"

"He would contract to do physicals for large companies, then he'd identify so-called hernias on the men. Next, working in the minor surgery suite of his private office, he'd make an incision under local anesthesia and perform a sham procedure, which was no procedure at all. Then, he'd sew the patients up."

"You've got to be kidding."

"No, I'm not. As the years went on, I ended up operating on a few of them for real hernias, and when I went in, there was no evidence of anyone having been there before. Virgin territory."

"What happened to the surgeon?" asked Chase, thinking in terms of imprisonment.

"Have you ever seen that yacht in the marina, the big one called "Bella Bassini," always docked by the yacht club?"

"Yes."

"That's his. He retired years ago, and he lives on the yacht. Rumor has it he paid twenty million for the boat. So, you can see why we're headed now for a backlash."

"But the cheaters will just continue. They're the ones who'll find a way around the rules, and the only ones punished will be those of us who do the right thing."

Chase agonized over the situation for several months, juggling his body chemistry all the while. It was becoming obvious now. *Someone*, after a hearty diet of nectar and ambrosia for months on end, meant: "Chase Callaway." The repeated message of Dr. Underhill, a call to action, was clear. Chase should organize the resistance movement, locally at first, then nationally. After all, as Southern California goes – so goes the nation, eventually.

Editor's note: Deleted here is a lengthy description of Dr. Callaway's founding of MPC – the Medical Preservation Coalition. Capitalizing on the newfound concept of IRAs, Dr. Callaway extended the idea to IMAs, individual medical accounts with gentle taxation of the accounts to supplement current government plans for indigent care. For Chase, this was not some ethereal vision; his idea was based on raw facts. He procured reams of governmental and health industry statistics, extending his work well past midnight, month after month, shaking out a mathematical answer to the future of medical care. He wrote a treatise. He wrote editorials. He found audiences. He found followers. And perhaps, the measure of success was that he found enemies, not the least of which was the A.M.A. In a published letter to the A.M.A. president, Chase charged the association with being a "wide-eyed dinosaur staring stupidly at the fireball of an asteroid." In reply, the president publicly denounced him in written response: "Beware the reactionary forces brewing through charismatic characters who pursue futile efforts from the fringe."

Insidious, it is. Brain chemistry can be altered with remarkable subtlety. Every move, every thought is a function of chemicals, neurotransmitters, sending trillions of messages every second, around the clock. The eyes are open, the tongue it wags, but instead of one word to make a point, there are two – the old word and, with it, the new word, a twist on the old. At first, no one notices, but then the core personality, a biochemical vat, begins to change due to the new ingredients in the stew.

•

In his rise to Chief of Surgery, Chase slipped into deep melancholy. He didn't recognize it as such. He was, quite simply, tired. *Too* tired, with so much work to be done to save American Medicine. Yet, with lime green microspheres, Chase could conquer his fatigue; he could both generate and harness his rage at will; and he could rail against oppressive politics and bad practitioners. Oddly, associates asked him, "Why don't you smile anymore?"

Day-to-day medical practice lost its luster. Every surgical case seemed a bother, always accompanied by an irksome caveat, if not worse. For instance, a new plague had appeared in Los Angeles and New York, monikers aplenty, such as "4-H Club" (homosexuals, hemophiliacs, heroin users, and Haitians), and the HTLV-III virus had been caught red-handed. Yet there was no diagnostic test and no cure. After removing a groin mass from a young man, wherein the knot proved to be a lymph node bursting with the bizarre bug, Mycobacterium avium, Chase called the referring physician.

"I think this guy may have that new HTLV-III virus."

"Yes, I've already treated him for pneumocystis. I'm sure he has it."

Chase was floored. "You knew? Why— What— The patient didn't tell me anything about having pneumocystis. Why didn't you tell me? For chrissakes, we can stick ourselves with needles during surgery. I never dreamed— Why didn't you tell me?"

"Because these patients have organized. They're being discriminated against. Then we're being told it's a violation of their rights to tell anyone if they have HTLV-III."

"*Their* rights? Dammit, Jack, what about my rights? What about the rights of the surgeon? We already have to worry that the hepatitis patients might kill us if we get stuck, and now we have to deal with this, too – and you don't want to violate *their* rights?"

Chase racked his brain trying to think through every second of the lymph node operation. Had he been stuck? Had he stuck himself? It was such a common event. The scrub nurse hands you the needle driver, you reach for it without looking back so as not to lose your line of vision in the operative field, the nurse doesn't see your hand coming, Bingo! Stick! If no hepatitis, then no big deal. Until now.

The word "patient" was once again being replaced by "adversary."

Chase knew something was changing inside, gradually, relentlessly, but he wasn't sure why. His handwriting, usually perfect, was deteriorating (similar to the decay of John F. Kennedy's handwriting over time, he thought, where historians explained the decline as a paradoxical measure of Kennedy's success). Then, colleagues began commenting on Chase's speech sounding "funny." Then, a few jokes were made about him dozing off in late night committee meetings. Dr. Zink insisted that Chase start taking vacations, something he'd never done before. Oddly, he felt worse after a week off.

Skillful balancing of blue vs. green microspheres, the V-doughnuts, and pristine white was becoming more difficult. He would oversleep on rare occasion, but any occasion in surgery was unacceptable when a patient is in the holding area ready for surgery. Also, he felt himself less tolerant of minor faults, barking at scrub nurses for slovenly reaction times when he, on the other hand, was quick and adept.

Had it not been for middle-of-the night emergencies, the titration of elixirs would have worked far better. Once, after trauma call, driving back home on the freeway after removing a ruptured spleen in an auto accident victim, Chase felt a gentle thump against his car. Then, a blaring horn. When he opened his eyes (realizing he'd been driving asleep), the side of his Cutlass had softly kissed the side of a semi. He was halfway in the trucker's lane. As the semi sped up to get away from the maniac, Chase could see the angry driver shaking his fist outside the window. When he got home, he was pleased to find there had been no visible damage to his car. In effect, he had overreacted, as had the fist-shaking trucker.

When the call came from one of the nation's largest insurers, Chase was ecstatic. David and Goliath. His Medical Preservation Coalition, the MPC, was bringing them to their knees. They were ready to talk. His editorials had worked.

In the Mid-Wilshire section of Los Angeles, Chase entered an office tower and boarded the elevator. He was full of pride and fueled by microspheres. On the top story, in a conference room with one glass exterior wall revealing the *HOLLYWOOD* sign in the distance, with the other three walls covered in dark oak, Chase faced a panel of men in three-piece suits.

"Dr. Callaway, we are most impressed with your research and your vision. Our people have combed the numbers you sent us, and we think we might be able to put together a nice little package for some of our customers – a health insurance policy that has cash value. We're excited, and we think this will allow us to compete more effectively with Blue Cross."

Chase had trouble breathing. *A nice little package? For some of your customers?* He had been expecting a total capitulation of their managed care plans, one insurance company at a time, starting today, right now, a complete surrender beginning with the men sitting before him.

His larynx tightened. His voice quivered. He started off slowly: "I haven't devoted two years to this project for— for— (his voice grew louder, then mushroomed out of control) for some *nice little package* as an option for the precious few. My organization, gentlemen, is not about nice little packages, it's about revolutionizing health care in America. It's about stopping managed care in its tracks. It's about...."

Chase couldn't understand why the meeting had ended so abruptly or why he'd been excused from the boardroom or why the company never contacted him again. Through a mist, he could recall an exchange of blank looks among those in the boardroom that day as he uttered his revolutionary words to their complete lack of understanding. Their dumbfounded expressions had been those of the blind leading the blind, unable to comprehend the naked truth sitting before them.

Editor's note: Deleted here is an exhaustive account of Dr. Ted Zink's efforts to salvage his young partner. From the beginning, their father-son relationship came naturally. Chase had explained how his true father had wanted him to walk in his footsteps, but Chase felt he was always walking in his father's shadow instead. This awkward relationship had contributed to Chase's desire to leave Texas. Other motivations for the move to California had simply not panned out. Songwriting with C.C. Chastain had fizzled, and music was no longer part of Chase's life. To inject "fun" (diversion) into Chase's life, Dr. Zink had repeatedly invited Chase to go sailing, he had insisted on playing racquetball regularly, and he encouraged frequent dinners with Zink's family. Yet, his junior partner's mood seemed to be on a one-way street, going the wrong way.

Chase's creation of the MPC organization, his editorials published in the LA County Medical Bulletin, his sparring with the president of the A.M.A., all seemed half-cocked and grandiose, different than the humble Chase he had met seven years earlier. Chase seemed to have passed from personal devastation to persistent rage and was now moving toward mania. On the other hand, apart from the port placement disaster, Chase remained highly skilled in the operating room with excellent clinical judgment, so Zink kept quiet, offering sailing, racquetball, and family dinners.

But when he heard Chase's version of the apparent fiasco in the insurance company boardroom, with Chase tone-deaf to the grandiosity he had displayed, Dr. Zink finally mustered the courage to confront Chase as they scrubbed for surgery one morning: "I'm thinking you ought to see someone for counseling." Chase laughed and reassured his senior partner: "All is well. Digging myself out of debt has been getting me down, but I can see daylight now. As soon as that's over, I'll be fine."

9
FOREVER ALONE AT THE TOP

Punctuated equilibrium is in play whether life is evolving or devolving. Since Chase's unraveling is best understood as *devolving*, it is worth examining both the punctuation and the equilibrium, since the road was not straight downhill.

When the young woman walked into Chase's office complaining of a breast lump, he thought, at first, his sister had escaped the grave. The patient had Annie's dark and distant eyes, but it was her waxen mask, lean and forlorn, that reminded Chase of Annie's fusion with her terminal condition. The resemblance went further, to the point that the woman's whispering voice, like Annie's, reflected exhaustion when she said, "I have a lump."

Chase thought he might have allowed a gasp to escape when he first saw her. He could almost hear his mother's voice as she awakened Annie each new day with "Morning, Glory. Time to rise and shine." In response, Annie would whisper, "Why?"

Though his sister had died as a teenager from cystic fibrosis, this patient, shaking with angst, was how his sister might have looked had she lived to age thirty.

According to new California law interjecting itself between doctor and patient, Chase instructed the woman to read the government-issued brochure describing the option of breast conservation (lumpectomy) if cancer were to be found. Then, according to hospital policy, he documented the fact in his pre-op note that she had read the brochure (though he had not personally read it yet). Failure to record this critical item would have prompted cancellation of the surgery according to the law, a bizarre scenario for sure. The young woman opted for lumpectomy, and it would be Chase's first.

Even though the conversion from Halsted radical to modified radical had taken place five years earlier, lumpectomy was still considered a criminal act by many surgeons. Others, like Chase, were oblivious to lumpectomy as a legitimate option. Definitive studies were still pending.

After surgical removal of the lump by Chase (the standard biopsy method), pathology revealed medullary carcinoma, a relatively rare type of breast cancer. Chase went to the hospital library. He studied. He looked at the pathology photographs, recalling that he had seen this medullary type a few times during his fellowship. Yet, the clinical implications had not occurred to him. The medullary type was unique in that it formed a convenient sphere, without the usual fingers of cancer creeping into neighboring breast tissue. Her medullary tumor was only the size of a marble, completely surrounded by normal breast tissue. He asked himself, for the first time – *why? Why remove the breast if the entire cancer was already out and in the pathology lab? I might have already treated her adequately with the surgical biopsy alone, assuming her lymph nodes are clear.*

When the young woman returned for a discussion about further treatment, she presented Chase with a copy of a newly published book, *Breast Conservation*, and told him she planned nothing beyond the lumpectomy. He had no idea there was a book devoted entirely to breast cancer, much less a text on such a limited topic. He read it in two days and was shocked to learn that the theory for saving the breast could be traced back 200 years, and that the first attempts to combine lumpectomy and radiation dated back to the 1920s, and that maverick surgeons had published ample supporting evidence for lumpectomy ever since, and that the Halsted radical had originally been accepted on flimsy premature results – no questions asked for decades afterward. He also learned that a large co-op had established a novel approach to surgical controversies by randomizing patients to different breast cancer surgeries, and that their clinical trial to prove the benefit of lumpectomy would be reporting 5-year results soon.

How had this escaped him? He had completed his surgical residency under a mentor who expressed a keen interest in breast cancer, yet no mention had ever been made of these international clinical trials based on the underlying biology of the disease. He had been taught only excruciating details on how a "good technician" performs a "good mastectomy." Surgical technique ruled everything. Understanding the disease itself meant very little.

Then, Chase's young patient reported that she had sought a second opinion at a new clinic called a "multidisciplinary breast center" in The Valley where a surgeon had abandoned his general surgery training to focus on breast cancer and to spearhead this cooperative effort. The patient described her experience in detail, with multiple specialists sitting in the room together discussing her case, all agreeing she was an excellent candidate for lumpectomy.

"But I still want you to be my doctor," she said.

"Why? I don't think any other clinic in the country is doing what you've described."

"Because...you may not remember, but when you called me the pathology report, it was December 24th, and you spent so much time with me, trying to calm me down. I thought to myself that if a doctor is willing to spend his Christmas Eve with a desperate woman, as rattled as I was, then I want that person there for me, forever."

Chase had forgotten it had been Christmas Eve. He only remembered that he had imagined himself talking with his sister Annie and listening to her make a crackly effort to get her words out.

Within weeks, Chase visited the new breast center in The Valley and was astonished at the concept. He also learned, remarkably, that there were two scientific meetings each year where the subject was limited entirely to breast cancer. Remarkable! An entire conference for one disease. One of the two meetings was to be held in San Diego in a few months.

He attended this meeting where he discovered that it was sponsored by numerous professional organizations, but with the glaring absence of one College – his own. General surgery claimed to be the specialty that managed breast cancer from beginning to end, but where were they? Radiology, gynecology, pathology, radiation oncology, medical oncology, cancer societies, and so forth – they were all represented – but no surgical sponsorship whatsoever.

More shocking, Chase listened to presentations for five days covering the new implementation of mammography into routine practice, new evidence for the safety of lumpectomy, and a host of novel concepts. Yet, the distinguishing memory of the conference was this – he had recently passed his board-certification with flying colors, *but* – he had not studied one word, not one fact, not anything, that was presented during the five days of the conference. It became clear to Chase that a revolution was about to occur and that his specialty, known for its swagger, was sitting on the sidelines.

Later that year, at a national meeting of general surgeons, Chase attended a break-out session on breast cancer where those at the podium who endorsed lumpectomy were met with hisses and boos from the audience. Something was amiss. A serious disconnect was at work here, with two distinct worlds inhabited by two distinct life forms.

At the same event, Chase stumbled into his old mentor, Thatcher Nolan Taylor, M.D., where conversation turned to Chase's initial struggles to survive California, finally yielding a successful practice that was now, sadly, being crushed by managed care. Chase explained to T.N.T. that his primary mission in California was to expose managed care for what it really was – rationed health care delivery with medical decisions made by insurers.

T.N.T. squashed his former student's jingoism with quick and precise strokes. "Chase, medical politics is a dead-end path. Let me suggest something. You never expressed interest in academics, I know, but if you ever decide to come back to Texas, I'd like to see you consider a teaching position. One of our faculty members is retiring in a few years, so I'll have funding for a slot. The radiologists are planning to open a mammography center, but radiation oncology is the driving force here, and I'd like to make sure that surgery maintains control on how breast cancer is managed. You would be my first choice to head up that program."

Chase tried to contain his enthusiasm. "Might be good timing. I've been watching the developments in breast cancer. Even went to a meeting in San Diego. I *do* think there's going to be a revolution surrounding breast cancer very soon when those lumpectomy trials present their final data. I swore I'd never return to west Texas, but I'll sure keep it in mind."

"I read your recent editorial on managed care, by the way, in the A.M.A newspaper, and I have to admit, the poem at the end was very clever. Quite lyrical. We all got quite a chuckle out of it back in Texas. Still, I'd hate to see your talent wasted on medical politics."

Chase was doing more than "watching the developments" in breast cancer, as he had implied. He was reading and studying at a frenetic pace, and he was negotiating with Palmetto-Ciena Hospital to reproduce the prototype in multidisciplinary breast care that had been achieved in The Valley. Aware that expertise was often impotent without credentials, he was exploring the option of further specialization beyond general surgery.

However, the only option, as the lead surgeon in The Valley had done, was to engage in a one- or two-year fellowship in "surgical oncology," a new concept, ill-defined. Yet the programs that Chase reviewed seemed to be fixated on chemotherapy and "fighting the medical oncologists" for territorial rights, a sharp contrast to Chase's growing belief that the territorial boundaries should be broken down. Surprisingly, breast cancer was only a small part of these surgical oncology programs. Nowhere could he find a fellowship dedicated entirely to breast cancer.

So, he decided to continue what he was doing – intense self-education. After all, he was an autodidact at heart. This was the approach used by all pioneers in the formation of new medical specialties. Who trained Harvey Cushing, the father of neurosurgery, in the art and science of neurosurgery? No one. Cushing, like so many great men of medicine, taught himself.

Chase started to lose interest in his Medical Preservation Coalition. Yet, he couldn't disappoint his followers, however many there might be. Plus, he couldn't refuse the president of the Los Angeles County Medical Association when asked to write another editorial in the *LACMA*

Bulletin, especially after the invitation for him to join the Editorial Board.

Then, before an audience of 80 physicians near Newport Beach where a rally was organized (by Chase) to spread the word about the MPC, he had a panic attack at the podium. Palpitations, sweating, shaky voice, terror, and get-me-out-of-here panic. It happened when an audience member stood and shouted that Chase "didn't have a snowball's chance in hell" of stopping the juggernaut of managed care. Chase attributed his panic attack to sloppy chemistry. He had titrated incorrectly, forcing him to call a recess after the Q&A and rush to his car in the parking lot where he kept antidotes to all miscalculations. By the time he had corrected the chemistry, the audience had left. After that, he began a concerted effort to wean himself from all pharmaceuticals, trying a variety of methods that ended up with one common feature – they didn't work.

Chase believed that the "quiet voice of the Lord" could sometimes be one's own will searching for validation, and that such self-delusion was responsible for many of the great calamities of humankind. So, he usually ignored quiet inner voices and waited for Heavenly Shouts.

Such a shout came when Chase discovered, overnight it seemed, that he could not bend his fingers without lancing pain in his knuckles. He dismissed the pain at first, likely due to minor arthritis from trauma, invoking the memory of the punch to the wall at his grandfather's funeral. Then there was the street brawl when he'd been robbed after the car wreck, where his knuckles took a beating with each blow to his attackers. More than five years had passed since these events.

But the pain became steadily worse. If, during a difficult surgical procedure, deep in the abdomen, his partner Dr. Zink rested a metal clamp against Chase's knuckles, he yelped. Most of the time, however, he simply grimaced quietly behind his mask, clenching his teeth in pain as procedures became torturous. Yet, the less-demanding breast cancer surgery was remarkably pain free. Was this a Heavenly Shout?

As time went on, he found he could no longer make a fist with either hand, the right side worse than left (he was right-handed). Each new day began with Chase running warm water over his knuckles to allow the flexibility to earn his living. Of course, the chemicals of pristine white were now completely justifiable, whereas emotional pain does not count.

With the escalation of pharmacologic intervention, Chase's personality change was so dramatic that C.C. Chastain was prompted to intervene. They met at C.C.'s house. "Listen, buddy, California is filled with kooks, especially in medicine, so you might be blending in just fine with these nut jobs. I don't know. But you're not the same person as when you moved out here. You act different, you talk different, and frankly, I think you're on something."

"Well, that's an astute observation, isn't it? I suppose you haven't noticed the white powder flakes in your moustache?"

"Easy, dipshit, that's from a powdered donut. Nothing interferes with my work. Or changes my personality. Maybe it's just because my style is consistent. Consistently an asshole, yes, but buddy, at least I still laugh. You haven't smiled in years."

Chase was caught, and he knew it. He lowered his head and spoke directly to the planks of C.C.'s hard wood living room floor, mere steps away from the grand piano. "I guess I need help, C.C. I've done everything imaginable to stop on my own. Can't go twenty-four hours clean, though. Anxiety moves in at six hours, then panic at about the twelve-hour point, then unbearable terror by eighteen hours, out of touch with reality. My record is twenty-two hours. Helluva a record-keeper, I am. I've recorded every attempt. I'm not sure what to do. I can't let anyone know. They destroy addicted docs, as you know. No matter what they do, no matter how clean they get, no matter how many years of sobriety, no matter how accomplished they become, they're stained for life. The whispers behind the back, the speculation about relapse with every little thing that happens. Docs love to slap the scarlet letter on their competitors. I won't let myself be part of that. I've got to get help *quietly*."

C.C. Chastain agreed to help. He arranged for Chase to dry out in the privacy of a motel room across the street from Disneyland. Chase chose the Fantasyland motel, surrounded by animal topiaries, as he wanted to retrace his steps to the happiest moment of his young life, on Opening Day. Peeking between dusty curtains, Chase could see one turret of the Magic Castle, and he could still hear Walt's words: "To all who come to this Happy Place – welcome."

C.C. stayed in a room next door to Chase, checking frequently on his friend, the intent being to allow Chase's humiliation to remain semi-private (also allowing C.C. to get paperwork done during the withdrawal).

Chase spent the next few days in his self-constructed hell – tingling panic that made his skin sizzle, roller coaster emotions that took him to extremes, tyrannical dysphoria that demanded self-harm, all while pleading with God to take him off the face of the earth. As the false molecular messengers swam away from his neurons, his brain screamed for repair, pleading for the quick-fix chemicals to return, rather than the slowpoke natural ones. Drenched in sweat one minute, freezing the next, puking, heart racing, doubled over with abdominal pain, then relentless muscular twitching and cramps. Sleep was measured in minutes, and the worst part was that there was no end in sight. No improvement over time. No hope, it seemed.

At one point, when symptoms subsided, and he thought it must be over, Chase tried to stand up from the bed, but his legs buckled and he fell to the floor, face first. He could not stand up, though he did manage to reach the adjoining wall to pound, alerting his friend next door. C.C. thought it best to call an ambulance, but Chase begged him to hold off.

Face down on a stinking carpet in a rathole motel – this was devolution. Whatever the cause for his collapse, a half hour later, he managed to stand.

When it finally ended, four days had passed. It was horrible but would have been impossible without the buffering effect of a few V-pills (diazepam) that had helped him through the worst of the ordeal.

Chase felt like a new man, free of the handfuls of chemicals he had been taking to get through the day, half of which were simply to counteract the side effects of the uppers, downers, and pain relief. What a blessing it was to be rid of it all. Almost all, that is. As for the diazepam, he would simply wean himself gradually and be done with it. After all, the V-pills were nothing more than a mild sedative, the housewife's drug of choice.

Rumors hit Far West Texas College of Medicine that, after nearly a decade gone, Chase Callaway was coming home. As one old friend on the medical school faculty said when he heard the news, "Now people will know what we mean when we give grades to our medical students with the comment, 'This student reminds me of a young Chase Callaway'."

Then – delay. The retiring surgeon at Far West Texas, whose position Chase would assume, decided to keep working another six months to a year. Chase's heart sank. This surgeon would have to vacate the spot before a salary would be available, and Chase was stuck in a nightmare. Not the nightmare of his recent past, but a growing problem he had inherited as Chief of Surgery. He had hoped to extricate himself from the crisis through permanent transport to Texas.

A scoundrel surgeon, with whom Chase usually steered clear, had been in a long-standing battle with the previous Chief of Surgery, now the Chief of Staff. The controversial surgeon, Dr. Kelso, was a "professional assistant," a hulking presence with curly gray hair, smarmy charisma, comical to some physicians but irksome to others, such that he had few direct referrals. His unpredictable behavior caused most to shy away as his child-like jesting could turn malicious without warning. Without referrals, he made his living by covering the E.R. and assisting other surgeons, usually at night. Chase had asked Kelso to be his assistant only one time out of desperation, and he swore "never again."

On that occasion, Kelso's non-stop commentary was: "You ought to do such-and-such instead, like Dr. So-and-So does it," tailored to the exact opposite of whatever Chase was doing at the time. Plus, Kelso had the peculiar habit of angrily blaming all illnesses on the patient. "Damn, here we are in the middle of the night, and if this asshole had simply addressed his diverticulitis electively, we wouldn't be here now. Shit, it looks like a goddam grenade went off in this abdomen. You can't recognize squat with all this peritonitis."

Kelso had repeatedly tried to take over the case to the point of having the operating room table raised above Chase's preferred level, allowing comfort for himself at Chase's expense. "Too high," said Chase, "please bring the table down where I can see what I'm doing."

And then, Chase had to forcibly stop the surgeon from the blind riveting of hemoclips into pools of blood, without clearly identifying the responsible vessels.

Hemoclips were tiny V-shaped strips of titanium, applied with a device that closed the arms of the V around the open end of bleeding vessels. In general, Chase used them only rarely because they tended to slip off later if there was ongoing manipulation in the abdomen. Nevertheless, he abhorred the random jamming of the Vs, especially when targeting a squirting stream of blood, rather than identifying the open end of the actual vessel. During this one-time exposure to the professional assistant, blood kept pooling in spite of Kelso's rapid-fire hemoclip applications that did nothing other than drive Chase to the point of rudeness. "Please stop with the hemoclips. You don't know anatomically what's at the bottom of that pool of blood. If you can see the actual vessel, then okay." Dr. Kelso didn't say another word for the rest of the case. If only Dr. Zink had not been on vacation, Chase would have avoided the man completely. Never again.

Over the years, Kelso was frequently charged with inappropriate behavior – threatening the nurses, threatening other doctors, threatening administration, and even threatening patients in the emergency room. Once, he told an injured gang member that he was going to use him for target practice just as soon as the kid was patched up (Kelso made no secret of the various firearms he kept in his car). Oddly, his threats were made with a smile and clever wit, offering him refuge when confronted, as he would claim to be "joking." Finally, Kelso crossed the Rubicon of Unacceptability when he humiliated a Sister, a young nun who crossed his path one night in the emergency room of what was now a Catholic hospital – "I may have some bad habits, but I'd still like to explore yours." It was time to do something.

The first option was to change hospital by-laws in order to allow major cases to be performed without a first assistant. This would have squeezed Dr. Kelso out of Palmetto-Ciena without any confrontation. However, the surgical staff fought this with vigor, since all seasoned surgeons had longstanding associates that could turn a challenging solo operation into an orchestral arrangement. Furthermore, since it was *possible* to do these cases without another surgeon of equal skill, insurers would soon discover this and put an end to a major source of revenue for the surgical specialties. When a change in by-laws was voted down as an indirect ploy to oust Kelso, everyone knew it was going to get ugly with any other option.

Chief of Staff, Gavin March, started proceedings against Kelso in the form of a mandatory psychiatric evaluation. The report was so damning in its description of a paranoid sociopath with borderline personality that the Medical Executive Committee voted 9 to 3 to hire security guards for all future meetings, and to accompany committee members on their hospital rounds. As a member of the Medical Executive Committee, and no friend of Kelso, Chase was among the 9 who voted for the security guards in yet another surrealistic saga that seemed like a never-ending curse. Calling ahead to the ward to make rounds: "This is Dr. Callaway, and I'll need security on Unit 300 in about 10 minutes, in order to make rounds. Thank you."

But the good doctor Kelso was not easily subdued. Over the years of assisting other surgeons, he had kept a detailed log of their "errors and unnecessary surgeries," and when Kelso was finally told he was going to be dismissed from staff on behavioral grounds alone, he submitted his file of "improprieties" on Chief of Staff, Dr. Gavin March, to the state Medical Board, the American Board of Surgery, and the American College of Surgeons. Suddenly, Dr. March was embroiled in a fight to save his own career, his own livelihood, his own reputation, and he was forced to recuse himself from all further actions against Dr. Kelso. With Dr. March hog-tied, the responsibility for continuing the fight against the recalcitrant Dr. Kelso would fall to the Chief of Surgery – Chase Callaway.

Chase knew he could not handle another personal attack against his character like he was witnessing now with his friend, Gavin March. He had been through enough the first time around, years ago, when he naively showed up at the Ciena hospital believing collegiality was the norm for physicians.

In desperation, Chase called his future boss in Texas, Dr. Taylor, pretending everything was hunky dory, hinting at the possibility of an earlier return to Texas. "Chase, I'm sorry, but we have limited funding for salaries here. I don't have the money for new faculty members until someone leaves. We're highly dependent on VA funding, and I need five-eighths FTE freed up before we bring you back to Far West. We're certainly eager for your return, by the way. I can't recall getting so much positive feedback from the faculty in other departments..."

Chase couldn't sleep. Thank goodness he'd only allowed Dr. Kelso to assist him one time. Would Chase be safe with only a single case? Kelso claimed his files included "facts" he'd gathered from all sites around the hospital, not just the operating room. Some believed he had stolen physician files from the medical staff office. Whether or not this was true, Kelso boasted that he could destroy any doctor on staff that he wanted to. For Chase, it could be deadly. Such "facts" would include those accusations against him when he began practice at Ciena. He imagined those resurrected "facts" being sent to the same governing bodies where Dr. March's files had landed. Thus, insomnia, night after night, week after week, month after month.

He couldn't sleep without diazepam. Yet, as he tried to wean himself, it was one step forward, two steps back. The insomnia was crippling, and the longer he held out, the more sedative he took to overcome the increasing anxiety. In no time, his "weaning" resulted in a quadrupling of his usual dose.

He tried switching to "safer" substitutes (misguided by pharmaceutical sales pitches), other drugs in the same family, but nothing helped as his tolerance grew and grew. This was crazy! He had kicked a much more dangerous habit on his own, a multi-drug addiction wherein each agent by itself was more deadly than plain old benzodiazepines.

As the number of pills needed to sleep increased over time, he began to study the pharmacology and physiology of diazepam withdrawal, shocked to learn that abrupt discontinuation of the benzodiazepine family of drugs could lead to seizures and death. He had to wean, and he eventually had to stop. Plain old Valium had a dark side that few knew about at the time.

But every attempt to taper led to such profound anxiety, onward to panic, that the idea of going without was inconceivable. In one fitful night, believing that he would never fall asleep again, he took two, three, four, a total of nine tablets of a benzodiazepine sleeper new on the market, and he was still awake all night. With escalation came more tolerance, and with tolerance came a rapid and deep descent, once again.

The phone call from Dr. Kelso to Chase was the most terrifying event of everything that was happening at the time. "Chase, I understand you're taking over for Gavin March on this witch hunt going on at Ciena, so I'd like to sit down with you and talk things out, if that's okay. Listen, by the way, I was assisting an orthopedic surgeon in Santa Monica last week, telling him about the craziness going on there at Ciena-Palmetto, and I mentioned your name. He told me he'd been on call one night about seven years ago when he fixed a broken ankle on this elderly lady whose husband claimed she'd been assaulted by an intoxicated physician. The surgeon didn't know you personally, but the name Callaway stuck in his head because he was from Texas and he'd heard of your father through basketball, or something like that. Anyway, I found the story very fascinating, and it could be one of the things we talk about when we get together."

Chase could barely catch his breath. The horrible episode with its year-long aftermath had, remarkably, been kept out of the medical community. Until now. Not even his partner, Dr. Zink, knew of the million-dollar civil suit for "assault." Plus, there were the two malpractice suits as well, serving as handmaidens. Only a few friends knew of the civil suit and the later imprisonment of Sheldon Rose and his wife after their attempt to scam the sitting president.

Chase managed to answer, "That's a complicated story, but rest assured I did not assault anyone. They were scam artists." Yet, Chase knew it would be juicy fodder for Kelso, and that the madman could take the story anywhere he needed to take it.

On October 19, 1987, Black Monday, the stock market crashed. Chase had moved all his savings into the market, trying to accumulate assets as quickly as possible since it was becoming increasingly clear that his career might be short-lived due to sheer exhaustion. After the crash, in order to recover, he poured his remaining assets into his old HMO nemesis, for whom he'd worked years earlier. Professional investors were calling it the "darling of Wall Street" as HMOs were clearly the way of the future. *If you can't beat 'em, join 'em.* When the HMO declared bankruptcy a short time later, Chase was staring at the prospect of having to start over – again, still in debt.

Some of his physician-friends in Texas had already paid off their homes, and others had retirement plans fully vested. Although starting from scratch, he maintained optimism. *Plenty of time left. After all, I'm not even forty.* Still living in his breadbox apartment on the 13th floor, with his grandfather's books, many of them still entombed in cardboard boxes as his furniture, he kept alimony going while also continuing support to Sukie Spurlock. The money issue would take care of itself, he thought. Eventually.

Then, Chase realized he was having memory problems, and he wondered if it could be related to his escalating daily dose of diazepam. He couldn't remember some of the details surrounding the heated controversies at Department of Surgery meetings, most notably the status of legal proceedings against Dr. Kelso. He forgot he was supposed to assist his partner Dr. Zink one morning on a colon resection. In another example, after highlighting in yellow the key parts of the only major text he could find on breast cancer, preparing for his career change, he went back for a second reading of the highlights (as he had done in medical training with near-total retention), but had little recognition. It was as though he were reading the material for the first time.

When Dr. Zink confronted Chase about his shaky memory, Chase sensed his own impending meltdown. "Chase, I didn't think too much of it at first. But then, I've had to cover for you on days when you forgot that you had patients in the Palmetto office. Most of the things have been minor, admittedly, but last weekend, when you were covering, you forgot to make rounds on that wound infection I admitted late Friday evening."

Chase chose this moment, in a spectacular attempt at diversion, to reveal to his adopted father, Dr. Zink, his plans to return to Texas. He had dreaded the moment for months, but he was pleased that his partner accepted the move without criticism or condemnation.

Dr. Zink said, "I think your experience here was too much for anyone, Chase. Truly unbelievable. I get that. I wish we'd never sent you into the Ciena quagmire like we did after the hospital purchase, especially after your initial blackballing there. We pulled you out of the dirt only to throw you back in, when we should have kept you safe at Palmetto for a good while to let you recover. We're losing money on that hospital anyway. Wish we'd never bought it. Still, someone else should have cleaned up the mess there. Not you. And now this horrible Kelso deal, where we're all worried about getting sued, or worse, and you're sitting at the front lines on that. I'm terribly sorry to lose you. You're like a son to me. But it's not just your memory, Chase. You don't seem to have the same oomph as when we first started working together. I said it once in the past, but I think you ought to consider some counseling before you go back."

Chase understood how his behavior might appear strange to Dr. Zink, but there was no mystery to it. He was addicted to benzodiazepines, and he knew it. The only question was how to extricate himself. His ongoing study in the medical library had revealed an alarming fact – that, while these drugs were considered by the public to be innocuous, the grip of physiologic addiction matched that of heroin once high-dose tolerance had occurred.

But this is how Chase answered his partner's comment about counseling: "I was watching that new movie channel, you know, the one that's playing the old black and whites. The ending to one film used the phrase, 'No man is a failure who has friends.' Other than you and my old friend C.C. from medical school, I don't have any friends here. I woulda counted fifty or so people back in Texas as friends. After all this time, two friends and a handful of semi-friends. Those judicial reviews during my first few years, I'm sure that alienated docs even though I was in the right. The brotherhood of silence is real, you know. Now, taking on Kelso is gonna be a duel to the finish. I can't do it. No telling what that nut job will do. But I need to get rested, and I need to get back where I have friends, where I trained, where my reputation is rock solid. Where people know me. That's all I need."

While he was talking, a great fear swept over Chase, a fear worse than head-to-head combat with Kelso – the fear of a medical disaster in his practice unless he kicked the benzo habit soon. Better to stop practicing now than risk an adverse event that could tarnish his reputation even in Texas. So far, his memory loss had caused little harm, but Dr. Zink's concern indicated to Chase that the dam was getting ready to break.

He continued, "Ted, I'm going to stop practicing now. I know it's still months before my job opens up in Texas, but I need to quit. This Kelso thing is the most depressing prospect I've ever faced in my life. He's a madman pushed into a corner, and he's out of control. Look what Kelso did to Gavin March. I don't know anyone finer than Gavin, and now he's fighting for his professional life. I'm next in Kelso's crosshairs, and I can't take it. My term is over soon as Chief of Surgery, and everyone is expecting me to be Chief of Staff, but I can't face Kelso's lunacy. Those proceedings are going on way longer than we expected. I can't last that long."

Chase left Dr. Zink at the Palmetto office and returned to their secondary office in Ciena where he turned out the lights and buried his head in shame. There, his office nurse reminded him of a post-op patient, waiting for the past hour, a woman whose life he had saved, albeit temporarily. He had forgotten she was on the schedule. The woman was Chase's age, and she had presented with a ruptured appendix. In fact, the rupture was due to a colon cancer that had obstructed the opening of the appendix. In addition to peritonitis at the time of surgery, she had countless tumors multiplying throughout her abdomen. Now, she had completed chemotherapy, but the cancer was raging again.

"Why is she here?" asked Chase. "My part is done. The medical oncologist takes it from here."

"She wants you to take care of her through the dying process," said his nurse. "She didn't bond with the medical oncologist. She said he was like a robot. She wants you to help her from here on."

"I can't," he said. "I can't do this anymore."

Paralyzed, he couldn't get up from his desk to explain the situation to his patient. He was completely drained, and there was nothing left to give. For another thirty minutes, the woman sat in the exam room, waiting for Chase. The nurse kept checking on him every few minutes, perplexed as to the doctor's paralysis. Yet, Chase had to wait for the pills to start working before he could walk into the exam room and tell his patient (and his nurse): "I'm sorry. I'm quitting practice, and I'm moving back to Texas."

Over the next few weeks, he closed his practice and retreated to his apartment where he could formulate a strategy for weaning from diazepam, pressure-free of work demands.

When he received the notice of yet another allegation of malpractice – his third – he was in his sixth day of tapering the drug in a four-week strategy, as outlined in the medical literature. After reading the charges, he triple-dosed himself lest he kill someone in rage. The plaintiff was a man whose life Chase had saved after ruptured diverticulitis, the very operation in which Chase had been assisted by the nefarious Dr. Kelso.

Now, years later, the plaintiff had been facing prostate surgery, which led to an IVP study of his kidneys, which led to the discovery that one kidney was not functioning, which led to a retrograde IVP, which led to the point of obstruction being a solitary hemoclip, a metallic V that had clamped the ureter, the collecting tube that extends from kidney to bladder, and destroyed the kidney through back pressure.

The small diameter ureter had been buried in the cake of peritonitis at the time of surgery. The kidney loss had occurred without symptoms. The discovery of the offending hemoclip came through serendipity. Chase never used a single hemoclip on the case, whereas Dr. Kelso, the mad riveter, was not named in the lawsuit. Only Chase.

"Settle, just settle," Chase yelled at his insurance company rep. "I have no defense. It's captain of the ship. I'm responsible. Yes, I saved the guy's life, but what does that matter nowadays? We're not doctors anymore. We're ducks at the carnival where the ungrateful get to take potshots at us. We're nothing but freakin' lottery tickets. Bingo. Bad result? So what if you saved my life? I want my money. I want my entitlement. Well, I don't care if this is a mark on my record for the rest of my career. I don't care about the freakin' Big Brother national data bank they're putting together so that this kind of crap will stay on my record for everyone to see for the rest of my life. I just don't care. I don't care about anything anymore. Just settle. Whatever the guy wants, give it to him. Give him his damn lottery winnings." The insurance rep was stunned to silence.

After that, weaning from diazepam became even more difficult. He forgot to eat. He forgot day versus night. He was out of work, coasting, careening. He received a birthday present in the mail from his parents, and it took a few moments for the correct word – wristwatch – to come to his lips.

He had to get clean before going back home to Texas. Yet, every attempt to decrease his dose, even a little, sent him into a jittery state of dread and fright. Without his diazepam, the sound of a dripping faucet punched holes in his brain. A door slamming stopped his heart. The light coming through the plate-glass wall in his apartment blinded him, so curtains remained closed. The sheets of his bed formed a blanket of thorny spines that penetrated his skin. The fear of opening his apartment door was too great to bear. Yet it all disappeared within minutes after a single pill, and he was normal once again. There was no doubt about it. He was not in denial. He fully appreciated and acknowledged his predicament. Yet, what he didn't understand is why the grip was far more powerful than his multi-drug addiction from Disneyland Days.

One night, or perhaps day, he turned on the television and saw a faith healer speaking directly to him, eye-to-eye: "There's someone out there, watching right now, you know who you are, with a Valium addiction. You are in its grasp, and it's strangling the life out of you. You've tried everything, but nothing works. Well, just place your hands on the television screen and pray with me, and you will be healed."

"Yes. This is the miracle I've been waiting for, the miracle to prove that God is still alive in my life. I won't need to wean at all. I won't need to taper. It's over, and I believe it's over." Chase prayed along with the TV image. His fingers spread over the cathode-ray tube, and he could feel the electrons beating against the phosphor coating on the inner surface of the glass. Too, he could sense energy pierce the tube as those released photons that formed the face of the preacher now entered his fingertips, then his brain. He was healed – for the next eight hours.

For it was then that his heart started to race, his hands began to shake, his breathing quickened, and he felt panic rattling his bones. He rushed back to the TV set, but the photons forming the face were long gone. Instead, emaciated dogs and cats awaiting euthanasia filled the screen, along with a 1-800 number to stop the carnage.

Something was wrong. Chase prayed again, believed again, begged again, but he felt worse. He couldn't stop moving, pacing in circles faster and faster, wanting to call for help, but not wanting to reveal his nightmare to anyone. "Oh, please, Lord, do not let me go into full-blown seizures. That would be the end. Everyone would know. I'd rather die. Take me if it's your will."

Chase grabbed the Bible of his youth, rarely opened, breathless as he read the highlighted areas, as if a youthful Chase, strong and full in faith, were talking to the weathered and beleaguered Chase twenty years hence. "What would I have told myself today...back then? What advice?" He raced through the pages, feeling worse by the second. "Oh God, no, please no," as he felt himself spiraling into panic, his arms and hands beginning to twitch uncontrollably. "Heal me, please."

He couldn't stand it another second. He felt the terror of a hornet's nest disturbed, but the startle response persisted rather than the quick scare of the usual wasp encounter. Angry insects all around. Buzzing, attacking, the panic did not waiver, the insects didn't back off – not until Chase grabbed his bottle of Valium and popped untold milligrams of instantaneous relief.

What had he done wrong? Why hadn't God delivered him? He considered the strong likelihood that one must be in good grace to receive a blessing or a cure. Fervent prayer was critical. Foxhole prayers are low yield. Then, over the course of the next few days, he tithed 10% of last year's net to Varsity Voyagers, earmarked for The New Bloods, his old folk group. Days later, he sent an additional check to bump his tithe to 10% *gross*, fearing that he was trying to short-change Providence. He sought a church in his area to help him hold it together until he could get back to Texas. Within the city limits of Ciena, however, there was only a Buddhist temple. He would need to travel to other suburbs next Sunday in order to find a church in the same vein as west Texas.

Before that next Sunday, though, Chase received a sickening letter in the mail. His malpractice insurance carrier claimed that Chase had not been insured by their company at the time of the ureteral injury and kidney loss from the V-shaped hemoclip.

Chase had been switching insurance companies regularly for the past nine years, as physicians scrambled for the best deal amid skyrocketing rates. With each switch, it was necessary to request "tail coverage" by defining the exact time period the new company would be insuring. At first, he held hope that, in his muddled state of mind, he had simply submitted the current claim to the wrong company. As it turned out, however, when he found his records, the shock left him breathless – in his illegible handwriting on his current application, he had written the wrong dates of coverage for the "tail." When Dr. Kelso violated the abdominal cavity with his arsenal of metallic Vs, Chase had unwittingly been practicing *bare* – he was totally uninsured at the time and now without legal representation.

"How much do you want?" Chase asked the plaintiff's attorney, explaining his situation. "I'd rather not pay for a lawyer, if you're going to be reasonable."

"My client is an older gentleman and will be happy to settle for a hundred thousand. That's very reasonable for a kidney in today's climate."

"I don't have a hundred thousand. I don't have anywhere near that. I've had a run of bad luck. I don't own a home. I drive a beat-up '80 Cutlass. I'm sending money back home, alimony and whatnot. I just wrote a big check as part of a charitable donation. I have very little savings left, and I'm not working right now."

"Well, you certainly don't *have* to settle. We can always go to court, but you know how juries get carried away in the award process. After all, my client is missing a kidney."

"Your client is lucky to be alive. I can settle in installments. How about that? Ten thousand a year for ten years?"

"You're asking for an interest-free loan from my client? Not going to cut it. If we do installments over such an extended length of time, then our request will double. That would be $200,000 over the next seven years. I suggest you take out a loan and pay a lump sum now to my client."

Awash in diazepam, a broken man, Chase said, "Okay. A hundred thousand lump sum now. Just give me time to establish myself with a new bank in Texas. I'd never qualify for a loan here."

The job at Far West was finally open – that is, it would officially be open in three months. Plenty of time to wean himself in a peaceful environment, away from Kelso, away from a resurrection of the Sheldon Rose incident, away from the encroachment of managed care that would ruin private practice, away from the litigious patient population, away from a lifetime's worth of horrible memories. To compound it all, he had not written any lyrics with C.C. in nearly a decade of lost opportunity in Los Angeles.

C.C. Chastain agreed to drive Chase back to Texas, pulling a trailer full of belongings, the same items Chase had brought with him to California. Breaking even, however, was not the case. He was now under a significant debt burden with more on the way, worse off than the day he'd finished his residency. His brief career of high-volume, fee-for-service surgery, shortly after joining Ted Zink in his surgical practice, had not lasted long with the abrupt introduction of managed care that hurt on two fronts – slashing the fee schedule and dictating referral patterns according to contracted agreements. His practice overhead had been double what his colleagues back home were paying, yet managed care reimbursement in Southern California was lower than fee-for-service in Texas. He had fought so hard to secure his place in L.A., but now it was all going up in smoke. Instead of anything positive to show from these years, he would be limping back home, saddled with an oppressive addiction and crippling depression.

On the drive back to Texas, C.C. explained to Chase that he had a new songwriting partner, and that their studio was decorated by his partner's Gold Record hanging on the wall, a single hit from years earlier. C.C.'s new partner was hopeful that the Gold Record would not leave him floundering in music history as a "one hit wonder." They both believed that with hard work and a little luck, they could land a hit, offering companion gold to the solitary trophy on the wall. In silent response, Chase recalled how a ticket to stardom for C.C. and himself – after their song was stolen – was now a distant memory, melding into nearly ten years of harrowing surrealism.

A tune began to play in his head while he and C.C. drove through the Petrified Forest, one of those songs that you can't shake. He had not thought about it in years. Indeed, it was a song of Chase's own making, written as a child under the direction of his Sunday School teacher, Jewell Pollard, who had ended up in a vegetative state in the Dungeon at the local insane asylum where he had worked as an aide. There, he had taught the song to Ivy Pettibone, an inmate at the same asylum. Now, he was silently repeating the words of his song to the melody of "Chopsticks," and dreaming of asylum for himself.

> *Zanda the Panda*
> *Alone in a land-a*
> *Where bears do not live*
> *But a storm...blew him out to sea.*

> *In a palm tree*
> *He did land*
> *Don't you see*
> *Forever alone at the top.*

> *He cried, boo-hoo, boo-hoo. He wanted bamboo, he only boo-hoo'd*
> *Boo-hoo, bamboo, boo-hoo, I want to go home. I want to go home...*

10
FOOTLOOSE ATOMS IN THE LAKE OF SULPHUR

As the Greeks would have it – "tomos" meaning *cut*, while "atomos" indicates *uncuttable*. Rudimentary atomic theory was initially proposed more than 400 years before anno domini, the original thought being that if matter could be infinitely divided, then it would be impossible to reassemble. Yet, disintegration and reintegration were obvious in nature. Therefore, infinite division was impossible. Matter must be reducible, *only to a brink*, whereupon the splitting stops. At that point, one encounters "atomos." No further cutting.

Atomos was an ideal depiction of Chase Callaway, as he had been reduced to disconnected and deranged atoms, swimming free in brimstone broth, oblivious to future reassembly.

From tape recordings and log entries he made during this time, he could reconstruct only a patchwork of events. The following is what seems to be true.

Upon checking into his new apartment at the outskirts of Matherville, C.C. Chastain helped Chase strategize the withdrawal plan. They had both studied the matter, and C.C. believed in trying the 3-week approach, while Chase held on to the 4-week plan. C.C. won the debate and helped place diminishing doses of diazepam in 21 plastic baggies. They knew the science, and they knew that the risk of seizures would be greatly reduced by this gradual tapering (not to mention abrupt withdrawal carried a small, but significant, risk of death).

Ideally, these baggies would have been distributed one-by-one by a neutral party, but C.C. had to get back to L.A., and there was no one in Matherville that Chase felt he could trust. Importantly, the excess from Chase's supply, no longer obtained easily through generic pharmaceutical warehouses, was confiscated by C.C. Chastain as he left town. Chase would be in charge of the tapering, alone. At least he was free of all external stressors that had plagued him during the final months in California, and his new job was still months away. Tapering should be a snap.

Chase had stopped by the home of his parents shortly after initial arrival in Matherville – his way of warding them off from his apartment where he would become increasingly symptomatic during withdrawal.

However, Wes and Ramona Callaway paid an unannounced visit to Chase's apartment on Day 9. His withdrawal symptoms were escalating, and he was sure now that the 4-week approach would have been wiser. He wasn't confident that he could hide the anxiety from his parents.

Ramona tried to make small talk. "You know, Chase, it pains us to say it, but Livvy was better off without you. You were so selfish in that marriage, why, I don't know what happened to you. You weren't that way before medical school."

Chase was troubled that his mother would spring something like that on him, so long after the fact. Considering his fragile state now and all he'd been through, the divorce was more like a tornado spin-off from the larger hurricane. Why bring it up now?

"Which way is your bathroom, son?" asked his father. "The old prostate doesn't let me have much of a break."

Chase pointed to the hallway. "There, on the left."

In a wicker basket beneath the bathroom sink, Wes Callaway discovered 12 baggies containing diazepam. "What the hell?" he muttered to himself. "That explains why he looks so bad." Quietly, he emptied each of the baggies into the toilet. And flushed. He then returned to the living room where he announced what he'd done for Chase's own good.

Editor's note: Dictations and writings made later by Chase describe the scene that followed. Suffice it to say that when the screaming stopped, Chase vs. Wes, with Ramona as referee, his parents left in a huff. Chase kept screaming until they were out of sight: "You're a doctor, for god's sake. You oughta know what happens. Seizures and death. That's what happens."

Chase goes on to describe the 72 hours that followed, the peak period for suffering seizures or death from sudden diazepam withdrawal. He had no safe way for rescue, short of walking into an emergency room or rehab unit and admitting to the world that he was addicted. It would be career-ending even before his new career started.

He made a trip to the drug store for antihistamines and anything else that might "slow" his brain, which was moving into overdrive. He also bought two bottles of antacid, as he could feel his stomach catching fire. With anxiety mushrooming, he knew he would not be able to venture from his apartment again, not until this torment was over, dead or alive.

Then he remembered a pharmaceutical weapon he had purchased for a recent attempt at withdrawal back in California. His research indicated that the beta-blocker propranolol was supposed to counter many of the effects of diazepam withdrawal, slowing pulse rates, minimizing tremors, perhaps preventing seizures. How could he have forgotten? The cannister of 1,000 pills had not even been opened. He felt relieved to have a solid crutch to lean on.

Electric ripples burrowed beneath his skin, slowly at first, unbearable by the next day, heralding worse to come. Nervousness became anxiety that became panic, and it didn't stop there. Chase opened the large plastic bottle of beta blockers and downed one.

"999 to go," he said aloud to himself. "I hope I have enough." Over the next 12 hours, he took four more of the beta blockers as his symptoms were escalating in spite of the propranolol.

Forty-eight hours later, Chase's arms and legs were jerking every few minutes, uncontrollably. Once, in attempting to scratch an itchy spot on his nose, his fist slapped him in the mouth and bloodied his lip. Before it could happen again, he held the offending fist with his other hand. He had not been able to sleep, so this deprivation was now compounding the effects of withdrawal.

He could no longer tolerate the irritating blood coursing through his arteries and veins. Red corpuscles clattered and banged against the walls of his capillaries as they passed, causing interminable torture. Even the air swooshing in and out of his bronchial tubes irritated the cilial lining of the cells like a hurricane blowing palm trees to the ground. Each beat of his heart was certainly the last as this pounding, cramping muscle was nothing more than a grenade with the pin already pulled. He gulped more beta blockers.

Finally, he buckled and caved, calling for an ambulance.

"I've been taking these beta blockers," he said on the phone to the dispatcher. "I've lost count. Maybe seven or eight of them, but they're not helping. I can't take this anymore. Something horrible's gonna happen. I've got to slow my heart rate down. My pulse is 160 and rising. My heart's gonna explode."

At the same time, he felt a bizarre depersonalization, as if this entire nightmare were happening to someone else, and he was simply a spectator. Oblivious to reality or risk, he swallowed more beta blockers.

Purple halos surrounded everything in the room. Then, bells and sirens began wailing, louder and louder. His medical mind knew these symptoms as auras. Auras meant seizure activity was imminent, and seizures meant the entire world would find out the truth about him, if he lived, that is.

His disembodied brain was able to sit as judge, and – at this point – the brain decided enough was enough. It tried to feel the presence of God, but there was nothing. It tried to recall a fragment of love that might connect him to a person or a single thing on the planet, but there was nothing. It tried to conjure a future, a purpose for his life, but nothing. After years of torment, the lure of eternal peace was compelling. Tranquility was guaranteed if he quit toying with beta blockers and simply swallowed the entire one thousand.

Editor's note: Paramedics found Chase as a quivering mass on the floor, his back arched, eyes rolled back, blue in the face and blood pouring out his mouth, in full-blown status epilepticus – a continuous, relentless seizure with a 10% mortality rate. In short order, the *ambulance took him to Permian Medical Center where dedicated physicians saved the life of one of their lost.*

Editor's note: *The narrative is lost at this point, given that Chase's memory of the ensuing events was erased, perhaps thankfully so. From the medical records, however, it can be reconstructed that Chase remained unstable for ten hours in the ICU at Permian Medical Center. Intubated, monitored, and restrained, it was touch and go. What reversed the symptoms most effectively was, of course, the administration of diazepam, the very thing that had started it all.*

Chase later described only one memory associated with his stay in the ICU – hearing his mother's voice: "I never should have had children. I didn't think anything could be worse than what we went through with Annie, but I was wrong." Chase made the choice to believe it a false memory, part of the wild dreams he experienced while consciousness was lost.

Once that he was extubated and transferred to the ward, he regained an element of memory, though it was still not clear what truly happened and what did not. Nurses recorded a host of injuries sustained by the prolonged seizures, plus the medical traumas imparted in the ICU. Split tongue, now sutured. Split lip, also sutured. Both wrists red and swollen from repeated arterial blood gases. Throat raw from intubation. Phlebitis in both arms from IV meds. All muscles frozen in pain from the status epilepticus. Worst of all, he was addled. Touched. Unable to think clearly. One nurse charted that Chase had claimed to have taken 1,000 pills of the beta blocker propranolol. By the fourth hospital day, his thoughts cleared, and he felt reasonably well.

Returning now to the narrative...

Chase became wildly loquacious, regurgitating his California story to anyone who would listen, most notably his treating physicians whom he'd known nine years earlier during residency training. For some reason, they were not the least bit interested. His former co-residents listened, stared, nodded, and left the room without any reaction to

Chase's catharsis. Not a single question was posed about his remarkable experience in California.

Then, a smug, irritated psychiatrist with thick glasses and a stringy combover stormed into his room, quarrelsome a priori, announcing that Chase had one option in his future – drug rehab. Switching his weight repeatedly from one foot to the other, scowling and impatient, the shrink demanded agreement on the spot.

When Chase replied that he only needed to "dry out," the psychiatrist grew red-faced. "You have no choice in this. I'm telling you the score whether you like it or not." A long finger of condemnation pointed toward Chase's face.

What is *wrong* with this guy, Chase thought. *What kind of shrink comes in and begins a new patient relationship with a fight?* There wasn't an ounce of sympathy, empathy or concern.

The shrink continued, "Look, pal, the only reason you're not dead right now is the IV diazepam they gave you to break the status epilepticus, *and* the diazepam, mind you, that you're getting right now. *You're back on your drug of choice.* That's why you're feeling so chipper. Take it away, and you're nothing but a heap of frazzled nerves. The whole thing happens over again."

The sickening horror struck deep as Chase realized the ordeal wasn't over yet. He had to withdraw – still. He was in the exact same predicament as before, even though he was functioning on roughly one-half of his customary daily dose. Perhaps, he could still withdraw at home, according to his original plan. Only this time, his parents could monitor and distribute the baggies.

Each day closer to discharge, Chase noted that the mist surrounding his initial seizure activity at his apartment was starting to clear. When the nurse whom he'd befriended (and told of downing a thousand pills) made rounds, he told her, "You know, it's sorta crazy, but I think my mind has been playing tricks. I remember telling you about the thousand pills, but I'm not remembering that it really happened, even though I was sure it happened when I told you about it."

"Well, your drug screen showed the beta blocker along with diazepam."

"Of course. I took quite a few propranolol, but I think it was only six or seven, not a *thousand*."

It had become painfully real to Chase that he might have put the noose around his neck if the "thousand" version of his story had slipped out to the community through this nurse, or anyone else to whom he might have related this questionable account.

The more he resisted drug rehab, the more the psychiatrist chose to rant, rave, and belittle with every visit. "You don't have anything to say about it, buddy. You're an addict, do you understand? That's the absolute bottom in medicine. You've bought yourself a ticket to rehab whether you like it or not, and you've still got de-tox ahead of you."

Tough love? Chase didn't care. The guy was repugnant, and Chase couldn't imagine that he'd ever considered psychiatry as a specialty for himself. Without any training at all, he had more empathy in his little finger.

Phlebitis ate away the veins in his arms, and the infected hematomas from multiple arterial sticks at both wrists required incision and drainage. The chunk of missing tongue left him mumbling, helped in no way by the row of stitches inside his lower lip. Teeth were loose. Aching and bruised muscles simmered with anger at what they'd been put through. Then he began to ponder his shaky future.

Sure, after rehab, lots of doctors go back to their nice little private practices where their patients know them, and their staff loves them. People will forgive you when they know your heart. But I'm not going back to anything. I'm starting up. New practice, hundreds of new colleagues at the med school plus a thousand other staff. I'm supposed to be Chief of Surgery at the VA hospital for the next few years, and I've never even met those people. I can't face them fresh out of rehab. No, I'm getting out. I should never have gone to medical school in the first place. I've been spiraling down ever since I left music for medicine. It was a horrible mistake. If I go to rehab, it makes it official. Everyone knows. Career over.

Upon discharge, he was given a modest three-day supply of diazepam, a charitable offer when compared to his own father's plan of cold turkey. The three-day supply came with a reserved room at a new drug rehabilitation facility in town called Riverdell.

As soon as he was back at his apartment, Chase immediately went to the cupboard where he kept the large bottle of propranolol. Clearly, it was not empty. As he unscrewed the lid, he honestly didn't know what to expect, but the bottle was full. For some reason, in a fleeting thought, his brain had chosen a false memory. Why had he blurted out this false memory of intent, securing the misinformation in the medical records? Then again, what did it matter? His reputation was permanently ruined, regardless.

There was precious little time to consider the options. The diazepam would run dry in three days. Even then, it was a stretch using a dose far less than what he was used to. Fearful that he wouldn't have enough drug to get him into a controlled situation, he called Riverdell to confirm his admission, only to learn that they were working him in on a Sunday evening, five days from now, rather than Friday afternoon. Not good. He could keep withdrawal at bay for three or four days with his limited supply, but by his calculations, he would be experiencing the first stages of withdrawal by Saturday or Sunday.

When Chase's parents dropped by, several times each day, it was the same conversation, ending with, "You're going to rehab." In his mind, he would answer, "No, I'm not," as he tried to think through alternatives.

However, when Thatcher Nolan Taylor, M.D. visited Chase at his apartment, everything changed. "Chase, I want you to know that your position in our department is safe, if you'd still like to join the faculty. Oh, sure, there are going to be detractors. As you might imagine, word about this spread all over town in about 15 minutes. The Chief of Staff at College Hospital asked if I was going to be comfortable letting you in the operating room. I told him quite frankly what I thought – that you're one of the most precise surgeons in the O.R. that I've ever trained, and that you back it up with an impressive intellect. He was a bit flustered by my insistence at first, but I asked him how in the world he could question your talent..."

Chase heard, at first, only the negative comments by the Chief of Staff, confirming exactly what Chase anticipated – bias, discrimination, yes, the whole package was there, waiting for his return, wrapped in a big scarlet ribbon of prejudice. Yes, that was the color. Scarlet. The scarlet letter "A" he would wear for the rest of his life. Every smug half-wit who wanted to take pot shots at him only had to shine a light on the scarlet letter of addiction.

Then came the positive. "...so, I've gone out on a limb for you on this one, Chase. I wanted you to know that you've got complete job security as far as I'm concerned. As I told you many years ago, and I still mean it, I'm not sure if I've ever trained anyone with more potential than you, that is, both you and Franklin Cooper. I'd certainly put the two of you at the top, and I've always found it apropos that the two of you became friends like you did. Certainly, you two are my pride and joy."

Franklin Cooper was already a rising star on faculty at Harvard, and Chase hoped that someday his old friend would return to Matherville to take over as Chairman of the Department of Surgery after T.N.T. retired. Chase knew himself well enough to know he couldn't take orders from anyone he didn't respect (sharply limiting the field to T.N.T. alone), and currently, there was the ever-looming possibility that his old nemesis from residency, Dr. Brick Dagmar, could assume the throne (not that it was an immediate concern).

Thatcher continued, "One thing, though, Chase. In order to come back to work, you'll need to go through with this rehab business. I don't know what they do in those places exactly, nor do I care, but the state medical board has really gone to the extreme when it comes to this alcohol and drug abuse issue. The way I figure it, there's no urine test for medical incompetence out there, which they've ignored for years. But since they can measure addiction when you pee into a cup, they've focused on that instead. You won't have a moment's rest unless you agree to go through this rehab thing. Of course, they have that new Riverdell facility right here in town."

With those few words from T.N.T., Chase's resistance melted. He made his decision to return to work as a physician, and he agreed to go through rehab. Whatever it took. T.N.T. was the most revered person in west Texas (as far as Chase was concerned), and he was the only influence on earth that could have guided him into rehab.

Wes Callaway insisted that he would drive his son to Riverdell on Sunday. Having run out of low-dose diazepam on Saturday, Chase was already anxious and trembling as he waited for his father. Every noise caused jitters. His pulse was 120. His shirt was saturated with sweat. From experience, he knew that the first thing he would need upon admission would be a fix. Another 24 hours without diazepam, and he could be looking at the same seizure scenario as before.

A rare winter storm, setting new record lows, had blasted west Texas that week, layering the city of Matherville with strata of ice. The drive would have ordinarily taken only 15 minutes, but the slip-sliding on ice was going to extend the trip to an hour – an hour of increasing anxiety for Chase. As they traveled a difficult road, there was no conversation. His father was stoic as he drove, staring straight ahead, both hands gripping the steering wheel. Wes's face was without expression, without blinking. Even the silence was odd, given his father's propensity to lecture. Had he traumatized his father to the breaking point?

Chase would have been at wits end simply going to a rehab facility, but to do so in early withdrawal, grossly magnifying his anxiety, was pushing him toward panic. To divert his rapidly increasing fear, he slipped into daydreaming about a "reason." He had to have a reason. *All things worked to the good for those who love the Lord.* There were no coincidences. Everything had a purpose. Everything had a reason. It was inconceivable, and unacceptable, that he might have endured these past years leading to rehab without a purpose. To invent a purpose, or simply a future, he forced an out-of-body experience and considered himself as a character in a book, a play, or even a song.

Each time the car fishtailed, Chase fantasized that they would slide off the road to an icy death for the both of them. Or, at a minimum, cancellation of rehab. It should have been a perfect time for a heart-to-heart conversation. Yet, it would not happen now, if ever. Chase stared at the floorboard the entire trip, trying to stop his hands from fidgeting and thumbs from twiddling, wiping sweat from his brow every few seconds. No matter how much he tried to place blame where it belonged – on himself – he was still furious with his mute father for disrupting the tapering strategy that led to the hospitalization that led to now. Chase hoped his father, like Abraham, might see a ram with its horns caught in the thicket by the side of the road, a diversion for sacrifice, a substitute for the burnt offering demanded by the Lord. Never had Chase felt so helpless, so devastated, so tiny, reduced to the smallest possible particle.

We know today that the atom is not the smallest particle. With protons and neutrons and electrons giving way to even smaller components of quarks and leptons, it drives the analogy further when Wes Callaway's car drove Chase onto familiar grounds whereupon Chase saw a sign that took his breath away: *Matherville State Mental Hospital.* Beneath that, another sign: *new name effective January 1, 1989: Matherville Mental Health Pavilion.*

"What? I didn't know— I thought we were going to a place called Riverdell. What's going on?"

"What did you expect? A country club?"

"As a matter of fact, yes. I thought we were going to a new facility. I can't go there, dad. I can't."

"Riverdell is what they call their drug unit. It's a separate building from the main hospital. It doesn't make any difference. You're going."

"No. Turn the car around. Dallas has several places I can go. Take me out of state, if you have to. I'm not going into a mental institution, not right here in my hometown."

A shouting match ensued, and Chase knew his life was over. The scarlet letter would be nothing compared to a stint in the loony bin. But he was in poor shape for a fight, jittery and wildly anxious, on the verge of another bout with major withdrawal. Instead, he collapsed, begging God for a reason, yet doubting there would be an explanation forthwith.

Wes Callaway spoke like a tour guide. "There's the Riverdell facility. You can see it over there. Like I said, it's completely separate from the hospital. For a while, it was a successful outpatient facility for the chronics, but when the money dried up, they either turned the patients loose on the streets, or the worst cases went back into the main hospital. Now the money is in rehab, I guess."

Chase recognized the Z-shaped footprint pattern of the facility, located just outside the walls of the insane asylum. It didn't matter that Riverdell was technically on the perimeter, it was all one big complex. His father parked the car at the administration building, not at the rehab unit. "They told me on the phone that we check in here first," said Wes.

Chase was instructed to sign voluntary commitment papers, printed on Matherville State Mental Hospital stationery. The word "Riverdell" was nowhere to be found. As he scrawled his signature, barely legible, he felt he had signed his own death warrant. Too depressed and too tired and too far along in withdrawal, there was nothing left to do but sign. *What's the next step of mental agony below crippling depression? It can't get any worse than this.*

Yet, before the ink was dry on his signature, as if to prove there are even smaller particles than quarks and leptons, the admissions nurse said to Chase: "Now, I must tell you that Riverdell is completely full, so you'll be housed in one of the regular wards until we've discharged some folks from the rehab unit. Our rehab program is simply busting at the seams. Currently, there are five rehab patients being housed in old seclusion rooms that we've recently converted to private rooms for overflow. You'll be the sixth. It'll take about a week or so to move up the ladder as rehab patients are discharged, and then you'll be transferred in with the rest of the inpatients at Riverdell. The good news is you won't miss any activities, daytime or evening. The only thing you'll do on the psych ward will be sleep."

"No, Dad! No! Don't do this to me!"

The threesome walked out of the administration building, following a lonely asphalt path toward the heart of the asylum. Since his father wouldn't listen, Chase begged God for deliverance. "Oh, God, please no."

"Why?" Over and over, he said 'why' to himself. Then he saw their eventual destination – Building 19 – where he had worked for years as a psychiatric aide, then later a frequent visitor while spending time at Matherville State in surgical training.

As the admissions nurse unlocked the door to 19, Chase considered the possibility that otherworldly moments like this had to have revolutionary impact, for without such importance, there is no purpose to life at all. He still had to find a purpose, a reason. And he had to find it quickly. For without it, he couldn't take another step. He couldn't enter Building 19 as a patient if the universe were ruled by chaos. Finally, through his mental groping, he struck upon a reason and secured it as truth.

Everything, he realized, had been leading to this moment. He and his father had been on a collision course for forty years. This, now, was the key moment. Yes, this was the purpose – to prompt Chase to say the impossible.

"You may say your good-byes," the nurse suggested.

He turned to his father. The barrier between them was greater than the walls of the mental institution, it seemed. Yet, the purpose was now revealed – being dragged to this point where immutable barriers are broken, then being forced to say the one thing that neither of them had ever said to one another. Yes, that was it. A reason. The past ten years of torment had all been leading to this point in time when he could finally say... in fact, he did say:

"I love you, dad."

His father's eyes were dead. Stone cold. Unblinking. Then, Wes Callaway's face twisted into passive disgust before he turned and walked away.

Thus, the shedding of the second exoskeleton.

In contrast to the first shedding where uncontrolled rage had prompted him to rip through the shell and emerge a scorpion, the second shedding was quite different – here, the burning lake of fire, located in a bottomless pit of perdition, simply melted away the exoskeleton, leaving alienated atoms to float free, perhaps to join together once again in a new form, be it Phoenix or be it Monster, but still floating free for now, waiting for direction.

The door to the outside world slammed shut, and Chase was led to one of the old seclusion rooms where he was locked inside for his own protection from the lunatics, the chronics, and the hopelessly insane.

11
TREPHINATION IN LIEU OF THEOPHANY

The clanking door of the windowless seclusion room sent a barbed spear into his heart. Reeling backward to the far wall, clutching the imagined hole in his chest, Chase's eyes fixated on the metal door where four vertical bars filled the envelope-sized observation window, covered by a sliding panel.

The scrape-thud of the opening panel was a familiar sound to Chase who had, many years ago, peeked through this very window to check on the crazy clientele, back when the seclusion rooms had been padded, floors and walls, with old mattresses. But now, the sliding window panel opened for *him* – scrape-thud. His escorting nurse was on the outside, her face striped by the bars as she said: "I forgot to mention, since today is Sunday, I won't have the standard de-tox orders until tomorrow morning, and you've already missed dinner. Lights out in an hour. Can you think of anything you might need?"

He could barely manage a response. "I'm withdrawing right now, you know. It was withdrawal seizures that got me here in the first place! I'm not so sure I can make it 'til morning. I'm starting to feel a lot like I did before. Before the seizures, I mean. I need help."

"Well, there's someone on call, so if things get worse, I can always page him."

"Things are going to get worse. Trust me. You'll need to page him...now."

"I'll check with the charge nurse. Anything else?"

Did she hear me? "Yes, one more thing. When I went through this before, my stomach was on fire with acid. I had to take antacids constantly. This time, the burning is already there. If I've missed dinner – well, I could sure use some antacid."

"That would take a doctor's order. I'll make a note of it for the morning."

"I'm not talking about routine heartburn. I'm talking about *fire* in my stomach."

"Again, I'll check with the charge nurse."

"In the meantime, how about a piece of bread, a carton of milk, anything to dilute the acid?"

She continued, unfazed: "We'll be doing a bed check every fifteen minutes." (suicide precaution) "Be prepared for the flashlight shining through this little window during the night. If you're awake, as most de-toxers are, just raise your hand so that the aide knows to chart how much sleep you're getting."

Scrape-thud. The panel covering the bars closed.

When panic is stretched from minutes to hours, it deserves a different name with a different definition. Anxiety is too weak. Extreme anxiety is still inadequate. Chase was about to come unglued, and hospital policy was doing everything in its power to make sure that happened. The most appropriate word for his state at that moment was "crazed." And it was getting worse.

He scanned the room, redecorated since its days as a padded cell. A private toilet and sink was new. A skimpy mattress was now resting on a frame. Yet, it was the same dank quarters where urine and feces and vomit had soaked the walls and defined the smell of madness. Perhaps the odor was long gone for other customers, but Chase could still remember, and he could still smell insanity.

The impact of it all struck Chase in one blinding – no, enlightening – flash. How, after praying and praying for years and years for deliverance from a series of tribulations, had it come to this? He knew his core, he understood his spirit, and he knew he could never shake this moment. As Chaucer's English allows double, triple, or even quadruple negatives, Chase would – never, no, not never – shake this point in time.

He might be drug-free soon, but there could be no recovery. All was lost. Suffering, as being good for the soul, was a lie.

"My God, my God, why hast thou forsaken me?" said the psalmist of both the Tanakh and the Bible hundreds of years before Jesus of Nazareth borrowed what had to be infinitely apropos. Surely, this was the loneliest feeling in the universe.

Abandon Hope, All Ye Who Enter Here. Chase remembered his grandfather's fascination with Dante, and he felt the true essence of this statement now. Chase had been a tourist in this branch of Hell years ago, and he had visited Bedlam, the icy dungeon of The Tower where the patients in vegetative states were held. Now he understood the full meaning of "lost hope."

There was no redemption. There was no erasure from his record. Even if the rest of the world never knew, he would always remember that he'd been locked in seclusion in an insane asylum. His pleas with God for deliverance had failed. His dependence on defining the "purpose" of his life was a pathetic joke. In fact, the very idea that there was a purpose to anything so enraged him that he felt a swelling within, a bursting that dated itself to 20 years earlier when his wife and parents had convinced him that he was "destined" or "purposed" for medical school.

Sure, Pandora let the evils of the world escape, but there was one thing left in the box – hope. Even the ancient Greeks knew the importance of hope. Now, as it turned out, for Chase, hope was a phantom. He had deluded himself that a God was directing him, that there was a purpose. Now, the very word "purpose" made him sick, as did the word "God."

Then he detonated. In a paroxysmal fit with clenched fists and neck muscles drawn into ropes, Chase began screaming at God – "Curse you" – he yelled over and over at the ceiling where a recessed light formed the center glow, right next to a small speaker. "You fraud," he yelled. "You can't even defend yourself when someone curses you. You spared me from death so many times, just to degrade me now? Just to drag me into the ultimate humiliation? Then again, why am I talking to you? You don't even exist! You're the lie of the ages, which makes me the greatest fool who ever lived. All these years of trying to explain horrible things according to your perfect will. You have no will. Purpose is a lie. All things work to the good is a lie. I'm so freakin' mad I ever spent one freakin' minute believing that you were going to deliver me from anything."

He paced the room like a caged animal, unable to escape himself.

"Freakin' answered prayer. Listen to me. Talking like a fool to a god I don't believe in. Well, here's one for you – why don't you come down here, show yourself for once, just one freakin' time, and destroy me. What? No lightning bolts? Big freakin' surprise. Come down here and kill me, dammit. I'm nearly dead already. No answer? Can't talk? Hell, I'll do it myself, then. I've been alone this whole time anyway."

The screaming offered no catharsis whatsoever – no, not never, no how. In fact, the wailing only served as fuel for greater shrieks and screams as he realized the level of insanity – true madness – he had topped. He couldn't stop himself repeating the same curses over and over. The rage surpassed any attempt at worthy description that I can offer now. Indeed, he snapped. He needed to kill himself, and to do it quickly, before the 15-minute bed check. His trip to the ICU had already churned through the rumor mill as an attempt to take his own life when, in fact, it was a pre-seizure delusion, part of the aura from acute withdrawal. But now, in truth, he wanted to die, and there was nothing to stop him. Nothing, that is, except for the fact that there was no way to do it.

He had been stripped of his belt and shoelaces in the admissions office. Maybe he could strangle himself with his shirt wrapped around his neck, but the maneuver required an impossible knot in order to maintain the cinch. Then, he recalled the bizarre collection of shadowboxes in the asylum's surgical suites where swallowed items that had been recovered from gastrointestinal tracts over the years were on display. One of those shadowboxes was filled with bedsprings an inmate had consumed, trying to eat the entire bed. Chase checked his own bedsprings to see if they could be dismantled. Swallowing was not practical, of course, but perhaps the open point of a spring could be used to stab himself or tear open a carotid artery. He yanked at the bedsprings, but nothing gave. Then he stood on the mattress and tried to break the glass that covered the recessed light, but it was plastic, lunatic-resistant.

Scrape-thud. A flashlight broke the darkness and bore a hole into his skull. "Everything all right in there?" came the soft voice of a female aide. "Lots of commotion going on. I thought you were one of our regular patients at first. I didn't realize you were a de-toxer."

"I— I need something," Chase said. "I've been without my Valium for several days now, and I'm going to— I'm going to start having seizures, or worse. I need someone to call the doctor. Please."

"I'll tell the nurse." Scrape-thud.

When the flashlight quit auguring his brain, he looked around the room a final time, unable to figure a way to end it all. He fell to the floor and curled into a question mark, sobbing, pleading to a god unknown.

As a blob in the center of the floor, he remained frozen and awake through countless trephinations by the flashlight every 15 minutes, each time lifting his hand to signal to the holder of the light that he was still awake. Sleep was impossible as his body vibrated with the ever-present threat of more seizures. In distant echo, he could hear the lamentations of the chronics on the ward, as they screeched and howled as background to Chase's total silence. Multiple times during the night, he moved from floor to bed and back again.

At dawn (he reasoned by counting flashlight assaults), he fell into a stupor of quasi-sleep, but this was abruptly interrupted by his own death rattle – an acid river from his stomach had filled his throat, then continued onward to fill his lungs. For a split second, he had a decision to make, for he knew he had aspirated acidic stomach contents in large volume and that death was there for the taking. If he could stave off the powerful reflex to cough, if he could simply hold it in, the acid would liquify his lungs and he would be done with it. *Just hold it in. Hold it tight.*

Scrape-thud.

The observation portal opened, but there was no flashlight. No face looking in. No one spoke. Between the vertical bars, a small white bottle appeared on the ledge of the small window, then someone pushed it through the bars, followed by two more like it. The three plastic bottles rattled on the floor like dice until Chase could read one of the labels –

antacid. Each small bottle was a single dose. Scrape-thud, the portal closed.

Who? Why? Someone is helping me after all.

He coughed. And coughed. And coughed.

I want to live.

At first, voluntary coughing got the process started, then involuntary spasms took over. He rolled onto all fours and coughed some more, gagging on the acid as it spewed onto the floor. Then, he crawled toward the three bottles, broke the seals, still coughing, and started gulping down the contents of each one. With difficult resolve, he intentionally aspirated the last bottle of antacid hoping to neutralize the acid still in his lungs. This, of course, prompted even more coughing. Then, he stood and stumbled to the bathroom sink where he began swallowing water from his cupped hands.

He coughed uncontrollably for several more minutes, until he felt a rib pop. "Oh, God, help me," he screamed. The pain of the rib fracture was excruciating, a spear thrust into his side with each hack. He couldn't believe it. Rib fractures due to coughing only happened to old people. How could his body be so decomposed?

The burning in his throat eased, but the coughing continued, each time followed by a shout of pain.

Cough. Spear to the rib, "God, no." Cough. Spear. "Please, no more." Cough. Spear. Cough. Spear. "Oh, god. Help me. Someone help me. Please God."

He eased onto his mattress where he pressed on the broken rib as a crude stent so that he could continue to clear his lungs. "God, help me. Forgive my rantings and ravings, please. I don't want anything from You anymore. No requests. No petitions. No escape from consequences. I just want to live...in peace."

Scrape-thud. The panel over the observation window slid open again, but still no face between the bars. Chase could see natural light in the hallway indicating that morning had indeed arrived. He craned his neck to see who might have opened the eye-level panel but saw no one.

Then, a fourth bottle of antacid appeared on the ledge between the bars.

He forced himself from the bed, bent at the waist and clutching his side to ease his rib pain. He walked to the door, curious, still coughing.

After he secured the bottle from the portal, two hands snaked their way through the bars, one hand oddly puffy, the other one scrawny, ten fingers dancing and wiggling for him to see. The owner of those hands was so short that their head didn't reach the opening.

"Soti medo, Doti," came a woman's odd voice from the other side of the door.

Chase reached for the wiggling fingers and held them in his hands through the bars. Z-shaped scars coursed up and down each digit, prompting recognition of his former patient from her fingers alone, though he had no explanation as to why one of her hands would have been so bloated. Years ago, he had repaired one of her birth defects, fused fingers (syndactyly), after countless delays. When he stood on his toes and looked out through the bars, he saw Ivy Pettibone, now with gray-white hair, but still home to that marvelous smile.

"Soti medo," he whispered back to her. "How've *you* been, dear Ivy? I've been on a long, hard journey. A journey where I lost my way. Now I'm home again."

12
STELLAR EVOLUTION

Shortly after Ivy had disappeared back into the bowels of Building 19 (still the experimental ward for pharmacologic research), the Riverdell aide rounded up the overflow druggies who were housed in seclusion rooms in order to herd them to the rehab unit.

It was, perhaps, at this moment that Chase appreciated the impact of the second exoskeleton shedding, prompting the need for subatomic particles to realign. Something was different inside. Something had changed, and not necessarily for the better.

When he recognized Ivy's fingers earlier, an old neural network in his brain, tucked away years ago, flashed the embryology of syndactyly before his eyes. He recalled that every human has webbed fingers and toes during fetal development – it is the lysosomes, little packets of digestive enzymes located inside all cells, sometimes called "suicide bags" – that destroy the webs long before we are born.

Just how many of those lysosomes have been unleashed in my own gray matter, considering that addiction, oxygen depletion during seizures, psychic trauma, all work to release the same "suicide bags," which then dissolve the neurons in the host? Is my brain the same as it was? Am I a different being now, with different chemistry?

As the rehab patients prepared to walk single file out of Building 19, Chase weaved a path to the Day Room to look for Ivy, but he was quickly steered back into the fold by an aide. The group marched out of

19, then off the main hospital grounds toward the rehab unit. Wind gusts and blowing snow from the worst winter storm in recent memory seemed to make the short walk last for miles.

A towering African American man in the druggie line, mid-thirties, shoulders bulging in a letterman's jacket, sidled up to Chase as the group walked through the blizzard. "I screamed my first night, too. Cursed God, just like you. Name is LeRoy. I'm your next-door neighbor 'til we get our asses bumped up to the drug unit. Two folks are being discharged today, I hear tell, so we're movin' on up to the east side, brother. Never thought I'd be on my knees begging for a bed in a rehab unit."

Chase could barely speak. Shaking, heart racing, startled by the smallest noise or distraction, all part of extended withdrawal, he managed only a few words. "Me neither," he managed. "Never in a million."

"What's your name, by the way?"

"Chase. Chase Callaway."

"Tell you what, Chase, I'll tap on the wall tonight, just to remind you that you're not alone."

The troupe battled through the winter storm, slipping across sidewalks and streets until they entered the Riverdell Rehabilitation Center. Chase was immediately spirited away for his admission history and physical by a moonlighting resident from the nearby Far West Texas medical school. He knew this would be the first of hundreds of humiliations in dealing with "one of his own."

Chase tried to make light of the situation, explaining his addiction while informing the young doctor how he'd once been a distinguished graduate of the same medical school. The resident was blank. No response. He had nothing to say, no support, no encouragement, only "I need to do a rectal now." Next, with the neurologic exam, when the percussion hammer hit Chase below the knee, his leg shot out and kicked the resident in the chest.

"Oh, my. You're beyond four-plus. Actually, you've got clonus. Look, your resting pulse is 160, and well, your neuro exam is alarming. You need some diazepam stat before we're dealing with seizures here. We'll try orally, but I might need to start an IV. The psychiatrist on call should have ordered you something on admission. Honestly, I don't know how you made it through the night. Just to let you know, it'll take weeks to dry you out safely."

Getting a fix provided overwhelming relief. Even a paltry 10 milligrams stat was enough to allow Chase to get a grip. It was the first time in nearly a week that his heart quit jumping out of his chest. The tremor disappeared. The sweating stopped. The internal jitters became tolerable.

Daytime and evenings at rehab were filled with classes, group therapy, individual testing and counseling. However, none of it impacted Chase in the slightest as, remarkably, he was still enduring detox. At least everything would happen in a controlled situation, without a well-meaning chump flushing his drugs down the toilet.

Then, night after night, tap-tap-tap, from LeRoy next door as the hall lights went out, reminding Chase that he was not the only person in the world who had dug himself into a bottomless pit.

The 21 days and nights of withdrawal were more prolonged than expected. He never would have been able to do it alone. The lengthy process made him realize how adapted his body had become, living in harmonious dependence with chemicals that demanded equilibrium first, escalation second. It had never been about the "buzz," but instead, only to feel what he thought he recalled as "normal."

Tapering was rapid the first week, then very gradual thereafter. In the process, every organ system in Chase's body screamed for relief. He checked his pulse constantly, and it never slowed below 130 those first three weeks, even at rest. He was always soaked with sweat. Every sudden noise, no matter how soft, prompted a reflex jerking, heart palpitations, then a new coat of perspiration.

Even his own coughing startled him, followed quickly by stabbing rib pain, which in turn startled him again. Everything twitched all the time – arms, legs, fingers, facial muscles. Sight unseen, his toes curled uncontrollably inside his shoes, his teeth clenched repeatedly, and butterflies swarmed through every sinew as he tried to force his muscles to lie still. He spoke very little, as quivering vocal cords betrayed the torture going on inside. He felt himself covering his mouth with his hand, hiding his twitching lips, still swollen even though the sutures inside had dissolved.

A chest X-ray showed pneumonia from his aspiration and confirmed his broken rib. Antibiotics were begun, but no analgesia beyond aspirin was allowed. The cough-rib combination tortured him every few minutes, through every day and all the nights. His GI tract propelled liquids through his system so quickly that he spent much of the day in the bathroom, and the non-narcotics that the doctors prescribed to plug him did nothing. His skin crawled, his stomach knotted, his eyes hurt, his muscles cramped, his hands shook. Every cell in his body had been squelched for years, and now, these trillions and trillions of cells were waking up, rebounding, finally, but overshooting their norm, as if celebrating their freedom.

Duration of sleep was documented with the flashlight through the window panel, and each time that the beam of light hit him in the face, Chase felt rage at the ludicrous idea of struggling to sleep knowing that the light would blind him again in another 15 minutes. Little wonder that not a single minute of sleep was documented by the aides during those first nights.

How he wished that immortality could be granted through six days and seven nights of wakefulness, as he recalled from an ancient, pre-Biblical myth. Better than Gilgamesh, though, who fell asleep quickly and lost the challenge, Chase made it halfway to immortality. On the fourth night, he fell asleep – for two hours near dawn, then three hours of sleep the next night, four hours each night after that. Throughout it all, each night, tap-tap-tap from LeRoy at bedtime.

Sometimes, too, the fingers of Ivy Pettibone would poke through the bars to say hello. Moments later, she would slide a paper towel through the crack beneath the bottom of the door. Written on the towel in spittle, each time, was her signature word, her only word – GOD – a testimony of her mother's instruction to a child denied normal speech. Ivy had compensated by training other congenital curiosities, such as her over-sized salivary glands that could direct streams of spit with firehose accuracy that allowed her to write her one and only recognizable word.

The bizarre nature of it all did not strike him as surrealistic, merely his new norm.

After two weeks in Building 19, he and LeRoy were transferred to the main Riverdell unit where they became roommates, along with two other "oldsters" (over 30). Chase was not yet fully weaned. He had another week left, though his symptoms had reached a plateau. The final 2mg. tablet on the 21st day was terrifying, even though the dose was laughably small. For three more days after coming off all chemicals, his withdrawal symptoms continued.

Deep depression settled in at the end of the withdrawal process. The rehab doctors ordered, oddly enough, psychotropic medication. Yet, something peculiar happened with all attempts to melt away Chase's depression with pharmaceuticals. The drugs backfired. Instead of helping, Chase was completely intolerant of three different classes of drugs – all of them causing such severe dysphoria that Chase insisted they be stopped. There was something peculiar about his new neurochemistry, he reasoned. Never before had he been intolerant of any mind-altering chemicals – all had been welcome. Now, however, antidepressants were clearly a poison of sorts. He would have to live as nature designed.

Overnight, it seemed, on the 26th day of rehab, his withdrawal symptoms disappeared. The day before, his pulse had been 130. Overnight, it slowed to 86. Profuse sweating stopped entirely. His voice was no longer shaky. His twitching stopped. Jerking in response to noise ended. His GI tract got ahold of itself. The depression was lifting.

The rehab protocol required a battery of psychological tests. Chase's level of depression nearly bottomed out the scale. The psychiatrists were quite disturbed that Chase continued to refuse all chemical interventions at this point, for he scored easily within the range for suicide precautions. In his mind, though, Chase was walking on air. The doctors had not been with him that first night in the seclusion room, so how could they know that he hadn't felt this good in years?

Other by-products emerged from the battery of tests – Chase had, indeed, suffered a degree of brain damage throughout his many tribulations. Somewhere along the line, he had developed an impairment of three-dimensional relationships. When he was slow to mimic various shapes using building blocks, the examiner commented, "Well, your impairment is mild. Unless you operate heavy machinery, or unless you're a sculptor, it's probably not going to matter."

"I'm a surgeon," he said.

"Uh, well, I knew you were a doctor. I didn't know you were, uh…it really seems to be minimal. I wouldn't worry too much."

Countering this soul-rattling confirmation that brain damage had occurred was the discovery that his IQ test established a new record for the rehab unit. The examiner seemed surprised at Chase's reaction to the good news. "I'm a little bothered," Chase said. "I took a similar test back when I was a psych major in college, and I was 158 back then. I'm not sure I can be happy about a twelve-point loss."

"Well, it's not necessarily permanent. You know, severe depression can lower your score. Besides, IQ tests don't enjoy the same degree of validity or prestige they used to."

Why did everyone keep talking about depression? It didn't make sense. He simply answered the questions on the personality profile truthfully. Granted, his answers didn't reflect the way he felt generally. Yet, it was the way he felt now due to the prospect of facing a lifetime of condemnation and discrimination.

For Chase, it was the reality of a tarnished future. For the present, he was feeling clear-minded joy for the first time in years. If his future were in music, both the addiction and the renewal would have served him well. But to face the world of medicine? No. Having seen in California how doctors can devour each other, he knew it could get ugly even in Matherville if his Achilles heel were drudged up and put on display every time there was some sort of conflict. Or, for that matter, not even conflict – success could be equally dangerous.

Despite the diagnosis of depression being handed him, Chase was surprised to enjoy other people for the first time in a long time. The foursome in his apartment often functioned as a comedy troupe. Chase heard himself chuckle as each of them admitted, through self-effacing humor, how pointless resistance can be in a treatment center. LeRoy was the life of the party with such soliloquies as, "Man, every time one of those counselor dudes tells me, 'your best thinking got you here', I just wanna choke the life outta the sunuvabitch. But you know what – I used to think, think, think all the time about how to beat this addiction, and look where I am, man. I'm in a fucking mental institution." Then all would laugh.

Group and private sessions with counselors could be brutal since honesty, the most critical feature of recovery, does not necessarily follow sobriety. Chase suffered along with the rest. One counselor made him admit, for instance, that patient care had been harmed one way or another by his addiction. Chase said the words to get the counselor off his back, but he didn't believe it in his heart. He was far too obsessive, far too thorough, and he truly believed that his talent was so superlative that it remained so even in addiction. In sobriety, he would have only been that much better, and he clung to the belief that, addicted to diazepam, he was a more outstanding surgeon than most were sober, and that he'd only harmed himself.

Not everyone withstood the personal interrogatories that could borrow from the Inquisition. One night, long after curfew, Chase heard the television playing in the lounge where group sessions were held. Curfew laws were strict, so there could be loss of privileges for the perpetrator, ranging from no phone calls to complete lock-down. Chase felt obligated to warn the offender, so he rose from bed and trudged to the central lounge where LeRoy was watching TV.

"I gotta remember who I am, man," LeRoy said. "I gotta remember who I am."

Chase sat down beside him on the couch. LeRoy was playing a videotape – Super Bowl highlights – while tears were flowing down his cheeks. "They won't let me see my kids, man. I ain't gonna lose those kids. My wife, she's so pissed. I know I can calm her down if they'll let me have a pass. But *they won't give me a pass*, just out of spite. I love those kids, man. These doctors, they're splittin' my marriage up, man, like how can I make up with my wife if I'm here in prison? I gotta get out. I'm forgettin' who I am. I gotta remember." He pointed to the television. "That's me," he said. "That's who I am. Not this cry-baby your lookin' at, Chase. Cocaine, man. Bad shit. It's ruined me. I ain't never gonna do it again."

"You're not 'LeRoy' are you?" Chase asked.

"Can't believe nobody figured it out. Kinda hurts my feelings. I'm a has-been, I guess." The NFL star held out his Super Bowl ring for Chase to see. "You're in the same boat as me, man. You and I, the way I figure it, you and I got more to lose than anyone else in this place. That's why I used my ring to tap on the wall while we were in the nuthouse. Lots to lose, you and me."

A curious friendship formed. The two were linked not only by what they had to lose, but also by the equalizing power of addiction. For the rest of their committed time, LeRoy and Chase spent their afternoon breaks, one-on-one, playing basketball in the gym. For self-validating his worthiness to play against a pro athlete, Chase dragged out his timeworn quip about having "sat at the far end of the bench at Far West Texas." In these afternoon games, he was still hampered by his broken rib, now a month old, plus a persistent cough, but he could still score points on "LeRoy" who, in testimony to the basic discontent of man, confessed that he would have readily given up his football hero status if only he could have been a professional basketball player. *Editor's note: a book length account of the rehab experience is deleted here, as Dr. Callaway tells the stories of his new companions, their past misfortunes, and their current struggles.*

As for rehabilitation, Chase was surprised that there was so much soul-searching work to be done after de-tox. Counselors talked about a new way of living, a new way of acting, a new way of reacting to life's curveballs. Initially, the principles seemed foreign to Chase. Then, however, he realized they were simply the Biblical paradoxes – "lose your life to find it," and so forth. Humility was supreme, and Chase couldn't imagine anything more humbling than what he'd been through. Did he really need to talk about it all the time in group sessions? Yet, it appeared humility was going to rule.

For instance, in his first trip to the cafeteria, where docs, psychotics, and druggies all ate in the same room, Chase gravitated to the shortest line for food. An aide grabbed his arm and jerked him away to the longer line, reprimanding, "Stay out of that line. That's for doctors only."

When a teen-age girl in the rehab unit slipped on the floor she'd recently mopped, cutting her lip on a coffee table, she showed her injury to Chase who pronounced "no stitches needed." Chase was sickened when the girl was scolded and privileges lost: "Lucy, you are *not* to bother Chase with anything like that again. He is not a doctor in here. Do you understand? He is *not* a doctor."

Certain afternoon classes were shared with the psychiatric patients, and Chase enrolled in "Health" where an instructor spent a great deal of time explaining how important it was to drink a large glass of water each morning in order to "clear the poisons." The schizophrenics sitting at the table on either side of Chase were enthralled by the prospect of such easy eradication of their demons. One of them said, "When I was on the outside, I'd back off on my meds just to the point when I'd start hearing the voices. But I'm gonna try drinking more water in the morning." Chase lowered his head and stared at worn linoleum on the floor. *If my friends could see me now*. Humility, indeed.

Chase was always on the look-out for Ivy Pettibone, but he did not see her after the move to Riverdell. He had managed to learn from the ward nurse that Ivy's swollen hand was the result of a radical mastectomy performed seven years earlier for breast cancer. "Didn't slow her down a bit," said the nurse. Chase also managed to learn that Ivy had done quite well with her roommate during an outpatient experiment in the apartments, but that the roommate had died two years ago – about the same time that they converted the facility into Riverdell Rehabilitation Center. Ivy had been shipped back to Building 19. Remarkably, she had been making some progress in her speech in the form of recognizable words, but this improvement was lost after her return to 19. Thinking that he might see her at the weekly dance, Chase was surprised to learn that the Wednesday night dances were no longer held.

Humility dogged the recovering addicts everywhere, even if watching TV. Once, when Chase and LeRoy were watching a Dallas Mavericks basketball game, LeRoy suddenly yelled out, "Look at that empty seat! That's my seat, right on the floor. That's where I should be right now!" The camera was focused on a Dallas Cowboy star, watching the basketball game court side, next to the empty chair. "We go to all the games together. I can't believe it. That's my seat. Whenever we get outta here, Chase, I'm gonna introduce you to all the guys." Then LeRoy named five teammates in recovery and five others who needed to be.

Then, the surf group known as The Pipelines had their first hit in 15 years, and their music video played regularly on TV while Chase was incarcerated. Their surprise hit brought forth documentary coverage, and one evening, Chase saw their mother, his former patient, being interviewed on national television. Years earlier, she had said to Chase, "I bet your mother is really proud of you." *If Mama Pipeline could only see me now, here in rehab, watching life go by.*

A few weeks after The Pipeline's mother was interviewed, Chase was watching TV in the main lounge when he saw Dr. Kelso introduced as the newly featured health reporter for a major network. Kelso was the charismatic and sociopathic doctor back in L.A. who had caused so much commotion at the Ciena hospital and was preparing to skewer Chase's reputation. Now Kelso was a star. This was how life worked, apparently – sour cream rises to the top. Chase would be making payments for many years on the loan he'd taken out to cover the hemoclip malpractice case brought on by Kelso. With the cost of rehab added to the burden – well – what did it matter, really? Chase was alive.

Chase counted the hours leading up to his discharge. He was anxious to get the worst behind him and get on with his life. Never had he been so anxious tracking time, but on his day of scheduled discharge, Chase's counselor called him into a conference room, stating, "The head of the Physician Recovery Program in Matherville has canceled your discharge. He says that two months is not enough time to treat a physician."

"What! I've never met this guy. How can someone not even on staff at Riverdell cancel my discharge?" Yet, there was nothing Chase could do. He knew the consequences of leaving against medical advice (AMA). All would be lost. So, he was able to test his newfound serenity, his gratitude in all things, his acceptance of life on life's terms – by fermenting in Whiskey Prison.

The program of sobriety depended heavily on a Higher Power, ill-defined for most, but clear to Chase. He would simply reclaim the God of his youth. However, it was not as easy as he imagined. He had trouble accepting forgiveness, not for years of past transgressions, but specifically, for his first night in seclusion when he had cursed God and dared him to come out of the Sky. If there were ever a clear-cut case of blaspheming the Holy Spirit, this was it. What folly that he harbored this same fear many years ago after declining to join a Bible study. Now, he had truly done it – a direct blasphemy of the Holy Spirit in its worst form. What began as a minor fear in years past blossomed into a bona fide phobia – *enissophobia*, to be exact – the fear of having committed the unforgivable sin, a welcome mat to the house of madness.

When he repeatedly asked for forgiveness, he somehow felt trapped in a recurring theme that had played out when he was a young boy, firing up his grandfather's altar calls by faking his redemption on a routine basis, forcing a cycle wherein he felt free to sin because redemption was only as far away as the next altar call.

Heretical thoughts began to plague him as well, as though his soul were trying to find refuge with a different God. For instance, his broken rib caused horrific pain during his stay in Riverdell due to the unrelenting cough from his acid-fueled pneumonia. Chase grew frustrated that healing was unusually slow because his coughing did not subside one iota over the course of two months and counting. How he prayed for the cough to stop, but nothing changed.

In his discouragement, a recurring thought of heresy evolved – his recollection of a Sumerian goddess who lorded over the healing of broken ribs. Nin-ti, or the "lady of the rib," shared the word "ti" with the concept "to make alive." He knew some scholars felt "Eve" from the Hebrew, meaning "to breathe or live," was simply an echo of this early myth that predated Genesis authorship. He had to stop himself from praying to Nin-ti to heal his rib and stop the pain, given that Yahweh had declined to help. Despite this confusion, when it came time in the group sessions to describe his Higher Power, he did not mention Nin-ti.

When his stay at Riverdell finally ended after two additional penalty weeks had been tacked on, Chase felt a new peace, a surprising reaction he had not anticipated. Perhaps, it was a manifestation of those well-worn lyrics, "Freedom is another word for nothing left to lose." He was alone, with nothing left to lose. He had alienated his parents, his ex-wife, and friends. His debt would grow to an unforgiving level. In an odd way, he felt invincible to the inevitable traumatic events that life most certainly had in store. The worst was behind him, and he could not be cut into smaller pieces. *Atomos* – no further cutting possible.

Next up – a humiliating return to society. As we know, the atom can be divided, and it might be the case that Chase's mind began its split at this point, opting to embrace antiquity as the key to tomorrow's vision. His checkered past would become his guiding light. "Purpose" took on a whole new dimension as it would require staggering feats – superhuman – to justify what he'd been through. Limitless energy and persistence would be required. He would dream big. Bigger than life.

When the nuclear fusion of a star finally burns out, there is no force to counter the gravity, and the star collapses in a cosmic instant. This dense, hot mass rebounds in an explosion of unimaginable power – a supernova. In this explosion, atomic nuclei are fused in different measures to make every element in the periodic table. These factories fling newly formed elements throughout space as the building blocks for new stars and planets.

While Chase waited on the curb outside the Riverdell Rehabilitation Center for his ride home, newly discharged, he stared at the empty horizon. He meditated. He prayed. He pondered the fact that he was made of stardust, an exploded supernova several billion years ago, ready now for new life. The past held the key to his future. Too, he would remember forever the sound that a Super Bowl ring makes when it goes tap-tap-tap on the walls of a seclusion room in a lunatic asylum.

As he saw his taxi approaching, he muttered to himself the lines of the Renaissance poet:

Midway on life's journey, I found myself
In dark woods, the right road lost.

13
THEODICY

Why?

A word so small, the question so simple, the answer so slippery. Still, Chase wanted to know – why?

Everything has a cause – a causal chain implies a first cause – God must exist as the first cause. Chase knew the principle of sufficient reason, with its ambiguous entrails, as defined by Leibniz. Of course, the cosmological argument attributed to Thomas Aquinas had been lifted from Aristotle who drew from Plato. Anselm's ontologic approach of *reductio ad absurdum,* on the other hand, required too much effort for a simple truth. God exists. Yes, everything has a cause. Yet, the problem for Chase was the chasm between "cause" and "purpose." Why?

Random verses of scripture were dangerous, he knew, so he embarked on deep study, beginning with the *Book of Job.* In its pages, however, Chase no longer recognized the Bible story of his youth. From the beginning, it was God who offered Job as a pawn to Satan in their chess match, a remarkably human game so very much like the myths of ancient Greeks who projected their own human foibles onto their gods. God said, in essence, "If you're so sure of yourself, Satan, why don't you take a crack at this fellow Job?" *What caprice. What whimsy. How could the God of the Universe do this?* The story wasn't a simple question of theodicy – reconciling the co-existence of evil and God –

rather, Chase was reading about a God who encouraged evil to have a sporting chance.

Enough heresy, he thought. Indeed, apostasy brought fatigue. *Don't think about it too deeply. Obviously, the purpose of Job's harrowing experience was to serve as an example for the rest of us who suffer. But what's the take-home message? Could it be that the Lord disciplines those He has called to great duty?*

Chase bookmarked *Job*, hoping to return. Yet, he also had to consider his grandfather's entire library that had been waiting patiently nearly 10 years for the first volume to be read.

A more incisive, more incriminating, more therapeutic approach came from Step Four in the 12-step program – "Made a searching and fearless moral inventory of ourselves" – where, rather than simply airing dirty laundry, one commits a sort of "automos," a cutting of the self through sharp introspection. That is, after listing every wrong done to, every wrong done by, every wrong perceived, the "automist" contemplates his *own contribution to his own misfortune*, even if it's only 1%, or less. With enough honesty and mental agility, one often realizes that one has invited evil to sup with oneself. Through this ongoing exercise, Chase felt his bitterness start to recede both from travails in California and the abject humiliation in store for him now.

Two weeks after discharge from Riverdell, those weeks spent in study and contemplation, Chase had to face a cast of thousands at Far West Texas School of Medicine, College Hospital, the VA Hospital, and a ten-acre spread of ancillary facilities, all filled with curious people. On the day that Chase made his appearance as the new Chief of Surgery at the VA Hospital, a staff party of the operating room personnel was in progress, celebrating someone's birthday. When Chase opened the door to join the group in the lounge, the buzzing stopped and every face in the room turned in quietude and stared at the freakish curiosity.

"Hello. I'm Dr. Callaway. I—I know a few of you from back when I was a resident here…"

No one moved. Only the beating of his heart sounded in his ears. He scanned the room, trying to make eye contact and smile at those whom he recognized from the past. Nurses in green bouffant caps, scrub techs, surgeons gathered around the punch bowl, most looked to the floor the moment his eyes touched theirs. The air in his lungs emptied, and he could say nothing further. He forced himself to the punch bowl, nodded kindly in lieu of conversation, and fielded perfunctory "welcomes" from some. Then he sat down by himself with his cup of punch. Celebration never returned to the room.

Later, he sat in the office of the Chief, alone, lording over his fiefdom, his head buried in his hands. How could he go on like this? How?

Later that day, the Director of the Impaired Physicians Program, Dr. Fred Crisp, met with Chase and explained the urine testing program, and how Chase would be voiding into a bottle twice a week for the next year. "Usually, we only do this for a few months, during the most difficult time. But you're in a highly visible position. You could hurt my entire program if you relapse. As a matter of fact, the statistics say you *will* relapse because you didn't go to the four-month treatment program designed for doctors." Chase considered this absurd, but he realized that he was a helpless pawn for Dr. Crisp who held Chase's medical license in a hip pocket.

So, for one year, twice a week, the Chief of Surgery took the elevators down to Employee Health in the basement where he was issued his cup. Then, a random male employee would escort Chase to the urinal and hover at his back in the tiny restroom to make sure there were no urine-swapping shenanigans going on. At the end of each and every moment of total humiliation, *one hundred times* in all, the Chief of Surgery would turn to the employee and say, "Thank you. I'm sorry to have troubled you." Usually, he was met with a silent smirk.

All buildings at Far West were connected by tunnels and overhead walkways to avoid the harsh wind and weather, but it forced Chase into close contact with hundreds of judgmental faces. He could have walked outside, but he chose the walkways to conquer his crippling fear of people and their condemnation, real or imagined.

However, at first, he couldn't make it the full two blocks from the VA Hospital to the departmental offices. His forced "hellos" to hide his humiliation completely drained him. He could only make it halfway, to College Hospital, where he followed the walkway into the building and rested (hid) in an empty patient room, a quiet hall, or even a bathroom stall, before he could muster the physical strength and courage needed to finish the trip.

Some passers-by in the walkways tried to help, though efforts usually fell horribly flat.

One day, a kindly old physician collared him in the walkway and confessed more than Chase wanted to hear: "I thought it might help you to know that I too tried, uh, *to end it all*, once. A malpractice suit pretty much destroyed me, similar to your deal."

Malpractice suit? This guy thinks my struggle is about a malpractice suit? Try three of them, bud. Try a fourth lawsuit on top of it all for alleged assault and battery. Try having no insurance coverage for two of the four suits. Try getting run out of town by a cadre of jealous, incompetent surgeons. Try getting threats from a sociopathic surgeon who has placed you in his crosshairs. Try rotting in hell for years, topping it off with a near-death experience. Add 'em all up, and a malpractice suit barely even scores a point on the stress chart for me. Malpractice suit? Gimme a break. Instead, of course, he said, "Thanks, I appreciate that."

The other surgery faculty members were awkward around Chase, but he knew this would pass with time. They knew him in his prime, so it would not take long for them to see that he was the same old Chase. Most notably, Chase was impressed with former classmate Porter Piscotel who offered both solace and advice, with a genuine and caring attitude, more than any other member of the department outside T.N.T. Chase couldn't believe that this was the same old DeLorean-driving, pipe-smoking hotshot, the guy whose hubris, years ago, had thrust him into greatness as the top student in their class, that is, when only the third year was considered. Porter's current nickname among the residents, "General Wooden Head," (a.k.a. The General), seemed harsh to Chase who found Porter a changed person and a new friend. Furthermore, Porter had opted to focus his practice on the most difficult surgical cases, technically, performing procedures that many surgeons dropped from their repertoire as soon as they hit private practice. Chase was impressed.

Editor's note: Many tales from the VA Hospital are deleted here as they do not advance the story, other than to point out how ill-suited

Chase was to be part of a Kafkaesque bureaucracy. He had agreed up front, however, to assume this post for several years until another new faculty member joined the department at the bottom of the totem pole.

In requesting a conversation with Thatcher Nolan Taylor, M.D., Chase felt that the momentum for his new and true purpose – a multidisciplinary breast cancer program – had stalled. He wanted to give his mentor a gentle nudge, prompting this meeting:

"Dr. Taylor, the demands at the VA are getting bigger all the time. Administrative folly, of course, but much of what they say has to be done regardless. I don't feel like I'm doing a good job. Maybe you should think about hiring a full-time surgeon there. The VA administrator is really coming down on me hard about faculty supervision. They don't count our chief residents as junior faculty. They say what we're doing is ghost surgery. They want paid faculty members in the operating room on all cases. And, they want a full-time Chief."

"Oh my, Chase. Don't let them bully you. Always remember one thing over there – in fact, consider this your job description for the VA – don't *ever* get fooled into building their Bridge on the River Kwai."

And that was that. T.N.T. told Chase to hang on for another year or two. Eventually, there would be a new faculty member, a new kid on the block.

Throughout this burdensome time of re-entry into society, Chase had to force himself every step of the way. He had to force an air of authority when he chaired a VA committee, he had to force authority when he served as a referee for arguments among VA hospital employees, he had to force authority as teaching assistant to residents in the operating room, he had to force authority when he instructed medical students. Inside, he was dying. Ashamed and horrified at his own behavior in the past, he felt transparent, as though everyone he encountered had witnessed every shocking moment of his life, all the way into the seclusion room at the mental institution. When he would try to convince himself that he was over-reacting, a well-meaning someone would convince him otherwise.

"How are you doing?"

"Fine, thank you."

"No, I mean how are you *really* doing?"

132

"I'm *really* doing fine."

"Well, I just want you to know, I've heard. And I understand."

"You've heard what?"

"Well, you know...I've heard."

The millstone around his neck did not seem to lighten over time. He was not plagued by cravings, so common with addictions. He was, instead, plagued by the horror of what had happened in his life. He had to generate something, a strength from within, that would allow him to walk the entire distance from the VA Hospital to the Department of Surgery without stopping halfway and hiding in a bathroom stall to catch his breath, avoiding oh-so-many people who had witnessed or heard of Callaway's Great Fall.

Then, without epiphany or fanfare, without effort or will, one day Chase awoke to a new world, a world of victory. It was so sudden that he attributed it to new neural connections in his brain, unencumbered by foreign chemistry, dendritic processes finally reaching the critical distance to allow sparks to cross the gap. For eight months, the extension cords of those brain cells under repair had been struggling to reach each other, unable to transmit a current. Plugged in, Chase was a new man.

In sharp reversal of attitude, he was euphoric. He felt he had an "edge" on the world since he had fallen into the abyss and had lived to tell about it. Somehow, this imparted a deeper wisdom, a better understanding. Perhaps, he was a little cocksure, even smug. When he attended Department of Surgery cocktail parties, Chase was mildly amused when the other faculty members began to slur their words and reveal personalities kept on ice during the day. Now, he was above that, even knowing full well that those same individuals were looking down on him.

In the months that followed, Chase realized that his ability to read and study and memorize had returned. Science had recently discovered that brain cells could regenerate after all, growing anew from neural stem cells. So, maybe he could recapture his lost IQ points.

It became clear that his "purpose" was going to be found in the breast cancer arena, but beyond the limited goals as originally outlined by T.N.T. All vectors seemed to be pointing the same way – his very early exposure during a fellowship to breast pathology and its confusing limitations; a few years later, his early exposure at the San Diego conference where he caught a glimpse of the revolution in breast cancer about to occur; the tragic toll on his personal health from working round-the-clock trauma such that "regular hours" were a must for him; the arthritis in his hands that made deep abdominal surgeries so difficult, yet no problem with breast surgery; his interest in plastic techniques and cosmetic outcomes; his ability to break down walls between specialties and build consensus; his ability to communicate with female patients in a gender-neutral fashion offering whatever time was needed; and related to this, his ability to experience and exhibit genuine empathy. The subatomic particles were realigning as part of the ongoing supernova. It was enough to consider once again that there was order among the chaos, and that Providence had a plan.

He began to scour his past, dredging up stories and events that fit nicely into a Master Plan, albeit ever cautious about magical thinking. He recalled the pregnant patient with metastatic breast cancer he had encountered during surgical training, forced into an abortion against her will, ostensibly to fight the cancer; he thought often of his medical school friend and foosball partner, Amy, who had nearly undergone modified radical mastectomy for a benign condition; he remembered during his pathology fellowship, sitting at the double-headed microscope with the famous surgeon and diagnosing a rare type of breast cancer, without pathology faculty present at the time (and how that surgeon later came to Chase's rescue during his assassination attempt at the Ciena hospital); and most of all, he never forgot the mysterious patient with medullary breast cancer who could have been a clone of Chase's deceased sister, a patient who inspired him to study the concept of lumpectomies and to visit the first free-standing breast cancer center in the U.S. She had an unusual grip on his psyche as it seemed to be sister Annie speaking to him from the grave.

Importantly, as leader of this breast center crusade, nearing age 40, he had no designs on personal gain or reward. He had been stripped of ego to an incredible extent, with the apparent purpose to invest himself in others, humbly encouraging colleagues, allowing a level of success impossible when the leader is all about personal accolades. Furthermore, with no children and no hope of such on the horizon, and with no wife nor hope anywhere on that same horizon, he could devote a superhuman amount of time and sublimated energy. So, with unstoppable persistence, he began his purposeful work.

He embarked on a ravenous interrogation of every aspect of diseases of the breast – the molecular biology of normal and cancerous tissue, anatomy, physiology, benign conditions, surgical trials in progress, breast imaging, chemotherapy and radiation therapy of breast cancer, plastic surgery principles, benign and malignant breast pathology, the epidemiology of screening, risk factors and genetics.

A new computer service in the department allowed the devoted librarian (who knew Chase as a resident) to generate abstracts of breast cancer articles published in the English-speaking journals. Chase asked for a list every month, and it took him at least 40 hours every cycle, reading most nights and weekends, to cover the summaries of 500 to 600 new publications related to "breast." He repeated this ritual each month. And he would continue to do it for years.

Aware of the difficulty in maintaining balance in his life, he began an exercise program, and he finally began to delve into his grandfather's books as well – books of theology, books of science, and the great novels. As part of this effort, he returned one last time to the *Book of Job*, which, by its reputation, should have been the most important book of the Bible for Chase.

Different translations bothered him, however. In the King James, it was "Though he slay me, yet will I trust him," while in the Revised Standard Version, it was, "Behold he will slay me, I have no hope." Big difference. Chase studied source material, Hebrew translations, all to dissect the cause of suffering and to reconcile God's blind side. Rather than provide the answers to suffering, however, it seemed that the *Book of Job* was pure riddle.

After stumbling with the overworked "hidden sin" excuse, that is, retribution theology, to explain Job's nightmare, Zophar and the other friends moved on to irritate Job (and God), coming from different angles to explain Job's curse, including the same fallbacks commonly used today. In the end, Zophar and his friends were reprimanded. To be one of the longer books in the Bible, yet so ill-defined with regard to its message, Job seemed uniquely frustrating to Chase. All those words of poetry simply to say, "God is inscrutable. Don't even try to explain evil in the world."

Chase also had to consider that, in contrast to his earlier assumptions, he and Job were *not* kindred spirits. Job cursed the world and everything in it, and he cursed the day he was born. But he never cursed God directly. Passive, unquestioning acceptance, even praise to God was Job's secret. No purpose. No reason.

When it came to "purpose," the *Book of Job* wasn't going to cut it. Unlike Job, Chase had cursed God directly and with full intent. Sure, he had been in the throes of addiction and withdrawal, his brain chemically racked and tortured. The fact remained, however, even though Job had tippy toed around a direct curse, coming from every possible angle, he never crossed the line as Chase had done. No comparison.

Then, oh my, that happy ending when Job's friends and relatives "comforted him over all the <u>evil that the Lord had brought upon him</u>..."

The *Lord* brought the evil? The Lord? The *Book of Job* wasn't the answer – it was the question.

14
DOVETAIL

Chase Callaway found both refuge and strength in his burgeoning vision – a multidisciplinary breast center that would serve as an example for the rest of the country, bringing what he had seen in the private sector of L.A.'s San Fernando Valley to the world of academics. So far, only one academic site had merged all treating specialties into a single clinic, but that was only half the story, half the need – the same merging of specialties was needed for the diagnosis of breast cancer, in addition to treatment.

Competition was almost non-existent (even M. D. Anderson had yet to adopt the new multidisciplinary concept), allowing a rare opportunity for Far West Texas University to pioneer innovation, rather than its usual struggle "to keep up." For once, the university could reach beyond its reputation as a "psychiatric center of excellence" or a "basketball dynasty." His alma mater could drive a stake into the ground and raise its flag to announce itself as the first university center in the U.S. that gathered all specialists having anything to do with breast cancer (and benign breast disease) under the same tent.

The gloomy atmosphere at the VA paradoxically nurtured his dream. In an odd way, prone to symbolism, Chase connected his childhood terror at the VA to his present circumstance. The pink skeleton he met 35 years prior had been a glimpse of his future – bones left bare after acid dissolved away vital flesh. Now, these bones would

137

serve as structure for a new being, colored by cause, tempered into strength well beyond what a normal life would have allowed.

With the River Kwai admonition in mind, he trimmed his VA efforts to a minimum so he could focus on the dream. Any VA duty not critical to a properly functioning surgical suite was dropped or avoided. For instance, when he was asked to travel to another VA in Texas to participate in the peer review of a "dangerous, paranoid, alcoholic surgeon," he said, "No. I was dragged into something like this in California, and it nearly killed me."

"But this guy's a menace," Chase was told. "We really need your help."

"Get someone else, please." Self-preservation had to supervene. Still, he lost sleep over his refusal, wondering how many patients might be harmed, or even die, if another crazed surgeon were on the loose. As with all such thoughts for Chase, they attached like barnacles and never let go.

He continued his obsessive study of breast cancer. So many controversies, it seemed, fell between the cracks left by traditional medical specialties. Who would fill in these cracks? Only someone comfortable in the mortar of the unknown, yet well-versed in all the specialties dealing with breast cancer, including the basic sciences and ongoing research. Cross-pollination of clinicians and researchers was critical for a true Center of Excellence.

Thinking decades in advance, Chase reasoned he would need to generate his own flock of professionals for the future. He began lecturing first year medical students on normal breast anatomy and physiology, second year medical students on breast pathology, third- and fourth-year students on the diagnosis and treatment of breast cancer. He developed month-long electives and summer-long fellowships that were always booked in advance.

Importantly, he shared his dream with his students – that is, developing the premier breast center in the country – and he challenged them to become part of the realized vision someday. He understood that lower tier universities only rarely improved their status by importing faculty from top tier universities. Often, these imports turned out to be the rejects of their "world class" institutions, while the good imports used a place like Far West as a short-lived stepping-stone to a more prestigious university.

Thus, Chase was highly devoted to nurturing the future stars of the breast program from the home grown. Once these Texas born-and-bred professionals took center stage, the top recruits in the country would seek out Far West for their careers. It had already happened in the psychiatry department, so the model was in place.

One other feature of his long-term planning for the Far West breast cancer dynasty – he encouraged female medical students and residents to devote their careers to breast cancer. "It's going to happen just like what's happening now in gynecology," he would say. "Someday, I won't be able to practice breast cancer surgery. It'll be almost exclusively in the hands of women. Hard to picture today, with 90% men, but mark my words."

In promotional speeches, Chase would point out that one of the first scientists to promote the "multidisciplinary approach," was an archaeologist who had achieved his fame right here in the Pecos region. Alfred Kidder had been the first to bring in ethnologists and linguists and ethnographers and the like. "Multidisciplinary" was born and bred in west Texas.

Chase agreed with innovators who said the word "multidisciplinary" was inadequate as it implied nothing about communication among the specialties dealing with breast cancer – radiology, pathology, surgery, plastics, radiation oncology, medical oncology, genetics, psychiatry, epidemiology, and the host of research disciplines. Instead, "*inter*disciplinary" was the better descriptor, and for this, Chase pictured a dovetail.

He developed 35mm slides for a presentation that gave pictorial life to his dovetail dream. Then he took this show on the road, visiting each clinical department at Far West and a variety of research labs where efforts could be applied to breast cancer. He was disheartened at first to learn there was no ongoing breast cancer research on campus, but talented people started coming forth, curious as to what this Dr. Callaway was trying to do.

Then, he was invited to speak to the Studebaker Medical Research Foundation, an independent research facility on campus, loosely affiliated with the medical school. There, Chase invited scientists to join him in his quest, with the research focused on premalignant pathologies, prevention, and early diagnosis. Other universities, larger and greater and well-established, had the reins in hand when it came to *treatment* of breast cancer. Therefore, Chase's ticket to a research niche for the breast center was in those areas of premalignancy that were being ignored by nearly everyone.

At the conclusion of the dovetail presentation, Chase was surrounded by enthusiasm. One scientist could apply his immunologic therapies to create a vaccine against breast cancer, another could apply her susceptibility gene to earlier diagnosis of breast cancer, another was designing a new hormonal compound for an unrelated reason, but after hearing Chase, it occurred to her that the chemistry she was using might be able to help prevent breast cancer.

The next day, a core group of scientists met for the first interdisciplinary breast cancer research meeting, and the faithful continued in this mission for the next ten years (the research foundation invited him to speak yearly, adding more scientists to the cause until it was the largest cooperative effort on campus). Yet, Chase knew this was the cart before the horse. In his vision, research was to be merged with the clinical program which, at this point, was almost non-existent. Patients with both insurance and breast lumps went to Permian Medical Center, not Far West's College Hospital.

Thatcher Nolan Taylor, M.D., had warned Chase upon his return to Texas, "You're going to have your work cut out for you. Your partner, if you want to call him that, will be a radiologist who, well, is a likeable guy, but when it comes to cooperation with surgeons, none of the faculty has had much success with Dr. Sherbert. But if anyone can make it work, Chase, it's you. If it doesn't work, though, we'll get rid of him."

What a wonderful position to be in, thought Chase, working under the most powerful man on campus in T.N.T. It was reminiscent of his relationship with Dr. Ted Zink in California. Nothing like being linked to the top dog.

"I don't anticipate any trouble with Dr. Sherbert," Chase replied.

He had learned his lesson in California. Physicians don't respond to duress. They barely respond to rules. Too, they tend to ignore guidelines. Chase would simply return to his pre-California natural self, the man who could get along with anyone.

As the dream took shape (as an idea only), clerks, secretaries, nurses felt no barriers with Chase and openly told him they would like to be part of his breast center and his vision, if it ever came to pass. Clinicians started to show excitement as well. Medical students began openly expressing their desire to become breast radiologists, breast medical oncologists, breast surgical oncologists, breast pathologists. One such student was Nola Kastl.

In their first encounter, Nola had rushed forward from the audience of first year medical students, stating how the vision was a "dream come true" for her. She had been wrestling with her purpose in life and her role in medicine, and Chase's description of the dovetailing of talented minds was "as though I were the only girl in the audience – that you were speaking directly to me."

Nola's pale, gray-green eyes were penetrating if not unsettling, and Chase could recall, at that first meeting, backing a few steps away as she spoke. Yet, she proved remarkably resolute, spending her free time with Chase in the operating room, seeing new patients, even looking up articles for him in the medical library. Then, when Chase announced that the most urgent need for his program was breast pathology, she proclaimed her specialty choice: "I'm going into pathology, Dr. Callaway. I want to join the faculty and help with your dream."

But Nola was still a student, so this answer to the current mediocrity in pathology was still years away. Of all his multidisciplinary studies, Chase spent the most time learning the controversies of breast pathology. He devoured texts, articles, fascicles, atlases, teaching slide sets, memorizing patterns and reviewing microscope slides on all breast specimens generated at the university. His concern? Unlike other areas of the body where the subjectivity of pathology often made little difference, Chase was impressed by the staggering clinical impact of taxonomy in breast pathology. A diagnosis of "atypical ductal hyperplasia" was ignored by physicians, but the very same pattern on the slide might be called "ductal carcinoma in situ" by a different pathologist, whereupon the breast would be amputated. Nowhere else in pathology did mere words have this much power.

"Pathology," he would say in his sermons that inspired students like Nola Kastl, "is the most important discipline of medicine, and it is the least understood by clinicians. Sadly, breast pathology is even ignored by many pathologists. There's an explosion of information happening right now, and few are paying attention. Many clinicians are foreigners to pathology. They treat words on a piece of paper. But cancer is like a country you've never visited. You can read about its history, you can look at brochures, and you can think you know the country well. Until you've been there, however, you don't have a true feel for it. Until clinicians travel into the microscope and realize the whims of pathology, they're always going to be stay-at-home tourists."

Chase traveled deep into the microscope. His private lessons came from a Hopkins resident-in-training who was spending a fellowship year in Matherville studying the rich teaching files of brain pathology (taken from the many autopsies performed on the mental patients over the years). She had also consented to be the instructor at Chase's new "resident teaching conference" in breast disease, and she spent an hour after each conference teaching Chase how breast pathology was interpreted "back East," in contrast to Far West.

One evening after conference, she said, "You saw what happened today. The same thing that happens most every conference. In situ cancer is called invasive due to the artifact of sclerosis. Invasive foci are missed and called in situ. A classic medullary cancer is not recognized, instead called a routine Grade 3 cancer. I can't recall a single conference where I didn't object to at least one diagnosis for the week. Let me be honest with you, Chase. You, a surgeon, read these slides better than any pathologist on the staff here. You know it already. And I'm concerned about your dream. Don't get me wrong. I've heard your presentation, and it's quite impressive. But pathology is central to everything. If you don't figure a way to get some degree of expertise here at Far West in pathology, it will bring down what is currently a house of cards. It will be your undoing."

"To tell you the truth, I was sort of hoping you would join us here at Far West. Dr. Dreiser told me he's been recruiting you to stay here in Matherville at the end of your fellowship."

"Therein lies the problem. I've heard Chairman Dreiser make that same statement to the powers that be – 'if only I could get Marsha Cohen to stay in Texas'. Just last week I overheard him telling your chairman that very thing. Chase, you've done an excellent job of putting pressure on everyone, it seems, because Dreiser is feeling the heat to find a breast pathologist."

"And?"

"And, the trouble is, Dreiser has never said *one word* to me about staying on faculty here. Not once. He's just another academic politician covering his backside. So, your problem is greater than simply not having an expert breast pathologist. This is a great medical center when it comes to neurology, psychiatry, neuropathology, and so forth. But I'm counting the days until I can get back to Hopkins. I wish you well, but best I can tell, you're being tricked by a lot of people paying lip service. If you don't have pathology, you don't have anything."

Her words were chilling. His only answer to the problem – Nola Kastl – was years away (if she even stuck to her pathology plans).

On the opposite side of the looking glass, basic science researchers, like the clinicians, were equally oblivious to the nuances of pathology. While attending a conference of PhDs held in Austin, in order to learn more about cancer research, Chase was astonished that a speaker showed a routine photograph of "atypical hyperplasia" then apologized to the audience for presenting something so alien. The speaker said, "Don't squirm. I know this is difficult for you all, but you're going to have to learn about these benign proliferative changes in the breast. For years, we've been studying breast tissue from surgical reduction procedures, calling it our normal controls when often it's not normal at all. As scientists, we must discover and learn routine light microscopy to understand what we're truly studying in the lab."

At that moment, Chase felt the donning of a laurel wreath. Medical advances were divided into "clinical" and "basic science" research, but the tie that binds was the stepchild of *pathology*. As a symbol of his crowning, Chase placed the microscope his father had used in medical school on his desk at work – a constant reminder of his mission to build his program on solid ground, the foundation of pathology.

Over a period of six months, Chase wrote a treatise on how to build a multidisciplinary – no – *inter*disciplinary breast center with research woven into every crevice. Over 150 pages detailed each step of the process, focusing first on how to make the center the most patient-friendly in Texas, if not the entire country. It would be one-stop shopping at its finest. No callbacks for abnormal mammograms. Everything done on the same day, including biopsy. Every detail of the biopsy procedure was outlined, including the warming of antiseptic solution before placing it on the patient's skin. Patient flow, patient care, support systems, psychological services, wigs, prostheses, educational mission, research agendas, all of it flowed onto the written page so that there could be no mistake about it. Chase Callaway was back, and he was about to offer the world something new.

Chase devoted one fourth of his "how-to" treatise to a financial pro forma he created based on two years of billing records from the Department of Radiology, where a steady 70% collection rate allowed easy prediction of revenues from mammography. Because so many services would be non-income producing, the break-even point would be 50 mammograms per day, which was exactly double the current volume at the university.

Key to the future financial integrity was the "technical component" of radiologic billing. The "professional component" earned by the radiologists would, of course, be subject to the university's taxation system wherein the radiology department and medical school hierarchy ended up with more than half. The technical component was the bulk of the bill, however, covering the cost and maintenance of the equipment, highly profitable once equipment had been procured and paid for. Chase's key concept for success was that education, research and indigent care could only be covered – assuming Chase could secure grant money for equipment – if the sacred technical component was left untouched by university taxation, which was merely the status quo. The university never touched technical components. The significant difference would be the technical revenue going into a new financial control point for the breast center. This new arrangement could certainly be housed within the radiology department, but the money had to be earmarked for the interdisciplinary center.

After reviewing Chase's pro forma, the CFO of Far West's College Hospital had nothing to add or subtract, and the accounting department of the medical school had nothing to add or subtract. No one could find a single flaw in his calculations.

One small obstacle – Dr. Aaron Sherbert, breast radiologist, had a personal maximum of 25 patients per day, all seen and well-cared-for during his four-hour workday. In Chase's view, a full eight-hour day would solve the problem, and the center would be self-sustaining. In Dr. Sherbert's view, a doubling of floor space and new equipment would solve all problems (though he did agree to a 15% increase in volume – an additional 4 patients a day). Chase had no doubt that Dr. Sherbert would come around to the magic 50 patients per day. As was his norm, he had made friends with Dr. Sherbert who was far cleverer and more entertaining than the portrait offered by T.N.T.

Upon completion of his treatise – "Establishing a Center of Excellence in Breast Disease at the University of Far West Texas" – Chase decided that he should get approval for the Master Plan from the master himself, Dr. Thatcher Nolan Taylor. Chase gave T.N.T. a bound copy of the manuscript and waited eagerly, but quietly, for the response. Three months passed before T.N.T. called Chase to his office to discuss the proposal.

"Chase, this is just wonderful."

"Thank you. Is my key strategy for the technical component okay? As a new control point? That's the only touchy issue, since that decision is really up to the radiology department. Admittedly, I don't know if I can get the mammography and ultrasound equipment through donations or grants or whatever. The current equipment needs to be thrown out, and clearly, the radiology department isn't planning to lift a finger. If I do get the equipment for Dr. Sherbert, the capture of the technical component is the absolute key to making this thing work."

"The university has never taxed technical fees, Chase. They only tax professional income. If you get the equipment, I agree the technical fee needs to go to breast center operations exclusively, which shouldn't be a problem as long as that control point is in the Department of Radiology."

"A completely independent control point would be better, but as long as Radiology lets me access that control point in order to run the breast center, that'll work. Another thing, I do feel awkward asking for the medical director fee that I'm sure you read about, but this project is consuming most of my time. Even after I'm replaced at the VA and I go full time on breast cancer, then running this center is going to cut into patient time and, of course, my income. The whole thing seems to be gaining momentum. I'm very close to a brick-and-mortar commitment from the hospital. I'm speaking to women's groups regularly to start building support, and—"

"No, I think the medical director concept is fine, Chase. I'm starting to feel a groundswell of support for you in the community, and I notice that you've got the director's fee kicking in *after* the center has a substantial profit. Are you prepared for no profit, in which case, there's no medical director fee?"

"I know it's possible, but I really can't let myself think about failing." Yet, what Chase thought was this: *It is becoming increasingly clear that this mission is providential, the culmination of my exile to, and exodus from, California and all that happened there. It is not only my redemption, but also my very purpose for being alive.*

Chase waited for Dr. Taylor to begin discussing, even criticizing, the patient protocols, the services, the organizational structure, the employees, the patient flow strategies, or something, but the room was quiet.

Chase had to break the silence. "I know it's going to be a few years before the current mammography clinic expands into what I've described, but there's a lot of work to be done right now, especially when I get the brick-and-mortar commitment. Work that I could delegate. I'm all over Matherville and surrounding towns promoting this cloudy idea called the Far West Texas Breast Pavilion, but in fact, the Pavilion dream is *me*. I used to have Dr. Sherbert helping me with these presentations, but he's pulled back for some reason. Is it okay if I start looking to hire a clinic administrator?"

"Oh, gosh, Chase, the department doesn't have money to hire anyone like that. FTEs are the hardest thing to come by on campus. Besides, with the Department of Radiology getting the technical component, they should do the hiring and firing."

Chase held back a gasp. *No money?* Construction costs were easy to secure compared to salaries, yes, but he couldn't imagine waiting to hire a clinic director until the doors were already open and revenue stream established. Was it conceivable that the Department of Surgery had no intent to invest in this project – that his own department was planning to control the clinical care of patients, but using "other people's money?"

With construction and equipment and start-up salaries, this was going to be a $4 million dollar effort on Chase's part, assuming he could raise the funds. He hoped to accomplish this task without the medical school (or any of its departments), being required to chip in. Yet, a single salary was too much to ask? Too, it was only for a few years, since that salary would eventually come from technical component revenues.

"I don't want to put a damper on your ideas," continued Dr. Taylor, "but be aware that most of these lofty ambitions simply never make it off the ground at a place like Far West. I'll do everything I can to help you get things to work, especially interfacing with other departments. But prepare yourself – sometimes we have to scale back our dreams."

Chase felt his redemptive dream slipping away, dragging his purpose along.

"But the concept," Chase said, "are you okay with the concept? I mean that's why you asked me to come back to Texas, isn't it?" He wanted to make sure there was at least one page they shared together.

"Yes, of course. I want the surgery department to control how breast cancer patients are managed at Far West. I'm behind you all the way on this, Chase, even though your dream is a whole lot larger than I'd imagined. However, money is always the rate limiting step around here."

"But is my general plan okay, as I've outlined in the manuscript..."

"Yes. All except...where was it...oh, here, page 87, where you use the word 'dovetail'. Dovetail is a word that belongs in hunting, perhaps, but it makes no sense here."

"Sir?"

"You're talking about how different medical specialties fail to communicate, that is, the breast cancer patients are told to have a mastectomy by a surgeon, then the radiation oncologist tells them why they should have a lumpectomy. Then you shift to a metaphorical angle where the medical specialties are too territorial, and that the key is to *dovetail* the specialties. What does that mean exactly? Dovetail is better off as a noun, not a verb. I'd cut the dovetail concept, or at least the word itself. Other than that, I think it's fine to show this around to the others involved."

"Dovetail" is a problem?

Chased owed his very life and soul to Thatcher Taylor who had silenced those critics opposed to Chase's return after rehab. What was happening here? The purpose of the treatise was to make sure that everyone was aware of his strategy, starting with T.N.T., followed by other departmental chairmen and university officials. Instead of discussing the multi-faceted content in Chase's body of work, however, T.N.T. was bothered by a single word? Incorrectly at that, given that "dovetail" could be either a noun or a verb.

Furthermore, no money to hire a clinic administrator to help get this thing off the ground? He had accepted the need for fund-raising for all infrastructure, and he was well on his way to success. *But no administrative help, no clinic director?* Befuddled and frustrated, Chase left the Chairman's office when T.N.T. gave the signal – that is, slapping both his palms on the arms of his chair, as if he were about to leave his own office (the visitor would mimic the gesture and leave without another word said). It was a reflex exit, a sign universally appreciated.

Thatcher Nolan Taylor, M.D. was a Dallas product, but he had attended medical school at Stanford, then his surgical residency at Mass General. Legend held that he had once been offered to serve as Chairman of the Department of Surgery at Harvard, but that his response had been, "When I look out my office window at the Matherville skyline, it's nice to be the owner of a good deal of it. I would not be able to claim that outside of Matherville." Indeed, Thatcher's wife was the former Gretchen Studebaker, and the T.N.T. family was heir to this corner of Texas. Husband and wife influence on the campus was immeasurable.

Chase knew Dr. Taylor was a dedicated champion of the status quo. Even though T.N.T. voiced support for a breast center, he was nervous about some of Chase's progressive ideas like breast conservation, shared decision-making, and immediate reconstruction after mastectomy.

On this Dovetail Day, Chase recalled how Dr. Taylor had been the grand champion of the King's English back when Chase was a resident. At the morbidity and mortality conferences, it was not unusual for Dr. Taylor to stop a Chief Resident mid-sentence, and say, "Doctor, a patient does not *drop* his hematocrit. The hematocrit may go down, but not because the patient dropped it on the floor." Indeed, Dr. Taylor's love of formality and tradition ran so deep that, as a student of history, he was fond of stating that, "After careful study, I've come to the conclusion that had I been living during Revolutionary times, I would have sided with the British."

Heretofore, Chase had considered Dr. Taylor one of the few true intellectuals he had ever encountered. However, "dovetail" could be a verb – a well-established verb – meaning to interlock into a unified whole. In fact, if Chase's treatise could be reduced to one word, he would pick "dovetail." More importantly, how had this single word been the sole point plucked from a 150-page manuscript, *after* the treatise sat on Dr. Taylor's desk for three months?

Editor's note: At this point in the document, the author departs from the subject at hand and delves into the mutability of the English language. He traces the changes from Old English to Middle English to Modern English. He describes the introduction of inkhorn terms, the Great Vowel Shift, and how "vulgar" language originally meant "of the people" only to be transformed into pejorative. He likens Dr. Thatcher Taylor to Mulcaster, teacher of Spenser, and later the head of St. Paul's school, who insisted on the status quo for spelling, while fighting (and losing) to keep out the inkhorn terms.

Then, Dr. Callaway reminds us of the thousands of neologisms coined by Shakespeare, proving how radical mutations are inherent in language as a dynamic, ever-changing force. From there, Dr. Callaway takes us to Samuel Johnson who, in prefacing his dictionary, chastised *lexicographers who tried to "embalm" their languages, to "secure them from corruption and decay."*

If Chase had been able to access the hallucinatory, prophetic vapors at Delphi regarding the Day of the Dovetail, this story would have taken a different turn. Instead, realizing that interdisciplinary dovetailing was so frightfully alien to clinicians, to the point of language muddling, he renewed his commitment to incorporate all disciplines that touched breast cancer at any point, *fusing them in his own brain first,* such that he could break through the walls of intellectual tribalism. He would be a unifying light through example. At least, that's the way he saw it.

15
MORNING, GLORY

The impediments to excellence ran from A to Z, and Chase came to believe that Far West Texas University was glued together with a bond of mediocrity. Whereas a normal human, as in *Daniel*, would have seen the handwriting on the wall and escaped to a routine private practice, Dr. Callaway was more like Belshazzar – blinded. For he knew he was no longer "normal." He had been through a personal firestorm, tempered in a manner that few physicians could imagine. For this, there had to be a purpose. And given such a purpose, it had to be super-charged with redemption, lest the firestorm be wasted where a candle might have sufficed.

So, when his breast cancer patient, 47-year-old June Nestle, was halfway through her post-lumpectomy radiation therapy, and the pathologist called Chase to admit a mistake in her diagnosis – that is, she didn't have breast cancer at all – he held his rage in check. Instead, it was that old nemesis, the benign mimic of cancer, a "complex sclerosing lesion." He wondered – can one physician sue another for malpractice? This was certainly his first thought, for the pathologist had quite simply laid Chase's neck on the chopping block.

While restraining his outrage, scrambling for a positive twist of some sort, Chase called a meeting with the Chairman of the Department of Pathology and offered this misdiagnosis as proof that expertise with the microscope was desperately needed for the upcoming, interdisciplinary breast center. The Chairman, Dr. Drieser, slithered in discomfort, embarrassed, humiliated, and fearful. Chase was "out there in the community" publicly stating his vision of a Center of Excellence, while Dr. Drieser was simultaneously applying for grants from Hardy Studebaker's Runnymeade Foundation for his own department. Would Chase reveal this grotesque story? That a screw-up of this magnitude had taken place *after* Chase had repeatedly warned of impending doom based on current practice standards of pathology at Far West?

Chase didn't breathe a word. Instead, he encouraged the surgical pathology staff to devote themselves to intense study of complex sclerosing lesions. Assuming none would comply, Chase procured every article published on the subject, memorized every photomicrograph in every text and every publication, and after six months of study, knew as much as any pathologist on the planet when it came to the many faces and the sly imitation of complex sclerosing lesions.

Pathology Chairman, Dr. Drieser, promised Chase that recruitment would begin "pronto" for an expert in breast pathology. In the interim, Drieser promised that two separate pathologists would review and agree on every new diagnosis of breast cancer. Chase thought to himself, *blind leading the blind.*

Dr. Aaron Sherbert, the breast radiologist, seemed to share Chase's vision about the Breast Pavilion. At least, he shared the part about doubling his square footage for breast imaging. When the two of them met with a series of hospital officials to outline the strategy of a Center of Excellence, Sherbert dominated the pitch, describing his cramped quarters as the most critical issue at hand. Chase repeatedly tried to steer the vision back to "interdisciplinary care" and "improved research opportunities" and "better student and resident education," but Sherbert persisted in reciting a litany of broken promises by his own departmental chairman, including the preeminent crime – no pay raise for himself – as had been promised him in the past.

Over time, Chase realized that he should make the pitch alone in order to stay on point. Understanding Sherbert's delicate feelings, though, Chase took great pains to share all credit with his radiology colleague. For instance, when a reporter for the university newspaper decided to do a story on Chase's vision, Sherbert "didn't have the time" to talk with her, so Chase made sure that half of his quotes regarding integrated breast cancer care were attributed to Dr. Aaron Sherbert.

But the 50-50 plan didn't work. Later, when College Hospital (a distinct entity from the medical school) announced they were going to launch the breast center dream with an $800,000 build-out, not by doubling the current space, but by *quadrupling* square footage, Aaron Sherbert's response stunned Chase. Sherbert slammed the door behind the exiting administrator who had announced the plan, and then he said, "Oh, I get it. I see it all now. You're going to take all the credit for this, aren't you? I knew it from the beginning. Then, I *really* knew it when you started bebopping around campus by yourself with your slide show. Remember, I started this mammography center from scratch, so I'm not happy with what's happening around here. I don't give a damn what they tell me, or what you tell me – I'm not gonna to increase my volume."

"Aaron, the basic premise of the project is increased volume. We can get the tech support for you to make it happen. With this quadrupling of space, you get half, which is exactly what you asked for. We have to show an increase in the number of cancers diagnosed and treated. It's really not an option. We have to accommodate more patients to make the breast center pay for itself."

"Look, I'm no spring chicken. I didn't take this job to work my ass off. I'm seeing twenty-five patients a day, and that's that. Well, okay, maybe four or five more."

"Aaron, we need to see fifty patients a day, most of them asymptomatic screeners, to break even. If I get you the support personnel, it shouldn't be that hard."

"I don't need your help. By the way, what do you plan to do with all that square footage anyway? You don't need it. I'm not settling for just double the space anymore. I need three-fourths of that floor plan, at least. Furthermore, I was promised a raise that I never got..."

The infected wounds in the Department of Radiology blistered, scabbed, and oozed on a regular basis. However, the problems didn't stop in the specialties of pathology and radiology. Faculty turnover at the medical center was abysmal – 80% of new faculty were gone after five years. Chase's answer to this crippling churn rate was to focus on home grown Texans, in sharp contrast to the medical school hierarchy where their geographical inferiority complex had them shooting for the elsewhere stars to the neglect of their own.

When a recruited medical oncologist from Memorial Sloan-Kettering was caught falsifying data to get a patient enrolled in a clinical trial, he was not dismissed. Dishonesty in research was deplorable. Fortunately, the problem self-corrected as the medical oncologist left of his own volition shortly after the scandal. Also leaving was his replacement, then her replacement, then his replacement, and so forth, such that Chase's patients changed oncologists with the seasons.

Was there even one quality department at this university?

"I'm sorry to tell you this, Chase, but my worst nightmare just happened," said the Chief of Radiation Oncology. "I just finished a six-week course of radiating the wrong breast."

Chase felt his face flush, followed by a cold sweat. His fingers began to twitch. He curled them in place, a death clinch ready to pummel. Again, can a physician sue another physician for malpractice? Chase had performed surgical biopsies on both sides (in the pre-core-biopsy era). One side was benign, the other side malignant. The radiation oncologist had radiated the benign side, discovering his mistake during the dictation of his "end of treatment" summary. The patient's normal breast was glowing. The diseased breast had been lying still, untreated throughout the process, any cancer cells laughing inside.

I can't stay here, thought Chase. These fools are intent on dragging me into courtroom hell. I cannot take another lawsuit. Multidisciplinary is nothing more than multi-exposure, multi-liability, multi-headache, multi-stupidity. I need to drop this whole idea and go into practice by myself where I'm responsible only for me.

But again, $800,000 from College Hospital was "in the bank," ready for him to use to build the Breast Pavilion, bricks and mortar only. How could he stop now mid-stream? He still needed a quarter-million dollars for mammography and ultrasound machines (of critical importance to justify capturing the technical component). He also needed donations for furnishings, a minor surgery suite, a library, and a large conference room for the interdisciplinary team. Too, he needed a clinic manager, to help him get the center up and running.

Yes, T.N.T. had given him total license to proceed, but without authority or money. College Hospital was going to build the shell of his dream, while the medical school was contributing nothing beyond base salaries already in place for staff physicians. He felt a strong urge to drop the idea entirely. Something wasn't right, and ground had not yet been broken. It was now or never, if he were to resign. Yet, it always felt like there was only "one more hurdle," so "surely I can hang on."

In the midst of his quandary, a providential encounter changed everything. After several years of barnstorming throughout Matherville and west Texas, including speaking engagements at Midland, Odessa, El Paso, San Angelo, with over 70 such presentations of his vision of the Breast Pavilion behind him (he would eventually triple that number), a young woman approached him from a large audience of breast cancer survivors. She was chemo-bald, but with a thin layer of black fluff returning. Still, she had bright eyes full of hope that overpowered her nervousness.

She said, "I want to help you. You're doing something great here, especially addressing the crisis in failed diagnoses. I felt my cancer for more than a year, but my gynecologist kept telling me it was nothing to worry about because my mammograms were normal. Now, my nodes are positive. Somebody's got to do something to make things better. I might be able to help you."

"How so?"

"Two women have been supporting cancer causes for several years in Matherville, but they just found out that the person they've been working with was caught embezzling donated money from the cancer society. They might be too burned out now, such that they won't help anyone. It's hard to trust humanity after that. I'd like to introduce you to them anyway. They're sisters."

Two weeks later, on the day of his presentation to the sisters, T.N.T. approached Chase in the hallway at the hospital. "Is it true that the Raven sisters are coming to the department today to see your slide show?"

"Yes, sir."

"Well, if you don't mind, I'd like to sit in," Dr. Taylor said. "If you can get them to back you, we've got a whole new ball game here."

Darby and Jody Raven were sisters who had married brothers, scions of a sand and gravel empire in west Texas. Remarkably, there was no trace of Studebaker blood in their line. They had penetrated the inner circle of The Colony Club the hard way, by tirelessly volunteering their time and effort to worthy causes. However, their claim to fame had come by lassoing a Ferragamo trunk show and bringing it to Matherville where they had raised the surprising sum of $70,000 for cancer research. Upon learning of the later embezzlement, they resigned from the cancer organization's board. Subsequently, everyone with a cause was beating paths to their two doors.

When the Raven ladies walked into the Department of Surgery, Chase couldn't believe they were sisters. Darby was small, almost fragile in appearance, a classic beauty with pale skin, a genuine smile, warm eyes, and modest dress. Jody was close to six feet, statuesque and tanned, her short golden hair spiraling away from her face as if fighting a windstorm, and in further contrast to her sister, she was drenched in glittering accessories. Both women were in their forties, about Chase's age, and there seemed to be a swift and natural connection among the three of them.

Prior to the meeting, Chase had learned that Darby had already been through the breast cancer experience, treated by none other than Thatcher Nolan Taylor several years ago. "We got it very early," said T.N.T. "In situ disease only. Thankfully, she's done with it."

In a Department of Surgery conference room, Chase presented his interdisciplinary vision as reflected through 35mm slides, more nervous than usual given T.N.T.'s presence. Chase carefully avoided the word "dovetail." At the conclusion, Dr. Taylor said, "I know this might seem a bit grandiose for what Far West is capable of doing. If anyone can pull it off, though, it's Chase. This is a huge build-out beyond your standard mammography center, requiring cooperation of multiple departments. No easy feat in academics. Chase is one of the few physicians I've known who is up to that task, a master communicator. As for the research vision, in just a few short years, Chase has learned the language of the basic scientists, a rarity for a clinician. Impressively, he's organizing the PhDs into an interdisciplinary team as well."

The Raven sisters nodded as Thatcher Taylor spoke, both of them smiling periodically at Chase. Then, they explained politely to Dr. Taylor that they were intrigued with the project and would give it some thought.

One week later, the Ravens' mother was diagnosed with breast cancer in Atlanta. The sisters saw it as a sign. They flew their mother to Midland, then drove her to Matherville where Chase Callaway performed the lumpectomy and lymph node sampling. Then, he coordinated both the radiation and medical oncology follow-up to be completed back in Georgia where the mother had moved after the death of her husband.

The Raven sisters had been skeptical about supporting the medical school at Far West since all breast cancer treatment would, by definition, take place at the teaching hospital, a step down from luxurious Permian Medical Center. However, a new VIP ward had recently opened on the top floor of College Hospital, another sign for the Ravens when their mother heaped praise on her caregivers at the teaching hospital.

Naysayers warned the Ravens about linking their names to Far West, forgetting that Darby Raven had already helped to establish an endowed chair in the department of pediatrics. Years earlier, she had lost a child, a three-year-old son, to meningitis, whereupon Darby launched a crusade to create the academic chair in infectious diseases.

The Ravens' physician-friends were most vocal in their criticism. "You two will be nothing but dilettantes. The med school will use you, abuse you, then spit you out. They've done it for years."

The Ravens would then reply, "But what are you doing at Permian to address the revolution that's about to happen in breast cancer?"

"What revolution? Is that what Chase Callaway is telling you? We treat four times the number of breast cancers as they do at the university. Not to cast seeds of dispersion, but surely you know about Chase, don't you? I'm talking about his personal problems."

The Raven sisters sought to learn exactly what they could about Chase's past, given several detractors who were happy to cast aspersions. After hearing sharply different assessments, they trusted what Thatcher Nolan Taylor said about Chase: "I don't know if there's anyone out there who can pull off something of this magnitude, other than Chase Callaway."

Shortly after their mother returned to Georgia, the Raven sisters took Chase to lunch where they announced: "We see something special here. Something we've not seen before in any of our charity work. We want to do whatever it takes to make it happen."

Within a month, the Raven sisters had organized a 32-member Advisory Board, half of whom were breast cancer survivors. Plans were made for massive fund-raising, not through fashion shows alone, but by applying pressure to every charitable foundation in west Texas, starting with the biggest of them all – the Runnymeade Foundation, headed by Hardy Studebaker.

Chase already thought it odd that T.N.T. had never arranged for Hardy Studebaker to hear his Breast Pavilion pitch. After all, Dr. Taylor was married to Gretchen Studebaker. Hardy was his brother-in-law. Hardy sat on the biggest pile of cash in Matherville, dedicated to making College Hospital and the Far West medical school a bright light in a dimly lit west Texas. Yet T.N.T. had done nothing to access the Runnymeade millions. So far. Chase figured that T.N.T. was avoiding anything that smacked of nepotism. It was the Raven sisters who arranged for Chase to meet with Mr. Studebaker, along with the CFO of Runnymeade.

In the departmental conference room where the Raven sisters had first heard Chase's prophecy on the breast cancer revolution about to unfold worldwide, but especially at Far West, Hardy Studebaker sat silently against the wall without expression. He was a wiry man with thinning hair combed straight back. Chase noticed that when the penultimate 35mm slide dropped into place, showing how breast biopsy tissue would be divided among seven research labs studying seven different approaches to the mysteries of pre-cancer and full-blown cancer, Hardy Studebaker shifted in his chair for the first time. Hardy glanced at T.N.T., then at his CFO, then to the Raven sisters, and finally, Chase. It was a generous expression, the welcome face of a benefactor. At that moment, Chase pushed the button for the final slide – a map of the United States colored blue, but with the arm of west Texas colored gold. Within that gold area was a lone star, designating the city of Matherville.

Chase said, "There you have it. Are there any questions?"

Hardy Studebaker smiled broadly and said, "We've been looking for a long time to develop our second Center of Excellence. We've been resting on our laurels in psychiatry for too long. I believe we just found our star."

Runnymeade made its first contribution to Chase's cause the next day, offering to buy all new radiologic equipment, a grant exceeding $250,000. Chase merely had to do the paperwork.

As part of his approved "aftercare" upon release from Riverdell, Chase had agreed to weekly counseling sessions in order to hang onto his medical license. Even though the requirement was only for six months, he continued seeing the counselor for the express purpose of ventilating about work. Dr. Don Cowling was pleasant enough, charging reasonable rates with a professional discount (perhaps because Chase complained bitterly about his oppressive debt burden). Another reason to see Dr. Cowling was the fact that Chase's 12-step group suffered collective fatigue from his constant complaining about the frustrations at Far West. Most of the sessions with Dr. Cowling could be summarized like this:

"I'm on automatic pilot now. I'm home free. What a miracle. You wouldn't believe how this is coming together," offered Chase.

"But you've been calling this a nightmare for the past two years. Do you really think all the problems are going away?"

"Oh, there's still a bunch of little things. Well, not so little if you're the patient. For instance, I can't get block time in the O.R., for the needle-directed biopsies. Without guaranteed operating time and space, the women lie there on the gurney, in the holding area, with needles in their breasts, waiting hours for biopsies, sometimes all day. That sort of thing I've got to correct. I've tried for two years to get block time for those women. No luck yet. But now, suddenly, Dr. Taylor, my boss, seems motivated to make things happen."

"How does that make you feel?"

"Good."

"Good?"

"Yep. Good."

"Okay. Let's move on. What challenges do you see waiting in the wings?"

"Well, you remember how much trouble I've had with the Department of Pathology. Let me tell you, when Dr. Drieser found out I've got Hardy Studebaker and the Runnymeade money behind me, do know what he said? He's going to try and recruit the top breast pathologist in the country, Donald Paglia in Boston. Says he's a personal friend. Unbelievable. Drieser was doing absolutely nothing but paying lip service before, and now he's going for Paglia? I think we're off and running. I may not need to keep coming here to cry on your shoulder."

Chase saw that everything was finally coming together. The hard part was over. He could sit back and let the excellence unfold.

In his obsessive pursuit of the Breast Pavilion dream, he had neglected to make time for Sukie Spurlock, his former nanny turned L.P.N., "fired and unemployed" due to Chase's profound idiocy as a medical student years earlier. Sukie had taken the blame, as charge nurse, for Chase's indiscretion as an orderly, in his mishandling (pilfering) of the Quaalude sleepers meant for patients at Building 19. Out of relentless guilt, Chase had sent Sukie a monthly sum ever since, going on many years now even though Sukie begged him to stop. He could not.

He had visited her briefly on several occasions since moving back to Texas, but no in-depth conversations. Poor health kept Sukie housebound at the outskirts of town. She had been evicted from her home near College Hospital when all the dwellings were razed in the name of progress, building up the campus into a medical empire. After moving to a new neighborhood where the Black residents lived barely above the poverty level, Sukie had been slowed down by crippling arthritis in her hips and knees, keeping her in bed most of the day.

Ramona Callaway, Chase's mother, still visited her daily, tending to her needs.

Chase pulled up a chair beside Sukie's bed, noticing her silver hair was still thick, and her caramel skin barely wrinkled. While advancing age can turn faces at rest into permanent frowns, Sukie had kept a peaceful joy in her visage whether smiling or not. She spoke in her usual soft voice, "Your mother says you only handle breast cancer patients now. That's wonderful, Chase. How did that come about?"

"Lots of things happened at the same time, pointing that direction. Doors opening, you might say, but really more like windows opening where I saw what was coming down the pike with a complete overhaul for breast cancer. However, when it came to divine intervention, one thing really stood out. A girl walked into my office in California with a breast lump. She was the key patient, charting my course. She was so much like Annie in appearance, even her voice and mannerisms, that I felt somehow my sister was reaching out to me from the grave, saving me from myself. You know about all the trouble I had in California. (Sukie nodded yes.) The whole time I was operating on this girl for the cancer, I kept hearing our mother waking Annie up every day, saying, "Morning, Glory." Then I found myself saying "Morning, Glory" over and over in my head during the girl's surgery until I thought I might be saying it aloud. That's when it all started, I think. She left an enormous impact on me. I never had much interest in breast cancer at all during residency. Now the dream for a cutting-edge breast cancer center is really happening. I know I've hurt a lot of people in the process of getting to this point in my life – mostly you, my parents, Livvy – and I hope to make amends where I best can, even though some bridges have been burned.

"Always good to make peace with the Lord as well."

Chase was amazed at Sukie's oneness with God. She was kind to all while living a life that baffles. When he considered her two children, both dead of cancer at such young ages, then her husband dying so young, yet Sukie continuing to praise her Maker, Chase had to admit that some lives were genuinely devoted to the Kingdom. She had lived what the *Book of Job* described – no evident purpose for the evil, yet offering unwavering praise to the Creator of All.

Chase said, "I've been trying to make peace with God as well," he said. "But I don't see clear answers to my problems, so I'm forced to take control myself. If I hadn't pushed and pushed and pushed, making a nuisance of myself, this breast center thing would never have happened. Never."

"It can be hard at times, I know. After your mother converted and made peace with the Lord, she had a million questions about why things had gone so poorly for her and your father."

"I didn't really know where she stood, God-wise I mean," Chase admitted, not recalling that his mother had ever *converted*. "I guess when Annie died, she turned to God."

"Oh, my dear child, let me tell you about your mother. Annie's death made her ever so angry with God. I didn't think she would ever get beyond it. But she did. Losing my babies allowed me to be a comfort to your mother in time of need. No, Chase, it wasn't Annie that prompted her conversion. It was *you*. When you first came back to Texas. She told me she couldn't live another day after she saw you in the hospital like she did, all hooked up to those machines, preparing to die. That's when she made her peace with the Lord."

Jarred into silence, a voice in his head began to echo with, "Morning, Glory. Rise and shine."

On the drive to his apartment, he tried to recount the number of bromides that Sukie had laid on him during their visit, that is, the ones he also recalled from his youth. He came up with six aphorisms, and as he thought about their simplicity, he realized their remarkable sophistication. Her repertoire included many more sayings as Sukie was a cornucopia of back porch philosophy.

"Morning, Glory," he whispered to himself.

16
ESCAPE FROM THE OSSUARY

Although one of Dr. Callaway's earliest memories from childhood was a pink skeleton popping out of a locker at the VA hospital, one cannot transfer adult miasma at the same hospital to such a remote, singular event. Yes, his father's presence there as a young man still trailed a mist of sorts. However, psychiatry claimed that a father's long-distance influence could be reduced to a minor issue, once recognized and processed.

It was the present tense that plagued Chase now, not the past. For instance, a collective memory was building, layer by layer, forming a solid wall of regret and remorse and humiliation by having to urinate into a plastic cup, twice a week, every week, with the mandated witnesses hovering at his back, eager to mutter about the ignominious Chief of Surgery to their friends in the canteen. Each time Chase provided the sample, he mentally walked through a checklist of all that he could be grateful for – starting with the fact that he was still breathing, in and out.

The director of the Impaired Physicians Group, Dr. Fred Crisp, insisted that Chase continue aggressive surveillance long after the average doctor-addict had stopped. Instead of three months, Chase would be served a regular dose of humility for at least one year. Crisp stated his case as, "We have a great and growing organization, but we have to reach more. You're highly visible and, at the same time, you're our key person here at the medical center. What I'd really like to see for the program, however, is an addicted departmental chairman to validate what we do."

Chase was turned cold by this zealotry and had no intention of becoming a poster boy. The weekly 12-step programs for impaired physicians had been established by Crisp to allow physicians to remain anonymous in their recovery, providing escape from their hometown medical practices. Doctors who had lost licenses, or were on the brink, attended the meeting in the basement of College Hospital once a week. However, for Chase, the College Hospital venue *was* his hometown. No escape for him. Chase objected even to the name of the group – Impaired Physicians – since "I may have been impaired while using, but now I'm anything but. Why doesn't Dr. Crisp use 'recovering physicians' like they do at other places?"

Dr. Crisp, an academic in his early career, had once been considered a hopeless case, specifically designing research projects where alcohol would be needed for the protocol, and for his palate. He lectured Chase at every opportunity, always managing to work in something like this: "It's not only your visibility, Chase. I don't trust the Riverdell treatment program. You weren't there long enough to do any good. The success rate is so much higher at Atlanta. In my opinion, you're a huge relapse risk, and you always will be. The counselors at Riverdell said you were an intellectualizer, and you brainy types are more likely to relapse and end up either in a mental institution or dead."

Chase replied, "Well, I've already been in a mental institution, and we're all going to die anyway."

"See, that sort of answer is a good example. I understand your type. I see it all the time. You're a maverick and a bit of a smartass."

The straw broke when Dr. Crisp decided that medical students needed to be educated on the addiction process, and he arranged for small groups to attend the Impaired Physicians 12-step meeting each week. Chase was flabbergasted. He was the only medical school faculty member in the group. The other recovering docs were cozy in their anonymity. Now, Dr. Crisp was dragging in the very students that Chase was expected to teach the next day. Chase felt he had become a zoo animal, and when he protested, the response was swift:

"Chase, you're not accepting your addiction. And let me tell you from experience, that spells trouble. Mavericks don't cut it in recovery."

Chase replied, "You say you're providing a safe haven for the docs in West Texas to come here without their patients knowing. Yet, you drag in non-addicted medical students to observe? To observe *me*? One of their professors? Well, my recovery is not a spectator sport."

"Every time I turn around, Chase, I see that you're speaking publicly somewhere about this breast cancer thing you've got going. I believe you're in the public eye every week. Do you realize the damage you'll cause the Impaired Physicians Program if you relapse?"

"*If* I relapse. That's the key word, isn't it? If."

This same conversation played itself out one way or another on a regular basis. Chase was sickened that he was at the mercy of Dr. Crisp, in that his medical license rested totally in the director's hands, and the two men did not see eye to eye. On anything. Chase came to believe that the biggest threat to his serenity, and thus relapse potential, was the serenity program itself, as offered by the state medical association. He became so troubled by this ironic threat that he finally took a stand, believing it better to lose his license than continue under the dictatorial reign of Dr. Crisp. He quit attending the Impaired Physicians meeting.

Chase's sponsor, a surgeon who worked hard at the 12th step by helping others, suggested Chase attend a different meeting. Different indeed. Instead of heads lowered, spirits cowed, this new group was loaded with wisdom and honesty and serenity, not to mention long-term sobriety.

The Nameless Group had been founded, Chase was told, by a geologist and a doctor some twenty years prior. As a result, most of the group members were oilmen and physicians. Long-term sobriety was the rule. Anonymity was respected. Conquering personal foibles was the centerpiece. Acceptance was the key. Wisdom flowed more freely than any arid academic department of philosophy. Chase couldn't believe the difference between the two meetings. These were men who had learned how to live, not necessarily through the meaning of life, but through the simple secrets of living well.

Release from the VA Chairmanship came shortly thereafter. Dr. Scott Mooney, a silver-haired surgeon fed up with declining Medicare reimbursement, had abandoned private practice at Permian Medical Center, then joined the med school faculty, agreeing to take over the VA Chief of Surgery position. Chase applauded his arrival, not only in that it allowed Chase to devote himself full-time to developing the Breast Pavilion, but also because he enjoyed Dr. Mooney's camaraderie. As opposed to academic surgeons with no real feel for what it's like in the "real world," Mooney had retired from one of the busiest practices at Permian. He and Chase were kindred spirits, or so it seemed.

Moreover, Dr. Mooney was not part of the primordial horde. The entire surgery faculty sometimes took hunting trips during the work week en masse, sans Chase, leaving him to cover all general surgical services at three hospitals. Now, Mooney could help Chase hold down the fort. Scott Mooney enjoyed golf. He was obsessed by golf. His only request to T.N.T. when he took over the VA position was that Wednesdays be reserved for golf.

Dr. Mooney did not approach the VA with the same laissez-faire attitude as Chase had been instructed. No avoidance of the River Kwai for Dr. Mooney. He went by the book. And since the book demanded that Dr. Mooney work on his golf day (three standing committee meetings on Wednesday), he was chagrined to resign himself to the fact that reserved time for golf had been an empty promise. The VA demands were immutable. It didn't help that Chase Callaway had left behind a mess of incomplete assignments.

With the arrival of Dr. Mooney on staff, however, Chase shook the skeletal ashes from his feet and put his heart completely into the Breast Pavilion.

"Ron Campion just called me," Chase announced upon walking into the office of Thatcher Nolan Taylor, MD. "College Hospital is planning to break ground for the breast center in November. It was only a promise before, but it's real now. I hate to mention it again, but I think we're going to need that clinic manager that we've talked about before."

Dr. Taylor spun around in his chair toward Chase, eyebrows raised at first, then furrowed. He slapped both his palms onto the armrests of his chair, then seemed to catapult to his feet. "Come on. Let's go right now, Chase. We've got to talk to Ron Campion. College Hospital just *has* to manage this thing. Turns out, the Radiology Department has refused. I want the clinical leadership to be in our department, of course – under your direction – but we certainly don't want the administrative headaches or financial responsibilities in the Department of Surgery. An academic department has no more business running something like this than if we were to administer the operating rooms, or minor surgery, or even the surgery clinic. No – this is a hospital responsibility."

Chase kept quiet but thought about his treatise wherein the entire financial structure was based on capturing the technical component from radiology. All "dovetailing" services were to be subsidized by this key financial source. Chase trailed his mentor out of the office as the chairman called over his shoulder to his secretary to alert the hospital administrator that the duo was on their way.

In their meeting, however, Ron Campion, the hospital administrator, didn't budge. "We are covering the building costs on this, Dr. Taylor, perhaps closer to one million than our previous estimate. Now you're asking us to run it, too? Wasn't this already worked out by the medical school? We have no intention of running a breast center. Screening mammography centers can be notorious money-losers. Everyone in the industry knows that. Right now, across town, Permian has the market share on mammographic screening and breast cancer management. Our offer was for bricks and mortar only."

As Ron Campion spoke, Chase was thinking about the certain death of the project if he lost operational control. Everything in Chase's grand vision depended on a single financial control point where the technical component could be banked. Yet, he was witnessing the official leadership without a plan of any kind.

T.N.T. didn't protest the flat rejection from the College Hospital administrator. In fact, T.N.T. seemed to roll over and play dead, resigned to the ugly fate of having the Pavilion in his department. On their walk back to the departmental offices, however, Dr. Taylor announced, "Well, the more I think about it, the Breast Pavilion belongs in the radiology department, and I'm going to head back there and put pressure on them to run it. I gave up too easy the first time around when they refused."

"But—but— the Department of Radiology has demonstrated over and over again that they're not going to lift a finger for the Pavilion's success. Worse, Aaron Sherbert is working hard to make my life miserable, Dr. Taylor. In fact, do you remember when I first came back to Far West, you said if Aaron didn't get with the program, you'd get rid of him. Well, sir, unfortunately, I think I'm at that point."

Thatcher Nolan Taylor kept walking as if he didn't hear Chase. Nor did he seem to have any recollection of having made such a promise. In truth, Chase had tried to hide the growing tension with Sherbert from T.N.T., as there had been a complete breakdown in his relationship with his radiology colleague.

Editor's note: Deleted here is a 22-page account of the ensuing battle between Chase Callaway and Aaron Sherbert. Conversations such as the following were recorded in detail, along with various supporting documents as if preparing for trial:

Sherbert: I'm not sticking around here to do that specimen X-ray. I leave at four o'clock whether you're finished or not. I've told you my policy before. I'm not going to fight that traffic. I told you a long time ago to schedule those needle-directed biopsies in the morning.

Callaway: "I've done everything imaginable to reserve morning block times in the O.R., and I've gotten nowhere, Aaron. You know I've begged Thatcher to intervene. This lady has been in the holding area for three hours now with a needle in her breast, and you're threatening to go home, without confirmation that I've removed the lesion?"

Sherbert: "It's not like I haven't made myself clear on this."

Callaway: "Okay. Go ahead, I'll read the specimen X-ray myself."

Sherbert: "That's unacceptable."

Similar confrontations with similar themes run throughout. The incidents culminate with Aaron Sherbert cutting off all referrals to Chase, just to let him know who was truly in control. Sherbert began sending all surgeries generated by mammography to Dr. Taylor and the other faculty. The siege lasted nine months, and Chase's income plummeted, given that half his income came from private patient care. He asked T.N.T. to intervene directly, but nothing happened. So, he asked T.N.T. for financial relief by letting Chase attend more often on the resident cases, which worked well to bolster Chase's income, but infuriated the other faculty members who took less.

Meanwhile, Dr. Sherbert invested a good deal of time in hallway politics, reminding everyone of Chase's addiction history. When that didn't win support, Sherbert called the Raven sisters and revealed how Chase was nothing more than a master manipulator with a sordid past.

All this transpired in the months before the meeting with Ron Campion followed by T.N.T.'s decision to go with the Department of Radiology where Dr. Sherbert was housed. The entire project was being held together by a thread, and now Chase could see that thread unraveling. He would not have the gumption to mention it again, so he delivered the brutal truth to Dr. Taylor – one of the two combatants in this war had to go, either Sherbert or Chase.

Much to Chase's surprise, T.N.T. did not intervene. He did nothing. So, Chase dreamed up an alternative for T.N.T., perhaps a less demanding task: "Simply name me as the Medical Director. If I have the title of Medical Director of the Breast Pavilion, then Sherbert will either leave, or he'll have to accept me as the person calling the shots. Everything revolves around titles here in academia."

"Of course you'll be Medical Director, Chase, but I'm not sure about the timing here." T.N.T. took no action. Meanwhile the Raven sisters and their Board were moving ahead full steam with fund-raising.

Insubordinate, but out of desperation, Chase went to the dean of the Far West School of Medicine, asking to be named Medical Director. Yet, the dean, the man behind the curtain, instead, gave Chase a homework assignment – "Write me a complete history of how this Breast Pavilion project began, and I'll judge the next step after that. And, while you're at it, please change the name of the center. The university will not accept the word 'pavilion'. The psychiatrists already pulled their coup years ago and got themselves disengaged from medical school authority. Now they're completely independent in their Psychiatric Pavilion, still claiming to be part of the medical school. We're not going to have that happen again. 'Pavilion' is unacceptable."

Returning now to Dr. Callaway's own writing:

On the day of the groundbreaking ceremony for the breast center, Dr. Aaron Sherbert, talented breast radiologist, stood quietly at the back of the crowd, not having spoken a word to Chase, the de facto breast surgeon, in nearly one year.

In apparent contrast to this absurdity was the Department of Pathology where the chairman had finally captured the vision, it seemed. Dr. Drieser announced he would recruit a dedicated breast pathologist, starting with the top name in the country. In fact, this very individual, Don Paglia, M.D. of Boston, had agreed to come to Matherville in order to swing the hammer as first blow to bring down the old walls of the space to be renovated, allowing construction of the Far West Texas University Breast Center (formerly known as the Breast Pavilion).

In preparation for the groundbreaking, Chase read Dr. Paglia's text on breast pathology for the third time, such that he was able to keep Dr. Paglia engaged non-stop for two days while Far West hosted the esteemed guest. Then, near the end of his stay, Dr. Paglia said to Chase, "Would you have any idea why Hardy Studebaker drove me around Matherville this morning, showing me houses? Not that I mind, particularly, but he was acting as if he were recruiting me or something. I have no intention of leaving Boston. Drieser knows that."

Chase's heart sank, once again. Drieser's "recruitment" of Paglia was a fraud. Drieser was still faking it, demonstrating to the Studebaker money how he was "going to start at the top by recruiting Paglia." Remarkably, he was willing to engage both Hardy Studebaker and Dr. Paglia in his mock strategy!

Unable to take it any longer, Chase confessed the nightmare to the Raven sisters. Thatcher Taylor had gone silent, focused entirely on keeping the administration of the breast center out of the Department of Surgery, while Chase was embroiled in civil war. The Department of Radiology took a hands-off position, hoping in secret that Aaron Sherbert would pack his bags, so that the blame could be laid on Chase, not their department. The pathology department was doing nothing to correct their deficiencies, other than staging a mock recruitment scheme. And this was only three of the involved departments. Meanwhile, the obvious authority in the hierarchy to referee and put things in order, the medical school dean, was concerned only that the word "pavilion" not be used.

Chase confessed all these things to the Raven sisters. "I've dragged you into this, and you've given your public endorsement, putting together the Advisory Board and all, but I don't know how we're going to get out of this mess. The groundbreaking ceremony was a total fraud. I'm sorry."

Tall, blonde, imposing Jody Raven took the lead. "We plan on raising money for you. Lots of money. Lots of money for you *and* the medical school. I can assure you that these people listen to money, and therefore they listen to community leaders. We've put our names on the line – with much criticism coming our way, I might add – and it will not fail. It can't. This is a disaster. I can't believe that Thatcher is letting this happen and not doing anything." (Chase recalled Thatcher Taylor's comment upon discovering that the Raven sisters had come on board: "I'm halfway scared of Jody, but she'll get anything done if she puts her mind to it. But when you need diplomacy, go with Darby.") Chase didn't see how diplomacy was getting him anywhere. Jody, the warrior, would take the lead.

Jody Raven made her plan quite clear to Chase. "Darby and I are going to have a little visit with the Vice-Chancellor of the Health Sciences Center. If that doesn't work, we're going to the president of the entire university. After that, the Board of Regents." Chase was skeptical at first. Vice-chancellors and presidents changed positions so frequently that, in his brief time already, Chase had dealt with three of the former and two of the latter. How could any promise be maintained?

But the Raven sisters declared war. Twenty-four hours after Chase had spilled his guts to the two women, he got a phone call from the Dean of the Medical School: "Dr. Callaway, I've been giving some thought to your proposed Breast Pavilion. I've changed my mind. It will be fine for you to use the word 'pavilion'."

"Thank you very much, dean," he said, smiling into the phone. "These ladies had already printed some invitations to a major fund-raiser with Breast Pavilion stamped on the front, so they'll be pleased."

The next day, Jody and Darby Raven asked, "What next? What's the very next thing that needs to happen?"

Chase replied, "I've got to get this project administratively in the Department of Surgery where I can control what happens and where we can manage the finances once we're successful. It's a risk because our current volumes won't support the new scope of the Pavilion. Thatcher has refused. Adamantly. He wants the Department of Surgery to be in control of breast cancer clinically, of course, but not administratively. He wants the finances as far away from the surgery department as possible. Then, Aaron Sherbert looks like he's going to run this dream into the ground. That's sabotage. To make matters worse, I can't get any support from anyone. All this has to be settled immediately, before the public finds out what a mess we're in. The Pavilion *must* be in the surgery department, and *someone* has to name me the medical director."

Two days later, Chase was called to the office of the vice-chancellor, along with Thatcher Nolan Taylor, M.D. The medical school dean and the Raven sisters were already gathered around the long oak table. The new vice-chancellor opened the meeting with a swift proclamation: "This Breast Pavilion, as I understand it, has the potential to become the biggest thing to happen to this medical center in recent history, especially when it comes to community support. However, no one seems to be willing to take charge. Therefore, I'm simply going to say it. I want this project housed *administratively* in the Department of Surgery. In addition, Dr. Callaway, you are to be the Medical Director."

Jody Raven looked at Chase and winked. Darby Raven smiled innocently.

So that's how things happen around here. It has nothing to do with the formal chain of command.

Radiologist Aaron Sherbert resigned from the faculty the next day, then he left the state of Texas to serve as director of a breast center in Orlando (one of many sites where he had been interviewing for the past year). Before he left, however, he stormed into Chase's office, threw the books and teaching materials he had borrowed from Chase over the years onto the desktop, put his finger in Chase's face and yelled, "You, sir, are a fucking snake." Fittingly, he had dressed himself in military regalia from his weekend duty in the National Guard.

Chase didn't care. He was relieved that the siege was over, the war was over, and he could focus again on the success of the Breast Pavilion. He could start sleeping at nights again. A new leaf, he thought.

"How did you do that?" he asked of Jody and Darby Raven.

"One lunch with Hardy Studebaker, that's all," they said. "Hardy runs the show here, not necessarily the hierarchy that you see day to day. The Runnymeade Foundation is the purse, and Hardy is the string to that purse."

Indeed, Hardy Studebaker called Chase a few days later and invited him to the Colony Club where Chase had the thrill of entering the exclusive Smoking Room. "Chase, from the first time you presented your vision to me, I told myself we were going to make this happen, come hell or high water. This project will not fail. The medical school has a reputation, rightly deserved, for fouling up everything they try. Those days are over. I want you to call me directly if anything isn't going the way it needs to. Here are the phone numbers for my homes in Hawaii, Mexico, California, London, and here, yes, here's the one in Milan. I want you to realize, too, that Thatcher has his hands tied much of the time. Old friendships, old favors, and so forth, can really bog you down when you're inside a bureaucracy for so many years. Thatcher tells me you're the right man for this job. With the Raven sisters behind you, you're going to have all of Matherville in the palm of your hand, if not all of west Texas."

The next day, Thatcher Nolan Taylor had the funds available for Chase to hire a full-time administrator for the Breast Pavilion. Chase's first choice was a young woman who had started a highly successful mammography screening center at Permian Medical Center. However, she came with a high price tag. In fact, her salary request would have made her one of the highest paid employees in the university administration. Still, T.N.T. agreed with Chase that she'd be perfect for the position, and he offered her the job.

Chase was sure she would accept this premier opportunity. After all, the administrative director would join the circle of social elite in Matherville as part of the job description. Yet, the prospective director balked. Chase couldn't understand it, since it was a nice salary increase for her. Yet, he sensed that, during negotiations, she had gradually lost her initial enthusiasm, finally becoming evasive. Chase said, "This is going to be huge, I promise. You're already a breast cancer activist, and you'll be running one of the most prestigious breast centers in the country when I put all the parts together. We have the jump on nearly everyone. I can only think of a handful of major medical centers that are as far along as we are."

Still, she wouldn't commit. Chase tried to reach her at home, calling in the off-hours, trying to capture an answer. Cat-and-mouse lasted for weeks. Construction of the Pavilion was underway, and the administrative details were dragging him down. He had other responsibilities, tutoring medical students, residents, committees, departmental meetings, and a rapidly expanding patient load as the first dedicated breast surgeon in west Texas. He needed the administrator yesterday.

One night when Chase tried calling her at home, still searching for her answer, the woman's husband answered the phone, "No, she's not home from work yet. She stopped off for a quick drink, so she'll be home any minute."

Chase called back later, finally catching her at home. She said, "Sorry, I haven't quite decided yet. I'm very troubled about something, though. You know, academic doctors are known for being good teachers, but...not so good with direct patient care. That worries me, being a part of something that involves so many specialties. I'm worried about the quality of medical practice."

"Oh, don't worry about that," Chase hedged. "This project has enormous support, and we've already got some key quality people. We'll be recruiting more to fill in the gaps. Now, you may have heard that we're a little weak in the radiology department, and that's the sort of thing that I'm—"

"No, Dr. Callaway, I'm not talking about radiologists, or any of the other specialties. I'm talking about – *you*."

Chase couldn't believe he'd heard her correctly. He was speechless.

"The word is out that you couldn't make it in private practice, that...that you were run out of California."

"You – Are – Kidding – Me."

"If I had more assurance that you were, well, if I knew what all the rumors were really about, you know, if I knew the details..."

Chase had only seconds to decide. He could tell her to 'go straight to Hell and take your impudence with you,' or...he would have to confess his full story. Her brazenness had caught him off guard. Perhaps, though, "stopping off for a drink" loosened her tongue and she meant no offense. Then she egged him on, "*If I'm going to work with you*, I really need to know the whole story."

Before he knew it, he had confessed the saga of his initial ouster at Ciena his first month in private practice. Too, he explained how he had overcome staggering bias and obstacles en route to becoming the youngest Chief of Surgery in the history of the very hospital where he'd been trashed.

"But what about...I mean, well, I'm concerned about your addiction history. How does that fit it?"

The rest of the story unfolded. He was desperate. She was an excellent choice for the position, and he had no other candidates with experience. At the end of his sordid tale of addiction and recovery, she said, "Thank you for sharing all of that with me. I'm going to sleep on it tonight, and I'll give you my answer tomorrow."

When he finished his story and hung up the phone, he was sick to his stomach. *Either I'm going to have the most loyal employee ever, if she sees the strength of my story, or else I just bared my soul and confessed my most intimate personal secrets to a near total stranger who happens to manage the competition's breast center.*

When Chase arrived at work the next day, his secretary told him that the candidate for the administrator position had already phoned her response: "Not interested."

"Is that all? No explanation? Is that all she said?"

"Yes. That was it. She said she was no longer interested, and there was no need to call her back."

17
BONE LOCKER

Yoking words to form neologisms, common in the Germanic languages, allowed the birth of "banlocan" in Old English – a union of *ban* for "bone" and *locan* for "locker." Banlocan meant a joint, a limb, or one's entire body. Indeed, our fleshy bodies serve as lockers for our bones. The more Chase Callaway tried to dismiss the pink skeleton in the VA locker as an odd coincidence (***Editor's note:*** *See* Nutshell, *chapter 23, for the story of the pink skeleton),* the more he came to consider the bones as an omen, part of the unshakeable curse that was sinking its tendrils deeper and deeper into his flesh, persisting now beyond the California experience and its aftermath.

Even those whose lives he touched felt the pain of the curse. For instance, when a prominent socialite, a breast cancer survivor, tossed her hat into the ring by joining the Pavilion Advisory Board, her Permian surgeon condemned her so vociferously that he brought her to tears. "Who does this Chase Callaway think he is? I've done over a thousand mastectomies, and he waltzes into town claiming to be some kind of guru. I can't believe you're going to support him. I'm the one that cured your cancer." She was stunned, yet more strongly committed.

Husbands distrusted Chase as well. A typical phone call would go as follows, "I don't know what kind of Pied Piper thing you've got going on, but my wife can't talk about anything else other than your Pavilion and its research agenda. She's very angry that her diagnosis at Permian was delayed, and her treatment didn't go particularly well either. It seems to me that your cause, whatever it is, has become an obsession for her. I'm just trying to understand what you're really doing with this Pavilion thing. What are you selling these women?"

He tried to answer: "Well, for one thing, the entire country is in the middle of a one-disease malpractice crisis where the failure to diagnose breast cancer has rocketed to the number one position. This is because of the false belief by clinicians that nearly all breast cancers can be seen on X-ray, so they are not doing biopsies on lumps you can feel, like they used to, that is, if mammograms are normal. It's a disaster. This particular scenario is exactly what happened to your wife. And that's just one example. There's a total revolution underway in radiology, surgery, oncology, plastics, you name it, it's a new world. At least, in a few places it's a new world. Most of the world is quite old, as a matter of fact."

Rip tides pulled in all directions. External to the university came: "Callaway does way too many lumpectomies." "Callaway does too many mastectomies with immediate reconstructions." "Callaway had the audacity to question our diagnosis on path. Can you imagine that, coming from a surgeon?" "Callaway is patient-stealing. If he does a second opinion, you can be sure you'll never see your patient again." Then, internally: "How dare you go out on your own trying to recruit a radiologist, Dr. Callaway? How would you like it if we in radiology hired our own breast surgeon?" And from Porter Piscotel, the surgical residency program director: "Chase, you shouldn't be promising your private patients that their surgery will be done entirely by you, rather than residents. This is a teaching hospital, so these women need to understand up front that they're going to have residents operate on them."

Chase persevered, speaking to foundations and charitable groups and social clubs. He made frequent appearances on local television and radio, all such efforts arranged by the Raven sisters, not only for fund-raising, but also to break the prejudice against College Hospital as the place reserved only for the poor, the prisoners, the uninsured, and the unwitting.

Yet, a pervasive dread grew worse and worse with each public performance, based in the fear that someone would shine a light on his past. "No—I'm—talking—about—you." The words from the candidate for administrative director of the Pavilion echoed through his mind every time he stood before a group, such that he came to loathe the demands for publicity. The truth was harsh enough, but clearly, his past was becoming even more grotesque through the power of eager tongues.

Still, he managed to capture hearts and vision, winning named donors for each room in the new Pavilion. Obsessed with maintaining long-term gratitude to all donors, he oversaw engraving for the plaques to be hung on the respective doors. Every detail for the new Pavilion was critical. Indeed, he sketched the cabinetry for each room, picked out wall coverings and furniture with the interior decorator, even hung the pictures (on the radiology side, the lead mammography tech did the same, exercising her flair for interior decoration).

All the while, he kept due attention focused on medical education as the incubator of his dream. Recalling how, as a medical student, he witnessed the surgery faculty cancelling most of their lectures, opting instead to schedule their private patient surgeries, Chase vowed to keep the medical students a top priority. "Who knows which one of them might end up playing a critical role in the long-term success of the Breast Pavilion?" he would say.

The three-legged stool of academic medicine – patient care, research, and education – was wobbly, he thought, since it was only the first two legs that coughed up cold hard cash for the university. Education – the mission most important in the eyes of the tax-paying public – made a soft peep as distant third. Never, over many years to follow, did Chase cancel a single lecture to the medical students. His teaching skills and dedication did not go unnoticed. The students regularly placed Dr. Callaway in nomination for Teacher of the Year.

Hardy Studebaker knew, however, that clinical faculty members experienced excessive pressure to make money for the university, with little incentive to teach. Accordingly, he established a grand financial prize called the Studebaker Master Teacher Award. Although Chase had won Teacher of the Year (the first faculty winner in the history of the surgery department), this was because the votes were cast exclusively by the medical students. In contrast, the Studebaker Award was chosen by a committee of faculty administrators, department heads, and former winners. The year that the Pavilion was being built, at the annual Studebaker Award gala, a tuxedoed Thatcher N. Taylor, M.D. leaned over to Chase and said, "I hope you're thinking about your future acceptance speech. You do realize that you'll be the recipient someday, don't you?"

One full year was needed for the construction of the Breast Pavilion, as the work had to be done in stages to continue providing mammography services. When finished, the plantation doors opened to a lavish sight unlike anything on the Far West campus – white wicker furniture, flowers on every surface, an etched glass profile of a woman with long, flowing hair draped from window to window at the curved front desk. There was one deficiency though (glaring for Chase, unknown by the patients) – no dedicated breast radiologist. Substitutes and contract laborers were reading the mammograms while the search continued for a specialist.

"Search" was a stretch. The radiology department did little to recruit. They lost a full year initially, unwilling to recruit while Dr. Sherbert was still gainfully employed on campus. So, while Sherbert interviewed for new positions coast to coast, the department denied he was planning an exit and did nothing. Even after Sherbert left, recruitment consisted simply of "asking around."

Radiologists specializing in breast cancer were a rarity, with few fellowships available. Without a skilled radiologist, the Pavilion was doomed. Chase spent entire days and weekends in the medical library, looking up journal articles about mammography in the *Index Medicus*, copying the names of the authors, and then contacting these same authors by phone or by standard mail, proclaiming that any mammographer willing to live in west Texas would be treated as the "savior" of the Pavilion. *(Editor's note: this tedious exercise in the library by Dr. Callaway was one of many labor-intensive tasks of the pre-Internet era.)*

His pitch was universally rejected. Not even a nibble. So, in desperation, he took a week off from work to camp out at a breast imaging conference in Boston to see if he could lure a radiologist into conversation and, possibly, drag said radiologist back to west Texas.

While he was attending this meeting, making some headway with two possible candidates, "someone" in the university hierarchy appointed a radiologist to be "savior" of the Pavilion – a young man who was completing his residency in radiology, but with little mammography experience and no expressed interest.

Chase was stunned, excluded entirely from the process, no interview opportunity, no input, ignored by his own chairman, as well as the radiology chairman. Chase then learned that the anointed radiologist was, in truth, needing to kill a year until he could start a fellowship in interventional radiology at the University of Texas Southwestern. Had T.N.T. known this was a space-filler year? Had the radiology chairman known? A one-year stopgap?

After shaking hands with his new partner, Chase gave his colleague unrestricted access to $400,000. The bounty ($250,000 in the first round; $150,000 the second time around) came from two grants *Chase* had received from Hardy Studebaker and the Runnymeade Foundation. The money was earmarked for additional mammography and ultrasound equipment, along with the newfangled stereotactic biopsy table.

Yet, the money sat idle for the entire space-holder year. The new radiology partner wouldn't spend it. "I'm still shopping around, looking for the best deal," he said over and over throughout the year. In fact, he was biding time until his fellowship began. More equipment meant more work. The new stereotactic biopsy approach would be a major shift in practice patterns, away from surgeons doing the biopsies, toward radiologists.

Fortunately, the new radiologist was pleasant and accommodating. After opening day, however, the Pavilion began losing money as predicted with low volume, and this "savior" of the Pavilion saw no need to help Chase promote the breast center and its unique feature of multidisciplinary care. At the time, no one in Texas, including MD Anderson, was offering this approach to breast cancer care – two multidisciplinary conferences every week, one to assure diagnostic accuracy (radiology, surgery, pathology) and the other to coordinate care (breast surgery, radiation oncology, medical oncology, plastic surgery, nurse specialists, prosthetist, social worker). Chase added another feature to the Pavilion repertoire not discussed yet by more than a handful of experts nationwide – risk assessment with special attention to the hereditary cancer syndromes.

As for the one-year radiologist, his arranged marriage with the Pavilion ended on cue. As before, there was no proactive recruitment of a replacement. So, what followed was a parade of semi-retired, semi-interested, semi-competent stand-ins, while the search for a breast radiologist went nowhere.

Chase had to talk himself out of quitting every day, watching the debt burden swell, but hanging onto his lofty purpose, claiming supernatural persistence and patience, attainable only by a superhuman who had been tempered by fire for this singular purpose. However, this self-delusional propaganda was wearing thin. Every day, by phone or in person, the Raven sisters encouraged him to continue. "Success is just over the horizon," they would say. Periodically, Hardy Studebaker would call as well, assuring Chase that the puppet master (Hardy), would not allow the Breast Pavilion to fail.

Yet, no one came to west Texas to interview for the breast radiology position. Indeed, why come to Matherville and earn a marginal salary in a department that did not particularly believe in the concept of a "breast radiologist?" Although the breast center had been administratively placed in the Department of Surgery (via the Raven sisters), the salary for the radiologist was still dictated by the Chairman of Radiology, supported by Pavilion revenues.

The radiology chairman was unyielding in his position – "A breast radiologist should be paid modestly at most. Why should a mammographer who works eight-to-five with no night call, no weekends, no emergencies, make as much as my faculty members who are working their tails off?"

One day when the Raven sisters dropped by the Breast Pavilion to console and encourage Chase, he showed them the mammogram-screw-up-of-the-day. "What is your eye drawn to when you look at this X-ray?" he asked them.

Jody Raven walked forward and touched her index finger to a bright spot that stood out from the surrounding breast tissue. Darby agreed, "Yes, that whitish spot."

"Well, that happens to be a breast cancer," Chase said, "but today's radiologist had a different name for it. He called it a 'normal mammogram'." (Chase watched the look of horror come over the two faces of the Raven sisters.) "Something's got to be done," he continued, "and it's got to be fast. These clowns are going to destroy everything we've done so far. The last semi-retired radiologist they sent me decided he should do an ultrasound-guided needle biopsy on a mass he saw. Great, I thought. Finally, someone is cutting edge. Doing these biopsies by ultrasound guidance is the new thing. Then I get the path report back. Cartilage, it says. The biopsy report said *cartilage*. I couldn't figure it out at first, then it dawned on me. If you don't know what the hell you're looking at on breast ultrasound, the ribs look like masses. The idiot biopsied a freakin' rib! Can you imagine what the patient must have felt when the biopsy gun shot into her rib to extract the sample? Jody – Darby – I am living in a nightmare from which there seems to be no escape. Each evening, to protect myself from getting dragged into court, I dictate my own radiology reports on my own patients if I disagree with the official interpretation. Are you getting the picture? Do you think there's another breast specialist on the planet having to practice like this? Having to live like this? I owe my life and career to Thatcher, and now I owe it to the both of you, but I can't take it anymore. Acceptance is the key to serenity, as they say, but what I'm living through is completely unacceptable. Acceptance would be a crime."

Later, in his head, he wondered: *Am I nothing more than Voltaire's foolish Candide? Am I dismissing strings of misfortune through the empty-headed philosophy of Pangloss, forever describing horror-upon-horror as the 'best of all possible worlds?"* Or, the modern version of 'everything works for the good of those who love the Lord'?

But there were no answers. Everything that could be done had been done. Quite simply, no warm body was willing to be part of a radiology department that paid bottom wage and where breast cancer was a low priority. Chase didn't care anymore about qualifications for his radiologic partner. His only job requirement would be a willingness to learn. He was helpless. The Raven sisters were helpless. Hardy Studebaker was spending the month in Italy.

Though every radiologist in west Texas had declined the opportunity already, Chase started back through the list again, beginning with his top choice, Molly St. Martin. He had left Texas before Molly entered medical school, so he didn't know her, but the effusive endorsements of Molly were universal. Her second-time reply to Chase was the same as the first: "I've thought about it quite a bit since we talked initially, but I'm really not interested. This person will be the key to your success, and he or she needs to be on fire for breast imaging, and I'm just not there. Mostly, I can't see myself being part of that radiology department. Historically, they've neglected breast cancer. I do applaud your efforts, though. We hear about what you're doing even here in Midland, but it's not the right spot for me. The training I received there at Far West in mammography was abysmal, and I was tempted at first to do something about it, but no thanks."

Making matters worse, the same month that the Breast Pavilion opened its doors, the medical school switched its billing system out of individual departments into a central office. Chase's pro forma for the Pavilion had been based on a steady, historical 70% collection rate for breast imaging over the past five years. However, centralized billing proved him terribly optimistic by converting this historical 70% to the new 30%, with no short-term improvement conceivable for at least six months. The Breast Pavilion, from Day One, with its stopgap radiologist not interested in improving volume, began losing $30,000 a month.

Though Chase's personal practice of breast surgery was growing rapidly, and the number of breast cancers being treated at College Hospital increased accordingly, the Breast Pavilion's financial control point within the medical school included only breast imaging. It did not include the positive fiscal impact Chase had on College Hospital, a separate financial entity. Since College Hospital had funded construction of the Pavilion, they were clearly due that benefit and remained quite pleased with Chase's efforts.

In order to stem the losses to the medical school, Chase convinced his chairman, Thatcher Nolan Taylor, to divert the university taxes pulled out of Chase's professional income to go into the Breast Pavilion account, but this relief was trivial when compared to the staggering financial losses on the mammography side of the Pavilion. No radiologist. No recruitment. Centralized billing a disaster. Meanwhile, Chase was totally powerless – and totally accountable.

Then, managed care made a swift entry into Texas. Chase's 70% pro forma collections became a relic. The dip to 30% after the switch to centralized billing would never rise again above 50% due to the limitations of poorly conceived sub-Medicare contracts signed by the university (to that point in time, no one had ever heard of contracting private insurance rates that were *below* Medicare rates).

Chase was in the bizarre, vulnerable position of having the most luxurious clinic on campus, bought and paid with donations and grants, but a cash flow problem that would ravage his dream. Insomnia worsened, serenity was lost, and his life revolved solely around patient numbers and financial reports and how to keep the plantation doors of the Pavilion open.

With recurrent insomnia now in its third year, starting when the feud began with Dr. Sherbert, Chase recognized the change in his personality. He had been through this before, only now he knew its danger. He had graduated from his sessions with Dr. Cowling as a counselor, but Chase's 12-step sponsor advised him to "consider leaving the university" and return to private practice. Yet, if he were to do that, his personal nightmare in progress for over a decade would make no sense. Exhausted, Chase met with the Raven sisters and warned them that the dream was on its final gasp. Their support and involvement had been "heaven sent" originally, so now, how could he explain the hopeless spot he was in?

Jody and Darby reminded Chase that they had organized a Chanel Fashion Show for next month with over 1,000 women planning to attend, and with money ear-marked for Chase's fledgling research agenda. Undeterred in his decision to quit, Chase approached Thatcher Nolan Taylor and said, at wits end, "I'm expected to address the audience before the fashion show, but I can't stand up before that crowd of women and tell lies. If you think there's any point in it, you'll have to do it. Do you know what I tell people when they ask me where to go for their mammograms? I tell them 'Anywhere but here at Far West'. I can't fake it. In fact, I've told the Raven sisters to dissolve the Advisory Board after the fashion show."

Not only did Dr. Taylor speak beautifully at the fashion show, but also the dean of the medical school appeared, promising the women of Matherville and surrounding cities that the medical school was "absolutely dedicated to making the Breast Pavilion a tremendous success." It was a "top priority."

Chase stood in the wings, listening to the ballyhoo. He had already contacted friends at Permian Medical Center to begin the process of abandoning ship. When he got back to his office after yet another day off-campus, he found a memo addressed to him from the silver-tongued dean who had just wowed the women with his support for the Pavilion: "The financial losses of the Breast Pavilion are so great that we plan to close your clinic the first of next month if the tide cannot be turned. As a short-term solution, you should transfer funds in your research account into your operational account to stem the losses."

"That money was raised for breast cancer research – period! Even if I made the transfer, it would only cover our losses for a piddly two months, solving *nothing* long-term, yet at the same time violating the promises I made to the donors. That money is *not* to cover the losses due to the pathetic billing service, or your lowball managed care contracts, or the fact that you refuse to offer a decent salary to recruit a radiologist. You lousy piece of —"

Alas, the words above were merely what Chase yelled into his mirror at home. In reality, he answered the dean with polite resistance, then hurriedly purchased a minus-80-degree freezer used in research to store tissue and blood specimens. Thus, the research account was emptied before any university official could pilfer the funds.

He was torn in half – one part wanting to escape, the other linked securely to his mission. The California tribulation and his subsequent near-death experience would have no meaning if he quit now. His past trauma had allowed an otherwise impossible humility to emerge. He had no personal goals for himself as a result – no lust for academic titles, no need for an impressive list of publications, no academic honors to seek, no ivory towers to climb. Instead, he felt himself forged into nothingness, an invisibility, a boneless spirit from which he could inspire others to make the Pavilion succeed – and, beyond that, to make progress toward the eradication of the disease he had chosen to fight.

Should it be any wonder that Chase escaped to peace and tranquility at the nearby mental institution? Indeed, serenity shifted his way whenever he traveled across Crooked Creek to the asylum where he had once been an orderly, a medical student, a surgery resident, and finally, a patient. Now he had a new role – Attending Surgeon.

A perennial legislative threat to close the maximum-security hospital made it mandatory that faculty supervise the residents in training with a magnifying glass. Oddly, the residents were scrutinized closer at this hospital than at the VA, or even College Hospital. At the other sites, the faculty would be working multiple rooms, if not multiple buildings, and attention was divided and sparse. At the mental institution's hospital, however, faculty could focus in a quiet, intimate setting.

The hospital without a name had to be kept open. No one wanted the lunatics and prisoners chained to their beds while being treated at College Hospital where momentum was building nicely to siphon the private clientele away from Permian Medical Center. Hardy Studebaker personally served as overseer for the success of the maximum-security hospital. Runnymeade money made it possible to maintain accreditation, and, as a by-product, it was the ideal scenario for residency training.

While working in the Surgery Clinic at the mental institution one day, attending surgeon Chase Callaway spotted Ivy Pettibone sitting in the hallway, holding her arm swollen by lymphedema. White-haired now, still with a cowlick rising above bobbed hair, Ivy's child-like face had a few more wrinkles, but she still had her infectious smile.

"Hello, Ivy. Long time no see. I never did get to thank you for those antacids you slipped me while I was in the seclusion room."

"Reti lati, dolaso dolati," she replied.

Ivy had undergone a mastectomy several years earlier, but when Chase looked at the surgical incision, he was surprised to see the pectoralis muscle missing, leaving rows of ribs covered only by skin. Her left arm was double the size compared to the right.

"I'm sorry it's so hard to get rid of this swelling in your arm," he said, reaching for the fat fingers of her left hand. "It's just one of those things that happens when we treat breast cancer."

Chase saw that the lymphedema in Ivy's hand was worse than her arm, and he wondered if his surgical separation of her fused fingers so many years earlier had predisposed her to having a worse case of post-op lymphedema. He could still see his old Z-shaped handiwork in the scars. Chase found it puzzling that she had undergone a Halsted radical even though the switch to modified radical had occurred 15 years earlier. He located her chart while she continued her gibberish.

Upon reading the notes, he was surprised to learn that she wasn't there for the lymphedema at all. She had been sent to Surgery Clinic because of a draining sinus, a long-standing blowhole in her mastectomy incision that had never healed.

"Wait a minute!" he said aloud to an uncaring hallway. "What's going on here? She's had this draining wound for *five years*, ever since her surgery! Wounds don't keep draining unless there's a reason." He quickly located the old operative note. The diagnosis for her Halsted radical was "lobular carcinoma in situ," an entity now considered only premalignant. It nearly took his breath away. The names of the surgeons were listed, and the intern on the case was now a Chief Resident. Maybe this resident could shed some light on why they'd done an obsolete procedure that, even when popular, would have been overkill. The attending surgeon on the case was listed as Porter Piscotel, M.D.

Step-by-step, Chase dissected the situation. First of all, the draining wound. He had the nurse place Ivy in an exam room where her row of bony ribs looked like an old-fashioned washboard, covered with a wet sheet. Her thumping heart caused the muscles between her ribs to vibrate with each beat. Chase had only seen a few Halsteds post-op, and this was one of the ugliest. Smack dab in the middle of the cross-hatched scar was a tiny hole that drained a drop of pus upon compression. Ivy kept smiling the entire time that Chase inserted a probe into the hole along a tract that extended at least three inches.

"Well, one reason for a draining wound is persistent cancer, but we know that's not the problem. With lobular in situ, she never had a real cancer in the first place."

"What?" said the nurse.

"LCIS. It's premalignant, if you accept that term. Preinvasive for sure. We don't really know the natural history in individual cases, but if you do nothing, most patients never develop full-blown breast cancer. So, her sinus tract cannot be due to a cancer she never had. I read in her chart that she had a wound infection after surgery, five years ago, and that they packed the wound open. Maybe she's got osteomyelitis of a rib. One thing for sure, this isn't right. This sinus tract needs to be explored."

Chase scheduled Ivy for surgery, and he explained to the residents why it was unacceptable to observe a draining sinus for five years, as if this should require any explanation at all. After the general anesthetic was given, Chase directed the resident to unroof the tract, that is, divide the overlying skin along the probe. When the incision reached the apex of the tract, the surgeons were shocked to find a wadded ball of gauze, not much bigger than an English pea.

"Good god," said Chase. "She's had a draining wound for five years just because someone jammed the packing up there too tight and forgot about it? And for five years, every resident who's gone through this training program saw her in the clinic and issued wound care instructions for the aides? And then, of course, each resident wrote 'Return to Clinic in 3 months' in the chart, which is convenient timing for follow-up because that particular resident will have moved on to another rotation."

Chase scolded the hapless resident who assisted him now. "Pus drains out of our bodies for a reason, no matter how long it's been going on. Don't ever be as negligent as your colleagues during these past five years. Twenty residents have signed off on this patient over that time frame, missing or ignoring an obvious problem. Don't ever—" He caught himself. He swore he would never chew on a resident (especially, an innocent one).

Too, Chase realized that all the effort he'd invested in Ivy over the years in getting her fingers freed from one another, only to have one of her hands ruined by inappropriate surgery, was contributing to his ire. Additionally, he had considered Ivy a friend, as they had played the piano and sung together on many occasions in his prior life.

Two weeks later in the surgery clinic, Chase found the sinus tract had completely healed. Once again, Ivy seemed to sense Chase's favor toward her, and she thanked him profusely, repeating phrases that Chase barely remembered.

Chase's fascination with Ivy prompted him to pursue her case further. He pulled the old microscope slides from the lab and saw that the pathologist had overcalled the LCIS. Using Paglia's criteria in his book on breast pathology, Chase knew the microscopic finding was not enough to call "lobular carcinoma in situ." The lobules were full of cells, all right, but not expanded by those cells. It should have been "atypical lobular hyperplasia" at most, for which there was no surgical treatment at all. Yet, here was Ivy – mutilated, her ribs bulging, her heart nearly visible, and her arm swollen for life. Her hand was so waterlogged that the very fingers Chase had once separated were now squeezed together in a bloated ball of elephantiasis. Chase was so disgusted that he didn't know where to turn. *And the other faculty criticize me for calling myself a breast surgeon.*

Later, when he inquired about details from the Chief Resident who had been an intern at the time of Ivy's surgery, the resident told him, "Yes, I remember the case well because Matherville State was the only rotation where I actually had time to read, and I didn't understand why we did the surgery that we did. After studying, I felt I knew more about LCIS than anyone else on the team. None of the residents or faculty seemed to know that some experts were saying LCIS isn't really cancer. But no one would listen to me. After all, I was only an intern."

"So, where'd the idea for a Halsted come from?" Chase asked. "The LCIS deal is bad enough, especially since the lesion didn't even qualify for that diagnosis. But a Halsted? That procedure had already been dead for ten years when you all operated."

"Dr. Piscotel. He was the attending. I remember. He said no self-respecting surgeon should be treating breast cancer if he's never done a Halsted. Then, I remember him saying something about how these patients in the mental institution serve humanity by allowing surgery residents to get proper training."

Far West Texas College of Medicine was teaching Chase to sublimate explosive rage. So, he set about yet another project – a training manual 88 pages long, written entirely for surgery residents, explaining the basics of breast disease. He was so frustrated and angry that he dictated the entire volume from memory, beginning to end, in one week, and his secretary turned it into a document. Chase paid for hundreds of bound copies to be given to current and future residents and medical students. The challenge of breast cancer surgery, he explained, was *not* in the operating room. Instead, the challenge was in understanding the biology of breast cancer, the natural history of preinvasive lesions, and so many things that had nothing to do with surgical technique.

Chase would need to overhaul medical education in breast disease at Far West. Lectures weren't enough. He would need to apply some pressure. Tests. Scores. Objective measurements. "We can't continue turning residents loose on society with Neanderthal attitudes about breast cancer," he would say, "even if the faculty doesn't care."

It galled him, too, that the residency program director, Porter Piscotel, would not include a rotation for the residents to the new Breast Pavilion for a three-month stint. Five years of training in general surgery, with breast cancer the most common malignancy to be treated by general surgeons in private practice, but no rotation under Chase's tutelage? His elective rotations at the Pavilion were packed with residents from gynecology, primary care, and radiology, but surgery residents had to beg the program director for even a one-month rotation with Chase. "After all, what's so tough about performing a mastectomy?" asked the Halstedian brain.

Many months were spent by surgery residents in rotation on sub-specialties where the general surgeon would never practice, of course. Most notably, eight mandatory months out of five years would be spent on the cardiac surgery service under Dr. Dagmar, even though the vast majority would never use those skills. Oddly enough, and perhaps unwittingly, the specialty of general surgery had turned upside-down, emphasizing skills that would not be used, while de-emphasizing skills that would be used.

Though Chase was often accused of trying to "create a new surgical specialty for which there is no need," he was opposed (at first) to the idea of breast-dedicated surgeons. "We only need breast-dedicated surgeons like me in academics to train the general surgeons about breast cancer. Because if we don't beef up training for general surgeons, you will see a new specialty emerge. We're in the middle of a medical revolution, like it or not, and there are those calling for a new specialty in breast surgery."

"What revolution are you talking about?" chimed the chorus.

Still, there would be no routine rotations to the Breast Pavilion for the surgery residents. Attendance at the multidisciplinary conferences was an optional alternative in lieu of a full rotation at the Pavilion, but average attendance varied between 0 and 3 out of more than 20 residents who were under no pressure to attend.

·　　·　　·

Within a matter of two weeks, Chase managed to tear through the red tape, arranging for Ivy to travel by van to see a physical therapist in Midland who was using a new technique of total body lymphatic massage for localized lymphedema. Ivy was escorted by the hospital's physical therapist who learned the technique and brought it back to Matherville.

Remarkably, when Chase saw Ivy again a month later, her arm was covered in a fitted sleeve that allowed her fingers to wiggle. The swelling seemed much improved.

"Soti medo," she said.

"Ivy, next time I get a chance, I'm going to visit you on the ward, and we'll play ourselves a tune."

Ivy reached for Chase's hands with her own and clasped them together. And in that moment, the totality of his mission flooded back into his mind. If he were to leave Far West now for Permian Medical Center, there would be no mission across town where profit was the primary driving force. Too many things had already come together at

Far West for him to quit. He had to get patient care up to snuff, he had to continue to grow the breast cancer research consortium on campus, and clearly, from what he'd seen with Ivy, he needed to champion medical education in breast disease.

But one dastardly image Chase couldn't erase from his mind was the wrinkled smile of the medical school dean, standing before a crowd of 1,000 women at the Chanel fashion show, while he promised, promised, promised success for the new breast center while, in reality, he was hammering 2 X 4s in place to cover the entrance to the beautiful southern plantation known as the Far West Texas University Breast Pavilion.

18
SEEDS OF WOLF'S BANE

Dr. Thatcher Taylor called Chase to his office, an odd request because Chase was the one who usually initiated meetings with his boss. In fact, he frequented Dr. Taylor's office weekly, at least, working, struggling, communicating, trying to convince. Gracious to a fault, T.N.T. obliged these walk-in meetings with Chase, always patient with what seemed to be a perpetual state of crisis. Each of these meetings ended with Chase apologizing: "I'm sorry to have dragged you into this latest breast center problem, but I can't seem to get around it." Then Thatcher would reply: "No need to apologize, Chase. This Breast Pavilion must *absolutely* succeed. This may be the most important thing in all my years as Chairman. Never before has the community of Matherville looked away from our rivals at Permian Medical Center and toward Far West for expertise. So, don't apologize."

But on this occasion, Dr. Taylor's tone was different. When Chase sat down across from Thatcher, the Chairman seemed to be squirming in his seat.

"Chase, I received a call today from the Impaired Physician's Committee. Fred Crisp said you've stopped going to your meetings."

Chase flushed with rage. He wanted to strangle Dr. Crisp, commandant of the committee who played poker with physician licenses. What irony that the greatest threat to Chase's serenity was the physician recovery program. "He called you?"

"Yes."

"Well, it's true, sorta. I quit going to *his* meetings. He was hauling in medical students to observe the group. Not med students with addiction problems, but med students interested in staring at the zoo animals under the guise of medical education. I think you can you imagine what it's like for me to be seen there, the only med school faculty member, then days later trying to be an authority figure for those same students."

Chase tried to talk calmly to cover his fury. "Let me give you the name of a different reference, and you can call him to find out how I'm doing. Dr. Steele is my sponsor. You remember him. Finished general surgery back in the sixties. I told him I was having a lot of trouble with Crisp from the very beginning, starting when Crisp canceled my discharge from treatment without ever having met me. Then, Crisp tries to make me his poster boy for impaired physicians. However, the final straw was his brainstorm to start bringing in med students for so-called educational purposes. This guy's a zealot. The second letter of A.A. stands for anonymous. When my sponsor saw this developing, he took me to a home group, a bunch of oilmen and doctors and other guys with many years of sobriety. I bet you know nearly all of them. It's a great group. Honest. Self-reflecting. If you check with Jack Steele, you'll find I'm there every week, contrary to Crisp's accusations. Every week."

"Well, pulling in students for observation is, admittedly, way out of line. I'll try to get Fred off your back. You know he wields a lot of power with the licensure board. If any recovering physician gets into trouble of any kind, the Board always turns to Fred Crisp for thumbs up or thumbs down, and he's got the sole authority there."

The big picture was sickening. As long as he stayed in medicine, Chase would have this ogre of addiction looming over him. Loom it did. Not a day went by that he didn't wish for a return to his life in music where his checkered past could only serve to augment a career. How had it come to this? No matter what he did, everyone would be watching, waiting for a misstep. Unlike a figure-skater, where the crowd is sympathetic with a fall, the addict is more like a race car driver where some in the crowd quietly hope for a crash.

Managed care insurers became even more of an enemy, demanding all records dealing with his addiction history before allowing him to be a "preferred provider" receiving reduced income. Added to the condemning records of three malpractice suits in California, Chase spent days on end putting together the documentation for one insurer after another, often requiring letters of support from colleagues before he was allowed to continue to practice.

If God opened doors, Chase couldn't see it. Slamming doors in his face? Why, yes. Every day, it seemed.

With no energy left for relationships, friends or lovers, Chase increasingly retreated to scholarly study. Amazed at the absence of breast cancer research on the Far West campus – including the independent Studebaker Medical Research Foundation where donations for breast cancer research were readily accepted then shifted to semi-related projects – Chase began cross-pollinating disciplines and arriving at novel hypotheses for diverse and unusual ways to attack breast cancer early in the process, that is, "pre-cancer."

For example, Far West Texas didn't even have the basic rat and mouse models in place for cancer research. So, Chase studied for months on the science behind these models while, at the same time, he scoured the campus for empty lab space that could be converted to a chemical carcinogenesis lab. At medical school graduation, once, he wondered if his goals were not turning into obsessions.

The faculty was required to sit in cap and gown on stage, many rows deep, under the hot lights, miserable for almost three hours. The back row, however, was so well hidden from the audience that many faculty members would simply slide on out, stage left, and leave the auditorium during the ceremony. One such June, when the outside temperature of 104 degrees dictated torture inside, Chase was sitting on the back row, where, over the course of the first hour, every other faculty member slithered out before the diplomas were granted. However, Chase had smuggled beneath his academic gown a research article that addressed the estrous cycle of the female rat, critical to understanding the standard DMBA model of chemical carcinogenesis.

Alone on the back row, he slipped the article out of the loose sleeve of his black gown and studied the reproductive cycle of the female rat, plus the differences between Sprague-Dawley and Wistar-Firth rats, and how dimethylbenzanthracene worked to induce cancers, all in the name of research. The sweat from his arms and the drippings from his brow combined to smear the underlined black, and the highlighted yellow, left over from the first and second times he had read the same article. He wondered: *Have I gone too far?* He would not ask himself this question again.

Chase insisted on making Friday his "academic day," a research day theoretically guaranteed to all clinical faculty members, but claimed by few – in fact, within the surgery department, claimed by no one. To take a day "off" for research meant no patient care, no income for the faculty member, no income for the general surgery section, no income for the larger surgery department, no income for the medical school, each of whom took their cut of revenue. Yet, the "academic day" was mandated in print in the Faculty Handbook, a document about which T.N.T. once said, half-serious, "I'd be very suspect of anyone who actually read the Faculty Handbook." Chase never admitted to reading every word in the book.

After claiming his academic day, amazing things began to happen. Researchers came out of the woodwork to become part of Chase's team. He helped all of them by reviewing their strategies, by offering correlating clinical information, and by reviewing their grant applications ("Wow. Thanks for the review and your commentary. Usually, clinicians don't read a word, then tell you that the grant looks great.)

Importantly, he was also able to dole out seed money from the nest egg that the Raven sisters had provided, money that Chase had hoarded against the attempted raids by the dean. Soon, researchers were generating data that led to grant funding and publications, plus collaborations across Texas and nationwide.

Chase shook his head in disbelief when former classmate Porter Piscotel grumbled with the implication that Chase wasn't pulling his fair share. "Academic Day?" Porter wondered aloud in a faculty meeting. "*Anyone* can excel in research if they have an academic day. In fact, most could win a Nobel Prize if they always took their academic day."

Chase marveled that listeners thought Piscotel was joking when he made such statements. The Nobel Prize reference was said without a smile, and nothing to support the idea that he was kidding. Porter routinely made comparable statements that Chase found hard to digest. Chase paid close attention to Porter who was no longer the nurturing friend he'd been shortly after Chase's near-death experience. As Chase grew stronger, the friendship became weaker, as though Porter thrived best when the other person was in a position of weakness.

Later, Chase would learn that one of the main reasons for Porter's disgruntlement had been the (misconceived) notion that each faculty member had a portion of their private care income diverted to the Breast Pavilion through the complex system of in-house taxation. Porter had "spread the word" widely, allowing drops of poison to do their thing. Even after discovering that this was not the case (and admitting his error), Porter remained openly cynical about Chase and the Breast Pavilion.

Chase's success in recruiting and coordinating the research community was, of course, not a solo act. While Chase might have been the composer, the actual conducting came from the diligent work of a charming couple – Gunnar and Freya Pixley – he, platinum-haired and diminutive, speaking with the English accent of his Yorkshire father rather than the tongue of his Norwegian mother; she, platinum-haired and diminutive, often speaking Norse. From this couple, Chase learned pure scientific method, how to dissect the published literature into its precarious origins, and, importantly, the politics of medical research.

Neither of the Pixleys had advanced degrees. Both husband and wife were products of the research underground, assistants who had worked in various labs for decades, learning where both the bones and treasures are buried in medical research. From the catacombs, where they had survived funding crisis after funding crisis, the Pixleys had been adopted by the surgery department.

Here, Chase found true symbiosis. He appreciated what it must be like for world class research centers where an idea becomes reality with a snap of the fingers. Indeed, it was Gunnar and Freya who implemented Chase's first step – establishing a chemical carcinogenesis model – through the installation of equipment, learning the chemical safety codes, gaining approval at animal rights committees, and on and on. It took well over a year and was funded entirely by fashion shows and other events sponsored by the Raven sisters.

Chase designed the first experiment. Freya carried out the steps with compulsive attention to detail, supervising the eager medical student who was Chase's understudy at the time. The outcome was successful, cancer being prevented in the animals through a first-ever pharmacologic manipulation. After six months of writing and referencing, Chase's article appeared in a prestigious research journal.

Unlike swollen-head academics who fight for the glory of first author status on publications, Chase placed the name of his medical student as lead author – Nola Kastl, the girl with brown bangs and pale gray-green eyes who had flown from her seat in the audience that first year in medical school to tell Chase she wanted to be part of his dream, his vision. Chase's reasoning as to why he gave the coveted first author position to students was that it might help lure them to a career at the Far West Texas University Breast Pavilion.

As a senior medical student, Nola enrolled in two electives with Chase and spent her vacation time with Chase as well, learning breast pathology, making clinical correlations to pathology, and studying research strategies. Chase had admired Nola from the beginning. She was a bit intense, but her raw intelligence and enthusiasm supervened.

In an odd coincidence, Nola was torn by the same three specialty choices Chase had once entertained – psychiatry, pathology, and surgery. It was a unique triplet in which the extremes of psychiatry versus surgery were pulled in yet a third dimension by pathology, a tripolar decision. Once Nola learned of her link to Chase through this triplet, she spoke about this coincidence to other students, the Pixleys, and anyone who would listen to the sound of fate.

Editor's Note: In Nutshell, *the reader learned about the genesis of the Meeker-Crim Prognostic Index, a tool developed by two academics -- a psychiatrist and an internist at Far West Texas College of Medicine who were both interested in the medical education process. Using a complicated formula to overcome subjectivity, Drs. Crim and Meeker were able to predict physician meltdown years in advance. But then, with the introduction of computers into research, they were shocked to find out that a better crystal ball for predicting self-destructive behavior among physicians could be extracted from a simple questionnaire when students listed their top three specialty choices for the future. For those few students who answered "psychiatry, surgery, pathology," in any order, outcomes beyond 10 years showed a disproportionate rate of burn-out, addiction, and suicide. Remarkably, this triad had a predictive value that was superior to the M-C Prognostic Index that had taken decades to construct. The two investigators – Meeker and Crim – had no idea how the triad worked. While Chase Callaway was aware of his participation in the development of the M-C Prognostic Index, to the editor's knowledge, neither he nor Nola Kastl ever learned about the ominous implications of the "psychiatry, surgery, pathology" triad.*

Having discovered his own knack for basic science research, Chase wished now that he had chosen pathology as his specialty when he had the chance, a lead-in to molecular biologic research. It was too late for him, but now he could live this dream, vicariously, through Nola, if she chose pathology and stayed at Far West. So, during their time together, Chase guided Nola with his praise and personal instruction at the double-headed microscope.

One day, she announced, "Dr. Callaway, I've finally made my decision. I'm going into pathology." She took a step toward him as they rose from the microscope.

"Nola, that's great. I'm really pleased for you." He saw that her arms were fumbling for a congratulatory hug, a gesture he thwarted by extending his arm and shaking her right hand. "Of course, in all selfishness, I'm hoping you'll stay here on faculty."

Her eyes dropped to the hand holding hers, then she looked up at Chase again before she continued. "Yes, I want to be part of— part of your master plan."

With nearly all daily contacts being female – employees, students, patients – Chase made the conscious decision to build an impenetrable emotional wall, given the potentially awkward (and ruinous) situations that could arise in his chosen sub-specialty. He placed his past securely behind the bricks, which allowed a non-threatening approach to patient care and a squeaky-clean interaction with female students and residents who rotated through the Breast Pavilion.

Another five years would pass before Nola would have her board certification, but Chase could wait. After all, it would take that long to put together the entire package anyway, for there was plenty to do in the meantime, trying to build excellence across all departmental boundaries.

The success of the chemical carcinogenesis animal model owed a debt to the behind-the-scenes grace of Hardy Studebaker who made sure Chase procured the needed real estate at the Studebaker Medical Research Foundation. The medical school didn't have the facilities to handle the dangerous chemicals, so the lab was established across the street at the Research Foundation, to much fanfare and some envy.

Porter Piscotel had previously lured T.N.T. into spending $60,000 of departmental money (indeed, using patient care income by the faculty, the very "sin" falsely attributed to Chase) on a white elephant research device that never yielded a scientific paper. Suddenly, however, Porter developed an interest in chemical carcinogenesis, and he jumped whole-heartedly and wide-eyed into the fray with his study of gastrointestinal cancers in hamsters. Chase was more than happy to share his spoils with Porter. With their friendship slipping, Chase wanted to reconnect, even if it took the sharing of lethal chemistry conjured in a lab that began humming away only after great time and expense.

Through many complicated experiments, Gunnar and Freya Pixley groomed Chase into a skilled researcher. Sometimes, however, the training dealt more with bizarre politics. "Chase, you have a lot of people on campus stalking you, knowing you have seed money. Beware of the Studebilkers," they once said. "They're nothing but parasites."

"Who are the Studebilkers?"

"Money-hungry researchers. Bilking dollars anywhere they can. They're the researchers on campus who spend all their time networking and conning the big money out of rich Texans. It's quite an industry. Grants have become too difficult. Too much time to write them. Only a few are funded. It's much easier to go directly to the money sources in west Texas. These informal grants are not all Studebaker money, of course, but the term Studebilker caught on. It's amazingly easy to separate an oilman from his money if you can convince him you've got the cure for cancer. It's utterly bizarre how these people, so cunning and sophisticated in amassing their fortunes, turn foolish when it comes to doling it out to science they don't understand. If you read the prospectus on any of these biotech companies that the Studebilkers are starting, you'd think Matherville was the only place in the world attacking cancer, diabetes, and heart disease. A rare project will actually succeed, of course, keeping the whole thing going."

"So, am I being called a Studebilker? After all, Hardy Studebaker is probably the reason I'm here. And T.N.T., of course. And the Raven sisters."

"You're no Studebilker. Your deal is different because it's real. The Breast Pavilion is the biggest thing around here in a long time. The research, for you, it's secondary."

"Well, it used to be secondary, but now I'm not so sure."

"You do have the gift," replied the Pixleys. "We hope you're with us full-time someday."

"Unlikely. I can't get through the endless series of unsolvable clinical problems at the Pavilion. Number one is the breast radiologist position, which is pretty much the same problem as our financial position."

In reality, the Breast Pavilion was nothing like it appeared in the society pages of the Matherville newspaper. The doors were open, yes, but the financial losses were overwhelming. And, the mammography services were being provided by the "rent-a-doc" approach, with patient numbers flat.

"Chase, I'm going to ask you to accept Dr. Bloom as your partner at the Breast Pavilion."

The unusually forceful command from Thatcher Taylor took Chase's breath away. Chase could mark the day and time when Dr. Bloom had started working part-time at the Pavilion, based on the steady stream of complaints. After blowing his cigarette breath in the patients' faces, he would flip the top of their gowns up, leaving them bare-chested, sitting on a cold exam table, then he'd stare at their breasts for what seemed an eternal minute of silence before crudely palpating each side. "Inspection is always the first step in physical diagnosis," he would explain to the shocked mammography techs and any medical students in the room. "Inspection first, palpation second. It's true for the entire physical exam that you learned as an MS-1, breasts included." The techs were pleading for Chase to "do something" to end Dr. Bloom's reign of inspection.

This was the hill to die on.

"No, Dr. Taylor, I'm sorry. I can't accept that." Chase felt horrible standing up to the man who had salvaged his career only a few years earlier.

"Now, Chase, don't be so impulsive with a knee-jerk answer. Couldn't you just accept Dr. Bloom three days a week?"

"And do what on the other two days? Celebrate? No, sir. I never thought I'd say this, but I will quit if he's named as our radiologist."

Thatcher Nolan Taylor, M.D. let out a sigh of exasperation and despondency as he lowered his head, staring at the pile of papers on his desk.

That was that. The rift was carved, and Chase knew it. He had not felt this distraught in his career since he'd announced to his California partner Ted Zink that he was returning to Texas. What desperation Thatcher must have felt, knowing that Chase had been begging to get this very same radiologist barred from the Pavilion. How could Thatcher cow down to the Department of Radiology? Where was the T.N.T., the power, that everyone talked about?

One admirable feature of Thatcher Nolan Taylor's general surgery section stood out in contrast to the rest of the medical school – remarkable stability over time. This peace was, in fact, due to T.N.T.'s clever assemblage of the faculty, picking his staff from former students and residents. Alas, the lingering, lifetime effect of the academic hierarchy was key. No former student dared to stand up to the revered Dr. Taylor, that is, until the day Chase Callaway told him, "No, sir. I'll quit if he's the choice."

In this sequestered stability of the general surgery section, Chase became an outsider. The mere decision to dedicate his practice solely to breast cancer was a grave offense to some, especially Porter Piscotel. Porter was an ardent believer in the jack-of-all trades concept of the general surgeon, an idea that had been breaking apart at the seams for decades. Chase made matters worse by convincing T.N.T. to let him serve as attending surgeon for all breast cancer cases done at the university. In Chase's mind, this would assure the right operation for the right patient, and would allow him, also, to monitor all the outcome data. In Porter's mind, the move was heretical, and he resented being cut out. He felt that his private opinions about breast cancer management were critical for a proper balance in resident education.

The estrangement worsened when Chase moved his office from the surgery department to the new Breast Pavilion downstairs. He grossly underestimated the importance of daily interaction among his peers. When Dr. Mooney, the VA Surgical Chief who had taken over for Chase, wandered down to the new Pavilion one day, he stuck his head in the minor surgery suite and proclaimed, "I think you're gonna see all of us faculty doing our minor cases down here from now on, rather than across the street at that dinky minor surgery room at College Hospital."

To which Chase replied, "You know, I realize I have a lot of real estate here. Just so you'll know, when College Hospital agreed to build the Pavilion, bigger than I'd asked for, I went directly to Thatcher and offered to share the space with the other faculty. He said, flatly, 'No. You can't have old men with their rear ends up in the air getting hemorrhoids banded in the same facility where women are being evaluated with breast problems. Women need to feel secure that nothing else is going on in that center besides breast care.' I mention this, of course, to let you guys know that I didn't intend to hog all this space. I have to admit, though, I think Thatcher is right on this one. Plus, look at the plaque on the door of this minor surgery room. The Kirkland Foundation donated their money specifically for breast patients. I know. I wrote the grant. Take a look at all the doors. They all have plaques of appreciation."

From then on, Chase's closest colleague, Dr. Mooney, began making cracks about Chase's luxurious furnishings and especially Chase's private bathroom. Over the next few years, Mooney would drop by periodically to tell a clever joke and to remind Chase what an inadequate job he'd done as VA Chief of Surgery. Finally, with amazing regularity on each visit, Mooney would preface his exit by walking beyond Chase's desk and pissing in his private toilet.

A primordial horde, upstairs in the surgery department, began to beat their drums.

The faculty also grew resentful of Chase's self-proclaimed "incompetence" in peripheral vascular surgery. Daytime incompetence was okay, but at nights and weekends, he should have pulled his weight.

Chase considered himself weakly trained in the first place (no fem-pops as a resident and no carotid endarterectomies), to the point he'd been unable to get privileges in California. Now, more than a decade later, his skills were completely obsolete, not to mention the vascular sub-specialty had been revolutionized by clot-busting drugs. So when he agreed to return to west Texas, a key part of the arrangement with T.N.T. was that he would not be required to attend on vascular cases, at any time – day or night.

After several years back in Texas, though, he discovered that T.N.T. had never discussed anything of the sort with the other faculty members. So when Chase was on call at night, he forwarded the vascular emergencies to the other faculty, under the assumption that everyone was on the same page. Totally embarrassed upon discovering the error, he called the primary vascular surgeon and explained.

The colleague replied, "Well, I'm glad you finally mentioned something about it. Bad enough to be on call, but having to cover for you on vascular has been a bit much."

Perhaps Chase didn't belong in the surgery department after all. Once, the entire faculty took the weekend off for a deer hunt, timing their venture when the Saturday Grand Rounds topic was "Alcoholism and Addiction Among Physicians." In one of the longest hours of his life, Chase sat alone on the elite front row, empty faculty seats on either side of him, with a crowd of residents and students behind him staring at the back of his head, the only known addict on campus. After that, it was safe to say that any resentment the faculty held toward Chase was mutual.

That same deer-hunting weekend, with Chase alone on call, a young man presented to the emergency room with a popliteal artery injury from a gunshot. Of all places for such an injury, thought Chase, the site where they criticized me in California for never having performed a fem-pop procedure, a gross deficiency in the Far West surgery program.

Chase couldn't find any faculty in town, including the Permian hospital, nor could he find the distal end of the blasted popliteal artery, which had branched already into smaller vessels. The Chief Resident had never treated such an injury either. After a failed attempt at a graft, the patient eventually ended up with a lower leg amputation, and Chase ended up with despondency brewing in rage.

Then, Sherri Kastor killed herself. The warning signs had been there.

Sherri was a soft-spoken surgery resident whom Chase had liked from the start. He had even tried to inspire her to consider breast cancer surgery as a career option. Yet, when the residents approached Chase, complaining that something was wrong with Sherri, that she was acting strange, Chase forwarded the information to the residency program director only to be rebuffed by Porter Piscotel.

Dr. Piscotel: "You know, Sherri did have some personal problems once, and I let her take a break from residency. She was doing a terrible job anyway. Poor motivation was her problem. But now, I can assure you, Sherri is a true gunner. Why, she stayed up all night recently taking care of a sick patient in the ICU while she had a bleeding ulcer of her own. True grit, eh? Her hematocrit was only 20%, and there she was, working away. She needed a three-unit transfusion the next day, once her bleed was discovered. No, she used to have problems, but she's doing a bang-up job now."

Even Thatcher Taylor was unconcerned: "Oh, Chase, I wouldn't worry about that. You'll eventually learn to take what the residents tell you with a grain of salt."

As Thatcher Taylor mouthed those words, as it turned out, Sherri was lying dead in O.R. #6 at the VA hospital, having started an IV on herself and infused enough Fentanyl to kill a horse.

Riding in Thatcher Taylor's car to the funeral, five faculty members described Sherri's flaws and how suicide, in the end, is not usually preventable. Chase wanted to claw his way out of the car. He had spent the entire funeral replaying every interaction he'd ever had with Sherri. What might have been done? What could he do the next time? He reflected on his own precarious moment in life, in the seclusion room, separated from death only by the absence of an obliging weapon. That experience gave him a different view on the world, perhaps a supernatural view. Certainly, an alien view.

The faculty response was the same as when a colleague departed the university for greener pastures – always the fault of the person who left. Condemnation of that person followed, along with a list of their shortcomings. The university was never at fault. No self-reflection concerning institutional weakness. Absolute preservation of the image. From this, Chase fashioned a psychiatric diagnosis applicable to the neurosis that seemed to enslave his alma mater – *malignant institutional narcissism.*

As Thucydides pointed out in antiquity, the reason history repeats itself is pride. Pride prevents self-reflection, the lack of self-reflection negates wisdom, and the lack of wisdom disallows betterment. And so, an institution afflicted with this collective thought disorder is forever trapped in its ugly cycle where it insists on a pristine image for the public. If that image is threatened, death to the offender.

A few weeks later, still ruminating on the suicide, still exhausted from his standoff with T.N.T. regarding the radiologist Dr. Bloom, Chase Callaway made his way to the operating room to perform a lumpectomy. The patient was elderly and frail, the cancer small, so removing the lump under local anesthesia was all that would be required.

But when he swung open the doors to the operating room, a full code was in progress, with the attending anesthesiologist and a resident both panicked, trying to intubate Chase's patient to establish an airway. A fiberoptic scope lay on the patient's chest.

"What the hell is going on here? What the *hell* is going on? This case was scheduled to be done under straight local!"

"We're having trouble intubating her."

"I can see that! It was scheduled under local. Did she arrest on her own? Spontaneously?"

As it turned out, the attending anesthesiologist had switched the case from local to general anesthesia, against Chase's orders, solely to allow his resident to practice fiberoptic intubation. The need for such practice was now evident – the resident couldn't do it, nor could the faculty member. Once the patient had received the paralyzing drug for the practice session, however, there was no turning back. Fiberoptic assistance was used (at that time) if routine intubation was unsuccessful. But the attending had reversed the sequence, "for practice," and instead of backing away, they had persisted for so long with their fumbling attempts using the new fiberoptic scope that the patient had been deprived of oxygen, launching a cardiac arrest, in full progress as Chase walked in the operating room doors. Such was a lumpectomy under local at the teaching hospital.

Murderous rage was Chase's new suit, and it fit him well. After the patient had been resuscitated from her physician-induced arrest, she was taken to the recovery room where, when she awoke, she was aphasic – unable to speak due to neurologic damage.

"Goddamit, I want a full investigation," Chase yelled over and over. "I want to know how this happened! This is not malpractice – it's assault and battery. Do you hear me? Assault and battery. If your chairman won't do anything about it, then I'm calling the D.A.'s office."

The faculty member blamed the resident, while the resident blamed the faculty, confessing that their department needed to improve "their fiberoptic intubation numbers," and that the patient had been talked into agreeing to a general anesthetic. When no action was taken by anyone, Chase called the Chairman of Anesthesiology, demanding official intervention.

Instead, the offending anesthesiologist faculty member approached Chase a week later and struggled to apologize, clearly under duress. Within two sentences, the blame shifted, inconceivably, to Chase when the attending anesthesiologist said, "You shouldn't do a case like that under local anesthesia anyway. We can control the situation better with the patient under a general."

"You sonuvabitch! How *dare* you tell me crap like that after what you did to my patient? I do lumpectomies under straight local every day in minor surgery. It's minor, minor, *minor*. Do you understand me? It's never, *ever*, under any circumstance, safer to give a general anesthesia for something this minor. I specifically scheduled her for a local, to be done in the O.R. only for closer monitoring than we do in the minor surgery room, and you turned her into your guinea pig just to practice your fiberoptic bullshit. What's more, how can you – of all people – talk about *controlling the situation* after what I witnessed when you couldn't even intubate her the old-fashioned way? Assault and battery, do you hear me? That's what it was. You stroked out my patient. Stroked her out, you asshole. As far as I'm concerned, you're nothing but a freakin' criminal in a scrub suit!"

Chase was uncontrollable, inconsolable, and his pleas to the Chairman of Anesthesiology went unheard. His letter to the dean went unanswered. His complaint to T.N.T. drew no response. Instead, it was duly noted that Dr. Chase Callaway had a temper problem to go with his history of drug dependency, and the hallway scuttlebutt around campus told how witnesses thought for sure that Dr. Callaway was going to kill the anesthesiologist. It was a juicy rumor steeped in truth, but with the emphasis on the remarkable, suppressed rage of the otherwise mild-mannered Chase Callaway. In the end, Chase's brouhaha accomplished nothing. No reprimand. No malpractice. No charges filed with the D.A. Nothing. Nothing, that is, other than increasing awareness that Chase Callaway could "go ballistic." Thus, a perfect example of "malignant institutional narcissism."

The patient gradually regained her speech over the ensuing weeks, easing the consciences of the guilty and the gutless, but Chase regained nothing. Another piece of his heart had been destroyed. His life at his alma mater was much like an experiment he'd performed as an undergrad in psychology. It was the classic rat-and-lever experiment. If there's always rat food after pressing the lever, the rat keeps pressing. If there's always an electric shock, the rat quits pressing. But if it's unpredictable, if there is chaos – shock or food in random order – the rat will retreat to the corner, shaking and drooling, unable to feed or care for itself until it dies. Chase was shaking and drooling.

Oddly enough, he was never tempted to resort to a chemical solution for his pathologic rage. His prior stint in the seclusion room functioned as his lever with its electric shock.

What is this curse? I'm simply trying to build a Center of Excellence. Yet, I seem to be the incarnation of Dostoyevsky's Idiot, or Voltaire's Zadig, simply trying to do what's good and simple, but only causing chaos and disaster.

He retreated deeper and deeper into himself and into the subterranean world of medical research. He found it increasingly difficult to pray for relief because an inverse correlation seemed to supervene – after a prayer of supplication, the opposite would occur. And with that, he quit pressing the lever.

Chase came to believe that an ethereal malevolence required an ethereal resistance, if not outright magic. One way or another, his suffering had to stop. He found his old talisman, the souvenir he'd taken from Grandfather Zebulon's library shortly before he had died – a wood-carved shell. Initially placing it on his desk at home, Chase often found himself fiddling with it. One evening, he was examining it closely where one surface was rough and unstained, as though broken off from a larger piece of art. Then the phone rang. It was his mother.

"Chase, you need to know…your father was diagnosed today with PSP, progressive supranuclear palsy they call it. Something's been wrong for quite a while, and we thought it was Parkinson's at first because of a tremor in his hands, then we thought it was Alzheimer's because of some dementia, but it looks like it's PSP, and it's going to be a tough time from here on out."

Chase hadn't seen his parents in months – not since his father's retirement party where Wes had spoken of his plans to do watercolors, woodworking and other crafts now cancelled by a future of relentless neurologic deterioration. It was going to be awful for everyone.

The curse flowed not simply through his father's shaky fingertips, but into Chase's hands as well. Chase's arthritis was getting worse, with constant pain. If that weren't enough for a surgeon's death knell, Chase began to develop a Dupuytren's contracture of his right hand, where thick fibrous bands were forming at the base of his fingers onto his palm, pulling those digits into a clenched fist. His ring finger was already curled completely and couldn't be forced straight. Other fingers were curling as well. Even breast surgery was increasingly difficult for him, and he didn't make it any easier on himself by opting to make tiny, cosmetic incisions that barely allowed room for the plastic surgeons to insert an implant. His meticulous skin closures that prompted plastic surgeons to coin the phrase, "a Callaway closure," were also increasingly difficult.

As his reputation as a breast surgeon had grown, it seemed the curse had grown as well, not simply with the pain and contractures of his hands, but miasma spreading into his patients. Pathology reports seemed to flow across his desk with unexpectedly bad outcomes. In situ disease turned out to be invasive. Lymph nodes thought to be negative turned out to be positive. With these bad reports came chemotherapy, and with chemotherapy came the need to place ports for drug delivery. In spite of his skill in placing these ports, the memory of that early death years ago in California began to haunt him. The sequence became Pavlovian – as soon as the bad pathology report landed on his desk, Chase slipped into a dark mood that lasted until the port was safely in place days later. Multiple patients in need of ports meant overlapping waves of this dark mood, or more accurately, a permanent tide.

"I don't get it. I take the patient to the O.R. with a diagnosis of early disease, and the next thing I know, I'm putting in a port for chemo. This is happening way too often."

"Oh, you're just imaging it," said his secretary at the Pavilion.

"Check the reports for the past year, would you? Let's see exactly how often this is happening."

In spite of his referrals primarily being "early" mammographic discoveries, where most of the time the positive lymph node rate would be around 20%, Chase's patients for the past year had metastatic tumor in the nodes 58% of the time. Something was wrong. Terribly wrong.

The curse is not simply impacting me and my family – it's impacting everyone around me, everyone whose life I touch.

PSP. PSP. PSP. The initials of progressive supranuclear palsy reverberated in his head all day, every day, as he thought through the disease complex and its progressive and ruthless symptoms, its dismal prognosis. It was not surprising then, with the mounting evidence for a family curse, that Chase noticed twitching in his right hand. First it was just the thumb, contracting on its own, then the index finger joined in the convulsions, jerking to meet the thumb in a pinching motion. So, for Chase, it became a progressive triad – arthritis with its red and swollen knuckles, fibrous Dupuytren's contractures that threatened to convert his hands to claws, and now, twitching spasms.

. . .

The young woman newly diagnosed with breast cancer sat with her husband across the consultation table from Chase, hopeful that she had found her healer. At the conclusion of their preoperative session, the husband offered, "Thank you for accepting my wife as a patient. Everyone says you have the best hands for breast cancer surgery in this part of Texas."

Chase held both his hands beneath the table, out of the couple's line of vision.

19
WHEN THE WOLF'S BANE BLOOMS

With Wes Callaway's diagnosis of PSP, and its promised progressive neurologic decay until death, Chase's heart softened. The custom-made cruelty of PSP was that it kept Wes from engaging all the hobbies he'd planned in retirement, leaving only books and TV for which his father had no interest. He'd been too hard on his father for too long.

Chase's parents had recently moved to the outskirts of Matherville where one could claim country living. Ramona asked her son if he would landscape a vegetable garden for Wes and her, giving Chase's father a motivation to keep moving. The two-acre yard was overgrown with weeds and brush, however, so the first step was to spray weed killer over the entire property, then convert about one-fourth of the yard to cultivation.

It was an arm's length effort on Chase's part, but an effort still. In all those childhood years of gardening with Sukie Spurlock, neither of his parents had shown much interest in getting dirty. Until now. So, while his parents were on a three-week tour of the Greek islands, Chase set about spraying many gallons of weed killer over the proposed plot. He took off a Monday for the spray fest, his first weekday off in a year.

His plan, after letting the weed killer work, was to dig multiple beds, landscaping each site with native rock, then planting a different crop at each location – eggplant, corn, tomatoes, cucumbers, green beans and watermelon, for starters. Between these vegetable plots, he would grow Wormwood Sage, Coyote Brush, and Snow-in-Summer.

By the time he sprayed the last of the poison, however, Chase felt a boring pain in his right eye. He went inside his parents' house, took two aspirin, then four, then eight, trying to stem the tide of discomfort that was scorching its way to his brain. He fell onto a couch waiting for the headache to pass. After an unknown length of time, the pain was complete. That is, the torture had filled his skull. Worse, he couldn't recall exactly where he was or how he got there.

Finally recognizing the inside of his parents' new home, he scanned the room for a telephone. He needed to call someone for help, but other than his parents, he could think of no one. Then it occurred to him to call the Raven sisters, but when he started to dial, he couldn't remember either of their phone numbers, even though he talked with them almost daily for several years. What day was it? Monday? *Can't be, or else I'd be at work.* For some reason, he still remembered his office number, so he called his secretary. "I won't be in tomorrow. Terrific headache. I'm sorta stuck at my parents' house. Surgery? Tomorrow? What kind of surgery am I doing? Well, I won't be able to make it." He hung up the phone.

Within minutes, it seemed, a bell was ringing. He answered the phone but heard only a dial tone. Perhaps the noise was a doorbell.

When Chase found the front door, he opened it and was shocked to see Dr. Thatcher Nolan Taylor, along with another faculty member whose name was escaping him at the moment, a very annoying lapse since Chase recalled that the other man had been a friend for years.

"What…why are you here? It's only a headache."

"Chase, we're here to help you. Your secretary said it sounded like you needed help…that you were confused."

The two men silently guided him to a Mercedes (Chase has no memory of any conversation that might have occurred).

Later, in the emergency room, a neurologic exam and a spinal tap brought forth the diagnosis of meningoencephalitis, and Chase was admitted promptly to the Intensive Care Unit. His brain was aflame, and the sound of his own groaning was foreign, coming from someone else. Hours later, it seemed, the Chief of Medicine walked into the room and proudly announced to Chase: "I've got good news for you. Your drug screen is all clear. The only thing in your system is aspirin."

"That's news? How is that good news? I didn't take anything other than aspirin, so I'd expect the drug screen to be negative. It's good news for you, maybe, and everyone out there waiting for me to relapse. But think. It tells me nothing about what's going on. It's bad new for me, not knowing what's happening."

Good news didn't travel as fast as the more plausible news, the morbid version that everyone expected, confirming their beliefs about addiction. A few faculty friends dropped by to console Chase, but when he tried to explain what was going on (to the best of his knowledge), they would ease out the door.

For those willing to listen, Chase tried to downplay it all. "Still not sure how I got sick. I think it was the weed killer. Like an idiot, since there wasn't any wind, I didn't wear a mask, and I was spraying for several hours. Now, at least, I know how my lab rats feel when we inoculate them with chemicals," he joked half-heartedly.

The widespread belief came clear when the hospital chaplain entered Chase's room, patting him on the shoulder as he said, "I've come to pray for you. Do you know yet where they're going to send you this time? I heard Atlanta."

"What are you talking about?"

"Why, to rehab." The pastor must have recognized the shock on Chase's face, as his own face scrunched into a puzzled look. "This *is* about your addiction, isn't it?"

"No-o-o. As a matter of fact, it has nothing to do with addiction. My head hurts like hell. The spinal tap led to a CT where there was a little something that led to an MRI where there was a different little something that led to a carotid angiogram where there was absolutely nothing, other than the fact that it made half my face feel like it was being blow-torched, which, by the way, made my head feel a whole lot better. After all that, I've got a diagnosis of meningoencephalitis, but no one knows why. Let me tell you, it's pretty darn scary when something terrible is in your brain, and nobody can figure out what it is. It's interesting, though – rather than ask for the facts, everyone has chosen to believe this was a relapse, with no evidence for that whatsoever."

The chaplain was contrite. "I'm sorry. I was just repeating what everybody's been saying— I just assumed— well, I came to pray for you."

"Don't bother." Chase couldn't believe the words that came from his mouth.

The chaplain apologized again and left the room.

On the fifth day, the pain subsided, and the episode of "idiopathic meningoencephalitis" was deemed a mystery, with several rare disorders still in the differential. Chase didn't buy the explanations. He had been spraying weed killer and inhaling the toxins for hours leading up to the headache.

Occam's Razor, he thought. Phenomena should be explained with the least number of variables. In fact, William of Ockham, the Franciscan scholar, probably wrote something along the lines of *entia non sunt multiplicanda praeter necessitatem*, but regardless, as part of the reductionist philosophy, William took a razor to every question. For Chase, the answer to this question was "weed killer."

The aftermath, though, was what nearly wrecked him even though the initial headache was gone. After discharge, returning home on extended medical leave, he found himself in the grip of overwhelming dysphoria. Not depression, but dysphoria. Everything in the world was wrong, hideous, horrible, intolerable. Love was a lie, joy was illusion, and every breath of air was nothing but noxious fumes perpetuating a living hell, taking him closer to death. He would never be able return to work. He hated work. The breast center was a pathetic, money-losing joke. He hated the very idea.

He knew how absurdly magnified his thoughts were as they played their tricks. Yet, knowledge that his dysphoria was foreign offered no respite, no insight. He remained swathed in total despair. He was terrified. Was this permanent? Had the meningoencephalitis forever altered his brain chemistry? Had a chemical carcinogenesis created a malignant soul?

Exactly one lunar cycle later, Chase's symptoms disappeared – overnight. He couldn't believe it. He was normal. Completely. Normal for him, that is. His enthusiasm about life returned. He felt the Breast Pavilion still had a chance, and he was excited about its future. He was even encouraged about finally bonding with his father in time of need. Yes, it was all part of Providence tempering his soul even further, to give him the superhuman strength needed to accomplish the impossible.

The Ubermensch was not merely a godless concept from Nietzsche, but had some common ground with the final product described by Kierkegaard in what some later called Christian existentialism. It was only after all powers of reason had been exhausted that man could reach for God. The man with greater reasoning and more questions would suffer a worse level of angst, more peril in the process of deconstruction and reconstruction. Yes, Nietzsche went hopelessly insane, perhaps because he had not taken the ultimate step of surrender as had Kierkegaard. God always works through paradox, so who was Chase to question the grooming he had endured?

This exhilaration lasted for – well – one lunar cycle. One month later, Chase woke up from a deep sleep to see "4:00 am" lighted on his alarm clock, with a sharp, boring pain in his right eye, much like the onset of his meningoencephalitis. Then, adjacent to the right eye, in a crescent pattern, a patch of skin tingled. He was not sleepy in the slightest, but wide awake with the poker in his right eye, then nausea, followed by the pain spreading through his skull like a brush fire. Stomach cramping drove him to the bathroom for the next hour. All of this was tolerable, but what was not tolerable was the relapse into dysphoria that followed. A flashback. The pain and nausea disappeared by mid-day, but the dysphoria held on. All was Hopeless. All was Lost. He hated everything in the world. *If this is the new me, I should end it all now. This was the primal question for Camus, and I answer "Yes." End it all now.* Chase barely made it through the day.

Remarkably, the dysphoria completely vanished by the next morning. The curse had lasted a mere 24 hours, resolved during his next round of sleep. It was as though the meningoencephalitis had returned as a refresher, to remind him that more tempering was needed to forge the soul of a nascent Christian Ubermensch.

One month later, he woke again at 4:00am sharp, a boring pain in the right eye, a crescent-shaped tingling of skin around this eye, a global headache, nausea, an hour on the toilet, all of which was followed by the hideous dysphoria. Once again, it was completely gone the next morning. He was fresh as a daisy after 24 hours.

Chase's neurologist could make nothing of his symptoms, which also included complete loss of smell, an ominous symptom on occasion. "Atypical cluster headaches," she said, trying him on a series of drugs that didn't help. Then, "atypical migraines." Later, "a bizarre sleep disorder" (to which Chase resorted to a concise prayer: "Guard my sleep.") Finally, his neurologist admitted, "I don't have a clue."

Then, one day while sweating on the treadmill (the gym was Chase's new answer to all ills), he caught a glimpse of himself in the mirror. The crescent of tingling skin by his right eye was pink bordering on red, a three-inch curve, a crescent moon, where the blood flow to the skin, now heightened through exercise, yielded the discoloration. The sight of the red crescent turned his blood cold.

Truly, a curse was at work, and it was more than mental. He kept a log of his symptoms, always starting with the 4:00 o'clock spontaneous wake-up and the pain in his right eye, the crescent of tingling skin, and finally, the worst part – the dysphoria that jeopardized the rest of the day.

The slightest frustration on a cursed day could launch him from dysphoria into a tirade. He didn't need a high threshold anymore. Soon, he realized he desperately needed to stay at home on such days since the curse was not going away until it had run its 24-hour course, 48 at the most. Cycle after cycle reinforced the permanence. Yet, such a need to stay at home was impossible. He had patients scheduled in the O.R. – breast cancer patients who needed surgery. He couldn't repeatedly cancel patients at 4:00 a.m., just three hours before he made the incision. No, he had to go to work. It was a hideous affliction, and one that he could do nothing about. He recalled the gypsy's poem from the classic horror movie, where a tortured soul deals with such a monthly curse:

Even a man who is pure in heart
And says his prayers by night
May become a wolf when the wolfbane blooms
And the autumn moon is bright.

Yet, a different internal voice tried to convince Chase that it was *not* a curse. Perhaps this latest development was more like Paul's proverbial thorn. Patriarchs who had come face-to-face with God always lost their glow over time. Entire nations lost their glow over time, forgetting freedom and deliverance. Instead of a curse, maybe it was a blessing designed to help him maintain the glow. With a lunar reminder, he could stay the course on this mysterious path that was being cleared for him.

For 15 years, all signs had been pointing away from surgery and toward – it was becoming clear now – the laboratory where his research would unfurl a miracle. He had been given a sneak peek at premalignancy in 1977, long before clinicians were made aware. Later, at Far West, he had made the pitch to researchers (and potential donors) that the Breast Pavilion would become home to the "molecular biologic Pap smear of the breast," while everyone else on the planet researched treatment *after* cancer had already occurred.

From human bodies to organs to tissues to cells to molecules to atoms, it was all happening to steer him back to his original goal, long before he considered surgery, even before he had considered psychiatry – rather, all the way back to childhood when he dreamed of making great medical discoveries in the world of research.

If he didn't respond to God's direction soon, the trials and tragedies would only continue. He'd been as blind as the Pharaoh of the Old Testament who tolerated ten plagues before releasing Israel.

Now that he saw God's plan, he would need to proceed cautiously. For even though Pharaoh acquiesced after ten plagues, his submission was only temporary. From *Exodus*: "And the Lord hardened the heart of Pharaoh king of Egypt, and he pursued after the children of Israel..."

Yes, it was disconcerting that *the Lord hardens hearts*. Could such hardening happen even to a man who is pure in heart and says his prayers at night?

20
QUANTUM LEAPS

What a peculiar twist of fate for the now-twisted phrase "quantum leap." In everyday use, it has come to mean the exact opposite of its true design – which is, the *smallest* possible change known in the universe, when an electron of an atom hops from one energy shell to another. Then, when enough photon-emitting quantum leaps occur, it results in visible light.

It was the tiny leaps that illuminated Chase Callaway's dream. One by one, after years of discontent and turmoil, the pieces began to fall together. Or, better said, the pieces were forced together. For when he reflected on his progress, each major advance had a common denominator – *enlightened insubordination*. Every critical hurdle he faced had been overcome through bypassing the academic hierarchy, achieved with the Raven sisters at his side while Hardy Studebaker was careful to remain invisible, or nearly so.

The effectiveness of this strategy was marvelous. With every new problem, the glass walls of academia grew thick and guaranteed that the solution would be both visible and impossible. For instance, when Dr. Callaway petitioned the dean and the vice-chancellor to recruit a medical geneticist to supervise the upcoming revolution in testing for mutations that predispose to adult-onset cancer, his letters went unanswered, his phone calls unreturned. Glass walls grew thick. So, Jody Raven swung her battle axe, Darby Raven wooed, and Hardy

Studebaker waved his wand. Into Chase's lap plopped a $100,000 grant to establish a program for the new discipline of breast cancer genetic testing.

Yet, when the Runnymeade Foundation published their annual report, the grant was credited to Thatcher Nolan Taylor, MD. A large photo of T.N.T. filled half of one page, while a description of the BRCA genetic testing program filled the rest. Chase's name was nowhere to be found even though he had single-handedly forced the issue and would be in charge of the new program.

This was the dark energy that accompanied each quantum leap – anonymity for Chase. He didn't mind, though, for it supported his contention that his trouble-filled career had stripped away personal ego, allowing him to thrive as the unseen power generator that would make Far West Texas University Breast Pavilion unique. Now, he was extending that concept to an obscure destiny in the laboratory where, as he'd done in the clinic, he would coordinate and unite all the players into a single cause.

Problems at the Breast Pavilion seemed to be melting away, save one – the critical position of breast radiologist (and with it, financial stability). Losses were accumulating at a rapid rate, insurmountable according to some, yet the Department of Radiology offered no help with recruitment.

Molly St. Martin, the "top female radiologist in Midland," had previously refused Chase's offers (twice). Dr. St. Martin was a general radiologist who had reservations about "painting myself into a corner professionally" by restricting her practice to breast imaging. Additionally, she had reservations about the Department of Radiology at Far West, and even some reservations about Chase Callaway. She had never met Dr. Callaway in person, but after his previous calls to recruit her, she researched his background, learned of his checkered past, and saw no reason to align herself to needless risk.

As a counterbalance, Molly's older sister had once been the college roommate of the ex-wife of Will Glendenning, one of Chase's old classmates in medical school (before Will dropped out to focus on a PhD). From that source – Claudia Glendenning, calling herself "number one fan" of Chase Callaway – Molly learned that Chase had been widely considered "Most Likely to Succeed" at every level of education. So, Molly decided to keep an open mind.

But then, an odd series of events occurred in Molly's life, leading her to Matherville. Her son wanted to play high school basketball, but Midland was a football town. Matherville, on the other hand, was the only basketball town in west Texas. Then, Molly's daughter was proving to be a standout in gymnastics, and the best instructor in west Texas was smack dab in the heart of Matherville. Finally, Molly's husband, a CPA, was offered a job in Matherville with a firm promising twice his current pay. While Molly prided herself in her detached rationality, even she had to admit that the stars align occasionally. All four members of her family, in a matter of six months, felt themselves guided to Matherville.

Dr. Molly St. Martin called Thatcher Nolan Taylor, M.D., and said, "Let's talk."

Then, Molly met Chase, dropping by his office one hour before her official interview with T.N.T. Chase was struck by her instant warmth and likeability. Since a breast radiologist assumes the role of primary care physician, first impressions were critical, and Molly had the knack. She was tall and lean, with auburn hair pulled into a bun, her dark eyes framed by large glasses that reflected powerful intellect, valid or not. Most importantly, she had that rare talent of transmitting instant camaraderie.

Over the course of one hour, Chase revealed the historical background and future plans for the Pavilion, along with the inside scoop about the Raven sisters, the "community support," and Hardy Studebaker. Most of all, though, he explained his style of management through encouragement, and how it had worked nicely for the employees of the Pavilion, as well as students and residents, *but* – had no impact at all on the academic hierarchy where all the barriers lay.

Molly seemed impressed, and she offered an occasional smile, but her eyes were piercing the more she spoke, leaving him slightly nervous. She looked at her watch while he was rambling about being first in Texas to introduce genetic testing, interrupting with: "I'm supposed to be meeting with Dr. Taylor now. Is he coming down here, or should I go upstairs?"

"He's on his way down, due any minute."

"Let me tell you in advance what I'm about to tell Dr. Taylor. I *am* interested in the position. I'm not asking for any more money than I make now, but if Dr. Taylor can match my current salary, I'll talk details."

Chase couldn't believe his ears. He'd been snarled in radiologic hell for six long years, two of which were after the Pavilion had opened its doors. Now, this lovely woman waltzes into his office and says that she wants to "talk details."

Once T.N.T. joined them, Chase knew his boss was impressed from the start. "Whatever you want," Dr. Taylor replied, over and over, to detail after detail. Thatcher had once confided to Chase that the "radiology problem" had become the worst nightmare in his 30-year career at Far West.

But then, Molly St. Martin dropped the bombshell. "And finally, I will not work at this university as part of the Department of Radiology. Put me in *your* department, Dr. Taylor, and we have a deal."

Thatcher Nolan Taylor squirmed in his chair, then one hand crept up the back of his head where he began to twirl his hair. "Well, that would, uh, certainly be unorthodox to have a radiologist in the surgery department, but I don't see why – well, I'll certainly look into it."

Molly continued, "It's non-negotiable, if that helps. I won't work in that department."

Before Dr. Taylor could answer, Chase was called into the hallway by the newly hired clinic manager at the Breast Pavilion who told him that a patient from Midland was not going to wait any longer. "She's new to you, and her X-rays are hanging in your office. If you'll just go in and say 'hi' to her, we can stall until you're done here."

Chase glanced at the mammograms, spotted the cancer, then read the radiologist's report that stated, "A skin marker was placed on the palpable lump, and there are no abnormalities beneath the marker." Yet, there on the X-ray, the size of a walnut, was a breast cancer. As often happens, especially in the elderly, the compression plate had dragged the loose skin forward during the X-ray, so that the lead marker on the skin was no longer overlying the cancer. Tunnel vision that burrowed only beneath the marker meant a missed cancer. The radiologist would have been better off if there'd been no marker at all, freed of the human impulse toward tunnel vision. When Chase read the name of the radiologist, he gulped, then whispered: "Molly St. Martin, M.D."

"Now *there's* a coincidence. She's about to sign a deal with Dr. Taylor for more money than I'm making," said Chase to his right-hand business manager, Christi Bloom, who was standing at his side. The twosome were speechless, for a moment.

"What do we do?" asked Christi.

"Nothing. Nothing at all. We've got to make a leap of faith here. Besides, she'll need to learn everything over anyway. Like I did, starting from scratch. She'll do it. I'm not too worried. Remember, everyone says she's the best general radiologist in the area."

Christi wasn't so sure. "Well, it's hard to believe she's in there with Dr. Taylor, calling all the shots right now."

Chase added, "But a big point in her favor – you'll never guess what she asked me earlier in my interview. She asked what *I* needed. Me. Do you believe that? I've not had a single physician working on this Pavilion deal ever ask me that. It's always what *they* need. Yet, Molly said she knew full well she was in the driver's seat on this radiologist position, so I should let her know up front what *I* needed, and she would include it in her demand list. My head is still reeling with that one."

"Well, what did you ask for?"

"Nothing at first. She caught me off guard. Then it occurred to me that, as much debt as we're piling up without the radiologist position filled, I'm never going to get that medical director fee I wrote into the pro forma. Never. It's a pipe dream, all while my surgical income is crushed by the demands of the Pavilion. So, given that one of *her* requests is that her malpractice premium be paid through the Breast Pavilion financial control point, well, I said I'd like that same perk she has *instead of* a medical director's fee. The amount is almost identical to what I'd originally asked for."

"Well, that doesn't do our Pavilion balance sheet any good," Christi said, ever watchful of the mounting debt. "As a matter of fact, two malpractice premiums are going to hurt pretty badly."

"At first, I know. But I've got a feeling Molly is going to make this place fly, and when that happens, we won't even remember expenses like this. We'll be paying our own way easily."

Molly St. Martin accepted the position.

Thatcher Nolan Taylor sent Dr. St. Martin one dozen roses, while at the same time confessing to Chase that Thatcher had lost a lifetime friend in the process. The Chairman of Radiology was outraged that the Department of Surgery would hire its own radiologist. Such a violation of academic protocol was more important than friendship, as it turned out. Chase felt no remorse whatsoever (of course, it wasn't his friend lost). T.N.T. had finally taken a stand, perhaps the most critical stand in the history of the Breast Pavilion. Now, the entire breast center was housed within the Department of Surgery, to a degree far greater than even Chase had imagined. Notably, each step of the way had been opposed by T.N.T.

Fellow physicians stopped Chase in the hallway to congratulate him on the capture of Molly St. Martin. There was universal love for this person that he barely knew. And when one of Molly's former classmates said with a wry smile, "Well, she's a great radiologist, but you better have your life in order," Chase let the comment slip by. It concerned him not. His life was coming into wonderful order, finally.

Indeed, the change at the Breast Pavilion was abrupt. When an electron jumps from one energy shell to another, there is no intermediate stage. It's circling in one shell, then instantaneously, it skips to another – just like that. The "quantum" applies to the abruptness, not magnitude. "Overnight," the Breast Pavilion became the cutting-edge center for multidisciplinary breast care in west Texas. Breast cancer surgeries had quadrupled at Far West during Chase's tenure, so far, but the primary beneficiary there was College Hospital. The critical component for financial success of the Breast Pavilion was that ever-lurking pot of gold – the technical component of the radiology fees where the money flowed toward the medical school rather than College Hospital.

Chase watched Dr. St. Martin soak up breast cancer knowledge like a sponge, all while offering patients personalized, sympathetic care. He was also intrigued by her leadership style, derived (she said) from a self-help book titled, *PEP* (Purpose-Effectiveness-Power). Molly, in fact, later admitted that she agreed to work with Chase only after recognizing that he appeared to be operating "naturally" by using the very principles outlined in *PEP*. The *PEP* book had sold countless millions and had created its own universe that extended from catch phrases on coffee cups to cultish seminars. The *PEP* lexicon of catch-phrases permeated conversations about business management, spoken by people who had never even heard of *PEP*, including Chase Callaway.

Fair enough, he thought. *She's studying breast cancer, so I'll study her book.* When he read *PEP*, he marveled at the simple espousals of common sense. Building a nest from the twigs of antiquity, the author had established himself as guru to millions even though openly admitting there was nothing new in the book at all. The author had simply organized classic concepts into the common language of our time. Chase was fascinated at the book's success, and he wondered if he could do the same thing if he harnessed the back porch philosophy of his nanny, Sukie Spurlock.

When he looked at the references listed at the end of *PEP*, he realized he had read half of the sources by age 18, and most of the rest by age 25. So, he felt a bit phony when he started incorporating the lingo into his speech to impress Molly. Be it a benign form of manipulation or not, it seemed to work well, for the transformation of the Breast Pavilion came from Molly's light, not his, photons emanating from her quantum leap.

Drs. Callaway and St. Martin quickly established patient protocols that would have set the curve for the entire United States, had anyone bothered to check. Women were not called back for abnormal mammograms – the work-up was completed on the first visit, including biopsy if needed, such that the national average of 40 days from X-ray to pathology was compressed to a *single day*. All biopsies were reviewed in an interdisciplinary diagnostic conference on Tuesday, then all new cancer patients were presented at an interdisciplinary conference on Wednesday, with all specialties in attendance, plus the patient. By Chase's reckoning, there was not another breast center in the country this efficient and this patient friendly.

The idea of interdisciplinary breast centers as the next step beyond mammography screening facilities was starting to appear in the women's magazines. When someone brought Chase an article about a medical mecca in New York having established such a center, anointing it as the "ultimate" in breast care, Chase realized what he'd accomplished locally. The Breast Pavilion was far more streamlined. He wrote the director of the "ultimate" center, describing how they did things at the obscure Far West Breast Pavilion, and received a response: "Congratulations. I've never heard of any center this advanced. Do the women of west Texas appreciate what they have?"

In fact, precious few understood. Far West Texas University wouldn't acknowledge its own Breast Pavilion. No advertisements. No public relations efforts. No coverage in its own alumni magazine, where Chase repeatedly begged that an article be devoted to the Breast Pavilion. One huge exception: the Raven sisters and their Advisory Board generated publicity through frequent fund-raisers. Though, for the average human, there was no explanation as to what was going on at the Breast Pavilion coupled to its research agenda. So, the citizens with money and power were fully informed about the Breast Pavilion, but not prospective patients. Not the public.

"If we're going to dig ourselves out of debt, we've got to have help," Chase pleaded on multiple occasions to the dean. "We've done something really special for this university. Are you aware that we've launched genetic testing after considerable red tape, and that the only two spots approved to do this in Texas are M.D. Anderson and us? Our numbers are improving through word of mouth, but we need to get into high gear to get out of debt. We need some publicity in Matherville and the surrounding area. All the pieces of the puzzle are now in place."

There was no response from the Far West Texas College of Medicine.

The bottomless pit of financial losses finally found its nadir. Patient numbers started to rise, but the Pavilion was already deeply in debt when Molly joined the staff. Chase monitored patient numbers daily, and had been charting the debt (unfortunately, housed in the Department of Surgery) every week for several years. Unable to face his own Advisory Board, he had cancelled meetings a year earlier. Yet, after

Molly joined the Pavilion staff, Chase reinstituted monthly meetings of the board where Molly endeared herself from the start by baking casseroles and cookies for each luncheon. New money was tapped. More talks were given. Chase filled his days with these comings and goings, barely able to maintain his practice. Always, he was focused five and ten years down the road.

Students were the pipeline for success. Chase continued his speeches in high schools and regional colleges, trying to attract students into Far West medical school and, eventually, the Breast Pavilion. "There'll be a place for everyone – radiologists, surgeons, oncologists, plastic surgeons, researchers, and on and on." He expanded the summer fellowship programs in order to accommodate more medical students where they could work side-by-side with Dr. St. Martin. Furthermore, he expanded opportunities for them in the research lab.

One unexplainable deficiency remained. As head of the residency training program in general surgery, Dr. Porter Piscotel still refused year after year to allow surgery residents to spend even one month under Chase. Each year as the residency rotation schedule was being compiled, Chase would say, "Porter, I'm telling you, the surgery residents are functioning at a very low level when it comes to breast. The first-year medical students rotating with me are amazed that our Chiefs don't even know how to hang a mammogram on a view box, and they sure don't know what they're looking at. Yet, I frequently have gynecology residents rotating with me. If general surgery doesn't get on the stick, we're going to lose breast cancer to the other specialties. Or, at a minimum, breast surgery is going to break off."

Porter looked intense, as if listening while wheels turned in his head. "You know, Chase, at the national level, the Boards don't require a rotation on a breast service. After all, most universities don't even have a breast center. But I'll tell you what. I don't like the way the radiologists have taken away surgical biopsies from us. I can put residents in the Pavilion if you'll teach them how to do those needle biopsies."

Chase wanted to yell his response, but he held himself in check. "Well, Porter, first of all, our residents have no business doing biopsies when they can't even interpret the images, or the thing they're going to biopsy. These are, remember, image-guided biopsies. They've got to have some core knowledge of interpretation. Get this – I've been administering written tests yearly, for about five years now, to both medical students who do electives with me, and to our residents. The medical students always score above ninety percent. The test is fairly easy. Well, guess how the residents do? They *average* fifty percent. Their average score is a failing score. We had a chief resident last year who scored 25% on multiple choice with four options on each question. Go figure."

"Chase, you don't seem to understand. Surgeons are procedure oriented. If you would simply teach them to do biopsies, they'd learn the background. We have a chicken-egg situation here. You can't expect surgeons to spend a long time in ground school."

Chase recognized a dead end, so he tried another objection to the biopsy issue: "But more importantly, I have a great working relationship with Molly St. Martin. She is teaching radiology residents how to do these new stereotactic biopsies. If I start encroaching on her territory – well – I can't even start to consider that. That relationship with her is very important to me now, after what I've been through with that radiology department. What's more, the very backbone of my philosophy, what makes the Pavilion work, is that I respect the territory of the other specialties. Once they see I'm not trying to take anything away from them, a spirit of cooperation just comes naturally. It's an interesting paradox that, if you respect territories, the walls between them seem to crumble. Try to break through those walls, and, well, that's the ugly side of human history, medicine in particular. So, I simply can't have surgery residents doing the image-guided biopsies."

Porter shifted in his chair, grunted a few times, checked his watch to remind Chase that the welcome was ending, then said, "Well, I hope you'll re-think that. By the way, the residents complain that you never let them operate on your private patients. How are they gonna learn?"

"Uh...Thatcher still does his own cases from start to finish. I really don't think I'm out of line here."

"Well, I can't remember the last time I didn't let the senior residents do at least part of the case."

"Our referred patients are plenty different, Porter. Some general surgeons don't want to do pancreatic surgery or the difficult post-op care, so they send you their cases directly. You've cornered the market on these very difficult procedures. This isn't the case in breast surgery. My patients don't come from other surgeons. Other surgeons are quite confident in their breast cancer skill set. My patients are self-referred. They've heard about the cosmetic things I'm doing, different than the community docs, even on lumpectomies. Very frequently, they ask me to *promise* that I will perform every step of the operation."

Porter frowned and looked at his watch again.

Chase could hear the strain in his own voice as he continued, "Back to residents rotating with me, however, I'd probably be more inclined to let them do part of the case if I was working with them on a daily basis, where I had confidence that they were reading and preparing for cases. As it is now, they send in an intern to be my first assistant."

"That's because the senior residents know they're not gonna get to do the case. It's a vicious circle. Another chicken-egg problem."

"I can see that. However, it's still amazing that the most common malignancy our residents will treat in private practice is breast cancer, and they don't even rotate on the breast service. Yet, they spend six months minimum, maybe nine or twelve, out of their five years of training on the cardiac service."

"Chase, I don't set the standards. There's the American Board of Surgery, the Residency Review Committee, and, too, Dr. Dagmar needs those residents on his service. There's a lot of work on that rotation. The care of the critically ill patient plays a crucial role in general surgery."

In the end, not a single general surgery resident spent even one month with Dr. Callaway at the Breast Pavilion during Piscotel's tenure as residency program director. Indeed, this deficiency became common knowledge among medical students headed for general surgery residencies. Fully aware they would *not* rotate at the Pavilion as a resident, it became standard to take a senior elective with either Dr. Callaway or Dr. St. Martin, understanding that this would be their only opportunity to attend "ground school."

Editor's note: Deleted here is a lengthy tale of Dr. Callaway's one attempt to let a chief resident do a critical part of a mastectomy – the axillary node dissection. Feeling the pressure from Porter Piscotel to let the residents do more (and hopefully softening Porter's position on letting residents rotate on the breast service), Chase decided to allow one of the chiefs to remove the axillary nodes, knowing there were several key structures that could suffer injury. It helped that this particular resident was widely considered the most gifted technician among the current batch of residents. In contrast to the proclamation made to surgical patients by faculty – "I'll be standing right there with the resident" – a mistake could occur with such rapidity, there was no assurance it could be stopped. In this particular patient, the chief resident was showing off his dexterity, operating way too fast, with Chase repeatedly insisting, "Slow down." Then a muscle jerked abruptly. "Oops." The long thoracic nerve, hidden by fatty tissue, was divided with a quick snip of the scissors. It would result in a "winged scapula," often believed a cosmetic issue only, but in fact, it created a modest functional loss with shoulder mobility. Chase was sickened, so much so that he could barely finish the case. After performing a nerve repair on the spot, there was some hope that the disability would be minimal over time. The next day, the resident proudly stated to Chase that it must have been a minor nerve because there was no winged scapula. When Chase examined the patient, however, the deformity was obvious, and it was because of the patient's obesity that the resident had not been able to appreciate the shoulder blade's new position. Chase said to himself, "And there you have it. The resident has already developed the most useful tool for a surgeon – denial." Chase never let a resident work on one of his private patients after that incident. The vicious cycle would continue.

Then, a different challenge arose when Chase encountered a force that was swaying top-tier students *away* from Far West for their residency training. Remarkably, the culprit was Thatcher Nolan Taylor, MD. Unable to let the incident go by, Chase met with his boss. "Dr. Taylor, I had a question about Lori Van Buskirk, one of the top students I've seen come through here. I learned about her in the undergraduate student newspaper years ago and started recruiting her the first day she entered med school. You know, she did that summer fellowship with me. I had sorta hoped she might end up as Molly's first fellow in breast imaging someday and maybe a partner after that. Well, I just heard that you landed her a spot at M.D. Anderson for her residency."

Chase struggled to avoid any hint of rebuke in his voice.

"Chase, I'm sure you're aware, for someone going into academics like Lori, that the location of your training is everything. You know as well as I do that, in actuality, geography means nothing, but unfortunately, the understood law of academics is location, location, location. It's why I asked you many years ago if you were headed to academics."

"I understand, but I'm trying to build for the future at the Pavilion with our best students." Chase realized his tone was turning sour, so he cut himself off.

Dr. Taylor looked at him for a moment before twirling a lock of his hair. Then he said, "Chase, for someone going into academics, Far West Texas is a dead end. You and I both know, for instance, that your friend Franklin Cooper is on the road to national prominence. It would be a professional death knell for him to come back to west Texas and assume the chairmanship here after I step down. I always try to put the individual ahead of the university."

Chase's heart sank. His good friend, Franklin Cooper, was the perfect choice to replace T.N.T. should the day ever come. Obviously, it was not going to happen.

Chase tried to see it from Thatcher's point of view. Was this anti-recruiting strategy of Thatcher simply an effort to compensate for his own regrets? Did T.N.T. feel he had settled for less than his potential? In all probability, yes. He could have been the premier surgeon in the country, president of the American College of Surgeons. Not after he chose to stay at Far West, however. Nevertheless, Lori Van Buskirk was not an isolated incident. In fact, Thatcher Nolan Taylor took considerable pride placing the brightest students at the best location, location, location.

At least Chase's protégée Nola Kastl was staying put. Nola was a workhorse. She had already consumed two textbooks of breast pathology while still a medical student. Now, as a resident, she could interpret slides with more expertise than the faculty. Sometimes, Chase worried that she was too devoted, for she had an eerie way of asking, "Please let me know what else I can do to help you. Your dream is my dream." Her deep-set, gray-green eyes would never blink and never stray as she spoke.

Nola was already commandeering the new video microscope (purchased through fashion shows) for the conferences, and she was establishing herself as part of Chase's team in the research lab as well, focusing on the study of premalignant breast tissue (again, funded by fashion shows).

Chase had introduced Nola to a research pathologist who was using a computerized microscope to study a variety of tissues, primarily brain samples from the Psychiatric Pavilion. Chase's vision was to use the unique scope on benign breast biopsies, converting subtle changes to mathematical quantities and thus, taking much of the wishy-washy human element out of interpretation. He believed the natural history, that is, the future probability of becoming cancer, might be predicted from these mathematical calculations. In order to forge the collaboration with the image analysis expert, Chase contributed $15,000 in seed money (funded by a single donor) as the first installment to begin the project.

One day, research assistant Gunnar Pixley stopped Chase in the hall. "I just heard you've been supporting Dr. Pierpont and his new microscope in the image analysis lab?"

"Why, yes. I'm contributing part of his tech's salary so that his lab will look at breast tissue, just like they're already doing on brain. Why?"

"I wish you would have told me. Pierpont's microscope is only a prototype, and it doesn't even work. It's been collecting cobwebs for nine months, the entire time you've been paying him. To make matters worse, Pierpont is a notorious Studebilker. He's a master at scrounging money from people. He can sniff out a pile of cash anywhere in the medical center."

"But...Pierpont tells me every time I talk with him that the research is going 'fabulously'. He says he's almost ready to write a paper."

Chase was furious. The donated money he had given to Pierpont was from one of his board members who wanted to honor her best friend, a young woman who had died of breast cancer. How could he ever face the lady again? Chase had been scammed.

He stormed into Pierpont's lab, and with a pointed finger touching the researcher's chest, Chase said, "Is it true your scope doesn't even work? That you have no data whatsoever?"

"Well, there's some kinks I need to work out…"

"So, nine months of nothing?"

"Well, that's one way of looking at it."

"That's fraudulent. Worse, you've defrauded the woman who donated that money. That money was entrusted to me to honor Her—Dead—Friend. I'm pulling my support of your lab, pronto."

Dr. Pierpont, of course, was outraged, as only those with exposed culpability know. Of course, the incident became one more example that Chase Callaway could be a hothead.

No more hand-outs to the scoundrels who lurked around these ivy-covered walls. Chase vowed he would do the research himself from now on. With Nola Kastl serving as his liaison to pathology, and with the help of the Pixleys, Chase's hand could be in everything, everywhere at Far West.

He would immerse himself in each project, making sure each donated penny went directly into productive research. 100% donated – 100% utilized for cancer research. No administrative overhead like the cancer societies and foundations. "100% donated, 100% used," became a new selling point in his presentations to the community.

Get involved in research, he did. A PhD in Italy claimed she had discovered a blood test to detect breast cancer in its earliest stages. Again, using donated funds, matched by the Studebaker Medical Research Foundation, Chase arranged to fly the PhD to the United States so that the Breast Pavilion could be the initial site of primary clinical testing. Chase called it "home run" research. If the test worked, it would revolutionize breast cancer detection, and Far West would be forever on the map. New forms of breast imaging were on the way, such as MRI, yet the expense for general population screening would be prohibitive. However, a positive blood test could be the revolutionary key that directed physicians to use something like MRI if mammograms were negative.

Chase organized campus experts from the biostatistics department to the basic scientists to clinicians, then wrote his first scientific grant to an improbable new source of money for breast cancer research – the Department of Defense – asking to refine the blood test, correlate its results with biopsy findings, then introduce a clinical trial. All this was predicated on the notion that, someday, proper patient selection would be critical for a second tier of breast imaging beyond mammography.

The Department of Defense slammed the grant to the ground with a low-score rejection. First, they criticized the absence of a breast cancer track record at Far West, specifically the principal investigator (Chase who, at age 45, didn't have a single grant to his name, not to mention his lowly "assistant professor" status), then they pulled the rug from beneath the very foundation of the grant, which had been predicated on the large number of cancers missed by routine mammography – "We're not sure how the Principal Investigator has arrived at these low sensitivity numbers for mammography. A 90% cancer detection rate with mammography is well-known and highly satisfactory, begging the question as to why a second level of breast imaging would be needed for screening."

Chase was undeterred. He saw the incredible potential of a blood test. He knew the limitations of mammography. He knew X-rays missed far more cancers than anyone was willing to admit. A blood test could fill the gap, guiding doctors to look harder, to use special techniques, to use the new methods of breast imaging that were still in development.

On the day before the PhD from Italy was to arrive in Matherville, Chase received a call from California. His old partner, Ted Zink, MD, the embodiment of healthy living, had undergone a one-vessel angioplasty that inadvertently caused a heart attack, which was complicated by a stroke that was then fatal. It was the domino effect, well known to practitioners, especially when working on fellow physicians.

Expected to serve as a pallbearer at the funeral, Chase said to one of Dr. Zink's daughters, "I...I can't make it. I'm sorry. I'm hosting a scientist that I flew here from Italy for only two days. I'm the one, you see, who got her to come to the U.S...."

In truth, there was no excuse, and this was reflected in his stumbling and persistent apologies. He was sick inside and ashamed of himself when he let the biblical mantra play in his head: "Let the dead bury the dead." He would not forgive himself easily for this decision.

In spite of the failed Department of Defense grant application (as well as local grant failures), Chase Callaway spent the next five years trying to facilitate research on the blood test from Italy, flying to New York on multiple occasions for meetings with venture capitalists and intellectual property law firms. In the end, it was a bust. Nothing ever came to pass. The test never made it to the U.S. for validation studies. It was a total waste of time. He could have written 10 or 20 scientific papers of no particular importance during the time spent on his "home run."

Chase still had great faith that, with the right collaborators, his research empire would blossom. For example, there had been a major coup already with one of his animal models. Working with an aggressive tumor cell line, injecting cellular suspensions, one of Chase's team scientists, Dr. Kesey, had cured the disease, at least in three rats. No one on campus had been able to slow these tumors, which killed within 30 days. Through laser destruction of the tumors when pea-sized, leaving the dead tumor in place for the antigens to arouse the immune system, then adding an immune-stimulating concoction, the three rats (out of 60) were not only cured, but when repeated cells were injected, the rats were immune. No cancers developed, no matter how many times the rats were injected – a sharp contrast to the 100% mortality in untreated rats. Dr. Kesey was ecstatic.

The timing was perfect. Immediately prior to this rat experiment, Kesey had been told that, at age 35, he was a scientific has-been. The CEO of the Studebaker Medical Research Foundation had told him to pack his bags. With heartless criticism, the CEO had maligned Kesey to the point where the scientist was quite depressed about his future. Chase had consoled Kesey and tried to help him find a job elsewhere, using every contact he had, but without success.

Then, the three rats. Cured. Future cancer prevented. As a result, the CEO of the research foundation met with Dr. Kesey, nullifying the earlier 'pack your bags' mandate, and instead, announced plans for a new biotechnology company based on the immunotherapy of breast cancer. Even Dr. Kesey joked about the prematurity of such a company based on three rats, but given his circumstance, he went along, nonetheless. Importantly, he would have a job. The CEO now had a justification for placement of donated funds that were earmarked for breast cancer – "We have recently cured breast cancer in the laboratory. All that's left is to transfer the technique into humans."

Freya Pixley had done the manual labor, Nola Kastl had helped with the pathology, and Chase had financed the study with his research slush fund (fashion show donations). Also, Chase had studied the aggressive cell line for years, trying to break its code. Yet, it had been Freya who kept the model running, passing cells from generation to generation, for several years before the big discovery. Chase had thought the model too costly and too virulent. However, Freya persisted. "Someone," she would say, "someone is going to come along and find something that works." She was correct. The running joke was that the company should be called Tri-Rodentia Technologies, but instead, Dr. Kesey underwent a transformation from outcast to Chief Scientific Officer of the new biotech company – Immunomodulator Technologies.

Finally, a success, of sorts, in the lab. It became harder and harder to trek back to the Breast Pavilion when the thrill of discovery was in the research laboratories. Chase was already on the precipice, considering how to finance a leap to the laboratory when yet another development shoved him one step closer to the edge.

Although he had escaped the influx of managed care in California, the wave caught him in west Texas, and Chase found himself once again begging to become a "preferred provider" as if this were an honor. However, managed care was not a fixed entity, and it gradually mutated into monstrous oppression as it sought any excuse to deny "providership." Once an applicant checked the Yes box on the insurer's application form, denoting "past history of addiction," he or she was no longer preferred.

Some insurance companies wanted lengthy explanations, others wanted endorsements from the chairman of the impaired physicians committee, others wanted letters of recommendation from colleagues swearing Chase had never been drunk in the operating room, and some wanted actual medical records from the Riverdell Rehabilitation Center where he had bared his soul to counselors – indeed, his most sordid confessions now lay in black and white print in the lap of some insurance company clerk. All this, to accept a reduction in his surgical fees.

Chase was nearing seven years of sobriety, yet the consequences of his indiscretions were gaining momentum due to managed care snooping, rather than fading with time. While his patients were being afforded all sorts of legislation to ensure their privacy, to the point doctors could barely communicate with each other about their care, doctors were treated with the opposite end of the stick – open records to the public that generated a media frenzy where the local TV stations ran features on "Dangerous Doctors in Your Town." These exposés were based on medical board actions against physicians, almost always related to addiction, and usually *after* the physician was many years into successful sobriety.

As he struggled to exonerate himself with insurance companies and clear his name, his reputation as *the* breast surgeon of west Texas continued to grow (no mind that he was the *only* dedicated breast surgeon in this part of the state). As his reputation grew, his detractors multiplied. Making matters worse, even though he encouraged all his second opinion patients to go back to their original surgeons, few did. Thus, each second opinion generated a new physician-enemy. While the surgeons of Matherville and neighboring towns tried to convince their breast cancer patients that there was no such thing as a "breast surgeon," the demand for Chase's services grew and grew. Now, Molly St. Martin was having the same effect on mammography centers in west Texas where patient numbers plummeted in favor of the burgeoning Far West Texas University Breast Pavilion.

This was the state of affairs when two radiologists from a competing mammography center felt it was their civic duty to contact Darby and Jody Raven, treating them to lunch and an eye-opening epiphany. The physicians felt "an obligation" to let the Raven sisters know they were supporting a drug addict who crawled his way back to Texas after getting kicked out of California.

The Raven sisters relayed the encounter to Chase. "We didn't want to tell you, but we thought you ought to know what's going on. This isn't the first time we've been taken aside," Darby said. "In fact, over the past seven years, this is the third time, is it not, Jody?" "No, the fourth," said her sister. "Jerks. Jealous jerks. All of them."

"I'm sorry," he said. "I saw it as remote history. I never dreamed it would haunt me like this. It's worse as time goes on, worse with longer sobriety, worse with greater success. I should have told you both the details at the beginning. It's just that I operate under the assumption that everyone around me knows the whole story. It was so public, after all. I always assume my track record in medicine speaks for itself."

"You do understand, Chase, that it doesn't matter to us," said Darby as she slipped her hand across the luncheon table and touched the back of Chase's clenched fist. "We did know. We knew all along, from the beginning, even before Thatcher gave you the nod. Then, of course, Thatcher assured us you were his favorite – you and Franklin Cooper. He said you two were the best. We trust his opinion totally. That said – we had other sources, other motivations, besides Thatcher." Chase couldn't imagine what Darby was talking about.

In a way, the two sisters had become a part of him – like a grace note to a musical note, or a flam in percussion, where richness is added by these nearly silent additions. The sisters added volume to his vision, Darby as the grace note, Jody as the flam. They had invested their reputations in him. For whatever their motivations, even beyond the influence of T.N.T., he knew he could never, ever, let the two of them down.

21
LE DÉJEUNER PERPÉTUEL

Editor's note: Parallel with his gradual deterioration, Dr. Callaway began recording brief notes summarizing all encounters, the vast majority of which are uninformative as it pertains here. However, his contact with the Raven sisters increased in frequency to the point he would chat on the phone with one or both every day, sometimes several conversations, sometimes quite lengthy. Fund-raising was taking a back seat to the internal politics that kept Chase preoccupied. He welcomed their counsel in all matters.

So many issues were at stake, the three of them decided to meet every Friday at noon for lunch (Dr. Callaway's "academic day"), to strategize for the next week. Indeed, communication among the threesome was so frequent, so intense, that one could say they were chained together in a perennial lunch.

The two sisters were such a stark contrast, it was hard for Chase to believe they had the same parents. In his writings, he would often refer to them as Kate and Audrey, fully aware that the two Hepburn actresses were not related. Still, Jody Raven shot straight from the hip, articulating rapid-fire, intimidating nearly everyone. Darby was almost a foot shorter than her sister, with a voice so sweet and soft that few were aware they had agreed to her bidding until it was too late to back out. Kate and Audrey.

What follows are several of the notations Dr. Callaway made from the Friday luncheons that continued over the course of several years:

Jody: I am fed up to here (gesturing) with our being called dilettantes, especially when it comes from my husband. He seems to forget that I have an MBA and was working as a financial analyst when he and I met. Darby, of course, was a medical technologist specializing in microbiology. We consider ourselves better armed than so-called "ladies who lunch."

Darby: Our lunches have been so helpful for me to understand the craziness that goes on down there at Far West. It's like a soap opera. We get challenged quite a bit by friends regarding our help with the Breast Pavilion, but our potential donors are always surprised at how much Jody and I understand. I know we've run you ragged, Chase, with everything from one-on-one meetings to large groups, but we've been remarkably successful.

Chase: Yes. Thank you, as always. We're at the point where we can offer to women what we've been promising for a long time.

Jody: Well, all the women on the Advisory Board are just gaga over Molly St. Martin. Are you finally happy, Chase?

Chase: Very. The Department of Radiology is mad as hell, but it was Molly who insisted on being in the surgery department. We'll still have some financial entanglements with them, but Christi and I hashed out a five-point plan for radiology to follow, as well as the taxation going to the university. I've run the numbers over and over. It's airtight. The perfect solution. We only need Thatcher to sign off on the five points.

. . . .

Jody: How is Christi Bloom working out as the business manager, or clinic administrator, or whatever you call her?

Chase: Perfect. She's a real pistol. Stands up to Thatcher in a carefully diplomatic way that allows her to be more effective and bluntly honest than I could ever be.

Darby: What's so wonderful about having her is that she was hand-picked by Thatcher himself, so he seems to roll with the punches.

Chase: Yes, Dr. Taylor knew her from her high school days. She was a classmate with his son. She's run various medical clinics since graduating from Vanderbilt. Christi has taken so much of the burden off my back. I hope I never look at another financial report as long as I live. Anyway, I appreciate you both chiming in to get her hired.

Jody: Well, we simply made it clear that if Far West expects the community support to continue, we needed a go-to girl whom we can deal with directly. I'm glad she's working out.

Jody: What is the latest on the debt, by the way?

Chase: Since Molly's been here, our numbers for mammography have gone up at an amazing rate. Still losing money, but the rate of loss is slowing dramatically. Problem is, centralized billing by the university is still terrible. All my projections were based on 70% collection rate, you recall. When we opened in September '93, centralized billing kicked in that very same month, and the bottom fell out. Unfortunately, after all this time, they're still only up to 50%. Worse, we've been told that rate is unlikely to improve because of managed care sweeping into Texas.

Jody: That's an easy fix. We arrange for the Breast Pavilion to do their own billing. Outside and apart from the university.

Chase: I'd say that's impossible.

Jody: Everything down at that hellhole is impossible!

Darby: But let's not forget that Hardy Studebaker has told us repeatedly, "Don't worry about the debt." Hardy is our greatest friend here, no doubt. I suspect he would pay off the debt personally if there was no other way.

Darby: We have a new project in mind. Jody and I have decided to form a new support organization in addition to the Advisory Board – Friends of the Breast Pavilion. Our problem has been this – we keep getting approached to donate money to breast cancer research through the various organizations out there, especially the Race for the Cure. All the breast centers in west Texas donate, except us. It looks bad.

Chase: But a university doesn't donate to others. We're the ones *doing* the research. We should be recipients, not donors.

Darby: Be that as it may, it doesn't look good. So, we hope to get 60 or 70 women involved for quarterly luncheons with guest speakers. Also, you've talked about beefing up your summer scholar program with more students rotating through the Pavilion. We can use extra money to help you there, making the Friends Scholar a prestigious award. Maybe more than one scholar each summer.

Jody: It'll be a slush fund in reality—money we can use as we see fit, without having to cow down to the nitwits in the dean's office.

Darby: Something else, before I forget. Our idea to start rotating membership on the Advisory Board is working just fine. We even have a waiting list. This should really improve our exposure.

• • •

Darby: I'm wondering if it will ever end, but we keep getting cornered by physician friends at Permian who try to diminish you, Chase. It's horrible, really, some of the things they come up with. It's so insulting to us, as if we're unable to judge character. Then, at the same time, apparently from a different universe, word spreads among your patients, our friends, how wonderful you were as their breast cancer surgeon.

Jody: The dichotomy is crazy. I'm ready to bitch-slap the next doctor who tells me that you shouldn't be practicing medicine.

Darby: How are you doing, Chase? Does any of this get back to you?

Chase: Not really. I have to remember that these guys – and they're all guys – are threatened by my claiming to be a breast surgeon. Most of the stuff is said behind my back. Some of them, by the way, qualify for a 12-step program from what I've heard. No, far and away, my biggest struggle is the lingering effects of that meningoencephalitis. I have these monthly spells, where I have no business coming to work.

Unfortunately, when you have patients on the operating schedule, you have to be there.

Darby: You've talked about that problem a lot. Does all this stress make it worse?

Chase: No, it's very organic, if you know what I mean. Physical, not mental. The symptom complex is unique, quite predictable, and I can only hope future episodes fade away because my neurologist is clueless. When it hits, I do everything I can to avoid interaction with others. I can deal with the physical symptoms, but the dysphoria, the psychic hatred of everything in the world, is a horrible experience. It's amazing how quickly it goes away, thank goodness. Usually within 24 hours.

Darby: So sorry. I truly am.

Jody: Speaking of what people say about our little team here, and you in particular, we also get questions sometimes about your availability (gesturing with air quotes). I might be out of line here, but you know me as well as anyone, I'm always out of line. I'm talking about your social availability. Are you seeing anyone?

Chase: Well, I'm still paying alimony, almost done, though that's not really an answer. Bottom line, I'm way too preoccupied now to consider a relationship. Half the days I come home screaming inside, sometimes screaming on the outside, and that won't work if I involve a girlfriend. For right now, I really can't focus on anything besides the success of the Pavilion. It's day and night for me. Friday and Saturday night, then all day Sunday, I read as many articles as I can, especially basic science. This "molecular biologic Pap smear of the breast" is a niche play that could put the Breast Pavilion on the map. There are drugs right around the corner that are going to prevent breast cancer, but we don't know who should be treated. A so-called Pap smear will tell us. Same for the blood test research. When MRI comes out, we'll be able to find virtually every breast cancer earlier than mammography and more reliably, but we won't know who to put on the machine. I need to master the basics on this stuff if I'm going to coordinate such a massive effort. So, I suppose the answer to your question is: "No."

Jody: Love your honesty. Dating can be a strain, a time sponge. Hell, marriage can be a big strain, as you know. I know your ex, and she seems delightful to me. Still speaks very highly of you, by the way.

Darby: Your private life is really none of our business, but I do know that a never-ending project like this, well, you can lose your identity. It can swallow you up. Maybe it's better that you aren't trying to work a relationship or raise children right now.

Chase: Not having kids is a huge deal to me. Only the childless know what I mean. Humans are hard-wired for that, so if you don't have kids, you end up sublimating that energy to nurture something else, even if that something else is misplaced. While I attribute my semi-insane level of persistence to an effort at redemption, I doubt I'd taken this course if children were in the mix. Of course, looking back, I wouldn't have needed redemption if children had been in the mix. Too late now. It's full steam ahead for me.

. . .

Darby: It is so interesting to me that we have Thatcher to thank for bringing you back to Matherville. We wouldn't be here without him. Yet, you had that turning point where you refused to accept the assigned radiologist, and it seems like he has slowed down progress ever since. Or, even caused things to stall. Could his age have anything to do with it? I'm just rambling, but it makes me wonder what his plans are for retirement, and who will replace him?

Jody: Bottom line, is his successor going to be friend or foe? We've stuck too many severed heads on pikes already. I'd just as soon get this Breast Pavilion on automatic pilot before Thatcher steps down.

Chase: You've heard me talk about my good friend Franklin Cooper?

Darby: Yes, you've mentioned him before. We'd love to meet him.

Chase: Thatcher's pet. There used to be two pets, but I've fallen way down the list since the discovery that I'm not housebroken. Anyway, Franklin and his wife were friendly with Thatcher's family to the point that Franklin became a second son. Heart surgeon now, working his way up the ladder at Mass General in Boston. Already, he's Chief of the Cardiac Section. Even though Thatcher says he's not planning to retire anytime soon, I wish he would bring Franklin back. I doubt it'll happen, though, as Thatcher once called Far West a "dead end" for the truly talented. And remember, he might have been talking about himself.

Jody: Well, let us know if we can help make that happen someday.

22
SOBRIQUET

"Chase, you've got to come down here – quick. Dr. Taylor is about to give away the farm. Everything." The voice on the phone was Christi Bloom, business manager of the Breast Pavilion.

"What do you mean, Christi? I'm taking my first vacation in years."

"But you're in town, aren't you? Listen. Thatcher struck a deal with the radiology department that will ruin us. We'll never be able to make ends meet."

Chase said, "What about our five-point plan we gave him before I left? It put us on a clear course, profit first, and eventually out of debt."

"Yes, and he tossed it all."

"You've got to be kidding."

"All five points. Thatcher agreed to pay the radiology department a fixed percentage of our gross."

"What? Our gross? Net would be ridiculous. But gross? We owe Radiology one thing – a single FTE for Molly's salary, and that's that! No percentages of anything. In my opinion, they don't even deserve that. They didn't buy the equipment – I got it for them – and they haven't lifted a finger to recruit…"

"Well, you better get down here and do something fast. By the time you get back from vacation, it'll be a done deal. I've run the numbers doing it their way. At our current volume, the percentage works in our favor, and that's why Thatcher fell for it. However, when you project it out, just as soon as we start to break even, we'll be held in check forever. We'll barely make a dime and we'll never be out of debt."

"I can't believe it. After everything we went through to finagle our way to get this project into the Department of Surgery, then Thatcher does this. It's mind-boggling. How can this happen? I'm on my way."

Christi added, "I've already told him the deal is unacceptable."

Thank goodness for Christi. She's the only one with enough guts to confront T.N.T.

After pleading and begging (and alienating) Dr. Taylor even more than the last "hill to die on," Chase forced all parties into further discussion. For Chase, this meant working on the next underhanded, insubordinate scheme, enlisting the help of the Raven sisters and Hardy Studebaker. The routine was exhausting.

As always, T.N.T. finally relented in the end, and the Department of Radiology received a flat monthly fee from the Breast Pavilion to pay for their lost FTE, an arrangement steeped in common sense.

Chase's deteriorating relationship with T.N.T., born from his relentless badgering, was countered by the burgeoning expertise of Molly St. Martin. She exceeded Chase's hopes, not only through her talent, but also in her popularity with patients. In addition, she turned out to be a remarkable administrator. Using *PEP* skills and jargon, she surrounded herself with a host of purposeful, effective, and power-filled women who managed the front desk, transcription, patient flow and breast imaging. Patient satisfaction skyrocketed, as demonstrated by an in-house survey conducted by the university where the Breast Pavilion scored well above the other 22 outpatient clinics in the 400-physician medical center.

Twenty patients a day became 30, which became 40, and 50 was in sight (Chase's original estimate for the breakeven point). However, the debt had been piling up for years and was nearly insurmountable. The more success the Pavilion enjoyed, the more grumbling Chase heard about the debt. It was as though everyone had expected the Pavilion to go bankrupt, so what did another $18,000 in losses matter last month? Or $13,000 this month? But when the Pavilion began to breathe life, every level in the hierarchy demanded their due. "The Debt" became a daily issue, discussed at every opportunity, by every administrator at the university who had ignored Chase's dream. At the same time, Hardy Studebaker was telling Chase, "Don't worry about the debt. If you get this ship turned around before it hits the iceberg, I'll take care of the debt."

Then, Thatcher Nolan Taylor walked into Chase's office one day and announced, "I think you ought to give serious consideration to putting Christi Bloom on extended family leave, or even letting her go entirely."

Christi Bloom had been instrumental in overcoming every assault made on the Breast Pavilion by the university. In the process, she had offended nearly everyone, such that she became the obvious choice for a scapegoat. "Oh, Thatcher...*no*," Chase said, disgusted. "We can't let the university pull our strings on this one. They've been trying to make Christi the fall girl on our finances from the day she started here. She's not the reason we're in debt."

Chase's salutation of "Thatcher" marked the first time he'd ever addressed T.N.T. by his first name. None of the faculty members called him "Thatcher."

"She's missed quite a bit of work," Thatcher said, "and that doesn't look good when the Pavilion is struggling so."

The words were chilling, as they had obviously been coined by someone other than Dr. Taylor. Chase replied, "Her mother, as you know, is *dying of leukemia*, and it's been a fairly hideous downhill slide. An ugly death is in the works. I've been very forgiving of her hours, it's true..."

Flashing through Chase's mind was the many times Christi had served as his "bad cop." Just weeks earlier, T.N.T. had laid out yet another awkward plan to help cut financial losses – moving the indigent care out of the plush surroundings of the Pavilion and making College Hospital absorb the financial crunch with a mammography machine in the basement. Christi had said "no" with a flourish: "Dr. Taylor, that move would ruin the educational mission of the Pavilion. It's bad enough that we don't have full-time surgery residents learning about breast cancer, but the few hours of training they actually receive each week comes from seeing the indigent patients at the Pavilion where we have both Dr. St. Martin and Dr. Callaway supervising on site every day."

Chase didn't possess half the chutzpah of Christi Bloom. A critical feature, in Chase's mind, of the good cop/bad cop approach was that the good cop always had to stand up for the bad cop when someone's job was on the line. Christi had taken enormous heat for the struggling Pavilion, but at the same time, had been a key to its success. And, always in the back of his mind, Chase could hear Sukie Spurlock's aphorism about being nicer than you have to be. Sometimes, Sukie added a twist at the end, customized for the occasion. In this case: "...because you never know if the person you're dealing with has a loved one on their death bed."

Chase refused to fire Christi, and he refused to force her into an extended leave. He was sickened now that his relationship with Thatcher Taylor had sunk so low. He owed T.N.T. his entire career, and now to be cornered into a position of adversarial management was sickening.

The good cop/bad cop scenario, though, had a completely different role for him in his relationship with Molly St. Martin. There, he was the bad cop. It began a few weeks after Molly had been hired as part of the Department of Surgery when the dean of the medical school called Chase to say, "Now that Dr. St. Martin has signed on the dotted line, your job, Chase, is to convince her to move back into the Department of Radiology."

"I—I can't believe what you're saying, dean. Molly's first and foremost— no, her *only* demand—more than a demand, a mandate, a prerequisite, was that she *not* be in the Department of Radiology. We *promised* her that."

"Well, nothing lasts forever."

Two weeks is a long way from forever, you sneaky jerk. Instead, he said, "You will lose her then. I guarantee it. And you will lose me as well. I can promise you this, and this promise *will* last forever – I won't make a single effort to sway her into the radiology department."

Chase didn't have a drop of diplomatic blood left in his system. Moreover, he realized that the leadership's ethics were nil. The comfortable duplicity by the dean, in such a gross violation of honor, spelled everlasting trouble, and Chase made sure to document these absurd interactions. In fact, as the dean was speaking on the phone, Chase was transcribing this into his notepad: "Dean says: Well, nothing lasts forever."

Furthermore, Chase decided to nip the continued harassment of the Pavilion in the bud. His five-point plan for financial success had been tossed in the trash, though he and Christi Bloom had been able to salvage point one, the fixed payment to Radiology. Four points were left, and they needed implementation immediately. The dean needed to know that Chase had support in his hip pocket. Bypassing T.N.T., the dean, and the vice-chancellor, Chase worked his connections (Jody and Darby) and brought forth a roundtable meeting chaired by none other than the president of the entire university – Elmo "Skip" Didion.

President "Skip" Didion was a brilliant Texas Congressman turned university president, often considered to have gubernatorial timbre, but who dropped out of politics to return to his alma mater and lord over a more manageable mess. His early years in the presidency had been marred by a pathetic basketball team, for which he had no reaction and no plan, nor did he care.

Soon, President Didion came to realize that a winning season was a direct correlate to alumni donations, so "resurrecting the great basketball traditions of the past" became a top priority, even though he detested the sport and its anti-intellectual trappings.

Didion hired a former NBA star as coach, then the team started to win, and donations started to pour once again. Having dreamed of Far West being on par with Rice and Yale and Harvard when it came to intellectual prowess (and endowments), Skip Didion learned the hard way that the heart of the university was basketball, and everything else was fluff. With his first great season behind him, and with popularity soaring, he moved on to his primary goal of enriching the status of the medical center.

The roundtable meeting, secured by the Raven sisters, involved the entire university hierarchy that had anything to do with the Breast Pavilion. On the day of the landmark treaty discussions, Chase arranged for a photograph of the group – President Didion at the head of the table surrounded by the Vice-Chancellor of Health Sciences, the medical school dean, Thatcher Nolan Taylor, Darby and Jody Raven, Molly St. Martin, manager Christi Bloom, and others, all smiling. Hardy Studebaker was in Paris, but he would have preferred to stay anonymous anyway. Chase documented everything (thus the group photo), because Far West history, it seemed, could be rewritten faster than he could make it.

In his presentation, Chase revealed the background of the Pavilion in honest, sordid detail, using 35mm slides, pointing out the unnecessary obstacles that had been strewn in his path from the beginning. If the Pavilion were viewed, he said, not as an individual financial control point within the university, but as a patient-garnering resource like a satellite clinic, then the net gain to the entire medical complex, including College Hospital, was a huge financial success. Instead, the Department of Surgery was saddled with the Pavilion's debt, while the other clinical departments were making off like bandits as the breast cancer numbers increased, not to mention various financial control points throughout College Hospital, all profiting from the Pavilion.

Chase had worked over these numbers, extracting data from every site that enjoyed a parasitic relationship to the Pavilion. He also showed charts and graphs of hitting rock bottom at the time Molly St. Martin came on board, with a logarithmic rise in patient volume and charges ever since, *unaccompanied* by a rise in actual revenue due to the chaos in centralized billing. His penultimate 35mm slide showed a goose laying 10 golden eggs, while tiny minions gathered the gold with one hand, wielding axes in the other.

"I'm only defining obvious and concrete revenue streams here. I'm not counting the new and positive way people are starting to look at the medical school here at Far West and at College Hospital. How do you count these intangibles? I think it's safe to say that the Pavilion has brought more attention to this medical school than any other project in the past thirty years, at least. If you exclude the Psychiatric Pavilion, it's probably the most visible thing that's ever happened here."

At this point in the presentation, the Dean of the School of Medicine quietly stood up and, without excusing himself, walked out of the room and did not return.

President Didion ignored the dean and said, "What do you need me to do? Why have you called this meeting?"

Chase had a final slide – the remaining four points of the five-point plan he had proposed several months earlier. "Beyond the done deal of paying the radiology department a flat fee," he said, "next, allow a reputable outside billing service to handle Pavilion affairs." After finishing the remaining points, Chase added, "if these requests are granted, we will turn this thing around immediately. I promise."

It was inconceivable that the Pavilion would be allowed to escape centralized university billing. Yet, President Didion waved his wand. "Consider all of these things done. Now, do we have any more business here today?"

Chase nearly fell out of his chair.

Afterward, Dr. Molly St. Martin dubbed Chase "The Rainmaker." She repeated this so frequently that it became a sobriquet, describing how Chase, "without ever having studied *PEP*," was a natural consensus builder.

Editor's Note: At times, this abbreviated version of Dr. Callaway's manuscript might become tedious with its focus on the financial aspects that surrounded the Breast Pavilion. Indeed, many problematic and fascinating stories have been deleted to preserve the essence of Dr. Callaway's eventual madness. The daily drain he experienced over many years, revolving around money and control left him in a chronically, exhausted state. Often, he would comment that the most amazing thing he did in his medical practice was to continue to smile whenever he opened the exam room door and greeted his next patient.

Molly and Chase became close friends. Over time, he filled her in on the early days of the Pavilion and how he had been compelled to be insubordinate every major step of the way. He also began sharing more intimate details on how the entire process had negatively impacted him personally through the perpetual "hills to die on" that he'd already faced. In short, he was exhausted.

Molly was a great one to offer her shoulder, but sometimes she would simply stare blankly as he spoke. He wondered if she were in some sort of *PEP* trance, contemplating his confessions in light of the *PEP* framework. If so, she said nothing of the sort. They could talk for an hour at the end of every day – then afterward, Chase felt energized. Some people sucked energy out of relationships, others gave. Molly gave, be it natural or through the magic of *PEP*.

Sometimes, there was a gap between Molly's interest in pop psychology and her ability to assess others. She could be off base when it came to brief evaluations that occurred when only minutes were available in the assembly line of screening mammography. One incident made Chase wonder how she could be so astute and savvy in her business dealings, including personnel management, yet...

"Chase, I'm sending over a lady right now who thinks she has a lump. I didn't feel anything, and I don't see anything on imaging, but she's convinced. You'll like her. She's a nuclear physicist. Leads a fascinating life. I had a nice long chat with her."

Chase walked into the room with a medical student trailing behind. The middle-aged woman ignored the entry and stared at her laptop computer, her gray wig sitting catawampus on her head while her jaw was grinding away against imaginary cud. After she spoke only a few words, Chase excused himself to the hallway, dragging the medical student with him.

"I'm sorry. It's never polite to laugh in front of a patient," he said to his student. "But I'm not laughing at *her*. I'm laughing at Molly. You see, the patient is obviously schizophrenic, and when Dr. St. Martin told me that the patient was a nuclear physicist, well, Molly has spent too many years in dark rooms looking at X-rays."

"How do you know she's schizo?" asked the student.

"If you paid attention on the psych rotation, it only takes a few seconds to spot it. Her affect, her speech pattern, the whole package. However, the kicker is the side effects of her drugs. The grimacing, the chewing – called Wrigley's sign for obvious reasons – these are symptoms not of her schizophrenia, but of the neuroleptic drugs she's taking to combat it. The Latin root of neuroleptic means "seize the neuron," and her neurons have been thoroughly seized. Now, watch. I'm going to flip open her medical record to her medication list, which I've never seen before."

And there it was – a list of anti-psychotic medications.

"Nuclear physicist? Really? When we go back in the room, look at her computer screen. She's drawing pictures on her laptop with Paintbrush."

This psychological naiveté of Dr. St. Martin aside, Chase grew to respect her more than any physician with whom he had ever worked. Similar to Molly's granting him "The Rainmaker" moniker, he returned the admiration by incorporating her name into his printed biographical sketch. Thus, he was never introduced before an audience again without mention of her name – "Dr. Callaway attributes the remarkable success of the Breast Pavilion to Dr. Molly St. Martin..." She had become an integral part of his success, both professionally and personally.

Molly and Chase grew so close they could read each other's minds. Standing over a patient, with his fingers on the breast lump, with Molly's ultrasound probe in hand, she and Chase could communicate to each other with their eyes. No verbalizing about the next step – the decision to biopsy or not was said without a word. When the telepathy was complete, Molly would simply say, "I think we should go ahead with a needle biopsy," and Chase would nod. Or, another scenario: "I think everything's going to be fine here," and they both would nod that, yes, they had successfully co-mingled their thoughts.

One day, after he and Molly co-discovered a cancer missed by the doctors at Permian Medical Center, Chase felt the urge to tell her, "I want you to know how much I appreciate your coming here to the Breast Pavilion. Other than my surgical partner in California, I've never had a working relationship this enjoyable. You really saved the day for me." He meant so much more.

"I feel the same way," she said. "For the first time in my career, I have a mission. And, you, the Rainmaker, provided that for me."

Chase replied, "Don't take this analogy the wrong way, but I'd like to propose a professional marriage. No matter what happens here at the Pavilion, I'd like you to know that I want to stick with you, even if we end up somewhere else. I've come to believe a good working relationship is more important than anything, bar none."

Molly extended her hand to his, "A professional marriage? I agree," she said. They shook on it.

How far he'd come. Years ago, such an exchange would be a steppingstone to physical intimacy. Something had changed inside. He wasn't the same person. In the reorganization of atoms, he had emerged with super-strengths, he thought. His trials by fire in California and its aftermath had taken him to a new way of living that few could understand, a calling that surpassed physical needs and pleasure. Furthermore, the nature of his specialty made carnality even more of a taboo. Never did he make a single move, or utter a phrase, which could be misconstrued by anyone, under any circumstance.

So, he found it implausible that the tongue-wagglers had a different take on his life where he was surrounded by so many women. Christi Bloom, the business manager, tried to sugarcoat the rumors for Chase. "I don't tell you most of it, Chase. It seems like people refuse to accept the fact that you have talent or vision. Since I've worked here, though, you've been linked to women off-campus and on-campus, including me. Now they've started in with you and Molly."

"It's so ridiculous, I can't even respond. I don't allow even the tiniest of openings for this sort of thing. The rumors are spontaneous combustion. They come out of nowhere."

"Yes, but you need to know about it. I guess they draw from your days as a resident, years ago, or so I'm told you. People are intrigued by you now. It's as though they're waiting to see if there's a chink in the armor."

Still, he considered how nice it was to have a completely clear conscience, to be able to ignore the rumors. What a paradox that, by erecting a partition between himself and the women around him, he had somehow opened a channel of gender-free communication. Yes, it was a hollow victory in some respects, but it was a victory, nonetheless. Lonely, yes. However, it was all part of the higher calling of his new life as the Ubermensch, or more casually, The Rainmaker.

23
RED GIANT, WHITE DWARF

Chase's nurse, an extraordinary woman whose healing grace was sprinkled over each newly diagnosed breast cancer patient at the Pavilion, had waited fifteen years past her own breast cancer before returning to work, drawn to Chase's dream. Diagnosed at age 32, her youngest child was now about to finish high school, the common goal line for so many young breast cancer victims.

Then she began to cough, for months on end. After her son's graduation, she submitted to definitive testing and accepted her death sentence in angelic stride. The cancer was back, this time in her lungs and her brain.

She continued to work as long as possible, wearing a wig now, not for the temporary hair loss of chemotherapy, but the permanent hair loss due to brain irradiation. The entire staff at the Pavilion felt their hearts chipped away daily as they witnessed her downhill course. She stopped working only weeks before her death. Manager Christi Bloom had organized a telephone chain to notify all Pavilion employees whenever the inevitable occurred.

Chase was at home, reading a breast cancer journal when the phone rang.

This is it, he thought.

"Chase? This is Karlyn. My cancer is back. It's spread."

The words took his breath away. This was not the call he was expecting. Karlyn was *not* the nurse about to die. She was a close friend from high school who had come to College Hospital two years earlier, quite reluctantly (and only because of Chase) for treatment of her "early" breast cancer. Her tumor had been tiny – a 95% cure – one you can nearly forget about. Yet, Karlyn was in the 5%. *How could this be happening?*

Chase's nurse, meanwhile, died the next night. He wrote a eulogy, more lyrical than prose. Then, on the way to the funeral, Chase slipped off the curb in the parking lot and sprained his ankle, landing on his right hand where the crippled fingers crunched together in agonizing pain. After that fall, his right hand would neither close nor open completely, and never without considerable pain. God's directives were getting louder and louder.

When people greeted him in the hallway, they would ask: "Are you losing weight? Are you limping? Have you been sick?"

Then, 5% Karlyn, with her original tumor only 8mm in size, died a few months later, completely unresponsive to chemotherapy.

.   .   .

No respite could be found in his personal life. His father's neurological deterioration was hideous. Wes could not hold his head still, so it rolled around on his neck as if held up by a Slinky. With eyes glued on Chase, Wes's gaze seemed fixed, but of course, considering the palsied head, Wes's eyes were forever swimming in their sockets just to look straight ahead. Then, with quivering, halting speech, his father would say, "You're only doing breast surgery? Why would you limit yourself so?" The swimming eyes telegraphed disapproval.

Chase would try to explain, but the eyes didn't understand, and the head rolled and bobbed and jerked. Then, in the next conversation, his father would ask the same question about breast surgery, as if trying to announce his displeasure all the way to the grave.

Wes's spastic movements grew worse with time, as predicted, and hospitalizations for pneumonia became part of the routine. Unable to swallow normally, Wes's food would make its way into his lungs, but the choking reflex was long gone – thus, pneumonia.

During one such hospitalization at Permian Medical Center, a Far West basketball game was being televised. Chase, seated at his father's side, was riveted to the television, where the Far West team was making its resurrection statement against a Division I team ranked #5 nationally.

"Dad, I think Far West is back, finally. The team looks really good today. President Didion says we're going to try for Division I status after this season."

By this time, though, Wes had lost the power of intelligible speech, and he only groaned, perhaps in response, perhaps not.

In an upset for the history books, the Roadrunners of Far West Texas won the game with a three-pointer at the buzzer. Chase shot out of his seat, yelling in frothy jubilation. He turned to look at his father, the greatest Far West player of them all, at least in the olden days. Wes Callaway was blank faced, a zombie stare, drooling, arms and legs jerking randomly.

Where is God? Over and over, Chase asked himself the same question.

.   .   .

In spite of the Pavilion's success, there was always a critical problem at hand. Notably, the revolving door at the university caused frequent disruptions in the interdisciplinary concept. Some of Chase's patients had their medical oncologist changing on a yearly basis, and some had two or three different plastic surgeons for their staged reconstructions. All newly recruited professors were paraded before the public as "a terrific addition to our faculty, bringing national prominence to the university," but no mention was made when they left Far West a short while later. Internally, though, the malignant institutional narcissism proclaimed this about the exit: "Glad he's gone, he was nothing but trouble."

Few of these tribulations crushed Chase's spirit as much as the ripping away of the genetic testing program that he had launched with the Runnymeade grant, allowing him access to the ground floor of this exciting new development.

Upon establishing his program among the first group of practitioners nationwide, Chase had been unable to recruit significant numbers of patients to justify the genetic counselor FTE he had fought for. Genetic testing for adult-onset cancer was new, and the public was skeptical and frightened.

To help recruit patients, Chase asked the medical center's PR department to issue a press release. When they declined, failing to see the importance or impact, he broke university rules and contacted local media directly. Instead of acknowledging Chase's extensive preparation and certification, however, one of the television stations ran a story on the identical BRCA testing program at M.D. Anderson. Dr. Taylor said to Chase, trying to ease his frustration, "This genetic testing program you started may be the first time in the history of Far West medical center that someone came out of the chute too quickly."

Then, two years later, the university decided to act on Chase's original recommendation to recruit a medical geneticist for all types of cancer. A "world famous" geneticist from Memorial Sloan-Kettering was a "terrific addition" that Far West featured on every television station, every radio program, every west Texas magazine, including the alumni periodical – *The Roadrunner*.

Chase was enthusiastic about the new arrival, at first. He believed that geneticists should work alongside clinicians when it came to high-risk patients, as these women often had questions that went outside the scope of strict genetics. This opinion was bolstered the first time he sat in with the new geneticist who was talking to a young woman recently discovered to have a deleterious mutation in the BRCA-1 gene.

"If I decide to have my breasts removed, can they reconstruct me at the same time?"

"No," said the geneticist.

"Excuse me," Chase said, "but, in fact, we reconstruct immediately here at Far West. It's become routine for us."

Then came the boom. The "world famous" geneticist strolled into Chase's office one day, stating, "As you know, the politics in academics can get sticky, so I'm going to say this straight out – I'll be in charge of your high-risk program from here on."

Almost speechless at the audacity, Chase said, "You mean the genetic testing part, don't you? That's only half my program. Many of my patients are referred because of tissue abnormalities that impart risk, nothing to do with genetics. I consider myself expert on the atypical hyperplasias, for instance."

"Well, in fact, I do mean your entire program."

"Now wait...I read my own slides to distinguish true atypical hyperplasia, plus I've formed a research team where we're studying the molecular biology of premalignancy."

"Your *entire* program."

Chase had no workable option but compliance. Even subtle resistance by Chase toward this "terrific addition" would have been academic suicide. The Far West administration was incapable of admitting one of its own graduates had achieved supremacy of a discipline.

Hostile takeovers, territorial disputes, all functioning at sandbox level. This was academic medicine. This was Chase's heart carved out and served on a silver platter to the new "world famous" cancer geneticist. Nothing collegial, no synergism, pure aggression, the music of malignant institutional narcissism.

But control of emotions is not the same as eradication of those emotions. Chase complained loudly and bitterly to Molly St. Martin, to the Raven sisters, to Hardy Studebaker, and to anyone who would listen how he had been stomped on by the latest golden boy who, predictably, would turn out to be sour. Several years later, after a bumpy course, the "terrific addition" would move back home to New York. Remarkably, to save face, Far West would continue to pay one-half of his salary in return for one-day visits back to Texas every few *months*. In addition, all East Coast honors and accolades awarded to the geneticist could be used by Far West in PR meant to deceive the folks of Matherville and west Texas into believing that he still worked at Far West. Underlings in the department joked about the "cardboard cut-out" they had for a boss.

Only Christi Bloom, Molly St. Martin, and the Raven sisters kept Chase motivated. Molly had been the key to their financial turnaround, and now Chase was ready to take the Breast Pavilion to some measure of national recognition.

"It ought to be so easy," he said to Molly. "There are so few people who've joined the breast cancer bandwagon at this point, compared to other specialties. We beat 'em to the punch. Most of the country's major cancer centers are trying to catch up, and I already have collected enough data to match the big boys. Too, the breast specialty societies are so small, why, you can network with ease."

Molly and Chase attended their first meeting together in New Orleans. Chase had been going for years to every breast cancer meeting possible, and Molly had started going to the breast radiology meetings as well. However, there was only one organization that included all specialties that dealt with breast cancer, a true multidisciplinary society. Here, the leadership committees were small and the chance to participate and rise in the hierarchy from the ground floor was a given.

He said to Molly, "During the business meeting at noon, you'll be able to meet everyone who runs the society. Many of the big names in breast cancer."

"I'm shopping during the noon break. I've got Christmas presents to buy."

"But, but there's so much networking we can—"

"Shopping," she said, and she walked away.

Her expression had been oddly stern, as if to say, "I set my own agenda, and I'm not influenced by others."

Chase went alone to the meeting. It wasn't really such a big deal, after all. Maybe, he'd been too pushy. Molly could make the Pavilion successful at home, while Chase could take care of the national reputation.

Back in Matherville, Chase showed Molly a flyer he had picked up in New Orleans, a notice of innovative technology being developed – a breast-dedicated MRI machine – a photograph of the future, Chase thought.

"Don't *ever* buy the first generation of new radiology equipment," Molly cautioned. "The price you pay for being first is that you'll also be the first to go obsolete. The second generation always comes out better than the first. Same goes for your idea about digital mammography, Chase. I know it's bound to hit the market, but we shouldn't be the first. I'll tell you when the time is right."

No urgency, he thought. He trusted Molly.

Then, on one of the cursed days of the lunar cycle when Chase awoke at 4:00 am with a boring pain in his right eye, he forced himself to work, as always. The dysphoria was oppressive, but at least he didn't have surgery scheduled on this particular day.

However, during a business meeting with Molly and key staff, Christi Bloom announced, "The transition to our outside billing service is going to hurt us pretty badly at first. Lag time looks like it'll be three months, so our gross collections are going to bottom out for a while. Also, Chase, since we shifted your surgery income into the Pavilion, your take-home pay is going to bottom out with it."

Chase lost it. He exploded. He had given ample notice for the outside billing transition to go smoothly. Unlike Molly's fixed salary, Chase's income was tied to production. Even more unlike Molly (and most physicians for that matter) Chase was in a precarious financial situation. He had already calculated that he would turn age 50 before he could start saving for retirement.

On any other day, it would have been "ho-hum," as he had come to greet adversity with serenity (or emotional numbness) over the tedious years at Far West. Unfortunately, it happened on "dysphoria day," curse day, with a crescent moon of reddish skin around his right eye. Chase's unbridled anger shocked Molly St. Martin as she had worked daily by his side for two years without ever seeing a display of temper.

Chase was so angry that he had to leave the medical center. By the time he cooled off, he realized how horrible it must have looked to Molly. So when he returned, he decided to confess all about his unusual syndrome. He explained every detail to work-wife, Molly, and how he dreaded coming to work on these cursed days. As an afterthought, he joked, "All the more reason for me to get to the lab where only the rats will hear me yell." He was serious about the lab – the long-term dream, supported by many vectors, was pointing that direction.

Molly didn't smile at his joke about the rats. She never said, "Oh, I understand now. How awful." In fact, she acted as though Chase had made up the whole story about the horrible bout with encephalitis. And, she had no questions about the bizarre syndrome that caused him so much trouble. Instead, she said, "My father never yelled. My husband doesn't yell. I have no exposure to that sort of thing, and I cannot tolerate it."

Crushed, he managed to argue feebly, "Well, frankly, I don't know anyone in my surgical circles who *doesn't* yell on occasion. Even the great Thatcher Taylor has been known to curse and throw an instrument or two. We work in a high-tension world, Molly. Cutting into people for a living takes its toll, I guess."

Molly gave him a withering look and turned back to the mammogram she was reading. She sipped her coffee and said nothing further.

The next day, dysphoria gone, Chase found a book on his desk – *The PEP Guide to Burn-out.*

Several months later, Darby Raven called him, bubbling with excitement. "Chase, I'm so thrilled I don't know where to start. Jody and I have come up with an idea that will get you into the lab. After everything you've been through, you deserve this, and you deserve it now."

His burden felt lighter merely from the music in her sweet voice.

"That's *if* Thatcher will go for it. You know how humble he is. He may not let me do it. Here goes...are you ready?"

"Yes. Completely."

Darby began, "You know, over the years, I've raised money for endowed chairs in the medical school. I don't know why I didn't think of this sooner. However, my plan is to raise money for an endowed chair to honor Thatcher. In his name. And you'll be the Holder. I've already got a name for it – the Thatcher Nolan Taylor Chair in Surgical Breast Oncology."

Chase couldn't remember Darby's exact words from that point on. Usually, he could recall conversations verbatim, but not this one. He was floating now. She said something to the effect of, "Calculate how much money you'll need to do whatever it is you need to do." He replied something to the effect of, "I need to pay off the Pavilion's debt first, then I need a research nurse, and I'll need money to hire a surgical partner so that I'm not a burden on the surgery department. I already have a partner in mind, and she can do the bulk of the surgeries. I'll be free to go to the lab. Once that's in place, I can build our research reputation so that the lab remains funded long-term through grants.

Editor's note: At this point in the document, the author tangentially skips from one unique research strategy to another, and he doesn't return to the subject at hand for another 36 pages. The strategies listed fall under two primary categories—"the molecular biologic Pap smear of the breast" and more reliable screening using a "blood test." Dr. Callaway points out that "little ol' Creighton University in Omaha" became the world's first center for hereditary cancer syndromes through the efforts of one man, a pioneer supported by his institution. The secret to this sort of success, he notes, is an agenda that has been overlooked by others.

Chase received a phone call from old family friend, nanny, and nurse, Sukie Spurlock. He felt bad that he hadn't contacted her in several months. "Chase, I want you to drop by my house and look at something. I know you're a busy doctor and all. I'm always reading about you in the newspapers, what with those fancy charity balls and the like. Still, I do have a slight problem to show you, if that's okay."

Sukie lived in a clapboard house in a borderline neighborhood after being relocated by the developers of the medical center at Far West, with their banner "5 million square feet of medical miracles during the next 10 years." To Chase, it didn't make sense for her to live like this. After all, he had been sending her money for years.

When he opened the rickety screen door and entered Sukie's home, he was surprised to see a group of Sukie's elderly Black friends, some with Bibles clutched at chest level, all gathered around her bed. They nodded in unison at his arrival, then parted to let him through.

"Hello, Chase, my baby. You are my baby, you know…can't recall if you were four or five when I started working for your family." Sukie motioned for her friends to step out of her bedroom. "I'm going to show you something now, and I don't want you gettin' harsh with me." One of the men, on his way out, uttered something to the others about Chase being a top cancer specialist.

When the room had cleared, Sukie pulled down the elastic band of her nightgown and lifted her right breast out, swollen three times normal size. Skin nodules were scattered over the surface – small cauliflower outgrowths, each with stretched skin, shiny and ready to burst. Chase remembered that both of Sukie's children – daughter and son – developed breast cancer in their youth. One of the BRCA genes might be ravaging this family. If so, it was a small miracle that Sukie had lived so long without getting cancer.

"I know what this is," said Sukie. "You don't have to tell me. In fact, I don't want to hear the word. I don't want surgery, no radiation, no nothing. My time has come, Chase, and I'm ready to join my other babies in Heaven. I hope you understand that. The reason I called is I was wondering if there's anything I can do for these knots on my skin to keep them from breaking open. I don't want to be messy or smelly in the end. I want my friends to visit."

Chase slid his hand across the surface of her breast, feeling each miniature cauliflower. "Sukie, I can try you on tamoxifen. It's a pill you can take here at home. It can't cure you, but sometimes it can make tumors shrink. Yours is pretty far along, and I've never used it for such advanced disease. I don't know, but we can give it a try."

"Good. Because I'm not leaving my house. I want to stay here and look at the pictures of my children every day while I prepare to meet the Lord. Chase glanced toward the top of her television set where she kept the pictures in four frames. From Sukie's perspective, she had four children: her two natural children plus the Callaway kids, Annie and Chase. Three of the four children were dead by "natural" disease.

"You all come back in here now," Sukie said to the group in the front room. The men and women ambled back in, slowly forming a circle around Sukie's bed. "We want you to know something else, Chase," added Sukie.

"What?"

"Our little prayer group here has been praying for you. I know from your mother that you're going through a lot right now. Still, we want you to know that we're praying day and night that you be the one."

"The one what?"

"The one who puts an end to this awful disease. Not in my case, of course. My time has come, and I accept that. But we're talkin' about everyone else. Cancer breaks too many hearts." Sukie gazed at him with her great wide smile that remained unfettered by time or disease.

Sukie had once been a second mother to him, as a live-in nanny and housekeeper. He looked at the floor to keep his composure, but then he felt foreign hands, one by one, pressing onto his shoulders until every one of Sukie's friends was touching him. He closed his eyes as they prayed. Inside, he was choking up. He could feel a lake of tears pressing hard against the dam – the thick, thick dam that protected him always.

When the Sun of our Solar System eventually begins to burn out, it will first become a red giant as the hydrogen-burning switches to helium-burning. Later, a white dwarf. The carbon core of a dwarf has no further energy source, so it will gradually radiate its energy away. Oddly, the more mass in a white dwarf, the smaller it becomes. But there is a limit to a white dwarf's mass, which happens to be 1.44 times the mass of our Sun, and this is called the "Chandrasekhar limit."

Thatcher Nolan Taylor, M.D. agreed to the endowment plan. He was reluctant at first since efforts like this often go to honor the deceased, or nearly-so, and he didn't consider himself in those categories. In addition to approving the concept, he also gave his nod to Chase's calculations on the target amount. It would, quite simply, be the largest endowed chair in the history of Far West Texas University – $4 million dollars –

an amount that would per annum generate peace of mind. The Raven sisters felt sure they could reach the target and more.

"I would like to get a plan in writing from you, Dr. Taylor, how I'm to use the money, making sure we're on the same page," said Chase who realized that envy of other faculty members would be a given, and that every expenditure would be subject to criticism. "My plan is this – first, before spending a penny on anything, even before I go to the lab, I've got to pay off the Pavilion's debt. It's an albatross, and it's making me and my staff miserable."

"Oh heavens, no, Chase!" T.N.T. became surprisingly animated, scrunching his face in disapproval. "Don't spend a cent on that debt. Now that the Pavilion's turning a small profit, Hardy will take care of the past debt, I assure you. I want you to use this money exactly as it's intended. Get yourself into the lab. It's what you've been wanting to do for a long time, and you deserve it."

Chase couldn't believe his ears. Ever since the endowment had been proposed by Darby Raven, he assumed the debt would come first. While Hardy Studebaker had been telling Chase "Don't worry about the debt" all along, the endowment might have been Hardy's answer, or so Chase considered. It was not a minor issue. By the time Dr. Molly St. Martin came on board, and the outside billing finally turned things around, the debt had grown to an oppressive $650,000. While the bleeding had stopped, the wound was deep. However, T.N.T. was telegraphing Chase that debt relief would come from somewhere other than the endowment.

"One thing more, Chase. We must be very careful about the wording in the endowment agreement. These are official university documents, governed by a set of rules unique for each chair. We must design the requirements for the Holder of this chair to be so specific that you're the only person on the planet who could possibly be selected. You need to have control on how that money is spent."

"Aren't I the only candidate? I mean, Darby is spearheading this idea specifically with me in mind – and at the same time, of course, to honor you."

"I've been in academics a long time, Chase, and trust me. Just when you think you've seen it all, someone surprises you still. The document has to be airtight."

Yes, thought Chase, "airtight."

...for I am at my Chandrasekhar limit. And this limit is, in its own way, a state of reasonable equilibrium. For if any additional mass is added to the white dwarf, it will explode through carbon detonation into the most powerful supernova known. On the other hand, if equilibrium is maintained, it's believed that the carbon core can crystallize and form a diamond more than 1,000 miles wide.

24
Z-SCORES

Tucked in hill country near Austin, at a lonely resort, PhDs and MDs packed the auditorium for the unveiling of new technology in cancer research – the latest version of a computerized microscope that converted entire sections of tissue into mathematical continuums.

Technology was already available to do this for individual cells, but not for entire slices of tissue where there were thousands of cells in the microscope's field. For cancer cells, such mathematical formulas predicted the degree of virulence, but Chase Callaway was in the audience for another reason entirely – to use the instrument on benign breast tissue as a predictor of future cancer risk. Indeed, this was the primary reason for the conference, co-sponsored by the inventor of the microscope and the National Cancer Institute.

The speaker, head of the Chemoprevention Branch of the NCI, said, "The next generation of PhD candidates can play all they want in the new world of genomics and proteomics...and, in twenty years, we'll have some of the answers we need. But for the here and now, we need to move directly to quantifying the expression of those genes and proteins by the morphologic features in the tissue itself, using this New Millennium Kruger 2000 equipment."

Chase's strategy was simple. Rather than relying on historical risk factors that may or may not relate to what is actually going on in the breast cells, researchers should focus on cells and tissue as the determinants of risk. Then, for instance, a drug like tamoxifen could be targeted against actual premalignant changes, rather than blindly using the drug to prevent cancer because of a positive family history.

The 76 members in the audience (Chase counted them…twice) were pathologists and basic scientists representing most of the major cancer centers in the United States. As the NCI leader spoke, his examples revolved around breast cancer, as opposed to the many other types of cancer, since this is where the technology would have immediate application, given that tamoxifen was the only FDA-approved drug to prevent cancer. This research strategy was based on "The Noah Effect" – or, "there's no point in predicting rain unless you build an ark." Tamoxifen was the ark. Now, it was up to medical researchers to predict the rain. The NCI had already adopted the New Millennium Kruger 2000, and research grants for Noah followers would be awarded to those facilities using the same equipment.

Chase had always loved this branch of pathology called "image analysis." Sadly, Matherville had a true national expert on the subject (one of the few national figures at Far West) – Dr. Pierpont, the very research scientist who had taken Chase's donated money and devoured it for other purposes in his lab while concealing the fact that his new microscope was a lemon.

But things were different now. Chase was going to be sitting on a pile of gold in the form of an endowment, and he would simply do the research himself, with the help of his pathology protégé Nola Kastl. The first step would be landing the Kruger 2000. Everyone in the room wanted a piece of the action, but only five scopes were available, and it would be another year before the next five scopes would be built.

The speaker, Dr. Renfro, continued, "This slide shows the results of the test all of you took this morning. Your scores are listed beside your initials." Dr. Renfro had shown a single microscope slide of early breast cancer called DCIS, and he'd asked the audience to write down as many parameters as they could, in three minutes, for measuring the aggressiveness of the abnormality.

Of course, everyone wrote down the basics: nuclear size and shape, the presence of nucleoli within a typical nucleus, overall architecture, and mitotic counts. Seven features was the average number noted by audience members. However, for one participant with the initials "C.C.," 16 features, many of which were ratios of two features, had been recorded.

Dr. Renfro pointed to the outlier and commented, "Sixteen features listed by this person is extraordinary, indeed, but here's my point. The Kruger 2000 sees and quantifies *one hundred* features. Scores on the hundred features are grouped into four categories: nuclear, nucleolar, cytoplasmic, and mitotic. Then, these scores are merged once again into what we call Z-scores, the final answer. This, of course, can be done on individual cells already, but the Kruger 2000 will do it instantaneously on entire tissue sections. The Z-score for benign tissue ought to predict the likelihood of future cancer; the Z-score on DCIS should predict the likelihood of future invasion; and, the Z-score on invasive cancer might help predict the likelihood of metastatic disease."

Questions popped out of the audience, and Chase was struck that these scientists were unschooled when it came to linking pathologic findings to clinical problems. "What difference does this information make? Does the surgeon do anything different for high grade DCIS versus low grade? So, does a Z-score really matter to anyone?"

Every question asked by audience members betrayed a dearth of the dovetail principle. Artificial divisions in both clinical medicine and in research, all in the name of "specialization," crippled progress. Or, so it seemed to Chase.

Finally, Chase spoke. "Clinicians are in a state of chaos right now regarding management of DCIS. Which sub-types need to be irradiated, for instance? Are there sub-types so indolent they don't need treatment at all? Or, does the type even matter? The clinical research here is an embarrassment because the basic science is ambiguous and the pathology subjective..."

Chase took command for the next five minutes as he lectured the group on the clinical controversies surrounding breast pathology, with special reference to premalignant states.

"You make some very good points," said Dr. Renfro from the podium. "As you know, currently, our semi-quantitative methods mean the human user still picks which cells to be studied. The Kruger 2000 removes most of the human bias by studying all cells at once."

Very quickly, the meeting became a dialogue between Drs. Renfro and Callaway. The rest of the room was silent. His laborious study over the years, daring to cross specialty lines, was evident now and finally paying off.

With his endowed chair on the way, Chase had included in his budget the expensive, computerized microscope, hoping to purchase one of the first five as soon as the money was in the bank. Under a new university policy, made possible through abundant dollars pouring in from basketball-loving alumni, all money donated for endowed chairs would receive matching funds from the university. Darby and Jody Raven had to raise only $2 million dollars, and the Chair would become $4 million with the stroke of a pen. If Chase could land the Kruger 2000, the resulting NCI grant (called an R-01 for original, investigator-initiated research) would be the first ever in the history of the Department of Surgery, and one of the few to be bestowed at Far West.

Chase had learned a great deal about the grant system for medical research, and he believed it to be the most bloated, twisted scheme imaginable, designed to perpetuate disease. Scientists spent most of their time competing for grants rather than applying their genius. Worst of all, success was measured in dollars received, not the eradication of disease. Universities kept score accordingly. The original goal had been forgotten. The surrogate became the mother. This was not a problem of form over substance – it was pure form.

President Skip Didion, for instance, couldn't finish a speech or a press conference without bragging of research conquests in terms of dollars, and how those dollars ranked with the top schools in Texas. Mastery of adjectives and numbers was his forte, whereupon he could always make his university "number one" with enough qualifiers. If successful NCI grants at Far West rose from a measly *one* R-01 to a piddly *two* R-01s, then the people of Matherville would hear, "Far West had a 100% increase in NCI grant funding this year. That's the greatest increase of any publicly-funded school with an enrollment above seven thousand five hundred in the nation." No mention was ever made of the fact that the top-notch schools were drenched in NCI money.

Chase, at mid-career already, felt he had little time to play these games. Even senior scientists had their grants funded only 20% of the time. Breast cancer was killing over a hundred women every day in the U.S. alone. Action was needed, not mindless tallies of research dollars captured.

One of Chairman Thatcher Nolan Taylor's charming qualities was that he did *not* keep score that way. Still, an NCI R-01 grant with the Kruger 2000 would be a nice feather in Chase's cap, and it might lower the heat he was feeling (or imagining) from colleagues envious of his upcoming Chair. It would do him good to follow the rules for once.

That afternoon in Austin, when the lectures were over, the crowd gathered around the Kruger 2000 to watch its marvelous software in action. Picture after picture popped up on the computer screen, rather than looking through the lens of a microscope, and the scientists watched the futuristic technology spit out Z-scores.

"All that needs to be done is labor," said Dr. Renfro. "Procure the tissue sections, capture the Z-scores, study the outcomes, and organize the continuums into proper groupings."

Troubled by something he saw on the computer screen, Chase asked, "Are all the calculations on the computer made at this particular power on the microscope? Or, does it adjust when you move from lower to higher power?"

"Always at this power," Dr. Renfro answered.

"But didn't you mention earlier that the observed field has to fill the screen with tissue for the Z-scores to be accurate? No white space?"

"Yes."

"Then you're going to have a problem." Chase felt a sea of eyes turning his way. He continued, "Some DCIS, especially when low-grade, has only a thin layer of cells lining the duct. At this power, part of your field is going to be white space. So, am I thinking correctly? Your Z-scores won't work in that situation. Furthermore, at this power, what I'm describing will occur fairly often."

Dr. Renfro straightened his back, his eyes dropping down to Chase's name tag, then he eagerly began to correct Chase, "Oh, but we've already had the system checked out by the top breast pathologists in the country. They've signed off on it."

While Dr. Renfro began dropping the names of famous pathologists who had analyzed the scope, the actual computer scientist who had invented the image analysis system sidled into the group and said with a gentle, whispering voice. "He's correct."

"What? But—"

"He's right," said Dr. Kruger of the Kruger 2000. "I can't believe we didn't think of that."

"But Dr. Paglia, Dr. Cooksey, Dr. Lemmons, the top men, how?"

"I don't know how," said Dr. Kruger, "but no one caught it. It won't be hard to fix, of course, but it's a tremendous oversight on our part. We'll need to be able to generate those Z-scores using at least three different powers."

"What institution do you represent?" asked the NCI's Dr. Renfro, turning back to Chase, straining again to look at the name tag. "Where's your work done?"

When Chase answered Far West Texas University, Renfro and Kruger exchanged glances as if to indicate that they hadn't intended to place one of their precious five scopes in the middle of nowhere.

"Well, who's your chairman? Are you in the pathology department or molecular biology?"

"Neither," said Chase. "I'm a surgeon."

Time can distort truth, and when Chase reflected on this instant in the years that followed, he could hear an audible gasp in the crowd. In fact, no such gasp occurred. It did not need to occur. The room was, however, very, very quiet.

When the day ended, Chase left for Matherville with the promise of the first Kruger 2000, plus an NCI grant application under his arm from the very person, Dr. Renfro, who selected the recipients. It would be a "first" for the Department of Surgery at Far West, its first R-01 grant ever for an original research project funded by the National Cancer Institute.

"Freya, you're not going to believe it," Chase said as soon as he got to a phone, eager to tell his cohort in the lab. "Success. Beyond my wildest dreams. We're gonna get the scope. A knockout in the first round."

Freya Pixley had tipped off Chase about the Kruger 2000 and the Austin meeting in the first place. "Before the scope gets here, I'll get certified as a histology tech," she said. "That way, I can help you with all your research. We can't wait until you're over here with us. We're clearing out lab space for your office already."

The histology tech was responsible for mastering the microtome, an ultra-sharp knife that cut through paraffin-embedded tissue, making ultra-thin slices to lay gently onto glass microscope slides. Freya was already skilled in immunohistochemistry, so now they would be able to do their own tissue processing and staining from beginning to end. Furthermore, with the recent development of laser microdissection, the key tissue could be photographed first, with a Z-score calculated, then the area of interest removed from the glass slide by the laser for DNA correlation studies.

Soon, Chase's team would have their full credentials. His former student, Nola Kastl, was about to finish her pathology residency. Though she would officially be in the Department of Pathology, she had already pledged her research career to Chase's cause.

Like the hundred variables that merge into a Z-score, Chase saw his entire life fuse into meaning. The loss of his agile hands, the loss of his marriage, loss after loss after loss, a hundred losses, all culminating now in a remarkable gain, an opportunity at last. One purpose, one mission, one reason, one Z-score.

25
LAWS OF ASCENSION

Perhaps it was the image of Porter Piscotel back in 1980 climbing out of his DeLorean, tweed jacket over his shoulder, pipe in mouth, which kept Chase Callaway at arm's length. Or, perhaps it was the fact that Chase knew Porter as a B-plus scholar who had blossomed into A-triple-plus on the clinical rotations, finally catapulting to greatness in surgery via geography Back East where he had been anointed. Porter had been blessed with extraordinary drive and energy and enthusiasm for cutting human flesh. No one, in Chase's opinion, was more eager (or capable) than Porter to tackle the most difficult operations imaginable.

When Chase returned to join the faculty at Far West, he had been leery about Porter. Chase was a contemplative Hamlet to Porter's action-packed Othello. No, that's not exactly the case. Chase took plenty of action, but only after filling his mind with competing viewpoints and warring paradigms. Yet, to his surprise, as Chase got to know Porter better, he appreciated what seemed to be a core of genuine kindness, a youthful, naïve optimism that was almost infectious. Random acts of kindness by Porter were the stuff of legend, usually involving patients in trouble, though not necessarily related to their illness. These stories provided great fodder for Porter's engaging wife who could spin mesmerizing tales at dinner parties regarding Porter's exploits.

When Chase returned from the Riverdell treatment facility, it had been Porter who had taken him under his wing and offered support. Chase finally admitted to himself that he had seriously misjudged Porter.

Alas, as it turned out, Porter's support was conditional, based on Chase's broken wing. As soon as Chase began to attract his following in the development of the Breast Pavilion, Porter grew distant. Indeed, the distance was inversely correlated to Chase's success, especially while Porter incorrectly believed his hard-earned income was subsidizing Chase's expensive dreams.

Porter Piscotel, MD seemed most at peace when either looking up or looking down. He thrived in his obsequious role to higher authority, most notably T.N.T., and he loved serving as patriarch to the residents in training, and as a god to medical students. When it came to equals, though, Porter's ability to interface lacked something.

When people asked Chase who would be the next chairman of the department, he answered, "Doesn't matter to me. I had always hoped Dr. Taylor would bring back my friend Franklin Cooper who's still at Boston, but Thatcher's a huge champion for letting his top students reach for the stars, so Franklin will stay in Boston, I'm sure. My guess is either Porter or Dagmar. Doesn't really matter. Both of them know how hard I've worked to make the Breast Pavilion happen, so I think they'll both leave me alone, especially after this endowment kicks in since I won't need to be crawling to either one of them with money requests."

Chase felt himself on the other side of the mirror from Porter in every respect. Porter's favorite word was "clearly," while Chase saw more haze. A chief resident confided once to Chase: "You know, before you got here, we didn't learn much about breast cancer, so I took the short course at the College of Surgeons meeting, and I couldn't believe it. Everything was controversial. But do you know what Dr. Piscotel told me when I got back and started discussing the controversies? He said: 'Forget that stuff. Stick to dogma'."

Chase replied, "The reason it's so controversial is because breast cancer treatment, stuck in a rut for many years, has recently been submitted to randomized trials, something surgeons have neglected since the beginning of time. The outcomes so far in these trials have been shocking. Wait until surgeons find out what happens to the rest of their cherished beliefs when dogma is randomized for study."

Thus, the difference. Chase felt dogma to be the enemy of science. Always has been, always will be. Erroneous dogma, in fact, forms the very basis for the history of science and medicine. Whenever Chase felt himself secure in his own dogma, he would think back to the oft-read lectures by Nobel laureate Richard Feynman, the brilliant scientist and physicist, who said we should always remain haunted by one critical word in science – *uncertainty*.

Uncertainty on the part of the doctor had to be hidden from patients for sure, but the danger was in hiding it from yourself. This is where Chase felt Porter crossed the line. Porter hid things from himself.

When Chase returned home and served his first month as attending physician at Far West, rounding with the residents on the patients of other attendings, he observed denial firsthand. The residents would say, "Yes, this is fluid coming out of the patient's surgical incision into a bag, but after pancreatic surgery, Dr. Piscotel doesn't allow us to call it a fistula unless it's over five hundred ccs during a twenty-four-hour period." Chase would reply with a smirk, "What do you call it when it's four hundred ninety ccs over twenty-four hours?" While grinning, they would answer, "Incisional drainage fluid."

Or consider the time when Porter did a Whipple procedure to remove a "pancreatic tumor" in a 26 year-old male, and pathology found "no pancreatic cancer." Rather than review the pre-operative studies so that everyone could learn something, Dr. Piscotel squirmed and coughed, announcing at morbidity and mortality conference, "Pathology is seeing some atypia on the slides, so it'll turn out to be a tumor of some sort." Chase had, in fact, been in the pathology department when the hooplah was in progress. The atypia was due to the inflammation of pancreatitis. No tumor. No cancer. The sad story here was not the unnecessary surgery – all the proper indications were there, and no one was placing blame – the sad feature was the refusal to learn.

Chase believed that acknowledging complications was every bit as important as skilled hands in the O.R. Since all surgeons have complications, post-op vigilance was critical. One could become "too vigilant," however. Indeed, hyper-vigilance had driven Chase into profound insomnia and anxiety over the years. So, an argument could be made, in fact, for ignoring complications. It ensured mental health – for the surgeon.

Porter Piscotel was a chauvinist and halfway charming about it. Not in the feminist sense, but chauvinism in its original sense – blind allegiance to an adopted cause. Nothing demonstrated this better than Porter's role as a rabid Texas Aggie. His constant belittlement of Far West Texas annoyed Chase to a degree, such that once, during a faculty meeting where Porter was locked in a soliloquy on the inadequacies of Far West compared to A&M, Chase said, "Porter, have you ever looked to see what's printed on your business card to see who you work for?" Chase was only half-way joking. The Callaway family was deeply embedded in Far West, and Chase was thrilled to be back in Texas, contributing to the potential greatness of his alma mater. He looked forward to the day when he could put the horrors of the Pavilion behind him and merge into the myriad alumni activities, most notably in support of undergraduate programs and the basketball team.

This same generic chauvinism permeated Porter's judgment when it came to applicants to the residency program. After a Texas Tech student entered the Far West surgery program and was found to be incompetent, Porter established an informal ban on all Texas Tech students. Each year, during the selection process, he would remind everyone: "We're not taking anyone from Tech. We had a really bad student from there once."

"Oh, that's just Porter," people would say, but Chase thought such pronouncements were not only authentic, but also unsettling. With every exiting faculty member bound for Permian Medical Center, regardless of the department, Porter was part of the chorus of institutional narcissism, devoid of self-reflection, with some extra umph: "I'm really surprised. I thought he/she was a better doctor than that."

Porter Piscotel penalized applicants for residency who, as med students, had been selected to Alpha Omega Alpha Honor Medical Society. He said they were, universally, "lousy on the wards." Chase recalled Porter's exact rank in their medical school class years ago. Porter was lost in the middle of the pack of 150 after the first two years, and still only 32nd in the class after his legendary straight-A third year. Porter didn't make the cut of the 14 students at the top. He had been denied the coveted AOA status.

So, one of Chase's first acts of appeasement shortly after returning to Far West as a new faculty member had been to nominate Porter as an honorary member of AOA. Year after year, though, the Chairman of Dermatology fought the nomination: "This is an undergraduate honor society only. Other schools induct honorary members, but that violates the spirit of the honor society. We don't do that here at Far West." Chase, holding back his personal reservations, would then relate how Porter had set the curve during their third year of medical school. However, the delayed induction of Porter to AOA was always voted down.

Chase was anxious about Porter's capricious nature, and perhaps he thought that his efforts to nominate Porter would circle back and win Porter's favor. Regardless, Chase brought it up at the AOA membership meetings every six months, until one occasion when the objecting dermatologist missed the meeting. After Chase's impassioned plea, Porter became a member of AOA, at the ripe old age of 45 – the first faculty member ever inducted to AOA at Far West.

From that day on, Porter never missed an AOA meeting or initiation, and his requirements for admission to the residency program changed on a dime. He wanted as many AOAs in his program as possible.

At times, it was easier for Chase to laugh. At one scientific meeting held on the Far West campus, the local faculty served as moderators at the podium for the out-of-town experts. Part of the moderator's job was to initiate the applause at the end of each question-and-answer period. In an oversight on the program, Porter served both as moderator and as a speaker in the same session. When he came to the end of his own presentation, and there were no further questions, Porter began pounding his hands together to generate applause for himself.

Chase was sitting in the applauding audience, next to the Pixleys, and when he lowered his head, gagging on his own laughter, he had to explain why. Gunnar said, "Oh, you're right. I didn't even catch it." Freya caught it only after Chase's explanation, then she, too, couldn't stop giggling. After Chase composed himself, he said to the two of them,

"It's sort of charming, in a naïve sort of way, but I couldn't stop thinking about Mike, Jane Goodall's famous chimp, the one that made himself alpha male, even though he wasn't the biggest or the strongest. He did it by banging two abandoned kerosene lamps together. He did it by making noise." Then, Chase quit laughing and thought to himself: *Don't feed chimps. They're carnivorous, and they cannibalize other monkeys. Respect homologies.*

Yes, Porter had a touch of Othello, the strong warrior personality, while, at the same time, he could be easily manipulated by certain parties skilled in the Art of Wormtongue, that is, sycophancy. Once, a good friend of Porter's convinced him to serve as a defense witness in a murder trial in another town, the defendant being a physician. Chase had an interest in the trial, for the accused was the very doctor Chase had been asked to nail by the VA years ago – a paranoid personality with untreated alcoholism, working at a small VA in Texas where he had offended patients, families, and staff for years. Chase, ashamedly, had declined to help based on his own exhaustion from a similar experience in California. Later, the lunatic physician was caught red-handed, injecting what most consider a lethal dose of potassium chloride into the IV of a patient whom he had threatened verbally earlier. The patient promptly died, and a murder charge was levied.

For untold reason, Porter's friend was able to manipulate Porter into believing this was a VA issue, another attempt by government bureaucracy to hurt its physicians. Porter was easily convinced to rally around the anti-VA jingoistic flagpole. "We've got to fight the VA on this one," said the friend, and Porter was always ready for a good fight. So, Porter drove to the small Texas town and testified in court that injection of that generous amount of potassium was "a perfectly reasonable and acceptable dose."

Jury deliberations took 22 minutes. The doctor, through Old Testament justice, was sentenced to death by lethal injection. When the murderer's picture made the front page of the Matherville newspaper, the court testimony, including the pronouncements by Porter Piscotel, read as colorful copy. Porter looked quite the fool, and he knew it. He tried to joke about his role, but to Chase, it fell quite flat. *How do you pick your battles, Porter? I've kicked myself blue for not helping to get rid of this guy years ago when I was given the chance. And you fight to keep him in business? Murder? For God's sake, man. And you joke about it?*

At first, Chase considered his observation of these "Porterisms" as a harmless game, but as time went on, a state of uneasiness bordering on imperilment began to overtake his thoughts, altering his opinion of Porter by returning to that "first impression," wrought from the DeLorean and the pipe. No longer were the incidents funny, given the consequences of such powerful bias, both confirmational and, to borrow a term from chemistry, conformational.

Residency supervision by faculty was a huge problem for Medicare reimbursement, not to mention the ongoing harangues by the VA. In fact, there had already been one FBI investigation into billing practices where the faculty had charged Medicare for cases in which there was no faculty participation, all the work done by the residents. The old system had, in fact, been preserved by T.N.T. who thought residents should learn to stand on their own two feet before going out into practice. Chase agreed. It was too bad that this era was ending through federal regulation. When Medicare representatives held a conference with the entire medical school faculty to explain the mandatory level of involvement required by faculty before billing could be allowed, afterward, it seemed that Porter had attended another conference entirely.

Chase thought the rules had been clearly stated by the Medicare authorities. For surgery faculty, this meant scrubbing in for the critical portion of the case. Stated alternatively, this meant scrubbing for nearly the entire case, except the opening and closing. It also meant rounding on the patients afterward, participating in the surveillance and care of complications, plus signing the residents' progress notes on a daily basis, *not with a simple signature*, but a written statement of agreement.

"What they're *really* saying is this…" said Porter after the meeting, whereupon he offered his own version of the dictum – "essentially no changes" in the status quo.

"Uh, Porter, I don't like it any more than you," said Chase, "I consider our Chiefs to be junior faculty. But that's not what the guy said. If we could continue exactly what we're doing now, they wouldn't have called this meeting, would they? We're being told to scrub in for everything but the opening and closing. If it's a ventral hernia, where the closure is, in fact, the key part of the case, Medicare says you have to be there for that as well. From now on, our times in the O.R. will be documented."

Porter replied, "No, that's not right. What he was *really* saying is this..."

<u>Conformational</u> bias. With *confirming* bias, one selectively hears only those things that support one's position. Yet, with *conforming* bias, one actually distorts and twists what has been said, a much scarier human foible.

In yet another way, Porter was a prototypical academic surgeon. Part of that prototype was a deep and abiding hatred, or at least a mocking distrust, of all other departments. If one of those departments served as your bread and butter, you feigned camaraderie in public, reserving scorn for private. In a word, other departments were the "enemy."

Once, when Porter was giving a guided tour of the Breast Pavilion to a Surgery Chairman from Up North, he bragged about everything in the facility, including Chase who was "a breast-dedicated surgeon." Odd, Chase thought. Porter had been openly critical of the breast surgeon concept from the beginning, yet Porter knew that having a "breast surgeon" was starting to pop up at the national level as being "cutting edge." But it was the next attempt to impress the visitor that floored Chase. "And," bragged Porter, "we even *took mammography away* from Radiology."

"You're kidding. I've never heard of that," said the visiting chairman.

"Yes, we got the position moved into our department. We're very proud of the fact that the entire Breast Pavilion is in the Department of Surgery."

"Well, good for you. Congratulations."

Chase was sickened. First of all, the takeover was a tragedy, nothing to boast about. That the Far West radiology department had been so lazy in recruitment was *shameful*...that T.N.T. had refused to put the administrative functions in the Department of Surgery until Chase pulled a backhanded stunt was *shameful*...that after Chase's insubordinate stunt, T.N.T. still tried to give all the profits back to radiology was *shameful*. T.N.T. had his back broken over it all, losing one of his oldest friends, the radiology chairman, and Chase was the backbreaker who was *ashamed* that he had to stand up to his savior-mentor on so many occasions, saying, "No...No...No." All of it was *shameful*. The whole story of the gradual co-opting of the Pavilion into the surgery department was repugnant in every detail.

Yet, here was warrior Piscotel, eyebrows raised, face aglow, oozing in his enthusiasm over snatching away mammography from the radiologists as one of the proudest moments in breast cancer history. And to beat all, Porter was inexplicably using the pronoun "we."

Finally, the visiting Chairman looked at Porter and said, "Well, we're supposed to be one of the top medical centers in the country, of course, but I've got to hand it to you – you're way ahead of us when it comes to breast cancer. I need to light a fire under some of my people."

Porter beamed.

In spite of this consistent pattern, disturbing to Chase but dismissed by others as "that's just Porter," there was a counterbalance of extraordinary unselfish behavior with effusive optimism by Porter, usually involving unlucky, downtrodden patients. Of numerous examples: a newly discharged patient, with severe unrelenting diarrhea post-op, discovered his house was on fire a few hours after getting home. He called Porter in a panic, even before he dialed 911, whereupon Dr. Piscotel drove across town to the site, picked up the patient, and took him to the Piscotel home where the unfortunate, semi-incontinent man stayed for two weeks in a bedroom with private bath made malodorous to the extreme. Porter's wife told a version of this story from her viewpoint that had audiences entertained no matter how many times they'd heard it. The message was clear – Porter Piscotel was uniquely willing to go to extremes that no one else would even consider. Yet, Chase noted the common denominator in every one of these stories – "downtrodden."

Why does the author of this treatise spend so much time belaboring the ins and outs of personalities too complex to understand completely... both Porter and Chase?

Because, on a chilly day in autumn, Thatcher Nolan Taylor, M.D. walked into Chase's office and sat down, slapping his palms on the arm rests, then speaking in a calm and gentle tone: "Chase, I need to let you know that I've been diagnosed with colon cancer. It's already spread to the liver."

"Oh, no... I'm sorry, Dr. Taylor. I'm so very sorry. What can I—"

"There's no hope really. Nothing you can do. I'll have the primary cancer removed with a short segment resection, just so I don't get obstructed, but I'm not even going to bother with chemo. Effective immediately, I've appointed Porter Piscotel as Interim Chair, and I'll be supporting him for the position permanently – if that's okay with you."

What an extraordinary gentleman, thought Chase. *If it's okay with me, as if that mattered.*

"Of course. Porter is fine with me – uh, great. He'll be a good Chairman."

26
VISION EXECUTED

On Day One of the new era, Chairman Porter Piscotel summoned Chase Callaway and Molly St. Martin to his conference room. Given that the Breast Pavilion was celebrating positive cash flow for the first time in its history, both Molly and Chase were eager for the meeting, anticipating a complimentary pat on their unified backs.

Porter sat at the head of the table, fidgeting, while the business manager for the department, Henry Rapier, sat to his right, taking frequent sips of Coke and wiping the condensation from the outside of the can. When it came to Henry and his numerical skills, T.N.T. had advised Chase upon re-entry to Texas to "double check all your monthly income statements." However, Henry had a remarkable skill as an able Iago, eager to manipulate any Othello willing to listen. T.N.T. didn't listen. Porter did. And Henry made no secret of his contempt for Christi Bloom, Chase's business manager at the Breast Pavilion, given that Christi had an annoying habit of routinely exposing Henry's mathematical shortcomings.

"The financial status of the Breast Pavilion has been a going concern for a long time."

Porter began the meeting as though he had twenty years of authority under his belt. He continued, "I've been studying your numbers in some detail." (Chase held back a guffaw, believing that Porter didn't do anything "in detail.") "Look with me, if you will, at the month of

August. Scroll down to your net loss. It has occurred to me that these ongoing losses can be completely erased, and the Pavilion will become financially neutral, through the simple act of cutting Christi Bloom's salary in half."

The first shot had been fired. Chase felt a boiling inside so torrid he thought he might actually reach across the table and strangle Porter Piscotel.

But he saw that Porter's hands were trembling, while Henry cast his eyes to the tabletop each time Chase looked his direction. *Two naughty little boys, seeing what they can get away with, now that "the gentleman surgeon" is out of the picture, dying.*

Barely clinging to composure, Chase managed, "First of all, you're only looking at one month, one point in time. If you examine the *years* of data, the *trends*, you'll see a very different picture. Secondly, if you're going to make major decisions based on a single month, why would you pick August? That's old news. Do you recall, or did you know, that it was August when the Pavilion was allowed to switch to an outside billing service? We had some bugs in the process, but after that, we've been sailing. Why don't you have September numbers here? October? I have them. We just had our best month ever. In the black, no less – without cutting anyone's salary. Besides, cutting a salary in half is absurd. If you want to fire someone (Chase looked at Henry), then you ought to just come right out and do it.

Porter began to stutter, head jerking, face contorting, his entire body twisting and turning. "Your losses have been staggering on this project Chase. Staggering. We've got to do something, and we've got to do it fast."

"We've already done it, Porter. We've turned the corner. Why aren't you willing to look at that? You're trying to create a crisis after the fact."

"Christi Bloom is responsible for this mess. I want her salary cut."

"That's the most ridiculous thing I've ever heard. I'm not going to tell her that her salary has been cut in half. What a chickenshit way to get rid of someone."

Chase, fuming, decided it was time to switch subjects and point fingers. It was a delicate issue that he had planned to pursue quietly and with diplomacy. No longer. "And by the way," he said, "we're missing a hundred thousand dollars."

"What do you mean?" Porter asked, shaken.

"Thatcher procured the money a few months ago from the College Hospital Foundation to help us at the Pavilion, but then his cancer diagnosis took center stage, and we've been unable to locate the money. Christi knows all the details."

Henry Rapier stared at the tabletop, his sticky fingers fumbling for imaginary accounting forms. Then, after an agonizing silence, he whispered under his breath, "I know where the money is. I'll take care of it."

Chase couldn't believe the swift admission of guilt. Had this stunt occurred in a bank, someone would go to jail. Instead, Henry stuttered through a labyrinth of moveable funds, transferring assets from one account to another, while one thing was clear – had Christi Bloom not been monitoring the situation, Henry would have succeeded in the robbery. Not for personal gain, but to get the money into an account more advantageous to his goals, and the goals of Porter Piscotel.

The gross embarrassment didn't bother Porter in the slightest (if he even understood what had just happened). He would not be distracted, and he persisted in his condemnation of the fiscal management of the Breast Pavilion since its inception. Molly St. Martin kept completely quiet during the ten minutes of gunfire.

On their way downstairs returning to the Pavilion, however, Molly had plenty to say. "My goodness, he's got a lot to learn. I'm going to give him a copy of the *PEP Guide to Leadership*."

"Don't waste your time, Molly, it has nothing to do with leadership. I've known Porter a long time, and he never changes his mind about anything. Proverbs 12:15, the way of a fool is right in his own eyes. He can't see through the prison bars of his own bias. He's a selective listener. Plus, he's a twister, someone who twists the square facts until they fit the round hole in his head. In a word, after what we just saw happen in there, I can guarantee you that our goose is cooked."

"Seek first to understand," she kept muttering as a mantra. "Seek first to understand. It's the very first principle of *PEP*. He didn't ask us one thing, not our perspective, not our plans, not our forecast...nothing!

I can't believe it. I've never seen anyone like that hold such a prominent position."

"Tell you what I'm going to do," Chase offered. "I'll make an appointment with Porter one-on-one, so that he doesn't have to flex his muscles to impress his goon Henry, then I'll explain the history of the Pavilion. He's completely lost on this. I don't know if it'll work, but I'll try it. The crazy thing is that Porter is basically a nice guy, and he's going to be popular with the other faculty. I mean, his first official act as Chairman was to give all faculty members a raise. How 'bout that for an opener? The problem is trying to pry open that steel-trap mind after it's closed. Frankly I've never seen it happen."

But an appointment did not come easy. In contrast to T.N.T.'s open door policy, Porter's schedule was always full, jammed packed, it seemed, with Porter leaving every day at 5:00 p.m. sharp. You could set your watch by the sound of his door slamming shut. Porter was first to arrive every morning, for sure, but Chase considered an abrupt conclusion to each day a marker that things were left undone. Medicine doesn't allow such rigidity.

"Looks like I can finally work you in at 4:45 next Thursday," said Porter's secretary.

"I need more time than that," replied Chase.

"That's the time slot he gave me."

At 4:45 p.m., Chase arrived. However, when he tried to squeeze the history of the Pavilion into 15 minutes, Porter interrupted him mid-sentence, every sentence.

"Look," said Porter, "Thatcher was frugal, and I am frugal. You've been downstairs spending money like there's no tomorrow, and it's going to stop."

The sound of hammering in the background (carpenters at work expanding and renovating T.N.T.'s old office for the new chairman), made it difficult for Chase to concentrate.

"What are you talking about, Porter? Listen to me. The plush furnishings were all donated, just like the artwork and everything else down there, so it bears no relationship to our debt or our cash flow. It says absolutely nothing about our spending habits. Those donations, by the way, came through a huge time investment on my part—"

"So, explain why your malpractice premium is paid by the Pavilion," added Porter, "what do you call that? Thatcher felt very strongly that faculty should pay their own malpractice."

"I call it my medical director fee, agreed to by Thatcher. If anyone has a right to complain, it should be Molly. She earns the bulk of Pavilion income. My malpractice comes out of our hide at the Pavilion's control point. Remember, it's the technical component from mammography that runs the Pavilion. And the capture of that technical component comes from our owning the imaging equipment, the very equipment that *I procured*—"

"You mean *Thatcher* procured."

Chase took a breath and continued. "Come on, Thatcher rubber-stamped my grant. I had the vision for the radiologic equipment to be part of the surgery department, and Thatcher agreed only after being forced into it by the vice-chancellor."

"There's still no reason why your malpractice should be covered. All the rest of us pay our own."

"That's not true anymore. Molly's malpractice is covered by the Pavilion. I spend more than half of every day on Pavilion problems, which limits my surgical income. I had a medical director fee written into my pro forma, but it became obvious it would never happen. Thatcher agreed that I could have the malpractice premium paid *in lieu of a medical director fee*. Remember, it's coming out of money that Molly and I generate, mostly Molly. However, if I hadn't procured the technical component before Molly got here, there would be no Breast Pavilion."

"That's where you don't get the big picture, Chase. The Pavilion debt appears as part of the Department of Surgery financials. You're making my whole department look bad."

Chase looked at the clock on the wall. Only minutes remained. "Thatcher always said the Pavilion was the most important thing ever to happen during his tenure. He let the debt accumulate knowing we would eventually work our way out. Now that we're in the black, it's going to happen. Have you seen our growth curve? We're hitting sixty patients a day now, with no slowing in sight. When we get going full steam, my malpractice premium is going to be a drop in the bucket. Even though Thatcher told me *not* to use endowment money to pay off the debt, that's still my plan, and I'm assuming you'll agree." (Chase did not mention the fact that Hardy Studebaker had told him for years not to worry about the debt. If Chase could make the Pavilion profitable, the accumulated debt would be "handled.")

Porter was unfazed. "The way I see it, you've violated almost every rule in academics to get where you are with the Pavilion. So, it's time to start playing by the rules. One of those rules is, we don't pay *any* nurse sixty thousand dollars a year. I'm not going to approve your request for the research nurse."

Argue him into a corner, then Porter will change the subject. How did we move to the hiring of a nurse? Chase felt his knuckles hurting, his fists clenched so tightly as to cut off the blood supply. "Porter, we already had an open FTE at forty-five thousand from my nurse who died. Did you hear about her? That she died of breast cancer? Well, the extra fifteen thousand a year is going to come out of the endowment. It's all in the paperwork I submitted, an absolutely neutral event financially for the surgery department. This nurse I'm hiring has special certification in oncology, and we're expanding her role to supervise all clinical research at the Pavilion."

"You're stealing her from the oncology unit, and that causes problems there. Of course, that's been your modus operandi all along, hasn't it? Some of my faculty are still upset that you stole Katelyn out of minor surgery already."

"I didn't steal Katelyn. She *asked* to come on board at the Pavilion. She really wanted to get out of minor surgery at the hospital. Frankly, she was tired of getting jacked around by the surgery faculty."

"Well, Dr. Bright is very upset about it."

"Dr. Bright was the worst offender. You oughta hear Katelyn's stories of the stunts he pulled in minor surgery, doing cases that should have been done in the operating room."

Porter's back log of criticisms was going to be limitless. He twisted the band of his wristwatch with increasing frequency, and the bell was about to ring when he added, "Oh, by the way, I was very pleased to learn that Henry found a hundred thousand dollars that we're going to give to the Pavilion to help out with your debt."

"You're saying Henry *found* a hundred thousand?" Chase was dumbstruck. He was unable to speak, given that his brain was shouting: *Were you in the same room with me when that sneaky bastard as much as admitted he'd intercepted the money? Money that T.N.T. procured for us in the first place? Did you catch the fact that he had no intent on sending it our way, until Christi Bloom caught him red-handed! That's the sort of trickery that Christi doesn't allow, and why he wants rid of her! And it galls me to no end that you think I'm stupid enough to buy into your lying bullshit.*

Alas, he said nothing of the sort, as the clock struck 5:00 p.m. Chase was excused.

How much was Henry contributing to this turmoil between the department and the Pavilion? Just as T.N.T. had advised, Chase always reviewed his financial statements from the university (i.e., Henry) on a monthly basis, and there were regular errors. Not the errors of embezzlement, but the errors of ignorance, as evidenced by the fact that the faulty calculations might go either direction. This was the same Henry, after all, who had once told Chase, "It's important to remember that there are two different ways to figure percent, and they give you different results." So, when Chase found an error the very next month, he dreaded the conversation.

"Henry, I found another error on my statement this month. This one's not in my favor, either. I don't have the same leeway for errors as most physicians. I cut it very close at home financially. This time, I've been short-changed by over a thousand dollars."

"Oh, yes, I see. Sorry, I'll get that corrected. I'll put what we owe you on next month's statement. Listen, while you're here, you need to know that Christi is really hurting you down there in the Pavilion. She's bad news. Let me give you some sage advice. As long as she's there, it'll never end for you."

Chase snapped. "Henry, let me tell you something you may or may not know. Hardy Studebaker is behind the Pavilion in every way. I can assure you, he's not going to let it fail. And it's certainly not going to fail because of Christi Bloom."

Chase knew it was a mistake the minute he let the Studebaker name slip. Since the earliest days of the Pavilion, he had kept his mouth shut regarding the Hardy Studebaker devotion to the cause. After Chase's slip, of course, the inevitable happened. Word began to circulate that Chase was "constantly" name-dropping, even threatening others, by calling on the name of the mighty Studebaker.

Chase scheduled appointments with Porter three more times during the next few weeks, all three being cancelled before they finally met on the fourth attempt. At the end of the fruitless meeting, Porter said, "One more thing, Chase. You're going to have to learn that Hardy Studebaker does *not* run this medical school."

Oh, yes, he does, thought Chase.

After that statement by Porter, Chase phoned the Raven sisters. "Somebody's got to do something, or else we're dead in the water. Porter's going to destroy everything to prove his point. And the problem is, he has no point." Next, Chase called Hardy Studebaker at his home in Hawaii, recounting every detail of the multiple attempts to chisel through Porter's skull, complete with Porter's naïve boast, "Hardy Studebaker does not run this medical school."

One person that Chase did not contact was Thatcher Nolan Taylor, M.D. How could he? It was so ridiculous…so petty…so unnecessary, after all that they'd been through. Chase was too embarrassed when visiting T.N.T. at home to drag a dying man into such a ludicrous, juvenile squabble.

Darby Raven recognized the implications immediately. After all, she was several hundred thousand dollars into a $2 million-dollar fund-raising campaign for the endowment. "We better get some sort of assurance, right now, before we go any further, that Porter intends to let you control the money in this endowment," she said. "I'm calling a roundtable, and Chase, I'm not going to invite Jody. We've already had one meeting together with Dr. Piscotel on our own shortly after he took over, and he was so intimidated by Jody that when she started talking, he started fidgeting, almost shaking, and when she asked him a question point blank, he knocked over his glass of water. Got all over Jody's dress. I mean to say, I think the poor guy nearly had a heart attack trying to talk to us. It should be just you, me and him."

On roundtable day, in the patient education library on Pavilion turf, Darby Raven said, "Dr. Piscotel, I'm sure you realize that we've targeted two million dollars for the Chair. With matching funds, it will become four million. Even though we're primarily honoring Dr. Taylor through this endowment, we are also honoring Chase and what he's done to create the Breast Pavilion. We're raising this money under the assumption that he will have complete freedom to use the money as he sees fit."

"Why, of course," Porter said. His hands were resting on the tabletop, fingers interlocking as if to denote calm assurance, but twitching, separating, interlocking again. Then his hands began to bounce up and down as a unit on the wood surface. "Chase will be able to do whatever he wants," said Porter. "The spendable interest, I think, will be in the vicinity of one hundred ninety-five thousand per year."

Porter detested Chase's "community support." It had been cheating as far as he was concerned. If you need money, you write grants. Indeed, Chase had written multiple grants to various foundations and community groups for the start-up funds in the creation of the Pavilion, but those didn't count in Porter's mind. Scientific grants were all that mattered when you were keeping score. You don't go begging from rich people. Especially, rich women. Porter was nervous around women, in general. However, around rich, powerful women, he was a certified bumbler.

After Darby had whipsawed Porter silly with nothing but pure sweetness and her gentle spirit, Chase finally spoke. "Porter, we've not been off to a good start, but let me just say this. If you sit back and let us do our work, we at the Breast Pavilion will do nothing but make you look good. You are welcome to take all the credit. Just let us do our thing."

After the meeting, related or not, the rumor began to roll around campus: "Can you believe that Chase Callaway is capitalizing off Dr. Taylor's terminal cancer? Raising money for himself based on the impending death of Dr. Taylor? Taking advantage of this wonderful man before there's even dirt on the coffin?"

Chase was devastated by the implications. "Don't they know that the Raven sisters started fund-raising for the endowment *before* Thatcher's cancer was ever diagnosed? We had opened the account, the first wave of letters had already been mailed, and the money was arriving before Thatcher ever got sick. Don't they know?"

"As a matter of fact, they *don't* know," said Chase's confidant in the lab, Gunnar Pixely. "I can't tell you how many people I've had to correct. It's pervasive, I'm sorry to say."

"Makes you wonder if my old buddy Porter isn't out there spreading the lies himself."

Gunnar said, "The problem is that the first widespread publicity about the endowment didn't come until after Thatcher was diagnosed, so it's an easy rumor for people to believe. Interestingly, though, did you know that Porter has started his own fund-raising for a second endowment to honor Dr. Taylor? This, in fact, *did* begin after Thatcher's diagnosis."

"What?"

"Yes, it's actually going to help us in the lab. Porter's going to fund a Chair for a faculty member willing to devote more time to helping the residents in their research."

"Fine. All power to him. Maybe that'll take the heat off me."

"Don't be so sure. Remember, in academics, when donations are made for a cause, there are all sorts of games you can play, and it starts as soon as someone pulls the check out of the envelope. Put your business manager on alert. When money arrives for the Thatcher Taylor Chair, not stated for which of the two endowments it's intended, you can rest assured where Henry Rapier is going to deposit it."

Fortunately, the major gifts were coming from foundations where Christi Bloom was tracking the funds. Yet, Chase remained unsettled. He still wasn't convinced he had control of the upcoming endowment. Some decisions were, by their nature, joint decisions, straddling two income sources. For instance, Porter was standing his ground, blocking the research nurse hiring, even though her extra pay would come from the endowment. Chase needed to hash this out with Porter, once again, along with the other plans Chase had for the endowment. He needed a meeting.

But the meeting never came. Chase tried for two months to get an appointment, but there were never any 15-minute slots. Trying to catch Porter in the hallway didn't work either. "Not enough time right now.

Later." Finally, Chase orchestrated an appointment by having Porter's secretary piggyback 15 minutes onto a meeting the dean had called to discuss the status of the Breast Pavilion. It was perfect timing. The dean would see the ever-improving cash flow, then the money coming in for the endowment, and then Chase would ease into his private discussion with Porter at the end.

But as the meeting with the dean came near a close, Chase saw the ominous signs of a rapid exit by Porter. He was fiddling with his watch, twisting it around his wrist, glancing at it repeatedly, then suddenly the identical move that had worked so well for T.N.T. over the years – Porter slapped both his palms on the tabletop, turned inward so that elbows pointed outward in the breeze.

Chase glanced at Molly. She saw it coming, too.

Don't do it, Porter. Don't you leave this meeting early. We've agreed to work out the details of the endowment right now. Today. You promised.

"Excuse me, dean, I have to get to another meeting." Porter walked out.

He's a chimp, imitating Dr. Taylor. Body language. Syntax. Self-effacing humor. But he's completely missed T.N.T.'s decency, honesty, and fairness. How could I ever have been frustrated by Thatcher in light of this parody?

Finally, Chase put his intentions for the endowment in print. How ludicrous, he thought, to be forced to communicate with one's Chairman only through writing. On the other hand, documentation could come in handy.

Chase gathered the perfect words to show how he planned to generate a base salary for a partner in breast surgery – first, by giving up his rotation at the VA and replacing that half-FTE of his salary out of the endowment. No gain in income for himself, but he could parlay the VA half-FTE into a full FTE by using the endowment to fund the other half, thus enabling him to hire a partner (another one of those "joint decisions" where both Pavilion and department shared expense). Thus, without altering Porter's departmental overhead one penny, Chase would have a surgical partner. She would do the bulk of the breast cancer surgery, spend the requisite time at the VA monitoring the residents, and at the same time, free him for the lab and his research vision. Thatcher Taylor had actually approved the plan (before the cancer diagnosis), though it had never occurred to Chase to get this in writing from T.N.T. He didn't need to under the old rules.

In addition, the VA would be happier with Chase's plan, given that Dr. Mooney, who had taken over for Chase as surgery chief, was insisting that the surgical faculty start "earning their keep." In fact, the Department of Surgery had always made off like bandits with major salary support going to the faculty for very little time spent at the VA. Some of the paid faculty members, in fact, never set foot in the VA hospital. Now, with T.N.T.'s River Kwai philosophy all but gone, Mooney was free to stick to the rules, and Chase's partner would be able to put in the required hours at the VA. Everyone would benefit, it seemed – Chase, his partner-to-be, the Pavilion, Dr. Mooney at the VA, and the Department of Surgery.

Porter Piscotel never answered Chase's letter, not in writing, not by phone, not in person. Porter simply took Chase's VA salary (as suggested in the letter) but used it instead to hire a personal friend who was willing to make the VA his primary practice site. Good for Dr. Mooney who was ready to leave the VA for golf, good for Porter's friend as the new VA Chief, good for the VA. However, one-third of the spending power of the endowment would be gone, and nothing had changed, except at the VA. Chase would have an extra morning each week, free of the VA responsibility, and that was that. An extra half-day, but otherwise status quo. The endowment earmarked for breast cancer had the VA as its primary beneficiary.

Chase had seen the standard template for university endowments, and it contained a statement specifically prohibiting this very shell game. Apparently, replacing salaries with endowed funds, then stealing the money away for pet projects by departmental chairmen had been a tried-and-true practice. Thus, the reason for the official prohibition. However, Chase's endowment was not yet official. Money was still being raised. Yet already, one-half of his base salary had been taken away to help Porter's friend.

Then things really turned sour. The university's matching program was backlogged, and all parties were shocked to learn that Darby

Raven's $2 million would sit idle for one year until the next round of matching funds turned it into $4 million.

"Can't we use the interest on the two million in the meantime?" asked Chase.

"No, the endowment is not an official entity until the matching funds are applied," answered the university.

This delay spelled trouble for the Breast Pavilion where the budget had already been formalized with the endowment income figured in. Chase had hired the research nurse over Porter's objections, histology equipment had been purchased (in anticipation of the Kruger 2000), and worst of all, half of Chase's base salary had been taken away, all while the endowment was still in the incubator.

"Porter, I'm sorry to stop you here in the hallway, but I guess you heard that we have to wait a year before we can use the endowment. We can't touch the two million already in the bank. I'm obviously upset about it, and especially with my VA base gone now, I'm not sure exactly, well, it's a little unsettling—"

Porter was glancing at his watch.

"I'm in a hurry, Chase. What are you asking?"

"Well, most importantly, I'm curious to know how I'm going to get paid? It's only a problem for one year, of course, until the endowment kicks in."

"Don't worry. I'll talk to the dean about it. The department doesn't have the money, but he'll have to use a slush fund of some sort. I was as surprised as you about the endowment. I'll take care of it." And he was off.

Hmmm? That wasn't so hard. He was actually halfway decent about it. Acted like he'd already thought it through. Miraculously, Chase's next paycheck contained his full base salary. For once, Porter had pulled some strings. A crisis had been averted.

The next month, the cash flow at the Breast Pavilion suffered a sharp reversal into the red, adding once again to the enormous debt incurred pre-Piscotel.

"What's going on, Christi?"

"I don't know. It was so sudden. Just when things were looking good. Henry gave me the numbers, and for some reason he's got us down with a huge increase in employee salaries. We haven't hired any new techs, though.

After reviewing the numbers, Christi approached Chase cautiously with the news. "Chase, they added your base salary to our monthly expenses, all of it. This is going to drive the Breast Pavilion into another eighty thousand dollars of debt before we can access the endowment next year."

"Dammit, that sneaky son-of-a-bitch. How dare he pull a stunt like that? Out there squawking to everyone about how I'm running the Pavilion into the ground, while he jumps the gun on the endowment and uses it for the VA, throwing more debt onto us? Without so much as a whisper to me! That's the truly amazing part – he doesn't' have the decency to tell me about an eighty-thousand-dollar dump onto our heads. He told me he'd get the money from the dean. What a communicator! It's bad enough he's violated every one of Thatcher's directives, bad enough that he's broken the rules of endowments, but now he's taking this out of our hides and driving us back into the red. What a wonderful deal that endowment turned out to be – no partner, no free money for the microscope, and now we'll be deeper in debt than if the endowment had never happened. Wouldn't the donors be thrilled to know what a profound impact they've had on fighting breast cancer?"

Chase was inconsolable. He called the dean's office and demanded an emergency meeting. While he waited, waited, waited for an appointment, he called the Raven sisters and Hardy Studebaker. He and Molly strategized. And they waited, waited, waited for a meeting to be arranged.

In the meantime, Chase caught Porter in the hallway. "How could you move my entire salary into the Pavilion *without even telling me?*"

"Hold on. Where else would you expect me to get your salary?"

"From the dean, *just like you said you were going to do.* You're the one who jumped the gun, hiring your buddy at the VA before the endowment was open for use."

"When did I tell you that I'd get the money from the dean?"

"In our conversation in the hall, the very day that we both found out the endowment was on hold."

"I don't recall any such conversation."

Hopeless was the only word that came to mind. Chase updated Darby and Jody Raven who, of course, notified Hardy Studebaker at his home in Milan.

Then, weeks later, a "major meeting" was finally scheduled by the dean. Molly & Chase were told to appear at the dean's office, where Porter Piscotel was already seated at the conference table. The Vice-Chancellor of Health Sciences was standing at a blackboard, ready to serve as moderator.

The vice-chancellor began, "We've just concluded a pre-meeting with Darby Raven and Thatcher Taylor's wife (Gretchen Studebaker Taylor), and I excused them from this portion of the meeting. I was pleased to learn that Thatcher is doing reasonably well, agreeing finally to go ahead with some chemotherapy. Now Chase, let's start with what I believe to be the problem…"

Seek first to understand…seek first to understand…how can you tell me what the problem is when you've never had a conversation with me or asked Molly one single question?

"…and I've come to the conclusion that this is merely a simple lack of communication."

You've got to be kidding. Is this Candid Camera?

Chase managed to say, "What are you saying? I've tried to communicate everything going on at the Breast Pavilion to everyone. I make phone calls, I write letters, I send memos, I let everyone know what's going on all the time. Communication is my forte, and I do it – or try to – non-stop. How could the problem be a lack of communication?

"Well, it seems that Dr. Piscotel has been left out of that loop. You've not really been communicating to him."

Chase was on the brink of exploding. What kind of mediator passes judgment without hearing the facts? Chase didn't know if he could contain himself or not, but he tried to speak calmly, "I initiated…multiple attempts…to meet with Porter. When I did manage to get an appointment, he'd cancel. If I tried to catch him at the end of another meeting, he'd get up and leave early. He—"

Porter spun around in his chair to pierce Chase with a hawkish look, eyebrows furrowed. "Oh, Chase, that's the most ridiculous thing I've ever heard. My door is open all day every day, and I'm there *every night* until 7:00pm. You could have met with me any time."

Chase wanted to coldcock him with a closed fist, but he took several breaths, knowing he was losing his grip. Chase said, with great restraint, "Let me just say I've tried my best to communicate, so let's move to the problems at hand, and the problem is this. The shell game that is being done with that endowment is expressly prohibited in the regulations. You can't come up with a better example of how to violate the terms of the endowment. I surrendered my VA salary under the premise that it help fund a partner for me. Granted, I know Dr. Mooney is short-handed over there at the VA, and it's a completely legitimate need, but that doesn't detract from the fact that the endowment is earmarked to benefit the Breast—"

"Look here, Chase," interrupted Porter, his voice condescending and derisive, "when you signed up to work for the university, you agreed to spend twenty hours a week at the VA. When you surrendered your salary, you freed up twenty hours a week you wouldn't otherwise have. That's how the endowment pays you."

Chase exploded. The white dwarf exceeded Chandrasekhar's limit and the detonation began: "So that's the lie you've been infecting everyone with. I wondered how you had rationalized it in that warped mind of yours. The VA is a fraud, Porter, and you know it. The twenty hours is a fraud. None of us do it. It was set up that way even before Thatcher became chairman. You don't spend your twenty hours. I don't spend mine. If you're gonna stick to the letter of the law for once, then all of us are guilty. You included. I'm required by the department to be there on Fridays, and that's that – no freakin' twenty hours. The residents are usually done by noon, so it's more like four hours. Even then, my briefcase is full because of the Breast Pavilion, so I'm working two jobs at once. There's no freakin' twenty hours coming out of this deal, and you know it, Porter. I can't believe you'd stack a lie on top of a fraudulent VA system to justify the fact that you've screwed this endowment and the people who donated to it. You lying piece of shit. *I quit!* You people are batshit crazy. There's a nuthouse across the street, and I can assure you there's more integrity over there than any of you can possibly muster."

Chase stormed out of the room to strike a deal with Permian Medical Center. On the way, he phoned Hardy Studebaker in Milan to let him know he'd resigned.

Molly St. Martin was livid, both at Porter and Chase. She stayed in the conference room after the explosion and used her diplomacy to quell the situation. Later, she called Chase at home and asked him to cool off. He didn't. He had one more scheduled surgery the next day, then he was packing his bags. This was a level of anger that would not dissipate. He had sought happiness in medicine for 20 years, and now that he was on the brink, a lying little snit was going to destroy it all.

In the middle of breast cancer surgery the next day, as he was dissecting out the intercostobrachial nerve in the axilla, having trouble focusing on his work, Dr. Darlene Wheatley rushed into the O.R., and said, "Dr. Callaway, the president of the university is on the phone, line two at the front desk, looking for you. I told him you were scrubbed in, but he wants to talk with you anyway – *now*. I'll scrub in until you get back." Darlene was a chief resident in general surgery, and Chase had planned for her to join him as a partner in breast surgery upon completion of her training. Thus, her future was on the line as well.

Chase left the O.R., and Dr. Wheatley took over.

On his way to the telephone at the front desk, he grumbled, "What people seem to forget around here is that the nature of our work is inherently stressful, but that doesn't stop them from piling it on."

On the phone, President Skip Didion rambled non-stop about how wonderful Chase was, how the endowment was going to be the largest in the university's history, and how it would be highly visible. "Highly visible," he said over and over. "You've got a new chairman with big shoes to fill, and there needs to be some forgiveness on your part. I think you'll see a different Dr. Piscotel from now on. We're going to cover your salary until the endowment starts up, then we're going to cover the salary of the partner you want. That'll leave the endowment full again, just like you intended. If something doesn't go right in the future, I want you to call me directly. I mean it. Dr. Piscotel is a good surgeon, and we don't want to lose him either. If worse comes to worse, we'll figure out a way to keep you here at the university. So I'm asking you to stay."

That afternoon, Porter Piscotel appeared in Chase's office at the Breast Pavilion and apologized. It was a first.

"I'm sorry, Chase. The breast center's been losing money for years, and I saw myself as the white knight who could ride in and fix it instantly. I'm sorry, and I'd like you to stay."

"Fine. I'll stay, Porter. The president has corrected all the issues with the endowment. But please, *please* let me run the Pavilion. You don't have to do a thing. I said this before – if you'll just sit back, I will do nothing but bring honor to this department and to you. I'm very good at administration and inspiring people and making things happen, and so is Molly. We work together beautifully, and we'll make this place a wild success."

But when Molly found out Chase and Porter had struck an armistice, she was upset, mostly because she had been completely left out of the negotiations. She made her point painfully clear to Chase: "I told you once before that I don't like shouting. I don't like tempers out of control. What I saw the other night in front of the vice-chancellor…well, let me say this, if that ever happens again, I'm not so sure about the professional marriage agreement that we've made."

"Molly, I'm sorry, but if I walked you through the entire history of the Breast Pavilion, long before you got here, you would find major hurdles, not minor, I'm talking hill-to-die-on-struggles, and *not one* of those battles was resolved through diplomacy. I've found only two techniques work at this place – insubordination and/or threatening to quit. We wouldn't be here, *you* wouldn't be here, if I hadn't taken those steps. That's the horrible reality. I hate it as much as you do, believe me."

"Well, that's not all I'm upset about. You negotiated a settlement with Piscotel without me. It was premature."

"But he's apologized. The endowment's intact again. We still have to wait a year, but we're not going to get killed financially in the meantime."

"Doesn't matter. Porter is a wounded animal now, and that's dangerous. I don't trust him for one minute. Show me what you got in writing."

"Well, uh, nothing's really in writing. But, well, President Didion is all over this."

"A leopard doesn't change his spots. If anything, Piscotel has more motivation to hurt you now, Chase. You think you've won, but you just humiliated a very insecure person who will lie in wait until the right opportunity comes along. To be blunt, I should do our negotiating from now on. I'm a tough cookie. *Calm* and tough. I don't need to yell. We could have used this opportunity to move the Breast Pavilion out of the Department of Surgery, to get as far away from Porter as possible, so that we could answer directly to the dean. I know the dean hasn't been much help either, but rest assured, the dean will cow down to the Raven sisters and the Board every time. This was our big chance, and frankly, I think you blew it. Porter Piscotel, Dr. Piss-and-Go-Tell, is now our boss – forever."

•   •   •

Remarkably, Chase Callaway was nominated for the Hardy Studebaker Master Teacher Award a few months later. He was a perennial nominee and one-time winner of the Outstanding Teacher Award voted on by medical students, the only past faculty winner in the history of the surgery department. The Studebaker Award, however, was a lifetime honor, the medical school's ultimate prize. The whole package came with a dinner gala that honored the winner's entire family, along with a generous round of publicity.

Finally, Chase thought, things were starting to turn. Three nominees were up for the award, one generated by the medical student body (Chase), one by the faculty, and one by administration. The final choice was made by the medical school administration in concert with all past winners of the Studebaker award.

Then, through the rumor pipeline of administrative assistants, Chase learned that he had won. Chase's father was in bad shape, deteriorating neurologically, and while Wes Callaway wouldn't be able to attend,

Chase arranged for the gala to be video recorded so that his father could see that his son had finally made something of himself. Of course, his mother Ramona would attend the awards dinner. Chase had hoped Sukie Spurlock could make it as well, but she declined due to illness. All the sacrifices were finally paying off. The Breast Pavilion was on automatic pilot.

As the event drew close, Chase was increasingly bothered that he had not yet received official word of his winning. Then, one morning, in bold headlines in the Matherville newspaper, he read the name of the Studebaker Master Teacher Award – Dr. Benjamin Sandusky. No one had an explanation. His rumor sources were shocked. A few days later, Chase met one of the past Studebaker Award winners in the hallway.

"Chase, I'm sorry about what happened, though I really don't know *how* it happened, to be honest."

"What do you mean?"

"You won the Studebaker Award this year, at least that was the score when I left the meeting."

"Well, in fact, word leaked out saying the same thing. I was told I'd won and to prepare my speech."

"At the end of the meeting, the dean thanked the former winners for being there, and I thought the meeting was breaking up. In fact, I was the first one out, so someone must have pulled something at the last minute. Several of us left the meeting at the same time, so maybe they did a recount, or re-vote or something."

Chase was puzzled, but not terribly disappointed.

Then, the "highly visible" endowment, as repeatedly described by President Skip Didion, followed the same perplexing path as the Studebaker Award. When time drew near to activate the fund, Chase received the official endowment documents in the mail. It was pitiful – the name of the Breast Pavilion was incorrect, the name of the Endowed Chair was wrong, there were 23 typos throughout the document (Chase counted), and most implausibly, the paragraph with the header – "Changes to the Endowment" – referred to "the protocol as outlined in Paragraph 11." However, *there was no paragraph 11*. "Perfect," said Chase. "But what I really like is the list of signatures at the bottom, the people who have signed off on it already. That says it all." The Chairman of the Department of Surgery, the Dean of the School of

Medicine, the Vice-Chancellor of Health Sciences, and President Didion had all scribbled their names above their lofty titles on a piece of crap. "This place is nothing but a ship of fools," he said.

Chase sent the document back, unsigned, careful to point out in gentle detail the numerous errors. "For a bunch of academics who are always hiding behind propriety, this shows just how much attention they pay to the rules. None. They make them up as they go along."

Chase focused intently on the endowment wording that prohibited the classic shell game. He had already seen Porter work this one over. Chase wasn't alone when it came to the shifting of funds from one shell to another. Once, he had arranged for the departmental librarian to receive a $5,000 donation from one of Chase's benefactors. "Oh, please don't give it to me yet," said the librarian. "Dr. Piscotel will just lower my budget next year by five thousand."

One phrase in the endowment bothered Chase at first, but then he dismissed it – "If the Holder of the Thatcher Nolan Taylor Chair of Surgical Breast Oncology leaves the university, all principal and revenues will default to the Departmental Chairman." Oh, well, it didn't matter. He wasn't about to leave now. With Hardy Studebaker behind him, along with the Raven sisters, a host of angels in "the community," the president of the university, and finally, considering the purchasing power of the endowment, he could tolerate Porter Piscotel, no matter what the chairman tried to pull. Yes, Chase was planted for life.

Chase wasn't the only one who had to iron out deficiencies in the endowment document. The Raven sisters had taken a copy of the agreement to terminally ill Thatcher Nolan Taylor who was quite disturbed by the sneaky "tricks." For example, 20% of the earned interest was *not* the standard amount to reinvest in the corpus. The standard was 10%. This would have cut into the spending power of the endowment to benefit the university's gold reserves. Also, the entrusted Chair Committee, required to monitor Chase's activities, had no representatives from "the community." Remarkably, there was a glaring absence of Darby Raven's name! This was not a "good faith" effort. Thatcher had specifically requested that Darby be a Trustee. Through his dying breath, he pulled strings one last time, and Darby was given her rightful place. Finally, everything was in order for the launch of the Thatcher Nolan Taylor Chair of Surgical Breast Oncology.

Traditionally, with newly endowed chairs, there would be the initial press release, special PR events, a reception, and embossed announcements mailed to all faculty members. With this "highly visible" endowment, though, Chase thought there might be even more. Mostly, he wanted his father to see the hoopla (since there would be no Master Teacher award). Wes Callaway wasn't expected to live but a few more months. Chase was forever bothered by his father's disgust over his career choice: "You're only doing breast surgery? But why? That makes no sense to me." In fact, Chase could not recall his father ever having expressed pride for his son.

Chase and his mother believed Wes Callaway could still comprehend his surroundings, but his speech was gone, so Chase already knew he'd never hear "Congratulations." Perhaps, Chase thought, he still might be able to read something in his father's eyes once the announcement was made about the Thatcher Nolan Taylor Endowed Chair of Breast Surgical Oncology.

But there was no press release, no reception, no gold-embossed notices mailed to the entire faculty. Nothing. Chase waited weeks, then months. Finally, a letter arrived from the Office of the President of Far West Texas University. In its entirety, it read as follows: **"This certifies that the actionable item is now enforced."**

"What the heck is this?" Chase said aloud to himself. "Junk mail?"

He scoured the letter for some sort of indication as to why the president would be writing him in secret code. Then, he deciphered the mystery. The answer was located at the bottom of the letter, far left-hand corner, small font:

Re: Thatcher Nolan Taylor Endowed Chair

And with that, Chase Callaway assumed the title of "First Holder of the Thatcher Nolan Taylor Endowed Chair in Surgical Breast Oncology." The "high visibility" of the most heavily funded academic chair in the entire university meant, in fact, that no one in west Texas would ever hear about the endowment again, as long as Chase Callaway held the Chair.

27
PAX ROMANA BREVIS

"Molly, now that the fireworks are over, would you give some thought – no – would you *please* take over the Pavilion management on a day-to-day basis? You already run the radiology side, but I'm talking being the interface with administration, too? The combat days might be over, but I'm at wit's end. It's going to be diplomacy from here on, and that's your thing."

"Yes, I'd be happy to do that. Sort of a good cop/bad cop approach?"

"I suppose, but preferably 'no cop' on my part. Off the record, of course, just an agreement between you and me."

Although he was thinking this – *I've been beaten to a pulp, nothing left inside, and I'm totally dependent now on your remaining strength.* Instead, he said this – "I plan to drift into the lab, now that the endowment is kicking in, and I'd really like to keep a low profile from here on. I'll still serve as attending on the breast cases in the O.R., of course, and teach in the clinic and run conferences and so forth. But if you don't mind, would you meet with Porter, by yourself, whenever he gets in one of his maniacal micromanaging moods? For that matter, with anyone who tries to strong-arm us?"

"Well, I don't want to meet with him any more than you do. I'll say it again, we should have held out for a better deal – a deal that excluded Porter entirely. I don't like it one bit that we're still under him and that we're back to square one, and that I wasn't a part of that decision. But, yes, we have to move forward."

However, the good cop/bad cop angle didn't work out exactly as Chase had hoped. The bad cop was still needed too frequently. Molly faced each challenge forthwith, but when rational diplomacy didn't work (as was the rule), she made a U-turn into Chase's office. Once again, it was time for Chase to do his "thing." His "thing," of course, was hardline ultimatums. More often than not, Molly's diplomacy ended up in the black hole of academics. No response, no action, for that matter, no acknowledgment.

The peace was short-lived, even though the Breast Pavilion had turned the corner into profitability, albeit still with its past debt. As though they had been "flies on the wall" to the unofficial good cop plan for Molly, the dean and Chairman Piscotel decided to double-team her, in full ambush. Inviting her to a lovely breakfast at the faculty dining club, Piscotel worked himself into a frenzy, throwing the financial reports onto his Belgian waffles, nearly shouting, "I personally contribute more to the surgery department with my patient care income than the entire Breast Pavilion. That's outrageous and it should be embarrassing for you and Chase."

Chase was stunned, later, when Molly told him of the encounter. "But did you remind him of the fact that we have a little thing called *overhead* that you and I are trying to cover? To the tune of one million freakin' dollars a year? We have fifteen employees. He has one. We have equipment overhead, we have—well, I'm not gonna preach to the choir, sorry, Molly. Our situation is not even remotely related to an individual faculty member. In fact, it's frightening that he would make such a comparison. It's just another typical demonstration of his warped sense of justice and what a blooming fool he can become once he closes his mind. But my, oh my, he can be the nicest guy in the world when he's not trying to destroy something."

"Well," said Molly, "that's not even the bad news."

Chase braced himself.

"He wants to start applying the university and departmental taxes to our gross income, not just our professional fees."

"He wants to tax the technical component? That piece of shit! That was my ground rule from day one on this project years ago. That was the very bedrock of the Breast Pavilion's financial success. Thatcher assured me that no one in the university taxes technical component income. If Porter does that, we're ruined. What did the dean do? Did he just sit there as usual, the bump-on-the-log act he's mastered so well?"

"The dean said nothing, but he was nodding a big fat yes."

Chase was sickened to his core.

"You were right, Molly, you were right. I should have listened to you. A leopard doesn't change his spots. I should have known."

"Not to rub it in," she said, "but I knew it within ten days after you buckled prematurely."

"How so?"

"We had a donation from one of our patients of three thousand dollars to the Pavilion for the express purpose of Christmas bonuses for our employees. I should have given it directly to the girls, but I made the mistake of running it through the university. Piscotel refused to give the money to our employees, saying that it set a bad precedent, that the department didn't have the money to do that for all the other employees, and that a clinic like ours, still in debt, had no business giving out bonuses. Piscotel had his lackey Henry apply the donation to our debt. So, I slapped a big sign on his office door that said, 'Bah Humbug'."

"I gotta admit," said Chase, "I knew about the employee bonus-bashing. Hardy Studebaker called me on it, so I had to get the scoop."

Molly looked surprised. "Studebaker called? Why didn't you tell me?"

"First, it made me sick to realize you were right about Porter. Second, it was the first time Hardy has ever criticized me. Hardy is now trying to act as a mediator so that Piscotel and I don't kill each other, and he told me it was probably unwise to be giving employees bonuses when we were barely profitable. Can you believe it? Piscotel had worked the Christmas bonus story into an unrelated conversation, as an example of my fiscal irresponsibility. When Hardy called me to slap my wrists, you should have heard him backpedal when I explained that it was *donated* money *earmarked* for Christmas bonuses at the Breast Pavilion. He says, 'Oh, I'm sorry, Porter didn't tell me it was donated money, he just said you were burning money as usual, handing out unauthorized bonuses. I told Hardy point blank to be very careful, that this was exactly how Porter operated, spreading half-truths and leaving out the key information, all perfectly crafted to make me look bad. I also told him that if another donor did the same, that you and I were going to ignore the university rules and give the Christmas bonuses directly to the employees."

"We've *got* to get out from under him," Molly said. "And don't beat yourself up. Remember, I was the optimistic one after that very first meeting with Porter when he tried to cut Christi's salary in half. You said our goose was cooked way back then. You were absolutely right, and I was the Pollyanna."

Chase shook his head in disgust. "Do you realize that if the standard physician taxes are applied to the technical component, the Department of Surgery will get four hundred thousand dollars a year, while we go belly up? Before, they tried to kill the golden goose by squeezing its neck, but Porter has a freakin' axe in his hand. Oh well, it's so outrageous that Hardy will put a stop to this nonsense pronto. By the way, Hardy told me once again not to worry about our debt. He assured me he's going to take care of it – all six hundred fifty thousand."

"Well, perhaps Porter's hissy-fit at our breakfast was the best thing that could have happened," said Molly. "Now I know. Now I'm committed. One way or another, I'm going to get us out from under Dr. Piss-And-Go-Tell."

Molly defined her mission according to *PEP* protocol, and she dragged Chase into meetings with various faculty administrators to assert the Pavilion's independence. However, the dean said "no" and that was that. They would never be free of Piscotel. Chase marveled at the irony that he was helping Molly undo what he had worked so hard for in the first place, that is, when he had forced the administration of the Breast Pavilion into the Department of Surgery, very much against T.N.T.'s will. Remarkably, now that the breast center, primarily a radiologic program, was inside the surgery department, they couldn't get it back out (even though the dean had once told Chase to push Molly back into the radiology department).

Molly wouldn't give up in her quest to free the Pavilion from Porter's grasp. Chase, on the other hand, thought the conflict would die out as soon as Hardy Studebaker covered the debt and told Porter Piscotel to keep his grimy hands off of the technical component of the Breast Pavilion.

In The Smoking Room at the Colony Club, Hardy Studebaker fiddled with his magic wand while his guest, Chase Callaway, spoke: "Porter is not going to get off my back until the debt is gone. I'm sorry, but that's the way it is. I'm perfectly willing to pay it off with the endowment, but Thatcher was emphatic with me, that he didn't want the endowment used to pay off debt."

"I agree with Thatcher, Chase. The reason I've waited this long to intervene is that I had to be sure the bleeding had stopped. I didn't want to bail you out earlier if the losses were never-ending. However, you've finally pulled out of the nosedive, and your growth rate is just wonderful, actually. I've been raiding the Runnymeade Foundation for the Breast Pavilion in the past, close to a million already, so I'll be going to the College Hospital Foundation Board. The Breast Pavilion has been a windfall for them at the hospital, of course. They've already donated a hundred thousand toward the debt problem, as you know."

"Yes, the hundred grand that nearly slipped away..."

Later, when Chase received a copy of the grant request to the College Hospital Foundation, he was shocked to see that the letter was not from Hardy Studebaker requesting the money for debt relief – it was from Porter Piscotel. "Oh, please no. Surely, they're not trying to patch things up between Porter and me by trying to make it look like this was Porter's idea."

To be sure there would be no confusion in the future, Chase called Hardy to complain. The response was cool: "Porter was required to write the letter, Chase. Calm down. The College Hospital Foundation doesn't give grants to faculty unless there's a supporting letter from the departmental chairman. I've already taken care of this for you, Chase, so you can relax. Things should be just fine from here on."

Two weeks passed when Christi Bloom burst into Chase's office, beaming with news. "You're not going to believe this. I can get us one million dollars, I'm almost positive."

"For the debt? Are you talking about the six hundred—"

"No, unrelated. Something out of left field. I'm talking about the Texas health and welfare system. A friend of mine, Dr. Meyerson, is one of the higher-ups now, in fact he's the highest up, and he just tipped me off to a one-million-dollar surplus. The only thing is – the money has to be earmarked for educational purposes."

Chase's mind raced through the possibilities. This was too good to be true. Laboratory equipment for research was the first thing that came to mind. He had always wanted to perform laser microdissections of tissue on microscope slides, so that the researchers would know exactly which cells were being studied after their DNA had been amplified. It was a perfect match for the Kruger 2000. The computer would store the photographic image of the tissue, provide the Z-score...

No. This is no time to get greedy. Laser dissection was not really "educational" in the strictest sense. The financial success of the Pavilion was due to Molly St. Martin. She should be recognized. "I have an idea," Chase said to Christi, "let's use the money for an endowment for Molly. With matching funds, it will be a two-million-dollar Chair. Can we call that 'educational'?"

"You were reading my mind. That's exactly what I was thinking. How great is that! Two major endowments for you both. But here's my idea. You're gonna love this. We have an opportunity here to show Piscotel that we're self-sufficient. That we don't need him. I've talked to my doctor-friend, the grand poobah now, and we're going to stage a meeting, acting as it were, so that it looks like we're negotiating for the money."

"Good idea, Christi, and we'll let you do all the talking. It'll let Porter see how connected you are. Maybe he'll get off your back, taking Henry with him. This is working out so well I can't believe it. A million dollars. Out of nowhere. Man, when it rains...when it rains..."

The staged meeting took place a week later. Porter Piscotel, with the uncanny knack of knowing precisely when a speaker's final word was uttered, marking the moment with a snort and a fidget, lassoed the periods at the end of Dr. Meyerson's sentences and roped them into his own opening words. Christi Bloom couldn't even enter the conversation as a postscript. Nor could Chase. Nor could Molly. The meeting became a two-man dialogue between Dr. Piscotel and Dr. Meyerson.

Chase was astonished that Porter was answering questions, *incorrectly*, about breast cancer, breast centers, and specifically the Breast Pavilion, never coming close to the truth, but hugging confidence all the way. Chase, Christi, and Molly found themselves in an eye-rolling contest. *Amazing,* thought Chase, *he doesn't even mind that we see him as a fool and a fabricator. He'll dominate a room at any cost. It's an addiction. He can't stop himself.*

Then, Dr. Meyerson shocked everyone in the room, including Christi Bloom, when he said, "This money was originally earmarked for hospital-based education, so it has to go to College Hospital or its clinics, *not* the medical school per se. The Breast Pavilion is a clinic under College Hospital, is it not?"

Chase looked at Christi as their eyes widened in shocking realization that the million dollars was about to disappear. How had Christi missed this key requirement? The Breast Pavilion had no direct ties to College Hospital. It was entirely housed, financially and administratively, within the medical school, a separate institution. Oh, well, thought Chase, it was a pipe dream anyway. We're going to be just fine without the million.

"Yes, absolutely," announced Porter Piscotel with his signature gusto. "The Breast Pavilion is considered administratively as part of College Hospital."

"Good. I don't see any problems then."

Nearly speechless, Chase was forced to confront Porter afterwards in the hall outside. After all, if the money were procured under false pretense, there could be nasty fall-out. "Porter, College Hospital contributed big time by funding our original bricks and mortar, but we have no connection to them now whatsoever. None."

"I know, but obviously, we have a lot better chance at the money if we're part of College Hospital." Porter's eyebrows were bouncing in childish delight.

Chase had tried to give Porter the benefit of the doubt before, cloaking Porter's prevarications in terminology like "conformational bias," but there was nothing sophisticated about Porter's approach at all. Porter knew exactly what he was doing every time he opened his mouth.

The same day, Chase wrote a letter to Dr. Meyerson clarifying the relationship of the Breast Pavilion and College Hospital. "You may have developed the impression from our meeting last week that.... let me apologize if there was any confusion on this point...College Hospital was, indeed, responsible for building the Pavilion, but we currently have no ties...we are administratively housed in...the chain of command is as follows..."

A phone call from Dr. Meyerson to Christi Bloom indicated that Dr. Meyerson was extremely grateful for Chase's letter, as his honesty would have an enormous impact on how the paperwork would be filed.

A week later, two events occurred within hours of each other. Landmark events. Chase was notified that the $650,000 debt been erased; and secondly, the million dollars was bestowed on the Breast Pavilion to administer in whatever manner Chase, Molly, and Christi so desired. Chase's secretary began wiping away tears at the news. Other employees laughed, others cried. One mammography tech developed a flyer that read, "Ding Dong, the Witch is Dead, the Debt is Gone, No longer in the Red," and placed copies around the Pavilion. The dark and ugly clouds of failure that had loomed over Chase and his dream for so long had disappeared. The war was over.

The Raven sisters called an emergency Board Meeting to announce the news. They surprised the group of women with a champagne breakfast, catered by the top chef in Matherville (from The Colony Club). Corks popped, and the ladies were soon giggling with delight. Chase took pictures of the occasion – his favorite was Molly St. Martin standing between the Raven sisters, both of whom were filling Molly's glass with spirits as the three angels bathed in the champagne.

Two weeks passed. Silence only from the Department of Surgery upstairs. Then, one afternoon, Porter Piscotel charged into Chase's office, beaming. "Chase, have you heard? I just got the news. The debt is gone. All of it." He plopped into the chair across from Chase's desk, sitting straight and smug.

Chase scrambled for words. "Uh, yes, Porter, we knew about it two weeks ago. In fact, we had a party here in the Board Room on the day it was announced."

Porter's face melted, and he slid into a slouching position in the chair. "Well, I, uh – I turned in the information for the foundation, and I've been out of town, so—"

What's he struggling over? Is he going to claim that his letter did the trick? That he's somehow responsible? The same guy who was trying to tax us into oblivion is now going to claim status as the savior. If so, I'll nip that in the bud." Chase said, "If I didn't seem worried enough for you, it was because Hardy Studebaker told me a long time ago that he was going to take care of the debt."

Porter turned red and purple and white and blue. He fidgeted, twisted, coughed, snorted. Chase halfway expected steam to spew out of both ears. "Uh, good. I just came down to tell you...in case you hadn't heard." Then he slithered from the chair and rushed out of the room.

Chase called after him, "And we got more good news, Porter. We got the million dollars from Dr. Meyerson, to boot." But Porter was already beyond ear shot, apparently, as there was no response to the news about the additional million.

When Molly St. Martin came into his office and shut the door behind her, Chase thought it would be a thank-you for designating the million dollars as an endowed chair for her. Instead, Molly said, "Chase, there are issues we have on the radiology side that I spare you from since you have so much on your plate. In trying to sort out the conflict, well, my bottom line is that it's time for you to put the wheels in motion, documenting or doing whatever the rules are, with the intent to let Christi Bloom go."

Chase tried to catch his breath. Cat fights in the Pavilion were not unusual, but he stood as far away as possible. Caring for breast cancer patients was a huge stress, and when the university added its own unnecessary obstacles hurting the Pavilion, it was too simply too much – far too much to tolerate internal bickering.

"But, why? How could we possibly...? Christi just now landed us *one million dollars.* I had nothing to do with it. Nor did you. She did it all by herself. It was *her* connection to Dr. Meyerson that's one hundred percent responsible. We've earmarked the money for you."

Molly replied, coolly, "I've been analyzing the psychodynamics around here regarding considerable dissension, and I've concluded that Christi is the common denominator. We cannot be an effective, purposeful organization with Christi at the helm of our business."

Chase was sickened, not by the charges against Christi so much as the ice in Molly's veins. Molly. Always so cheerful, so witty, so skilled, so charming, so sweet...so deadly. He couldn't believe it. So, it wasn't disgust Chase felt – it was *fear*. He wondered, for a split second, if he were ever to look backwards at this journey, at the backside of the signposts, would he, in fact, peg this moment as the worst of many wrong turns?

"Molly, I can't. Not after a million dollars. I don't care what she's done. Here I am, thinking we should be giving her a finder's fee. Of course, we'd get killed for that."

Molly glared at him, unflinching. "Okay. You'll see. Things will get worse, and you'll just have to find out for yourself. I know you and Christi are close, but mark my words, you'll be looking for the way out of a mess soon."

That strange, surrealistic episode aside, there was peace at the Pavilion, at least in its operations. After nearly a decade of anxiety and anger, the hard battles were over. Chase celebrated by declaring a week off for himself. He would spend some time with his father, and he would read and rest.

So, when his phone rang at home, he ignored it. Then, Porter Piscotel began leaving a recorded message. Chase couldn't believe it. He couldn't even get an audience with Porter at work, yet the chairman was calling him at home?

Woefully, Chase could tell with the first sentence that Porter's voice was bristling with restraint. Anger oozed out of each syrupy word: "Chase, I'd like you to explain...well, I just found out...the million dollars...I didn't know about...well, we need to have that sort of thing communicated...I'd like, at the next faculty meeting, for you to explain the million...we can't have things of this magnitude, well, just be prepared to explain how..."

Uh-oh. Porter was livid. But why? How could a departmental chairman be angry about a million dollars?

When Chase presented the story of the windfall at the next faculty meeting, he almost apologized for the wild success. "Yes, we've been very fortunate lately. However, if you want to know why all this happened – the endowment, the debt relief, the million – I'd have to say because I've kept in close contact with many donors, always making sure they're informed, always assuring them their money would be spent exactly as intended. Every penny. This hasn't been easy, nor did it go unrecognized. These donors are usually ignored after they sign their checks. I've not done that. I've had a lot of positive feedback in Matherville from patrons saying they've never had anyone so compulsive about how money is spent, with long-term feedback. As a result, we've had lots of very generous people contribute to our success."

When Chase sat down next to research buddy Gunnar Pixley, Chase whispered, "Man, I've never seen such angry faces in my life. Three faces, that is. Scowling at me, glancing at each other. Piscotel, Dagmar, and Dr. Judy. But why would Judy care? I have no association with him at all. He's a trauma surgeon, about as far removed from breast work as possible."

"Oh, you're just imaging things," Gunnar said. "You did great."

"I'm getting nervous. You know, after all the good news, I went ahead and ordered the Kruger 2000 microscope. Now I'm thinking I should have cleared it with Porter. But you know why I didn't? Because he's totally irrational when it comes to me. I think he'd try to block the purchase of the microscope, even though I bought it entirely through the endowment. After all, it cost a quarter-million. I don't understand why he's so angry about this most recent million bucks. The bloody truth is that I did try to tell him one day about the money, but he was scrambling out of my office so fast I had to call the words over his shoulder. I'd just caught him trying to take credit for our debt relief and he couldn't run away fast enough. I was three feet away from his back side when I shouted out the million dollars had been granted, but he was literally deaf with rage."

Confirming Chase's fears, a few days later, one of the Chief Residents who was scrubbed in with Chase on an axillary lymph node dissection, said, "Man, did you ever make the big dogs angry somehow."

"What are you talking about?"

"I did a Whipple with Dr. Piscotel this morning, and all he could talk about was how you stole a million dollars that had been earmarked for the new trauma center."

"Trauma center? What new trauma center?"

Chase called Dr. Meyerson at the Health Department to investigate. Indeed, after the staged meeting where Porter had made his bold and misleading statements about the Pavilion, Porter had called Dr. Meyerson later that day, telling Meyerson that what the surgery department *really* needed the money for was a trauma center. Dr. Meyerson said to Chase, in relating the phone call, "I told him it was a done deal. That you already had the money. He was pissed, to be honest. I couldn't believe it. A million dollars and the departmental chairman is pissed? I told him that we could re-visit his trauma center next year if there was another surplus, but he couldn't cool off."

Thatcher Nolan Taylor was on his deathbed now, homebound. Chase had desired, desperately, on many occasions, to inform his old mentor of the tragedies at hand imparted by Piscotel. Yet, how frivolous. How insensitive. Whining to a dying man about worldly concerns. All becomes trivial compared to death, thought Chase, so he had dismissed the idea. He always wondered, however, if Dr. Taylor had not somehow, perhaps inadvertently, encouraged Porter in his crusade against the Pavilion.

"Oh, that's impossible," said Darby Raven. "Dr. Taylor loves you. You can't imagine the wonderful things he's said about you from the very beginning."

"But Darby, think of all the times I had to stand up to him. To go around him. Through him. Christi, of course, was borderline rude to him sometimes, trying to get him to take a stand. I think it's very possible that Dr. Taylor issued a benign word of caution to Porter that was misconstrued. Thatcher could easily have said something like, 'the

Breast Pavilion has been an albatross, and you're going to have to be very careful with Chase.' Thatcher might have meant, 'careful not to upset him,' or who knows what? But Porter might have taken it as a mission to apply the thumbscrews on me. Kinda like when Henry II said in so many words, 'Will no one rid me of this turbulent priest?' and his knights filled in the blanks, assassinating Beckett."

The next weekend, Chase was on call for emergencies at College Hospital when the chief resident phoned him: "One of Dr. Piscotel's private patients needs to go back to the O.R. Stat. I've been saying this all week, but today the kid is going downhill, and I'm afraid he's going to perforate his gut, if he hasn't already. It was a post-op ostomy closure we did last week.

"Where's Dr. Piscotel? He likes to handle his own patients whether he's on call or not. Have you tried to reach him?"

"He's in Midland. They're giving him an award – West Texas Physician of the Year – or something like that."

"Ah-h, yes. I'll be right in. You know what they say: 'Never let the sun rise or set on a bowel obstruction'." It was faulty cliché, however, as the presence of a bowel obstruction was not always straightforward. Chase quoted it in jest, seeking a morsel of humor anywhere he could find it.

In this case, it appeared that the sun had risen and set at least seven times while the residents had been assured that the patient would "open up any day now."

The complication herein, post-op bowel obstruction, was often difficult to distinguish from post-op ileus where the bowel simply quits contracting for a few days. All general surgeons know the agony of waiting for the bowel to wake up after surgery. Even when a mechanical obstruction was the cause, it was more of a fluke than anyone's fault. It "came with the territory."

But when Chase reviewed the records and X-rays prior to the emergency surgery, he felt that the indications were there for re-exploration a week earlier when things turned south, exactly what the residents had concluded. Still, it could be considered a judgment call. Either way, faced with the same circumstances, Chase would have been documenting the status of the patient in detail every day, or even twice a day, as to whether or not a return to the operating room was indicated. After all, a delay to the point of bowel perforation could be fatal.

Rather than a concerned account of the events for the past week by the attending surgeon, however, the only notes in the chart were those of a third-year medical student, a violation of both in-house rules and outside regulations. There was no evidence that Porter had even made rounds on the patient. The dictum was well-known and clear: "If it's not documented in the medical records, it did not happen." Chase's flaring anger was calmed after the residents assured him that, indeed, Dr. Piscotel had made rounds every day. Apparently, Porter had been too rushed to leave tracks.

Emergency surgery was performed by Chase and the Chief Resident. Perforated bowel was repaired, and the underlying obstruction corrected. The patient recovered nicely and was discharged five days later.

Perhaps, it was the award for excellence that was presented on a Saturday night in Midland, at the exact moment when Chase was operating on the patient with a week-old, post-op bowel obstruction, or maybe it was simply the trip to wit's end – regardless, anger never left Chase's heart from that moment forward. It coursed through his veins, then oozed from his capillaries, out his pores. He was sapped by the restraint he needed to keep from lashing out at the object of his anger. Inside, a lethal rage was growing like a malignancy.

28
NECROPOLIS

Three people key to this story died within a matter of weeks, only two of whom were worthy of headlines in the *Matherville Daily Texan*.

First, Chase's father. Dr. Wes Callaway was cremated, his ashes scattered like seed over the lawn at the Far West Texas Field House where he had touched glory as a basketball star in the 1930s. A small memorial service was held, and eulogies came from old teammates mostly, his legacy being sport, not medicine.

Chase didn't speak at the service. Nor did he cry. Yet, a bitter thought gripped the son's mind during the funeral, fueled by his current disgust with the family's alma mater – *Dad still had all his marbles to the end. He could have, would have, appreciated my endowed chair, the 'highly visible' endowed chair, about which no one breathed a word, about which the confirmatory letter could not even bring itself to say 'congratulations', about which the word 'curse' might serve as a better descriptor.*

In his heart, though, Chase knew that prefab bridges could not span a lifetime chasm. Wes would have responded to the endowed chair with his usual, "Why would you want to limit yourself to breast cancer?" No, an alma mater might serve to suckle the child, but it's a rickety link to the father.

After the funeral, in the process of cleaning out his father's closet, Chase discovered two relics. First, a stack of newspaper clippings, not from Wes Callaway's basketball heyday, but instead, the local scoop covering the malpractice suit where his father's name was besmirched daily. (This was a "wrong side" mastectomy case wherein Wes Callaway claimed sabotage.) The clippings spanned two weeks, the duration of the trial, which his father lost.

Why embrace such punishment through this grotesque scrapbook? What was this syndrome that prompted his father to cling to the worst memories of his life?

Chase's other discovery was a Browning pistol, so small it seemed a toy, so cold it never felt heat, so old it had to be untraceable. Chase had no real interest in guns, but for some reason, this gray metal felt like potter's clay in his hands. He decided to keep it.

Ten days later, Thatcher Nolan Taylor, M.D. died and he, too, was cremated. At the funeral, the surgery faculty sat together in the same pew, but the illusion of amity betrayed the truth. No matter how Chase had tried to explain the origins of the endowment to his colleagues as pre-dating Thatcher's terminal diagnosis by several months, the fact remained that Chase was sitting on a whopping pile of cash. And that pile was a little taller, a little broader, no doubt, in light of Dr. Taylor's death sentence.

On the front steps of the Unitarian Church, immediately following T.N.T.'s funeral, Darby Raven sidled up to Chase and, touching his sleeve, said, "I'm nervous, Chase. I don't mind telling you. My brother is a molecular biologist at Cold Springs Harbor, and I was telling him about our endowment, and he says to me, 'Gee, why didn't you paint a big red target on Dr. Callaway's back and pass out machine guns?' I'm afraid he's right. I can't believe some of the whisperings I heard walking out of the service just now. The general consensus is that we enthusiastically capitalized on Thatcher's diagnosis and death."

Of the two men deceased, Chase needed the resurrection of Thatcher Nolan Taylor more than his own father. Chase's anger over Porter's scheming was barely containable, yet instead of this truth becoming known, his own reputation was being dismantled.

The third death didn't even warrant entry in the Public Records section of the Matherville newspaper, for there are souls who wander an entire lifetime without leaving visible tracks in the sand. Yet, their impact can be lasting.

By policy, when lifetime inmates at Matherville State Mental Hospital (a.k.a. Matherville Psychiatric Pavilion) died as wards of the state, unclaimed, their bodies were tagged for dissection at the medical school. Upon the death of Ivy Pettibone at age 66, however, a different fate awaited.

The course coordinator of anatomy rejected the body while still in the morgue. "Too many things wrong. That leg is a mess. And those scars on her hands indicate anatomic variants that complicate things for freshmen students, not to mention a difficult dissection. Of course, the radical mastectomy ruins our chance to dissect the axilla on that side. Nope. This body is unacceptable."

The new director of the morgue at College Hospital, now Chief of the Autopsy Service, was Nola Kastl, M.D., former student and pathology resident at Far West, now a faculty member, the same young woman whom Chase had inspired eight years earlier to commit to the Breast Pavilion dream. Traditionally, the autopsy service (and morgue) was delegated to the lowest faculty member on the totem pole, but Nola had volunteered.

In reviewing the chart to decide about performing an autopsy or not, she saw Chase's name scribbled in multiple locations, primarily related to office visits at the surgery clinic. She called Chase simply to let him know about the death, in case he remembered Ivy.

"I'm glad you called me," he said. "Ivy...well, it's a long story, but I'm very sorry to hear about this. Very sad. In fact, the ICU nurses were aware that I knew her. They called me while she was still fighting for her life. I got to say my good-byes."

"As it turns out, Ivy Pettibone is a special case," said Nola. "I've discovered in her records that she has a burial plot, arranged anonymously, and whoever did it included the stipulation of an autopsy. I'll let you know what I find."

In preparation for the autopsy, Dr. Kastl read as much of Ivy's medical record as possible, considering the many volumes. In her final days, Ivy had been admitted to the ICU of the un-named hospital at Matherville State. The clinical impression as to cause of death was listed as: "Overwhelming sepsis due to lymphangitis/cellulitis, a delayed sequelae of Halsted radical mastectomy."

Brain or no brain? This is the question that accompanies all autopsies where the brain is often left encased in the skull when presumed innocent of disease. However, this question did not exist for inhabitants at the asylum. Whether unclaimed bodies went to first year anatomy class or to standard autopsy, the brains were routinely studied. A new division had recently been established in the Department of Psychiatry – Stereotactic Behavior Modification – and the medical director, an M.D./Ph.D. from Harvard named Ray Divine, had met with Nola Kastl recently to establish a complex protocol for processing the brain in the detailed study of neuropathology post-mortem.

As part of the protocol, Ivy's brain was fixed for one month in formalin to stiffen the tissue from jelly to bologna, allowing thin and accurate slices for study. At the autopsy, each slice into Ivy's brain was completely unremarkable until Dr. Kastl reached Broca's area of speech articulation where she found a small arterio-venous malformation. Adjacent to the A-V malformation was an ancient scar, probably from a leak, located along the neural tract leading toward Wernicke's area for speech comprehension. For a moment, Nola Kastl thought the unthinkable: *What if this little lady was completely normal from the psychiatric standpoint? What if she's been locked up her entire life for a speech disorder?*

Prior to Ivy's death, Chase had crossed Crooked Creek to visit her in the ICU. When he arrived there, the residents were preparing to intubate her for the ventilator. "Ivy, they're just going to put this tube down your throat for a little while to help you breathe," he had said. "Everything will be fine just as soon as the antibiotics take effect."

As Chase had turned to walk away, he felt Ivy's hand grab his, and she pointed to the ceiling with her other hand. When he looked up, the only thing he saw was the speaker for the intercom system. He tried to placate her, but she persisted in drawing his attention to the ceiling. Her speech was garbled, as usual.

Then, a voice came through the intercom, "There will be a temporary power outage as we perform our routine test of the emergency generators. Do not be alarmed. The test will last only a few seconds, then we will go back to regular power."

Ivy looked at Chase and said, "God."

"Yes, Ivy, that's God."

She was intubated after that, and with endotracheal tube in place, she spoke no more.

As Chase left the ICU, he recalled the book Ivy had given him as a present long ago – *To A God Unknown* – borrowed, or stolen, from the asylum's library. He was years behind on his reading list, but he would move this volume to the top. After all, he had been dragging the book around for twenty years.

Ivy suffered a fatal cardiac arrest that evening. The antibiotics were too little, too late, to overcome the power of iatrogenic illness caused by those sworn to do no harm. A radical mastectomy for so-called lobular carcinoma in situ, a borderline pathology of uncertain natural history, had been performed for the practice of medicine, in a very literal sense.

Thus, three deaths.

But a fourth began its inevitable course shortly after Ivy's demise.

One of the surgery faculty members was on the phone, his voice shaky: "Chase, do you remember that young gal that I did the bilateral mastectomies on last month when you were out of town?" Chase had been in New York, lobbying to make the Breast Pavilion the primary U.S. site for research on the miracle blood test from Italy, now in his sixth year of negotiations and getting nowhere.

"Yes, how'd it go?"

"Well, there's a slight problem."

"What?"

"I did her biopsy here at College Hospital, and she would have been a lumpectomy candidate, but she wanted prevention against a future cancer because of her family history, and that meant bilateral mastectomies. Anyway, she wanted to go to Permian for a particular plastic surgeon, and I have privileges there, so that was that. We did her at Permian. Problem is, after the mastectomies, the Permian pathologists couldn't find any cancer. They saw a sclerosing lesion surrounding the biopsy cavity, so we all assumed I'd taken out all the cancer back when I did her open excisional biopsy. But the Permian pathologist asked for her biopsy slides from here at College Hospital, and they just called me saying the lesion was totally benign from the beginning, that it was nothing more than a complex sclerosing lesion."

Chase gripped the phone with a trembling fist, fighting the urge to throw it against the wall. He said, "Not again, dammit, not again."

"It's happened before?"

"Yes, several times, such that I've become expert on sclerosing lesions since these things can mimic cancer to near perfection. I catch them two or three times a year on patients from around the state when I do second opinions. How freakin' ironic that I've kept pathologists out of the courtroom, from every hospital in west Texas, *including Permian*, then it happens again here under my own nose. Well, you probably won't be sued, but who's the pathologist? They're gonna hang."

"Nola Kastl."

Inside, Chase wilted. Nola wanted to please Chase more than any other pathologist in the department, maybe more than any doctor anywhere. She was eager, new to the faculty, and now she would inaugurate her career with a lawsuit and a black mark that would never go away. It took little effort to recall the bitterness engendered in his own psyche after being sued his third day in private practice.

Not the public, not a jury, no one could understand how easy it was for this to occur with sclerosing lesions. Physicians couldn't understand, so how could anyone else? The discipline of pathology had walled itself off from clinical medicine years ago, so for cases like this, when things went awry, pathologists were held in siege. No one could help them. Complex sclerosing lesions could appear identical, virtually indistinguishable, from cancer. You had to be actively considering the possibility at the same time your eyes were scanning the tissue, or it could slip by the best of pathologists who, thinking about getting home before rush hour, might see it as "ho-hum, another breast cancer, fifth one today."

The Permian pathologists had it easy on this one. They had seen the outer rim of the problem, where the benign mimicry was obvious. When

Chase reviewed the biopsy slides, he saw that the central core was a near match for cancer. When shown fresh to eight faculty members later on, without any history afforded, five of eight called it cancer. It was a glaring example of how pathology was still an art, though wrongly considered the purest of medical sciences by the uninitiated.

"I have a one-hour lecture on this topic," said Chase to anyone who would listen in his fruitless attempts at catharsis. I've studied it for years. I've collected a large series, and I show the photos of benign next to malignant, and I ask the audience to distinguish. They can't. You have to back up, look at the overall pattern at low power under the scope, and get a Gestalt that tells you to stop and think and get special stains. Like the old trick of looking at the Greek vase and realizing it can also be two faces staring at each other, the mind rearranges the pattern of these lesions more clearly, and you see it's benign. In fact, once you recognize it, you wonder how you got trapped into even thinking for a minute it was malignant. The poor pathologists are nothing more than sitting ducks for the attorneys. However, since most patients have their definitive surgeries at the same hospital where the biopsy is performed, no one ever knows. Or, no one tells."

As weeks passed, it occurred to Chase that something had changed in his priorities. Not once did he consider the poor woman who had lost her breasts due to the "art" of pathology. Instead, he worried only about the fall-out from the inevitable litigation, and how Nola Kastl would survive the assault.

But Chase was not prepared for what happened next. When the lawsuit was filed, headlines in the *Matherville Daily Texan* proclaimed, "Young Woman's Normal Breasts Amputated at Far West Breast Pavilion." Then, TV cameras, some all the way from Dallas and Fort Worth, crowded at the southern plantation entry of the Breast Pavilion.

Shocked, Chase called the dean and tried to describe the circus outside his door, asking for advice. "Don't talk to the media," came the answer from the sage. So, outrageous claims and interpretations went unanswered. The Pavilion was publicly shamed.

"Why are these cameras pointed at the Pavilion?" Chase kept saying. "We don't do the pathology here." Yet, he knew it was an empty complaint. He was captain of the ship.

The stories were devastating, harping on the gross incompetence at the Breast Pavilion. "Inconceivable," said the plaintiff's attorney to the media. "This young woman has been mutilated, her life inexorably altered, her consortium confounded, her feminine identity ripped away, through sheer incompetence. She will never be able to breast feed...."

"Do you think we should explore the rumor that she just had an abortion?" asked one of the defense attorneys in response to the breast-feeding issue. The other defense lawyers joined in. "Also, have you seen the before and after pictures? I'm telling you she looks fantastic with that reconstruction." "Not to mention she had a family history of breast cancer. It's possible that this surgery saved her life." "And look, here's some evidence that these sclerosing lesions can actually turn into cancer if untreated. This article talks about the increased incidence of atypical changes and carcinoma in situ, and even invasive cancers, which come out of these lesions."

But nothing mattered. Chase was devastated. The media were killing his baby. His life was completely intertwined with the Breast Pavilion. Humans, he felt, deal with their own mortality through their children, or the legacy of their vocation, or the road to Heaven, any or all of these. For Chase, the Pavilion was, sadly, serving as all three. Without the Callaway bloodline going forth to a next generation, the Pavilion was most certainly his child, his daughter. The university had been strangling her from the beginning, and now the media were murdering his flesh and blood.

When he thought his depression to be at its absolute nadir, he got a phone call from a national magazine with a circulation exceeding 30 million. The writer was doing a story on the mastectomy victim, and they wanted to speak with the person responsible for the horror. Chase was so sickened that, after he hung up on the reporter, he had to leave the medical center, and he found himself driving into the high desert from which he never wanted to return.

Patients at the Pavilion began canceling appointments. Even Chase's private patients called and wanted explanations. Some brought the newspaper clippings with them to their appointments. "How could this happen?" they asked. "Did this happen to me? Did I really have cancer?"

Remarkably, and without explanation, Chase found himself collecting the newspaper articles, sorting them, saving them, as if embracing the humiliation would make it go away, exactly as his father had done with the malpractice suit headlines.

Making the situation even less tolerable was the fact that the lawsuit was against the ever-so-sensitive and sweet Nola Kastl, Chase's all-time favorite. He had spent years grooming her to become the lead pathologist for the Breast Pavilion.

The defense team was not willing to settle for the requested one million dollars for the plaintiff when, in fact, this was the average settlement delivered to those whose true cancers had gone undiagnosed, sometimes resulting in death. If a delayed diagnosis resulted in death, how could someone with a benign diagnosis ask for the same amount – one million dollars? No, for a benign, potentially pre-malignant problem in a high-risk patient, with an excellent cosmetic outcome, the defense attorneys were ready to fight, and Nola was going to fight with them. They would take this case to a jury.

Nola went missing for two weeks after the error, grappling with a "dark period" that, later, she refused to discuss. Chase knew her to be an excellent pathologist and perhaps his only hope for a quality program in breast cancer research. When she confessed that she was so devastated that she was thinking of getting out of medicine entirely, Chase decided to take their friendship off campus, and he invited her to dinner.

At an Italian restaurant near the Colony Club, Nola Kastl downed two dry martinis and a glass of Chianti before dinner. She became despondent as she described her frustration with herself. "You've trained me forever, it seems, about these sclerosing lesions. My mind was elsewhere, I guess." Without words clever enough to make the nightmare go away, Chase resorted to the only tool he had at his disposal – empathy. He confessed how he had been sued his third day in private practice and two times to follow.

While he pretended that he had survived the experience unscathed, he knew that, in fact, he had not. After considerable thought, he chose *not* to voice the following to Nola: *I've not been the same since. It permanently altered my view on humanity. It made me regard patients as potential adversaries. Unlike the younger Chase who was bursting with empathy, I have little of it left for this plaintiff and what she has suffered, only thoughts for myself, my lost redemption, the Pavilion's reputation, and for you, dear Nola. Most distressingly, I live in constant fear of it happening again. It's why I study breast cancer compulsively. Without doubt, my three lawsuits began a process that has now finally stripped me of all joy in medicine while, at the same time, turned me into an encyclopedia of breast cancer knowledge, with the hope of putting on the full armor to shield against attack.* Of course, he kept this to himself.

When he drove Nola home, Chase made the decision to walk her to the door. He didn't make that decision lightly. Fully aware that a sidewalk stroll redefined a relationship, and fully aware that the same neurotransmitters that fuel stress and anger are also at the heart of love and passion, and fully aware that those transmitters were alight in both his brain and Nola's, he still walked her to the door.

"Chase, if I can start calling you that now, after all these years of calling you Dr. Callaway, you do recall, don't you, how you and I are so very much alike? Remember how we both had that peculiar triad of specialty choices at one time in our lives – psychiatry, pathology, and surgery? No one else I know has claimed that same triad. Why would that be? Now I learn that you, too, were sued at the very start of your career..."

He was already nervous about his decision to walk her to the door, for now the cascade of intimacy so familiar from decades past had begun. Yet, he was safe, given that his heart had been lost along the way, and he considered it almost foreign that Nola might act like an adolescent forging a star-crossed pathway out of nothing.

At the front door, Nola turned toward Chase and waited an excruciatingly long time, it seemed, for him to make a move. He did nothing. She reached for his hand with both of hers.

"I don't want you to think I'm being forward," she said. "Maybe it's just the wine, or maybe just because I'm so shocked and confused right now, about having disappointed you so much with this lawsuit."

"Nola, I should tell you – this is complicated, but I just turned fifty, and probably too old for new or changing relationships, if you know what I mean. No, not too old. Too lost. I'm no longer the person I was."

She closed her eyes for several seconds, as if waiting for a kiss, then said, "I don't think you're lost," then she opened her eyes again.

Cavernous gray-green eyes had always been her most striking feature, and together with broad cheeks and wide mouth, she had a primitive appeal, a neolithic woman who did her own hunting and gathering and still felt lusty in the evenings.

He put a finger to her lips. "It's hard to explain, but when I diverted all my passion into the Pavilion," Chase said, "I had to let it consume me. I had to reach to superhuman levels. The obstacles were unbelievable, and I never would have made it if California had not turned me into sort of – well, a benevolent beast. A key part of my humanity was lost in the process."

Nola backed away. "You know," she said, "I suppose it's understandable. Some people, brilliant people I think, often have to rise above physicality."

"I don't really understand the power of obsession, and how it can work for good while destroying its host. Even before California, I was predisposed. And before that, I remember in college I got on a language kick and tried to become fluent in French, Spanish and German, all at the same time. I even read some novels written in the romance languages. Words have such subtleties, such nuances, that the translations to English always distort to some degree. The fullness can only be read in the original. One of the novels, written in French, where I made it through all the way, was one by Zola."

Nola took another step backward and put her hands on her hips, cocking her head as if puzzled by Chase's quick subject change.

Chase continued. "In Zola's novel, this adulterous couple is insane with passion for each other, and they conspire to kill the husband of the title character. The act of murder, as it turns out, requires so much passion on both their parts that afterward, there's nothing left for either of them. Instantly, and permanently, the lovers have no desire for each other at all. Can't even stand to touch each other."

"And that applies to our conversation...how?" Nola smiled as she spoke.

"Well, my passion about the Breast Pavilion has been all-consuming. It's robbed me of happiness and replaced it with horrific angst, yet it seems to have caused an explosion in my creative thought, especially writing. In Zola's book, the male lover starts out as a failed artist, a hack. After the murder, however, when he's haunted by the dead husband, miraculously, he becomes a world class artist. But *only* if he incorporates the face of the murdered husband into his work. Passion is a bizarre thing."

Nola shook her head in bewilderment, then said, "I'm not exactly sure what you're trying to tell me, Chase, but I've respected you greatly since the first time you spoke to our class years ago, and I guess it's been more than that for me, in a way. Whether you admit it or not, we have a unique bond, and maybe you're telling me that such bonds rise above the physical. That's okay. I can deal with that. For now, I just want you to know I'm terribly sorry and terribly sick about the mistake and the media frenzy, and everything. I'll make it up to you – somehow."

"Hard to figure how all this is going to turn out," Chase said as he inched away, back toward his car. "Or why any of it happened in the first place."

Then he switched subjects again. "You know, each neuron can have as many as ten thousand synapses, so when you multiply the number of neurons by ten thousand, you get a thousand-trillion synapses in the brain."

"O-kay-y. And?"

"And not a single one of the thousand-trillion touches each other."

"Not directly, but oh so close, and they still power each other."

"But no touching. Scientists argued about that for many years until someone simply looked under the microscope, and by golly, they don't touch. It's the neurotransmitters, the chemicals, that make the leap between neurons."

Nola shook her head, puzzled, then she smiled cautiously. "Very interesting, Chase. As always, you're loaded with facts that seem to be begging for metaphors. By the way, how did that French novel turn out, at least by your translation?"

"That's funny, I don't remember."

He did not want to tell her that the murdering couple forced themselves into a sham marriage that ended in a double suicide.

29
DEFENESTRATION

"I'm full right up to *here* with the in-fighting on my side of the breast center," Dr. Molly St. Martin said to Chase as she leveled her palm across the top of her brow. "It's time for you to start the protocol on Christi, whatever that takes."

A tight-knit cadre of employees had convinced Dr. St. Martin that all Pavilion day-to-day interaction problems would disappear if manager Christi Bloom were simply let go. Yet, this was a nasty act, beyond the purview of "purpose and effectiveness and power" (*PEP*) in its canned format, beyond the purview of a good cop, yet stock and trade for the bad cop – Chase – whose relationship with Christi predated Dr. St. Martin by two critical years that had kept the Pavilion breathing, albeit on life support before Molly arrived.

Chase felt alien to everything and everyone. He was alone in his fiefdom, servant to his own lordship. His battle cry had been synergy, his sword communication, and his divination had promised medical miracles. How could the mud and muck still be so deep?

Petty squabbles and office politics? How could they? In addition to his own nurse dying of breast cancer, at least half of the employees had suffered a major personal loss since the opening of the Pavilion. Christi's mother had recently died at an early age from leukemia. Who was next? Who would be the next to lose a mother, a friend, or be diagnosed themselves with some fatal illness? Life demanded communal support, and he recalled Sukie's old saw, "Be nicer than you have to be...," and how she filled the following blank with many examples, usually "...because you never know what cross that person might be carrying."

He was tired of swinging his sword, especially since he knew the most dangerous part of that weapon was the hilt. Now that he had relinquished day-to-day operations of the Pavilion to Molly St. Martin, he didn't want to fight with her, too.

Molly boldly (and Chase reluctantly), asked to meet with Christi Bloom in her office to outline the problems. After they sat in chairs across from Christi at her desk, Chase waited for Molly to explain the details, but she was dead silent, staring at her bad cop, waiting for him to begin the official reprimand.

Tired of fighting. Tired of turmoil. Tired of it all. With little comprehension of the nature of the problems, he lowered the boom on his good friend and confidant, parroting the charges as he understood them, which he did not.

Christi was angry at first, and then she cried. Chase longed to help, but he had nothing left to offer. Another friendship destroyed, another schism formed, and he couldn't seem to stop the momentum. His universe was crumbling quicker than he could patch it up.

A few days later, with the fallout over Christi still in the air, Chase negotiated the final details of the employment agreement with his new breast surgery partner, Darlene Wheatley. He thoroughly admired Darlene and was excited she would be his new partner, taking over most of the clinical care of patients.

As part of Chase's agreement to stay at the university, Hardy Studebaker and President Didion had corrected Porter's earlier raid on the endowment to fund a VA salary for his friend, by generating a base salary for Darlene.

All of Dr. Wheatley's requests were easily met until she added a final thought: "You and Molly both get your malpractice paid by the Breast Pavilion. I'd like that in my contract, too."

"Well, it's not really that easy or straightforward," Chase said. "Molly gets hers paid because she's on straight salary rather than production, and I get mine paid in lieu of a medical director fee, under an agreement I had with Thatcher Taylor before he got sick. Too, keep in mind that it's not really *paid* by the medical school or surgery department, in that it comes out of our own hide from revenues we generate here at the Pavilion. Not out of our pockets, for sure, but out of the money we earn for the university.

"But realize, Piscotel doesn't see it that way. He sees all of our expenses as coming out of the Department of Surgery budget. In fact, he sees it as coming out of his own pocket. You see, the Pavilion is a financial control point within a larger control point. You'd think, now that we're profitable, we could add whatever expenses we want as long as we stay in the black. But – not true. Welcome to the university. And, to boot, making it an even more sensitive issue, none of the other general surgery faculty gets malpractice coverage. So, to be honest, I don't think there's a prayer Porter will approve your request. In fact, after everything we've suffered with him, I can pretty well assure you he'll *not* approve it."

"It wouldn't hurt to ask, would it?"

Chase was tired. Very tired. "No, I suppose not." *What's the worst Porter could do, after all? Reject the request, fume some more, complain about my being financially irresponsible? But what difference does fuming make when the volcano is constantly spewing lava and steam?*

Chase wrote the request for Darlene Wheatley, knowing full well that it would be rejected. Still, he was careful to use humble, obsequious wording in his letter so as to minimize the steam. How pathetic, Chase thought, that he couldn't simply call Porter on the phone or talk face to face, man to man, like it used to be with Thatcher. Or, stroll into the office any time without an appointment. When it came to Porter and his skill in preserving deniability, it was best to put all these things in writing anyway.

On a lovely day in May, a day that would alter the course of the Pavilion and, for that matter, breast cancer treatment in West Texas, Chase woke up feeling good. Good meant that he awoke at a normal hour, without the lancing pain in his right eye that signaled the lunar curse and a day condemned to futility. Yes, he could make it through this one day, in spite of the ongoing, destructive publicity surrounding the misdiagnosis lawsuit and the "mutilating physicians" at the Far West

Texas University Breast Pavilion, and in spite of the internal hatchet job on Christi Bloom, and in spite of...

But when he opened his morning mail at work, the response letter from Porter Piscotel launched explosions in his brain causing all circuits from the cortex to the angry amygdala to short out, allowing primitive rage, murderous rage, to surface.

The Browning pistol. Between Porter's eyes. The back of Porter's brain would splatter against his pretentious awards hanging in cheap frames on the wall, while skull fragments shattered the discount glass. No remorse. None at all. A favor for the world.

In its entirety, the letter read: "Your request that Dr. Wheatley's malpractice be covered by the Breast Pavilion is emphatically denied. Furthermore, in keeping with my general policy of fical [sic] responsibility, in contrast to your policies at the Pavilion, I am rescinding your malpractice coverage as well. Your agreement with Dr. Taylor was arranged prior to the initiation of the endowment, so any medical director fee that you apparently feel entitled to, is superseded by the endowment."

Chase squashed the letter in his hand and pounded his fist on the desktop as he shot to his feet. "That goddam sonuvabitch!" He stormed down the hall to Molly St. Martin's office and said: "Read this."

His entire body quivered with restraint as she unwrinkled the letter and looked it over. In a way, he felt a strange sense of peace, the relief from anticipating a war now fully declared.

Molly raised her eyes to him and pleaded, "I know what you're going to do, and I know that I can't stop you. But – at least, let me have a copy of the original letter you wrote to Porter. I'll run the two letters over to the dean—"

"Screw the dean. Screw the goddam dean and every other lying worthless piece of shit at this medical center." Chase could sense that the basal ganglia were breaking down in his brain, with a Tourette-like language emerging, where profanity is stoked, and words of civility are lost.

"All right, then, I'll show the letters to the vice-chancellor, to the president if I have to. The contrasting letters show exactly what I've been trying to tell them all along."

"Ship of fools. They're nothing but a freakin' ship of fools. It doesn't matter what you do, they'll never change. It's Porter's favorite pastime, screwing us over."

"I looked over your letter before you sent it, Chase. Remember? You asked me to read it to make sure there was not a hint of hostility in it. But now, well, this letter from Porter is ugly. It's punitive. You know it, and I know it. He's obviously seething between the lines. And it fails to acknowledge that it's my income primarily funding the Pavilion, which includes both our malpractice premiums. It's not coming out of the surgery department, exposing Porter for what he is – vicious without cause. Let me handle this, please. Let me present the two letters side by side."

"Diplomacy doesn't work here. Why do you keep on with that? Once Porter decides to be an asshole jerk, he's relentless. His fake front to the world, phony humility, works like a charm, but at heart, he's a vicious mongrel and he's relishing in his power to break every promise T.N.T. ever made to me. But to use the endowment as his cover... I can't take it anymore. I'm not gonna be his Mahatmafucking-Gandhi. The endowment kicked in nine months ago. The terms were settled back then. If the malpractice perk were ending as part of the endowment, it should have been raised as an issue back then. No one said a damn thing. No one even hinted. This is so blatantly combative that— that—"

"I—I don't know what to say. Just try to hold—"

"There's nothing to say, Molly. Nothing. Because it has nothing to do with money, not with my malpractice coverage, *certainly* nothing to do with my original request for Darlene as a partner. This is about me and him. This jerk is not going to let up – ever! I gave him the benefit of a thousand doubts before, while we were in debt. I forced myself to understand why he was singling out the Pavilion for his special torture. But things are different now. The Pavilion is in tip-top shape – the best it's ever been – and yet, he doesn't care. He's going to harass me 'til kingdom come. Well, if he wants a battle, I'll give it to him."

No memory or witnesses exist for the next few minutes, but somehow, Chase landed upstairs in the Department of Surgery, banging on Porter's closed door. Nearly 20 years of unrelenting assaults had been thrown in his career path since the third day of private practice, and it was going to end now. When Porter opened the door, Chase didn't have to say a word. Porter knew by the fury on Chase's face why he was there. The smirk on Porter's face melted.

Waggling a finger at Porter's nose, Chase blurted, "How dare you pull a stunt like this?"

Porter backed away, stumbling over the plastic carpet protector on the floor as he wilted into his chair. To regain composure, he clasped his hands behind his head, rocked back and said, "Listen, when that endowment was drawn up—"

"Screw the endowment. My malpractice coverage is not tied in any way, shape, or form to the endowment. If it did, then why the hell didn't you say something about it nine freakin' months ago when it started? This is about *one thing* – your crusade to hound my ass until I quit and the big pot of money falls to you. The endowment is nothing but a pile of four million dollars in your jerk-o-vision, and it galls you that I'm the Holder of the Chair. For you, it has nothing to do with integrity, with honoring the wishes of Thatcher or the donors, or with educating our residents, or with eradicating breast cancer – nothing. It's nothing but cash for you to roll around in. Let me tell you something, you lying piece of shit…"

Porter had been shocked at first, but now with composure regained, he put his feet on his desk, arms still behind his head, smirk recovered. When dealing with a madman, one wins easily by simply keeping cool. "Chase, I should probably point out that you've not upheld the terms of the endowment."

"What? What did you say? What twisted lie are you trying to pull off now?"

Porter lowered his feet back to the floor, then stood eye to eye with Chase. Slowly raising his shaky finger, he pointed it between Chase's eyes. "You. You're not in compliance, my friend. How many NCI grants have you written since you've held that Chair?"

"Oh – my – god. I don't believe it. In nine months? How many grants, you say? You, who's never written a freakin' NCI grant in your life, who hasn't published an article in five years – instead, hauling in your prostitution money from pharmaceutical companies? Well, listen to this, you piece of shit – I'm finishing up the first NCI grant in the *history* of this department. Plus, it's almost assured I'll get it because of the impression I made with the Director of Chemoprevention at the NCI and my purchase of the Kruger 2000. Do you know a damn thing about any of that? This isn't like the white elephant cytometry equipment you bought for the lab with our departmental money – our hard-earned money – and then barely used. This is for real. Meanwhile, you convince all the faculty members that *I'm* the one who's been siphoning off their hard-earned money? You didn't believe me about departmental funds when you first took over, did you? You thought we'd been siphoning from the department. The Pavilion – no, not the Pavilion – *I* had to arrange the hiring of a freakin' independent auditor to come in and prove to you and the dean, and the cheating money men, that the Pavilion had not taken one dime from the private income accounts in the surgery department since its beginning. An independent auditor, for godsakes. Yes, the debt was housed in Surgery, but not a penny of our operations came from faculty income – your favorite way to discredit me. I wonder if anyone in academics has *ever* had to hire an auditor to fight the lies of his own chairman. Yet, with your highly selective memory, you probably don't remember anything about the auditor, do you?"

"Boy, you sure have an interesting twist on things."

"Don't accuse me of twisting anything. I used to think you were sort of an absent-minded professor, prone to distorting reality. I gave you every benefit of the doubt. But you know exactly what you do. You're a cold, calculating bullshit artist. When you apologized last year to get me to stay, it didn't take long to figure out that it was just more of your lying crap. Since then, I've written down every stunt you've pulled because, frankly, I figured we were going to end up in court. So, I don't even know where to start. Maybe with your business manager embezzling donated money that was intended for the Breast Pavilion, but went to the department instead?"

Porter grinned with mischievous relief. "So-o...you've been writing things down?"

"Yes," said Chase, curious at the calm in the storm, "every one of your stunts."

In what appeared to Chase as the expression of an imbecile who suddenly grasps the theory of relativity, Porter's smile grew even wider. "Documenting everything, huh?"

"Yes…reams."

"Ha! Hyper-documentation. That's a symptom of paranoia! That's mental illness." His eyebrows raised with childish excitement, and Porter looked as though he were about to pop the corks of a thousand champagne bottles.

"Oh, please. Spare me your Freudian crap. Of all the people I've known in my life, you are the *least* qualified to render a psych assessment of anyone or anything. I keep my memory accurate and pure, something you can't possibly understand. Know thyself, Porter, know thyself, even if thyself is a freakin' asshole. I document because I think we're going to end up in court. In fact, I'm sure of it."

Porter placed his hands on his hips, forcing a phony laugh as he retreated behind his desk and sat down again, rocking back, feet on desktop, arms confidently resting behind his head. The diagnosis was securely in place. "Dr. Callaway – (the condescension sizzled) – do you know who you're talking to? Do you realize you've just waltzed in here and – well, let me say it again – *do you realize who you're talking to?*"

Chase stared through the plate glass windows overlooking Crooked Creek, the mental institution forming the horizon. It was not a fleeting thought. It was a deep, compelling urge, and he could barely contain himself. His hands were itching to surround Piscotel's throat and throw the smug sonuvabitch through the window and watch his skull explode like a gourd on the concrete below. Chase felt his amygdala demand justice, while his frontal cortex screamed back, "Don't do it. Don't do it."

Chase turned and leaned across the chairman's desk, going nose to nose with Porter. "Yes, I know who I'm talking to," he whispered. Then shouting: "I'm talking to a B-plus overachiever, now a poser and a freakin' megalomaniac. You sat there for years watching Thatcher, trying to imitate him. You have no idea what made him great. None. The only thing you can do is mimic him, and it's pathetic, right down to Thatcher's gestures. There's nothing more repugnant than watching the rear end of chimp trying to climb the totem pole. You have no idea why the Pavilion is a success. You couldn't have pulled off anything like it in your wildest dreams. You were too busy stumbling over the 'yes, sirs' to Thatcher that come so easily for obsequious stoolies like you. *That's* who I'm talking to. So, run your little kingdom the way you want. I quit. Enjoy the four million. I'm sure you'll spend it on your trauma center, while you lie to the world and tell everyone that all the money went for breast cancer. What a bullshitter!"

When he stormed back to his office, Molly was waiting by the door. "What did he say? What happened?"

Chase was exhausted, and he could barely mouth the response: "What *could* he say?"

"I mean, what did you do? What did he do?"

"He said I was a paranoid."

"Paranoid? Where'd he come up with that?" Molly was visibly puzzled by the accusation.

"Where do all tyrants get it? It's their ultimate defense. Kick your opponent in the chest, then call him a paranoid when he complains of broken ribs. After all, who can see a broken rib? Like they say, beware all tyrants new to power."

Chase reached for Molly's hand and gave her a farewell shake. "It was nice working with you. I just quit." And he left.

Tires squealed as he escaped his alma mater. He pulled out his cell phone as soon as he had a free hand.

First, he called Hardy Studebaker. "Don't do anything rash just yet, Chase." The reply was swift: "It's too late, I've already quit. Thanks for all your help."

He called the Raven sisters. Jody fumed. She had put her personal reputation on the line for the Pavilion. "I've fought too many battles for it to end like this. That medical center will rue this day forever. I will damn sure promise that."

But Darby Raven clung to hope. "I'm so sorry, Chase. I know it's been so horrible for so long, but I believe part of you has known for a long time that you needed to leave. The endowment turned out to be nothing but a target on your back, and I'm sorry we did that to you. No one has ever said this, I'm guessing, but I suspect you stuck with it all this time, well, just for us. The ladies. You stayed for Jody and me and the Board and the promises you made us. I know you're too angry to think clearly right now, but don't give up hope completely. Please. We need you."

Darby's words clattered like pebbles against his armor of rage. In some ways, she was correct about his clinging to faint hope for an entire decade. After hearing her angelic voice articulate the power of promise, he knew it was time to cry, to release, to start sobbing. Instead, fury prevailed. For it was more than simple promises and personal indebtedness that had fueled super-human endurance – he had sought personal redemption for his own early failings in life, an opportunity now thwarted and lost forever. Accordingly, he discovered that the self-destructive fires of revenge pale in comparison to redemption denied.

30
MODERN PROMETHEUS

As blacksmith of the Olympian gods, Hephaestus was ordered to shackle the sole remaining Titan, Prometheus, at the whim of the new upstart, Zeus. Or, so Aeschylus tells us. While reluctantly forging the chain, Hephaestus laments: "Compassion will not move the mind of Zeus: All monarchs new to power show brutality."

All monarchs new to power show brutality.

While this scenario cycles endlessly, few care enough to stop the wheel from turning.

Editor's note: In the original document that exceeded 5,000 pages, Dr. Callaway offers nine historical examples that demonstrate the quote from Aeschylus above, culminating with Henri IV of France who ordered the decapitation of his close friend, Duc de Biron and Governor of Burgundy. As the duke's head rolled around on the floor, France's leading nobles who were challenging Henri fell to their knees in a trembling, sweaty heap, worshipping their king. Dr. Callaway then writes: "...so Lord Piscotel felt the most powerful surge in his life as he swung the axe to lop off my head."

At this point, the President of Far West Texas University, Elmo "Skip" Didion telephoned Chase and asked him to rescind his resignation. Again. Chase declined. Didion insisted. Chase declined once again...unless President Didion "promised to settle the feud in no more than 3 days," given that Piscotel would raise an army to destroy Chase if things dragged on. Didion made no promises, but insisted once again that Chase rescind, as he could do nothing if Chase had officially resigned.

Chase agreed, but only with the promise that any negotiated settlement exclude Porter Piscotel from Chase's chain-of-command. Skip Didion then stated that this would be impossible given that the endowment was parked in the Department of Surgery and that Thatcher Taylor's surviving family insisted it stay there. Chase replied, "Then I'll surrender the endowment if it will allow me to accomplish my goals. That endowment has been nothing but a monstrous monkey on my back from the beginning. A curse on my soul. Put me in another department, or let me answer directly to the dean, but I will not answer to Piscotel under any circumstances." I merely want to finish my work, my vision, without a nut job blocking me at every turn."

In the end, both President Didion and Dr. Callaway put so many qualifiers on their intent that it was difficult to say whether or not Chase had rescinded his resignation. Clearly, however, President Didion had opened the door, and Chase had set one foot inside. "You'll need to move very quickly," said Chase. "This will become a blood bath if things are allowed to linger."

Linger, they did. President Didion was thereafter "tied up" at the state legislature, securing next year's budget for Far West Texas University. At the same time, he was swamped with pro-Piscotel messages and letters from some of Matherville's finest. Too, he was overcome with pro-Callaway messages from others among Matherville's finest. In essence, it became a city-wide civil war. While Dr. Piscotel called in every chip he believed might assist him in battle, Chase Callaway called no one. So, when Chase received a phone call (finally) from President Didion who told Chase to "Call off your army," Chase replied in earnest – "I never called them to action in the first place. *Everything* has been their choice and their doing. The battle of slander is being waged by Dr. Piscotel, exactly as I predicted when I asked that you move quickly."

Yet, still no action on the part of the president. Instead, the war escalated into a conflagration with "The Letter." Sam Dinwiddie, the prototypical surgeon and role model for Porter Piscotel years ago, mailed a letter to all surgeons in west Texas and all graduates of the Far West program, announcing the heretical behavior of Chase Callaway and that he should be drummed out of the university. Indeed, Dinwiddie claimed to have launched his own investigation that included calling the dean and confirming that the Breast Pavilion was always meant to be in the Department of Surgery, and that Callaway's demand to move it out of the surgery department was throwing mud on the memory of Thatcher Nolan Taylor, MD. Of course, there was a "rolling over in the grave" cliché tossed in for good measure. In the end, the letter called for Chase Callaway's immediate firing.

Besides having already resigned, Chase was livid that the dean had uttered words so grossly incorrect and harmful to Chase. The truth, of course, lay in Chase's extraordinary efforts, bolstered by the Raven sisters (and behind the scenes, Hardy Studebaker), to get the Breast Pavilion into the surgery department in the first place. The facts were exactly opposite from what was being touted by Piscotel, Dinwiddie, and their blinded supporters.

When Chase learned that Sam Dinwiddie claimed to have uncovered the truth by calling the dean directly, Chase was sickened to his core. He telephoned the dean immediately, holding himself in check as he walked the Dean through the history of the Breast Pavilion, step by step, until the dean finally admitted, "I'm sorry. I'd forgotten all those details. Dr. Dinwiddie just caught me off guard."

But it was too late. Chase procured the mailing list of surgeons who had received the letter and began calling them one by one. They were, collectively, ice-cold in their response. Chase tried to point out that this battle did not have two sides to the story – there was absolute truth pitted against a big pile of garbage, and it was inconceivable that Chase was losing ground. It was painful to hear the voices of his colleagues so distant, without a shred of support. He didn't make it through one-tenth of the list.

He called the members of Thatcher Nolan Taylor's family who were in the Piscotel camp based on their erroneous belief that it had always been T.N.T.'s strong wish to have the Breast Pavilion in the Department of Surgery. Because this misunderstanding was opposite reality, Chase had to tread very carefully as he explained the source of confusion –

distinguishing between control of "clinical management" and "administrative control" when it came to breast centers. In fact, Thatcher had been uncharacteristically stern in his protest *against* having a breast center albatross as part of his financial control point. After experiencing the family's resistance to his explanation, Chase decided he would need to create a collection of documents, a treatise explaining the history of the Pavilion, along with the supporting evidence.

Chase even went to the remarkable extent of contacting the hospital administrator, Ron Campion, long since transferred to a hospital in Louisiana, to confirm the conversation that took place years earlier where T.N.T. had begged the hospital to manage the Breast Pavilion. The administrator remembered the tense conversation quite well where he had stood up to T.N.T. in his refusal to run the center through College Hospital. Chase asked Ron Campion to put his vivid memory in writing, but the letter came too late.

It didn't really matter, however, as Chase was getting bogged down defending the countless charges against him by countless enemies, most of whom he'd never met. What surprised him was not the propaganda machine that Piscotel effectively launched, but that the lies were embraced and believed so readily, by so many, without any opportunity for Chase to take the stand. When it came to his colleagues and his few friends, not a single person was interested in his position, and no one ever asked for his version. It was the widespread eagerness to adopt the Piscotel party line that eventually broke his spirit and, with it, his tenuous hold on sanity.

As a parenthetical comment, it was curious that Dr. Callaway maintained perfect sobriety throughout these years while losing his sanity. It was as though the most powerful psychotropic drugs – uppers, downers, and in-betweeners – were pointless as they would only bounce off his scarred brain.

Darby Raven, Jody Raven, or both, consoled Chase, in person or on the phone, every day for hours at a time. For the Raven sisters, the societal pressures had been immense. Advisory Board members had been hearing horrible stories about Chase, ready on a whim to forget all they had witnessed with their own eyes.

"It was our mistake to rotate Board members," said Darby. "Half the women serving now weren't around for those awful early years. Many members actually believe Molly started the Pavilion."

For Darby and Jody, defending Chase became a full-time job. Finally, they made an appointment with President Skip Didion to remind him of the powerful impact that "the community" had made with regard to the establishment and success of the Pavilion. After all, the twosome had raised, directly or indirectly, a total of $8 million dollars. For his part, Chase had presented his vision for the Pavilion and its future research agenda at more than 200 social gatherings in west Texas over the past 10 years.

The sisters made it through the maze as far as an antechamber to the presidential suite, only to wait several hours before learning that President Didion would not be able to make the appointment.

A newspaper reporter caught wind of the Matherville Civil War, and he contacted Chase for the story. Chase refused on the grounds it might interfere with negotiations. "But if this ends poorly, as I suspect it will, I'll be ready to sing. Give me your contact information." At this point, unless a reasonable option were offered, Chase fully intended to file a lawsuit against Dinwiddie and Piscotel for starters, if for no other reason than to get the facts made public.

The only heroic response to "the Dinwiddie Letter" came from Chase's radiologic partner, Dr. Molly St. Martin, who, after reading the slander by Sam Dinwiddie, and witnessing the melee that followed, announced, "In response to the offensive letter circulated by Dr. Dinwiddie and encouraged by Dr. Piscotel, I resign my position with this university. I will not work in a facility that is completely devoid of ethical standards. From what I know quite well in this instance, the actions taken against Chase Callaway are deplorable and without precedent."

President Didion was in a bind. As a natural politician, he knew to follow the polls, with principles being secondary. Best he could tell, the polls were split 50-50. From that, there was only one action to take, and that was no action at all. However, the resignation of Dr. St. Martin was another matter entirely, as she had become the heart of the Pavilion, and clearly the reason for its financial success. Pressure mounted.

Several weeks passed. Offers for jobs poured in from around the state of Texas for the team of Molly St. Martin and Chase Callaway whose multidisciplinary breast center had been the first in Texas.

The Far West situation was ugly beyond repair. Molly called Chase at home on a Sunday evening. "I've separated myself mentally from the university. I'm going to stick to my resignation. I'll not rescind. We've received some impressive job offers out there, but I can't seriously consider leaving Matherville now for family reasons, so it looks like Permian is our best bet. Let's head to Permian and do it all over again out there."

Although Chase was at great peace with this pronouncement, he had, minutes earlier, completed a 50-page detailed history of the Breast Pavilion that would serve as his defense now, or in court later, focusing on facts that would be new even to the family of Thatcher Nolan Taylor, M.D. (Eventually, the letter from the former administrator, Ron Campion, now in Louisiana, would be added). However, the document would serve no purpose if they were headed to Permian Medical Center, so he chose to shelve it. Besides, the battle had ended wallowing in the mud anyway, and he was tired of hollering into deaf ears. Did the valid history of the Pavilion even matter anymore? No one seemed the least bit interested in the truth.

The next morning, after Molly's Sunday declaration, Chase Callaway left a message with President Didion's office, confirming his resignation. It had been unclear as to his exact status anyway, but now with Molly leaving for Permian, he would stick with her no matter what. Whether this constituted a "second resignation" or confirmation of his first resignation was a moot point. Wherever Molly went, he would follow.

During this time of chaos, a devastating tornado cleared a path through west Texas, registering as an "F-5," costing untold millions in property damage as well as the loss of human lives. After Chase's now-legendary thrashing of Porter Piscotel (a.k.a. Chase's "psychotic break" by the Piscotel camp), Molly St. Martin began referring to Chase as "F-5" rather than her usual moniker where, in the past, she had called him "The Rainmaker." F-5 was not a compliment. She had warned him long ago that she could not tolerate shouting by anyone for any reason.

Pavilion employees heard the new nickname with striking frequency, culminating in: "Well, F-5 officially resigned today."

In contrast to the F-5, however, it was a silent whirlwind that breezed through the Breast Pavilion one day as Molly St. Martin was packing to leave for Permian Medical Center. With no advance notice, the wind whisked her away, nearly against her will, off campus. The whirlwind consisted of the Dean of the School of Medicine, the Vice-Chancellor of Health Sciences, and the President of Far West Texas University, Elmo "Skip" Didion. The triumvirate swept her up and carried her to lunch at The Colony Club and, as it turned out, landed her smack dab in the middle of the Smoking Room as the "first female in Matherville history to grace that particular enclave."

A newspaper reporter was waiting, camera-ready, for the historic occasion. The article would cover gender equality, the breaking of barriers, and hopefully, new directions in conquering breast cancer. Champagne flowed. Cameras flashed. In the process, the powerbrokers offered Molly the world. *Everything*. No more answering to Piscotel. Nor would she be required to return to the radiology department. She would be her own department, answering directly to the dean. There would be no financial barriers, and no more harassment. In short, she was offered everything that Chase Callaway had been lobbying for and had been attacked for doing so.

"What about Chase?" she asked.

"Well, his status won't change," said President Didion.

"But he'll quit if he has to answer to Porter, you know that."

"Well, all I can say is – his status won't change."

When Molly returned to the Breast Pavilion, the entire staff gathered around her, but she wouldn't say a word as to what had happened. Furthermore, she wouldn't go near Chase, telling him she needed to think. He knew it was something dreadful when she left early that day for home. The next morning, she informed Chase that she had decided to stay at the university.

"But what about me? You know I can't work under Piscotel."

"Your situation doesn't change," she said, "you'll be stuck in the surgery department."

At that moment – clarity came for Chase. In the words of Alexander Hamilton upon receiving the initial bullet from Aaron Burr – I am a dead man."

Editor's note: Pages to follow document Chase's uncontrollable rage (conversations below are either snippets or summations). Bottom line: in Chase's words: "the duplicitous Molly was planting her flag in his dead corpse."

He censored all comments to Molly at the strong advice from the Raven sisters who cautioned him: "Don't make her angry. We will get you two back together somehow, and we don't want to burn bridges."

In forced civility, Chase asked Molly, "What happened to your statement that you can't work in a facility that is lacking basic ethical standards? Specifically, as pertaining to my treatment? Dinwiddie's letter was the icing on the cake – the last in a long line of abuse by these jerks. What happened?"

Molly replied, "I guess you'd have to say that I remembered my mission to teach breast imaging to the residents. There's no teaching at Permian. Plus, my husband has pointed out that some people, no matter how good they are at heart, well, trouble simply follows them throughout life. Just an observation."

Oh – my – goodness. Now we have magical thinking that has labeled me with bad karma. Then again, when one considers a decade in California and another decade added now, maybe her husband is right. No one sees the California nightmare, but I have to live with it every day, and it's only paved the way for more of the same as I work to prove it wrong. Instead of proving anything, however, I'm dying of 1,000 cuts. No single traumatic event, but relentless torture one non-lethal cut at a time. Now that I think about, Molly's husband is absolutely correct. It's the Callaway Curse that I've always feared.

As Chase pushed and pushed her, Molly grew increasingly defensive, finally blurting out: "Chase, I told you early on, after that first temper tantrum of yours, that I could not work with someone who was that volatile."

"Volatile? Two or three tantrums?"

"When Porter wrote that hostile letter, I begged you to let me handle it, that I'd personally take the letter to the dean, that I'd take care of things. Instead, you storm up there to Porter's office like an F-5 tornado and destroy all chance we had for a peaceful settlement."

"Peaceful settlement? Can you name a single controversy that we've endured that was settled peacefully? And what happened to our professional marriage? Most of all, what about your phone call to me that Sunday at home when you said we were going to Permian? I had just written a 50-page document outlining and defending the truth, but I *didn't bother to show it to anyone since we were leaving.* You do realize that the next morning I resigned – resigned from the largest endowed chair at the university – *to follow you.* How can you ignore the fact that you called me for the express purpose of letting me know we were headed to Permian – *as a team*?"

"I don't know what I was thinking. Maybe my hormones were off…"

Editor's note: At this point in Dr. Callaway's manuscript, one can appreciate rage trending toward psychological breakdown as he launches a vicious tirade over the "hormone" statement. However, his anger is never expressed beyond this manuscript. Sparing the reader from this diatribe, the Editor chooses to move on to a later conversation:

"Molly, the Raven sisters have been feverishly at work, talking to us both, as well as university leadership, and they keep coming up with ideas to keep us together. Then you move your rook or your knight or even a pawn that keeps it from happening. I've got to ask you, do you want me here with you at Far West?"

"Yes, but it would start with an apology to Porter, no matter how insincere."

The Raven sisters objected strongly: "Chase, do *not* apologize. It will cast you in a bad light as the guilty party."

"But my goose is cooked. Don't you see that these job offers we've been getting, especially the one at Permian, are really for Molly? They don't want me. I'm nothing but competition for the general surgeons who practice there. Hospital administrators are incapable of appreciating indirect revenue streams. They want Molly where they can count each dollar in real time. She's the one who brings in the new business through screening outreach. Direct, easily measured revenues. When I try to show them the much greater economic impact of drawing newly diagnosed cancer patients into the system, they look at you stupefied. They can't comprehend it. I'm not even sure I have a solo offer. They're all tied to Molly. She has really done a number on me, not to mention that if she stays, she validates every damn lie that Porter has promulgated throughout this whole deal. The thought of that makes me sick. But I really have no choice. I have to apologize."

Darby Raven then said, "What's your status right now with the university?"

"Well, I've unofficially resigned, that is, through a telephone call to the president. But Molly says that Didion told her that I would have to accept the current situation with Piscotel, that is, I'd have to answer to him. That wouldn't be so bad, if you think about it, since Molly has managed to get the Breast Pavilion moved out from the Department of Surgery, which was our main goal anyway, to get away from Piscotel. I really wouldn't have that much interaction with Porter if Molly is answering directly to the dean."

After convincing the Raven sisters that he had little choice, and after getting the nod from Molly that she would, in fact, prefer Chase to stay at the university, Chase made an appointment to meet with Porter Piscotel.

Porter took the opportunity to lay out Chase's faults (insubordination had moved up to #1 on the list, passing fiscal irresponsibility as #2). Chase listened quietly, as he heard first-hand the outrageous version of events that Porter had been spreading to his superiors, his supporters, and T.N.T.'s family. It was sickening to hear what the world had heard, and even more troubling that Porter's pathology allowed him to believe the lies with all his heart. But Chase held his tongue. Then, he managed a global apology, confessing that he was willing to accept President Didion's offer and answer to the Chairman of the Department of Surgery, that is, the status quo.

"I don't know what you're talking about. There's no offer on the table for you. You resigned, and that's that. You're out, fella."

"Wh-what do you mean? President Didion told Molly that I would need to accept my current situation."

"And your current situation is anywhere but here. Your official status is not in question. You resigned. *Resigned.* Understand? I have a letter from President Didion about this right here on my desk to clarify any false claims you might make. You're out, and there's no return."

The conversation was so other-worldly that Chase could barely respond. Finally, pathetic drivel emerged: "But I'm in line for the first NCI grant in the history of the department. The Kruger 2000 is finally up and running, and the grant has been submitted. I've got the inside track because..."

"You're out, Chase. Now deal with it."

Stunned beyond all description, Chase walked the lonely hall back to his office where he closed the door behind him. A lancing pain pierced his side, and he doubled over, clutching his ribs. Never had his emotions converted to physical symptoms. He knew the sharp point of the spear was due to neurotransmitters out of control, telling lies to his brain. Yet, knowledge of this didn't help. He still couldn't catch his breath, nor stop the pain. Holding his side, he crawled to his private bathroom, finally grasping the countertop and pulling himself to a crouched position. When he looked at himself in the mirror, the scarlet crescent of skin around his right eye was radiant.

Molly St. Martin was beside herself. She'd heard President Didion with her own ears. What was Piscotel trying to pull? Frantic, she ran to a phone and managed to get President Didion on the line. Chase joined her, listening to half of the conversation:

"You told me that Chase would have to accept his role under Porter, the status quo...yes...yes.... oh, I remember now. No, you didn't say he'd be under Porter specifically. So then....no offer? No offer at all?"

Molly hung up the phone, and Chase said, "You misunderstood him?"

"Yes. He said your status would not change, *failing to clarify that your status was that you had resigned*. Even when I said you'd quit if forced back under Porter, he failed to make it clear that he was considering you gone. My misunderstanding should have been patently obvious to him. Instead of correcting me, he simply said, 'His status won't change.' I was tricked, Chase. They knew I didn't have the correct idea in mind."

"Okay, then. You're the expert negotiator. You had the opportunity right then and there on the phone, just now, to claim a serious and intentional miscommunication on their part, devious at best, and to insist that I have some sort of offer. And if not, then this trick of theirs was the perfect opportunity to save face and resign yourself. Molly, I have a copy of an e-mail you wrote to the Medical Director at Permian, accepting their offer for both of us."

"Things have changed, Chase. Also, when this is all over with, I'm going to get some counseling, and I hope you'll do the same."

I don't need counseling to determine right from wrong, Chase said to himself, while glaring at Molly. From that moment on, an all-consuming fury would worm its way into Chase's brain, leading him over the years to embrace permanent, deep-seated rage. The rage would have melted away over time, in all likelihood, if only Molly St. Martin had simply said – at any point in this long saga – that she was sorry. Yet, those words never came in any form. Not even a hint. Never did she demonstrate a trace of remorse. After all, using the principles of *PEP*, once a decision is made, one doesn't look back with regret.

In reflection, Darby Raven (ever hopeful to reunite the two physicians "at some point in the future") said, "You really didn't have a prayer, Chase. I recently found out that Molly has been telling board members that she was worried about your mental health. Her words. *Mental health.* When people asked what she meant, she would elaborate that she believed you to have seasonal affective disorder. Do you have any idea where she came up with that?"

"My god, is there no end to that woman's deceit? That's the sort of exaggeration a traitor uses to justify their actions when criticized. Burn-out, yes, but that was an open secret. Or, I don't mind admitting some OCD, with an emphasis on the 'O' that I harnessed years ago into the road toward excellence. But seasonal affective disorder? I'm recalling now what someone told me, shortly after we hired Molly. They said, 'you better have your life in order.' I see now what that means. She's a stern judge of anyone who doesn't meet her self-help standards. Here's what I'm guessing – back when I thought we were close, I told her that every major crisis at the Pavilion had started in October and lasted through the winter. It was nothing more than coincidental timing that became very vivid to me because there was a new hill to die on each year, starting within a few weeks of Halloween. Since Molly wasn't even around at the beginning, during these crises – remember, I was working on the future Pavilion *six years* before she came on board – she apparently didn't believe my simple explanation of the history of things. Then, using her highly developed psychiatric diagnostic skills as a board-certified radiologist, she labeled me with something she'd read about in one of her self-help books. With friends like that....

He continued. "Of course, I thought Dr. Mooney was my friend, too, but then I found out that he's been talking to all the surgeons at Permian, my future colleagues, and telling them that I'm a troublemaker. Worse, he's viewed as a neutral party by key people in the community, and he's been out there giving Porter's ridiculous version of everything. One time, after the feud began, Mooney came down to my office and I started to explain my version of events. He scampered out the door in a flash. Didn't even bother to pee in my toilet, breaking his long streak of territorial markings...."

After extended ramblings about Piscotel, Mooney, and Molly St. Martin, Chase said, "I seem to be in some sort of free-fall, Darby. And you know what? Because this fall is so foreign, so unbelievable – to everyone – even those who were on my side originally now exaggerate stories and buy into lies. 'Oh, he's always been so wonderful – must have been something awful that we were never told. Why else would they have canned someone of his stature'? These people are quoting from the *Book of Job* even though they don't know it."

Darby Raven said, "I know it's looking really bad right now, Chase, but please know, we'll help you at Permian. No matter how crazy it might seem, I truly believe Molly is going to come to her senses and see what she's done. When that happens, we'll get the team back together. I'm going to be so sweet and kind to Molly that she won't know what hit her. So, in the meantime, please drop the bridge-burning ideas, like the lawsuit you've mentioned. Keep the peace and take the high road. Always the high road. No matter what."

"Thank you, Darby. I do appreciate the fact that you and Jody have always stuck with me through thick and thin. Let's take the Advisory Board and make a beeline to Permian Medical Center. We'll do it again. Bigger and better."

"Oh, Chase, I haven't wanted to discuss it with you, given everything else going on. The Board won't be that easy. A lot of the ladies are alums of Far West, and their commitment is to the university. Then, Jody and I made a fateful error several years back when we decided to make the board a rotating commitment. We did it to expose more women to the Pavilion, but it backfired on us. Only a few members are still around from those early days when you were locked in battle all the time. They, of course, are puzzled by what Molly has done. However, most of our Board thinks that you and Molly started this project together. And gosh, switching subjects, I wish now you hadn't apologized to Dr. Piscotel – it's all over the city about your apology, and it's going to haunt us."

"That apology, you'll recall, is courtesy of the easily-confused and double-minded Molly St. Martin. If she had listened to the three stooges who hotboxed her at the Colony Club, she would have figured out exactly what they had done, and what they were trying to pull off. She held all the cards and could have had me right beside her. Then, after that, she *still* had another chance to redeem herself, but simply let that chance slide by, to my ruin. Darby, why can't you just tell the Board point blank what has happened here – the whole, ugly truth?"

"It's not that easy, really. Hard to understand, I know, but there's a different dynamic with each board member. Karen Wilson, for instance, already told me that we need to be looking for your replacement, and this time around, we need to find someone who's a better communicator."

"You've got to be kidding. When Porter took over, he essentially padlocked his door, cut the telephone lines, and cancelled all appearances. When it came to me, that is. He locked me out, dammit! Somehow, he has successfully convinced the key players of the exact opposite. Has anyone had enough smarts to check on my communication record back when T.N.T. was in charge? Or, the rest of the world, for that matter? Over the course of my entire career?"

"I did go a little nuts when Karen said that. I told her, 'Chase Callaway is one of the greatest communicators you'll ever meet. Don't believe the propaganda that the university is putting out trying to lay all the blame on Chase.' Although she understood better when I was finished, she's still committed to staying at Far West.

"Malignant institutional narcissism."

"I've heard you say it, but I'm still not sure what it means."

"It's my modification of Erich Fromm's term he used for narcissistic individuals who will destroy anything that threatens their carefully constructed image. I simply added the word 'institutional' based originally on the lack of self-reflection that I witnessed when I first got back to Texas, but it's so much worse than that. Its army of supporters will happily destroy anyone that threatens their image. I don't mean just a volley of insults. I mean complete destruction of those human beings that expose malevolence. Such an institution thrives on the jingoistic support of its leaders, and it grows by consuming the innocent, cannibalizing if you will. Molly St. Martin is now one of them. She's been swallowed up. Mark my words, she will never breathe a word of what really happened for the rest of her life. That's malignant institutional narcissism at work."

"Well, as crazy as it sounds, the details about what Molly has done are so shocking that I'm not sure many board members would even believe me, not to mention it takes an hour to lay out all the facts. I think we'll have seven or eight loyal supporters move with us to Permian, essentially those who were there with you from the beginning."

"Out of what? Thirty? Really?"

"It gets worse, Chase. To many, Molly is the hero of this story. She has *saved* the Breast Pavilion in their minds. They do not understand that her so-called victory was built upon the foundation that—".

"—that my severed head roll around on the floor."

31
COURT OF STAR CHAMBER

Business manager Christi Bloom crept into Chase's office, expressed her regrets about his improbable state of disgrace, then said, "This may seem cold, but I'm sure you're planning to take some items with you when you leave. Do you have a receipt for your desk?"

Reversal of fortune, indeed. Chase had protected Christi's neck from the university administration, from the recommendation of T.N.T., then Porter Piscotel and Henry, and finally, Molly St. Martin. Five saves. Now, Christi was making sure Chase didn't sneak off with university property.

Chairman Porter Piscotel, after the blow-out, in a startling and insincere turnaround, had guaranteed total job security to Christi and all of Chase's employees who were willing to stay on at the university so as to keep the mutiny of Chase as a solo act. When the Raven sisters asked Molly St. Martin about future monetary management of the Pavilion, fully aware of Molly's recent intent to dismiss Christi, Molly replied, "We can't fire Christi now. I need her for the transition."

Editor's note: Over the next 32 pages, Dr. Callaway describes a stream of former colleagues who filed into his office those last days, not bearing gifts of thanks, not bearing consolation, not bearing simple good-byes or gratitude or apologies. Instead, each petitioner wanted to suck the last drops of blood.

The pathology department sent a representative to strike a deal for continued service for his breast tissue specimens even though Chase would be at Permian where pathology services would automatically be done at that facility. Chase's most valued nurse ("excessive salary" according to Piscotel) explained to Chase the perks and salary she would require in order to move to Permian with him (Permian administrators groaned audibly and Chase feared he had jeopardized his own deal; however, Permian agreed to the terms, whereupon the nurse declined the offer). Research collaborators in various departments scrambled to get their data from Chase and discuss how they might proceed without his funding. Finally, Molly St. Martin, ignoring Chase's final appeal to reason and a continued collaboration, asked for Chase to leave all his educational materials he had developed over the years, from patient pamphlets to student handbooks to teaching videotapes.

His final day was a Friday, and Chase saved the hardest good-byes for last. Gunnar and Freya Pixley had recently completed their training on the Kruger 2000 computerized microscope. Pathologist Nola Kastl was the official captain of the scope, and she was there to say farewell along with the Pixleys. Freya hugged Chase. Nola could not look him in the face without crying. She slipped to the corner of the room to join a summer scholar whom Chase had recruited as yet another future piece of the dream, the top medical student in her class, now dumbstruck at her introduction to how sordid academic medicine could be. Everyone held back tears, as best possible.

"I just came from security," Chase said. "It was like the Dreyfus Affair, ripping off my epaulets and breaking my sword. They had a logbook that showed exactly which keys I had, and they took them from me one by one. It just about killed me to give up the key to this lab."

Gunnar Pixley left for a moment, then returned. "Chase, take this. It's only a symbol, I guess, but it's a master key, unknown by the security office. Only a few exist, and it's my only one. It's a master to the entire medical center. Every room. Every building. If anyone has ever permeated the entire medical complex like you've done over the years, by unlocking the doors that separate us all, I certainly don't know who it'd be. You understood us researchers like no other. You broke down walls like no other. If anyone ever had the key to a major breakthrough, if anyone knew how to unlock the mysteries of cancer through multidisciplinary research, it's been you. Consider this key a powerful symbol of remembrance."

Chase took the key from Gunnar, gave a last glance to the Kruger 2000 and said good-bye to Freya who had spent extraordinary effort in anticipatory training for that moment when Chase would be in the lab full-time. He said farewell again to Nola across the room with her student, whereupon Nola placed two fingers to her lips for several seconds, then held them out in a "peace sign" to Chase as he walked out of the laboratory, forever.

Driving home, he phoned Hardy Studebaker to thank him one last time for all that he had done.

"Chase, I'm very sorry. I want you to know I did everything I could."

Though it was difficult to judge sincerity on the phone, Chase thought it peculiar that the most powerful man at the medical center had not intervened at the end. As it turned out, those most jealous of Chase's relationship with Hardy had been correct all along in stating, "Hardy Studebaker does not run this medical school."

Chase said to Hardy, "Most of all I don't understand how there could be no compromise. I had several scenarios in mind – all of them getting the endowment off my back – that would have worked quite well, but not a single soul outside the Pavilion would talk to me once Porter launched his crusade. Rumors were swirling everywhere that were patently absurd. It was like everyone came out of the woodwork to join the thrill of destroying a life – mine."

Hardy replied, "You understand, though, that it was really only three surgeons who did you in."

"What? What are you talking about? Three surgeons?"

"In addition to Piscotel, Dr. Dagmar and Dr – oh, I can't remember his name. The one who wants to build a trauma center. Dr. Judy, that's it. The three of them formed an alliance and threatened to resign as a group if you were allowed to stay at the university in any capacity whatsoever. I could have persuaded my sister and the rest of the Taylor family to look at some options if it hadn't been for those three surgeons sticking together like they did. My sister Gretchen just wanted peace at any price, and she would have been open to several arrangements."

"I don't get it. This is nuts. I've never had a conversation about the Pavilion with Dagmar in my life. He didn't have a clue as to what was going on. Silly me, I even suggested him as a mediator at one point. As for the trauma doc, Ken Judy, same story – no interaction other than 'hello' in the hallways. He knew nothing about the Pavilion, other than the Piscotel version of my stealing a million dollars from their trauma agenda. I've never met anyone who can twist reality like Porter."

The eyes and ears are a poor witness to men with the souls of cannibals, Chase thought, recalling an ancient quote from someone.

Hardy continued, "I was at the meeting, Chase. Dr. Dagmar convinced the dean, the vice-chancellor, and the president that you were tearing apart the actual discipline of general surgery, that breast surgery was an integral part of general surgery, and that if you moved out of the Department of Surgery, it would fragment the specialty and would harm resident education."

"Did everyone really believe that rubbish? That statement is so wrong at so many levels I can't tell you. Dagmar was using the classic straw man argument – true in one sense, but totally unrelated to the issues at hand. Look at radiology. They lost mammography to us, yet the radiology residents rotated through, and their educational experience increased, not decreased. We didn't fragment radiology – we improved it. I can go on and on...for hours. I'm harming resident education? Good god, Porter Piscotel wouldn't allow surgery residents to rotate with me. And you know the main reason? You want to know what he told me year after year? That Dr. Dagmar needed the residents for his kiddie heart service. Go figure. I can assure you that the most wasted experience I had in residency was pediatric hearts. You get out in private practice, and you find out that the pulmonary guys, the cardiologists, the intensivists, *no one* lets you use anything you've learned. It was a shock for me. However, you wanna know the most common cancer that's treated by general surgeons? Breast cancer. Yes, and the residents at our beloved university never rotated at the Pavilion until *after* Porter handed over the residency program to someone else, who immediately started breast surgery rotations. So, these three knights in shining armor held their little court, and I wasn't given the decency to defend myself against such garbage?"

"Well, it's neither here nor there now, I suppose."

It is indeed both here and there, thought Chase. *You've been in secret meetings with these jerks who have whipped themselves up into a testosterone frenzy based on misinformation and outright lies, validating Freud's primordial horde, and where I wasn't asked to attend, and where there were decisions made about me and my career based on rules they made up as they went along. Henry the VII would be proud of his legacy. History repeats itself, but people are dead, eyes propped wide open for effect. How could you, Mr. Studebaker, sit in that meeting, knowing what you know, without stopping them? Have they sapped you of all courage? Or, did they offer to name another building after you?*

Chase had drifted off momentarily to Hardy's ramblings, but keyed back in again as the (former) puppet master said: "The point is that the final decision from the president came down to either letting you go or letting the united block of three surgeons go. Believe it or not, it was a close call. Truth is, Dagmar is near the end of his career, and if it had just been Dagmar and Piscotel, after what we've seen, it would have gone your way. But to lose all three at once? Thatcher was my brother-in-law, and I loved him like a brother, and I'll never know why he hand-picked Dr. Piscotel as his replacement."

"Let me assure you, if Thatcher hadn't believed Far West University was a professional dead end, he would have hand-picked my friend, Franklin Cooper, as the next chairman."

"Like I said, it took all three of them to win. It really boiled down to the third one, I can never remember his name..."

"Ken Judy."

"Yes, Dr. Judy. Turns out, we had picked him to be the force behind our next great center of excellence at Far West – the Level One Trauma Center. No one wanted to lose him."

Chase said, "Our Pontius Pilate President is claiming he deferred his decision to the Taylor family, and that *they* said to let me go. So you can imagine how much trust I have in what *anyone* says down there. Diogenes would be shit-out-of-luck at that place. President Didion simply two-stepped his way around the entire controversy so that he would personally come out smelling like the politician's stench of rose, didn't he?"

"Well, I must admit I'm very disappointed as to how this was handled."

"You know, in the Inquisition, they let the accused write down the names of people who had reason to hold grudges. Convictions were made only by neutral parties. Pathetic, isn't it, that there was more fair-mindedness in the Inquisition than the rights I was given. No forum, no chance for my own defense. Three certified jerks band together and toss accusations my way? Rapists and murderers have more rights than I've been shown these past few months. I consider the Breast Pavilion my child who was raped and murdered by the very people whose fingers are pointed at me."

"Chase, I know this has been tough on you."

"I do appreciate all you tried to do, but the word 'tough' simply doesn't cover it."

For Chase, the bottom of Pandora's box – traditionally occupied by Hope – was empty.

Chase planned to pack up his office at the Pavilion over the weekend while the clinic was empty, using his universal key for entry. He needed boxes for the move. Lots of them. His mind flashed back to the scores of boxes containing his grandfather's books, the containers long gone, and the books now fully exposed in his apartment. Early Saturday morning, he drove through the neighborhood to scout for boxes. *There, a dumpster with its door open, directly behind the bookstore.*

Peering through the opening of the reeking dumpster, he saw a cluster of intact boxes near the back of the cave, out of reach. He would have to climb inside, which required more effort and greater twisting than it would seem. Traipsing through the knee-high trash, he reached the boxes, firm as they were, clean as could be. Then his heart sank. The logo on one of the empty boxes, designed to ship compact discs, was for DoveWing Music, his old publisher that, thirty years prior, had released the music of The New Bloods. His knees buckled, and he sank to the floor of the dumpster trying to force tears that were no longer available, caressing one of the boxes, smoothing his palm over the winged logo, then staring at the steel walls of the dumpster covered with amorphous muck and slime, wishing he'd never have to leave its hold. He inhaled the perfume of his lost paradise.

· · ·

When his phone rang at home, he couldn't muster an answer, so he listened to Darby Raven as she left a message:

"I'm so sorry about all of this, and most of all, I'm sorry for you, Chase. I'd like to accompany you next week to meet the administration at Permian. I think we should promise them the moon, and by gosh, we'll deliver. I've managed to get seven board members to come with me from the Pavilion group, Jody included, of course. They're the old-timers, the ones who saw what you did at the beginning to make it all happen, disgusted with what they've witnessed at Far West. We'll add more members as we go. Just to let you know, I'm the only one of the Far West group who's going to stay on the board at the Pavilion, as odd as that seems. I have two reasons – one, to take the high road, trying to calm the storm, and secondly, to work on Molly to get her to come to her senses and join you at Permian someday. I swear I'll get the two of you together again. I'm sure of it."

32
MUTE TESTIMONY

The reincarnated Vision was more than anyone could imagine. Together, Chase and Darby Raven spent a month writing a proposal for an all-inclusive "breast hospital." It would be the first of its kind anywhere in the world and would be sponsored by Permian Medical Center. The facility would house breast imaging, surgical suites, medical oncology, plastic surgery flap units, and radiation oncology using new techniques specifically targeting the lumpectomy sites.

But it wouldn't stop with cancer. A host of benign breast problems and diseases would be included, as well as lactational services. Women would never need to go anywhere else for anything. It was the ultimate concept in one-stop shopping, a level of integrated care never before achieved, and perhaps never dreamed. The appeal (and envy) would not simply be in west Texas, but everywhere. People would travel from around the globe to see the pacesetter. Darby would head fund-raising (Jody was too angry to think straight at this point). The Permian administration was delighted, already thinking in terms of their negotiating power with third-party payors. Chase would be hired for the director's job in spite of the fact that he'd previously been "extra baggage" when Permian made the offer to Molly St. Martin.

In addition, there was a brilliant hook to tie the new "breast hospital" at Permian into the university's Breast Pavilion as a peace offering (Darby's idea; Chase's reluctant agreement). Chase would head a research initiative, based on the patients seen at Permian, linking to the PhDs that he had already organized at Far West. Chase would draw blood samples and save benign biopsy specimens, organizing them all into a massive research biorepository, each specimen linked to an exhaustive database. It would be a researcher's gold mine. Darby Raven called it the West Texas Breast Cancer Project, with start-up funding to be independent of Permian so as not to be a financial drain.

Ignoring his instinct for bloody revenge, Chase espoused a marriage of town and gown, natural enemies dating back to student riots of the Middle Ages. Yet, here in west Texas, of all places, town and gown would come together in a wedding of the minds. Surely, all would be happy with this arrangement. Even Far West Texas University shouldn't find blame with this effort. Everybody would win.

"This is the high road, Chase," Darby would say over and over, as if to convince herself in addition to Chase. "Part of me, like you, wants to wreak havoc on those who destroyed all you worked for. However, we must take this high road."

To start the ball rolling for the West Texas Breast Cancer Project, Darby organized a gala at The Colony Club. She invited several hundred potential donors, many of whom had been Chase's supporters in the past. Mostly, though, the guest list included fresh faces, with the hope that they might hitch their wagons to something new. Importantly, Darby invited Molly St. Martin so that Molly could see the future firsthand.

Chase spoke to the audience after dinner. Tremulous, he felt his voice starting to crack at several points in his rally speech, as if he were about to slip into a sobbing breakdown. Overwhelmed by the possibility of public humiliation if he should start to cry at the podium, he cut his remarks short and skipped to his conclusion. "Thank you for coming tonight. This project at Permian is going to be huge. For me, it's going to be a breath of fresh air."

Then, Darby spoke, praising Chase over and over, reminding the audience that he had introduced interdisciplinary breast care in west Texas, and that he had jump-started breast cancer research on the university campus.

She said, "In that spirit of innovation and courage, I would like to announce that we are establishing an award to honor the person, a lay person, each year, who has done the most in the fight against breast cancer." Darby looked straight at Molly St. Martin as she spoke: "We are calling it 'The Rainmaker Award'."

Chase didn't hear anything that followed. This award title was news to him. (The inaugural award was presented to a state legislator who, in the 1980s, had led the fight to force insurers to pay for screening mammography.) The chosen name of the award, dreamed up by the Raven sisters, was a secret tribute to Chase, his moniker as bestowed by Molly St. Martin.

But Molly didn't appreciate the insider satire. In fact, word got back to Darby Raven that Molly felt ambushed at the event.

After the speeches, a friend tapped Chase on the shoulder and said, "Boy, did you piss off a lot of people with that 'breath of fresh air' thing you said about Permian being better than the university."

"I didn't say that," replied Chase. "I was talking about me, that it was a breath of fresh air *for me* to re-start the research."

"Well, I was standing next to Layton Prudhomme, you know that real estate tycoon friend of Hardy Studebaker who's been buying up this part of Texas, and he was ticked. I heard him say out loud, 'We'll see about that. Sounds like Callaway didn't get the message.'"

Later, Darby said, "Oh, don't worry about it, Chase. They're jealous, like always, because they know what you're capable of doing. They know what you'll do at Permian and what will be impossible for them at the university. I probably shouldn't have invited some of that old guard, but after all, we're going to help the university research program big time."

Shortly after the Colony Club gala, the president of the Studebaker Medical Research Foundation, Greg Scott, was so swept up by Chase's vision (plus several lunches with the lovely Raven sisters) that he took it upon himself to announce he would give *free office space* to the Raven sisters at the medical foundation to headquarter and coordinate the West Texas Breast Cancer Project. After all, it would be the Studebaker scientists and the university scientists who would benefit, rather than Permian Medical Center.

Chase surfaced from deep despair. Free office space at the prestigious medical research foundation for the Ravens and their troops! His dream was still alive, albeit not exactly as he had planned. Breaking the spine of breast cancer was the most important thing – not his location. Remarkably, he would be able to access the research wisdom of the Pixleys, he could work behind the scenes with Nola Kastl and his beloved Kruger 2000, and he would be able to fuel every scientist on campus with more samples and more data than they could handle. *Behind the scenes, yes.* The direction of his life in medicine, he'd felt, was to work behind the scenes, even though it had never come to fruition.

Six weeks later, Darby Raven called Chase in his new office at Permian with horrifying news. Her voice, shaking with anger, was almost unrecognizable. Usually, the model of equanimity, Darby was nearly screaming. "I don't believe it. I've never been so insulted or humiliated in my life. Never! I don't know how to say this...."

"What, Darby? What?"

"They've kicked us out of the Studebaker Foundation. Kicked—us—out. We didn't even get the option to pay rent like others do. They flat threw us out on the street. They want furniture, computers, everything, out by the end of the week."

Something ripped inside. Chase, already aware of a murderous rage within, was ready to kill – literally. He wanted someone to die. And he wanted to be the executioner. His father's Browning pistol had been cleaned and serviced.

"Who did it? Who kicked you out?"

"It didn't come from within the Studebaker Foundation. I spoke to the president, and Greg was overly apologetic, totally embarrassed. He admitted his strings are being pulled by the powers above. But I can't figure out who that might be. I asked him repeatedly, but he wouldn't tell me. Said I'd be shocked to learn who was responsible, though."

Chase listened to her lamentations, a role reversal of sorts. Usually, he was laying his burdens onto her, but clearly Darby was deeply injured by the ouster.

"I'm too angry to talk right now, Chase. I'll call you back as soon as I have more information. As soon as I've had a chance to collect myself."

Chase immediately dialed the reporter at the newspaper who had called him months earlier about the brewing scandal. Chase was ready to sing. The entire world needed to know about this outrage, starting Day One at Far West, years ago. "Sorry," said the reporter, "I was told to bury the story shortly after the first time we talked."

"Wow. The hidden crime is even bigger than I thought."

Chase's rage left him paralyzed. He stared mindlessly at his stack of files on the "breast hospital," at his reams of paper on the West Texas Breast Cancer Project, at his research correspondence with scientists at the university, but he couldn't lift a finger to do anything.

After that, he forgot to eat, he couldn't sleep. He used what little energy he had left to restrain himself from doing something rash and crazy yet so well-deserved. "Who are these people?" he said aloud to himself. "How deeply does their evil run? We were trying to help them. *They* were the beneficiaries, not me."

He missed the call when Darby phoned him the next day, so he could only listen to the message she left on voice mail:

"Chase, I didn't think I could get any angrier than when I last talked to you, but I think I'm going to explode. It wasn't one person who threw us out. There were forty. Forty! Forty names on a petition, a Who's Who of Matherville. I saw the list that Greg received. I'm shocked beyond all words. I don't even know where to start. I counted many of those people as my friends. I can't tell you how I've helped so many of them and their families over the years. Still, when I saw the name of Layton Prudhomme I was especially stunned. I'd always counted him as a friend. Then, I learned that he'd been put in charge of prying me away from you. Do you believe it! It was Layton's job to manipulate me back to the university, while making sure you were disgraced forever. Layton's real estate interests at Far West, you know, are worth hundreds of millions, at least. Looks like he's willing to destroy anything or anyone who gets in his way. Who even knew he was in the mix with all this? He's a friend of Hardy's, but I had no idea he was involved until now. Well, that's the last straw. I'm resigning my position at the Breast Pavilion, and I'll never lift a finger for that university again. I'm just so angry. I can't calm down. I feel like I'm going to burst. I've never felt like this in my life. I'll talk to you later. Sorry for the long voice mail. I want you to see this list of forty as well. You need to know every name on the list. You probably count some of them as your friends, too. And you're not gonna *believe* whose name is at the top – the ringleader."

Chase was trembling, hands shaking and sweaty, and the noise of his own breathing sounded a storm brewing. He didn't know where to turn. He thought, *okay, okay, keep calm. Don't do anything rash. You can still pull off a miracle. You'll have to give up the Kruger microscope, of course, and all your relationships at the university. However, you can still link up with other researchers at other universities and those in industry. In fact, researchers from all over the world will want to access your biorepository. The only reason you were devoted to the west Texas venue was the lesson you thought you learned by going to California, making you a West Texas patriot – certainly, a wrong interpretation of the message as it appears now. Forget them. Forget transporting Far West to the front lines of research. Think globally. Tie your wagon to the top-notch researchers in the world who are already in the hunt to eradicate this disease. Most importantly, you have the ongoing and now exclusive support of the most beloved individual in Matherville – Darby Raven.*

Perhaps he drifted off to sleep that night, perhaps not. Visions by day are often mixed with dreams at night, so when the phone rang at 3:00 a.m., it seemed part of the reverie. Inexplicably, it was Darby's husband, Mark Raven, who had to repeat his name twice before Chase believed it. "Chase, I wonder if you'd be willing to come down and join me at the Permian hospital emergency room. Darby has had some kind of stroke or something."

Mark sounded remarkably calm. A small stroke should allow easy recovery, Chase considered as he drove to the emergency room. Darby was so young. Barely fifty. Perfect health. Always jogging. Always watching her diet. He had just talked with her hours earlier. Rather, she had talked to him, her words recorded on his voice mail.

When he arrived at the hospital, Darby was connected to a ventilator. Comatose. Normal blips on the monitor indicated that her cardiac function was fine, but she was non-responsive. Mark Raven was holding her hand through the bedrails.

A neurosurgeon, a co-intern with Chase 25 years earlier, was writing in a chart at the nurses' station, and Chase moved that direction. "Hey, Chase. This is a bad one. Midbrain. I can't do anything surgically. Know her?"

"Yes, a very close friend. How bad is it? I mean, is she going to live?"

"Let me put it this way. Judging from the size of the bleed and the location, it would be better if she didn't."

The words would not penetrate, bouncing off Chase and falling to the ground.

Chase joined Mark Raven at the bedside where the two of them stood waiting for a miracle until daybreak when they moved Darby to a room in the ICU, her heart still beating strong. However, Chase's belief in miracles had been stretched beyond its limit. Darby was the last angel, the only one left standing between him and a monstrous world with its teeth bared.

The social elite of Matherville poured into Permian Medical Center by mid-morning, joining Darby's friends and family near the bedside. Tears and prayers and wailing filled the ICU waiting room. The city was in shock. The crowd shifted like sand throughout the day, some returning every few hours, others arriving and leaving only once, but always a minimum of fifty as part of the tide. After the crowds arrived, Chase shied away, able to bear only a few minutes at a time, just long enough to hear, "No improvement."

In sickening coincidence, Permian Medical Center had recently announced the employment of Chase Callaway through a press release, and he was scheduled to appear on a local television show that afternoon. In a zombie-like state, he walked on the set, gave a fifteen-minute interview in which he couldn't recall a single word said, his only goal being the avoidance of an on-air breakdown, then he returned to the ICU vigil at Permian.

There, he was approached by one of the disillusioned Board members from the university who had followed him to Permian under the direction of Darby. "Here's the list," she said. "This is the infamous forty." Chase took the list from her. It was too horrible to imagine. How could people be so stupid and so vile at the same time? And so very proud of their dirty deeds to be willing to sign a petition like this? Then the Board member said, "You just missed Molly St. Martin. Probably best, though. After what she said, if you'd heard it, I think you might've killed her."

"Why? What?"

The board member said, "She took one look at Darby, turned to the person with her and said, 'My conscience is clear'."

"Her conscience? *Her* conscience? Did anyone tell her this is not about her?" How easily the conscience can be washed clean, he thought. I recall that Pol Pot uttered those identical words – "My conscience is clear" – when confronted with his life's deeds in the form of mass genocide.

When visiting hours were over, and after Darby's husband Mark left the bedside for a late-night meal, Chase slipped into the room, alone with Darby."

He embraced her hand with his, then leaned over close to her ear, whispering, "Darby, I am so, so sorry. I'm sorry you made the decision to follow me. If you'd dropped me like you should have, you never would've had to face such ugliness, such evil. I'm sorry, so sorry. Forgive me."

He recalled another circumstance, long ago, where he had serendipitously discovered his old Sunday School teacher as an inmate in the "Dungeon" at the mental institution next door, where only the "worst" cases, the vegetative souls, waited to die. In 4-point restraints, Jewell Pollard had not spoken a word in years. Yet, when Chase whispered his name over and over to elicit a response, she had turned toward him and said, "Zebulon?" This was his grandfather's name, so he had somehow made a connection with her, albeit weak.

But for Darby, there would be no connection at all. He squeezed her fingers, hoping for the slightest pressure in return. Nothing. Chase pulled himself away just as Mark Raven was returning to the bedside, to the love of his life.

Darby Raven died moments later.

⋅ ⋅ ⋅

Five pallbearers were family members, while Chase was the sixth, at the request of Darby's husband Mark.

Jody Raven was beside herself, but she did manage to say to Chase before the service, "If Porter Piscotel comes to this funeral, I will personally strangle him. I'm sick of hearing from my friends that 'where there's smoke, there's fire,' trying to cast doubts about you. The only smoke in this war is what Piscotel blows out his rear."

As the crowd filled the sanctuary to overflowing, Chase spotted the arrivals of Dr. Dagmar, the dean, the vice-chancellor, Hardy Studebaker, Layton Prudhomme, and other characters from the medical center who had been part of Darby's pink slip, those who had kicked her out of the research offices.

Mark Raven delivered his wife's eulogy, captivating the mourners with an effortless description of how things had transpired from his perspective. "We had just finished our evening wine, about ready to go to bed. It was a nice Chardonnay we had picked up in Napa last spring. We had been talking about our days, mostly Darby's days of late as she was involved with… well, things that were much more stressful than her usual. She had quite a few tales to tell, quite spirited I'd say, more than her usual tranquility, and then she says, out of the clear blue, 'Mark, I have this horrible headache. Do you think it could be the wine?' Then, she sort of slumps over, and…"

And now she is mute – forever.

Chase listened from the front pew. Darby's brother, the scientist from Cold Spring Harbor Laboratory who had told Darby that the T.N.T. endowment had done nothing but paint a large target on Chase's back, was seated next to Chase, sobbing. Chase was numb.

Then, when it came time to lift the casket, Chase took his place among the family members and grabbed the gold handle assigned to him. Yet, when he turned to face the crowd, his vision blurred, then focused again, but only on The Forty. Among the hundreds of mourners, forty faces stood out in a snapshot, none of them moving – all Forty fixed and rigid, in black and white, posed smugly for the photographer in Chase's mind.

This graphic and macabre branding of The Forty in his brain sent fire down his spine, splitting him lengthwise and tearing scales apart as he shed the Third Exoskeleton.

Beneath the final exoskeleton was nothing. Blackness. Eternal darkness.

This then, is the person I know. I am Chase Callaway.

．　．　．

At the Raven home after the funeral, I stood in a corner, counting from one to forty, then from forty to one, when I heard Hardy Studebaker approach Mark Raven and say, "It's never too early to start thinking about how we want to memorialize Darby. An endowed chair is always nice."

For weapons, they had influence and prestige and half-truths and schemes and slander and lies and machinations and power and money and, most of all, the willingness to eat their own. I had only one shield against the assault – a woman of virtue – and now she was dead, to be interred alongside my faith in a God who would intervene on my behalf.

33
LEPROSARIUM

Mark Raven called me one week after his wife had been buried.

"Chase, this might seem like an unusual question, but the funeral home told me after the autopsy, when they received the body, they couldn't find Darby's heart. She donated her corneas and her heart valves, but not her heart. They wouldn't have taken her heart without permission – would they?"

I paused. "No, but when they harvest the valves, they cut up the heart in the process, so it's pretty much in pieces. There's no soft or easy way to describe the process. Maybe the mortician didn't recognize the fragments of the dissected heart, or the heart might have been...uh, discarded...after they took the valves. It's unsettling, I know, but—"

"Well, that makes sense. I just wondered."

"Yes, of course."

I hoped it was the right answer, but it was hard for me to talk as I couldn't get around the oppressive symbolism, a poetic and tragic conclusion to the story of a woman heaven-bent on taking the high road.

I had not attended my home-based 12-step meetings regularly during the final crisis, but now it was time to say good-bye, for I had fallen into to a deep and dark well from which I anticipated no return. The group was worn out anyway from my incessant complaining that was only getting worse. Quite simply, there was no point in my casting a shroud of misery over the group, hurting the chances of recovery for some.

At my final meeting with this home group, I described the saga of Darby's death, though I downplayed its impact on me. I didn't relish anyone knowing that I, too, had been a casualty. Then, one of the members gave me a jolt, though perhaps it was nothing more than a shock administered to a disconnected frog's leg, a prep in biology class.

"Darby Raven? Why, her father was the founder of this group."

"Wha—?"

"Oh, yes. Long-time twelve-stepper. One of the original pillars here in Matherville. Helped hundreds get sober before he died, years ago. Had two daughters – Darby and Jody – and I forget how many sons. Just one, I think."

I had heard the founder's name mentioned many times over the years, but I didn't know Darby or Jody's maiden name, so I'd never made a connection. I tried to smile (but could not) at the notion of all those who had squealed to Darby and Jody about my history of addiction, unaware that each time someone pointed an accusatory finger at me, the resolve of the Raven sisters was only strengthened, in memory of their father.

Women have always been angels of mercy to me, while men stood by and mocked, or something like that. So said Edgar Allen Poe.

I knew my illness had moved well beyond the common defects of character and into the realm of dangerous decline, so little could be gained from a support group. I had entered a fixed, perpetual cycle of automated behavior over which I had no control. Periods of total calm, without emotion, punctuated by violent outbursts, screaming to the point of exhaustion – sweating profusely, heart pounding, vocal cords stretched and torn. No middle ground. No socially acceptable behavior. Always at one extreme or the other.

As with the leper who receives the rituals of death prior to entry to the leprosarium, so it was for me.

Editor's note: Although the story grinds down over the next several years to a stunning end, the remaining manuscript of Chase Callaway still has hundreds of pages left. With Dr. Callaway now accepting himself in the first person, the reader can easily distinguish between his writings and my condensations. On the other hand, his verbosity mandates my increasing editorial intervention.

Oddly enough, the bulk of his writings are theological, similar to the excessive religiosity exhibited by Sir Isaac Newton who wrote more about God than physics. Yet, rather than express opinions, Dr. Callaway's writings would be more in line with Voltaire who was also preoccupied with God, with whom he fought in spite of disbelief. Adept at quoting passages of scripture out of context, Dr. Callaway's writing became increasingly bizarre and incoherent, sprinkled with the repetitive self-absorbed theme of "I have been crucified with Christ."

He describes a preoccupation with past patients who later died of breast cancer, eventually communicating with them to offer apologies for his failure. He begins to carry on conversations with them as they return to life, at least in his mind.

The most crippling feature of his mental aberration, though, is the episodic rage that seems yoked to an internal clock. Tapes of injustice play in his head, over and over, each time gaining strength and culminating in a screaming explosion. If it occurs in public, he runs to his car where the reverberations of the screams are held within.

It's difficult to say how much of his leper syndrome is real. Yet, Chase describes patients diverted away from him by his former partner Molly St. Martin and staff at the Breast Pavilion. This trickery came camouflaged in the form of: "Oh, he only does research now," which was untrue. Worse, members of The Forty continued their group effort by diverting newly diagnosed patients away from seeing Chase. He would sometimes learn of the effort through a peripheral source, "Oh, she was going to come see you after she learned about her cancer, but then she heard all the bad stuff." Chase would say, "Bad stuff? Really? You mean the stuff about my encyclopedic knowledge of breast cancer, studying the journals all weekend, every weekend? Or, the incredible pains I take for superb cosmetic outcome, be it lumpectomy or mastectomy? Or perhaps it's catching the overstated findings on pathology, where she might not even have a true cancer. Is that the 'bad stuff' that she's been hearing? Or is it a question about my integrity, the charge made by a self-appointed lynch mob composed of half-wits who trip over integrity every day without even seeing it?"

A particular encounter deserves mention in Chase's own words:

When I left the office that day, I heard my name called out in the parking lot, but with a question mark at the end, as if seeking confirmation. "Chase Callaway?"

I was walking stoop-shouldered with my face to the ground. When I looked up, a young man moved away from his car toward me.

"Y-Yes?"

"I thought that was you. You don't know me, but my name is Jerry Day. I'm the pastor of Grace Church here in Matherville. I was making my rounds at the hospital just now."

My mind was blank. No recognition. I stood frozen while he continued walking toward me, his hand outstretched. "We've not met officially, but I'm thrilled to run into you here. It's been thirty years, at least."

"I'm sorry, I don't recall—"

"Oh, heavens, you wouldn't remember me. I was just a student living at a frat house in Austin when The New Bloods came and performed there. You were the emcee. In fact, it was your message at the end of the performance that led me to the Lord. I'll never forget that song, "One's a-Changing – the World's Re-arranging." I was a chemistry major, but I decided right there on the spot that I wasn't going to spend my life working on a better toothpaste – no, I wanted my life to count. I owe my love of the Lord to you. I'd heard recently that you lived here in Matherville now. Anyone who reads the society pages knows that, I suppose. That's why I recognized you, and I wanted to meet you and say thanks. This is really a special moment for me."

As the pastor walked away, I whispered to myself, "Oh, I miss it so."

Editor's Note: If the events are represented fairly by Dr. Callaway in his manuscript, then his paranoia about ostracism is at least partially justified. He describes being invited to speak at a women's group, only to receive a phone call later retracting the invitation with no plans to reschedule. More dramatically, Dr. Callaway was invited to "fire the gun" to launch the Race for the Cure at Matherville, but there were strong objections, and the invitation was revoked, with crushing impact on Chase who was struggling, yet again, to redeem himself. These events prompted fantasies of using his father's Browning pistol and firing at someone, anyone. Tales of ostracism and interference by The Forty and their extended fingers fill the pages. If only a tenth are true, it is indeed both shocking and heartbreaking. Back to his words:

Then, a well-meaning friend gave me a copy of a letter written by one of The Forty, one of the most politically powerful women in Matherville. The letter was addressed to President Skip Didion during the heat of battle months earlier. Somehow, my receipt of the copy was to help assuage someone's guilt, but it did nothing but fuel my rage. The letter described my gross lack of integrity, along with the need to oust me from the university and replace me with "someone that [sic] has ethics in line with the inmitable [sic] Thatcher Nolan Taylor, M.D." And so forth.

Blocked from responding to this letter in any fashion lest I make matters worse, I could only count the number of misspellings and grammatical errors in the obscene document. Consistent with the mysterious human tendency toward embracing abject humiliation, I kept the letter and read it many times, unable to throw it in the trash where it would have been more at home.

In a popular Christmas film, the protagonist is oblivious as to how his small contributions to many lives have generated profound and positive outcomes down the road. In contrast, I was completely cognizant of how I had impacted so many lives at such a cost. However, when in trouble, and when I needed those beneficiaries to line up in support, instead, they hurled bricks. Indeed, they took out lucrative mortgages with Potter, to force the Bailey Building and Loan out of business. This is why we call the movie a fantasy.

•

If it weren't for the "spells," I could probably manage, but it's the near-fatal attacks (at least that's how they feel) for which I need help. That help, by the way, must transcend cheap pharmaceuticals. The outbursts are not getting better. They're getting worse. I've moved to a remote location, not to benefit me, but to protect society.

The phrase "stabbed in the back" is commonly applied to the generic traitor, but its full meaning is much more – a well-placed knife in the middle of your back cannot be reached by the victim. It cannot be removed. It will remain there while you writhe in agony until death, be it moments away, or years. The only poultice that allows you to live with the pain is an apology from the attacker. I've often thought that if a single voice, out of this cast of hundreds, had said, "I'm sorry," then the entire history of this saga would have been rewritten. However, I assure you, not a single soul has opted for: "I'm sorry." Instead, the cannibals have feasted.

I scream. I scream at so many players in this game. Forty players to start with. Had there been only a single traitor, a single backstabber, a single liar, I could focus and adjust, perhaps. But with so many, I cannot focus. The spells are global. Tapes play in my head. Conversations. Countless conversations. The hard wiring of what was once my remarkable memory is now stuck like a needle on an old 45 record, playing stories over and over, the words being the same every time. My obsessive thought disorder, once harnessed to amass mountains of knowledge has been rendered useless.

The memory of these conversations abates in no way. When I hear these voices from my past, I start answering them as I should have at the moment, as noted in my writings here. I get louder and louder, repeating myself in italics until I'm screaming and cursing in capital letters, then bolded caps, in the vilest fashion imaginable, profanity indicating the same neural pathway as Tourette's. Oh, my poor basal ganglia! I want these people to suffer…and suffer horribly.

The screaming lasts for several minutes each time, until my heart is pounding, and I fall to the floor in exhaustion, drenched in sweat, struggling to catch my breath. For a moment, I am at peace, albeit from sheer fatigue. I sometimes shower twice or three times before I can leave the house. Then, the tapes play, and the anger builds again, its orgiastic nature unquenched by brief climax. Back on my feet, I shake my fist so hard against the mirror that my right shoulder and elbow are now plagued by chronic inflammation. Switching to my left fist to shake, that side now suffers as well. Sweat streams as I shout, and I cannot stop until the volume amplifies to maximum intensity. My voice is raspy from nodules that reside in tombstone rows on my vocal cords.

I calibrate and monitor my anger using the windshield of my car where drops of spittle coat the inside glass from my persistent screaming, uncontrollable even while driving. Over the course of one tank of gas, the inside of my windshield becomes a matrix of dots, in some areas nearly a smooth sheet of spit. Yet, not one iota of improvement since I began counting dots per square inch (DPSI). Each time I fill my tank with gas, I ask myself, "Can I make it through one tank without screaming?" No. Not even close. Each time I go to the gas station, my ritual includes counting and recording the number of dots per square inch in a specific site, then a wet cloth to clean the inside of my windshield, hoping always that this will be the last time, swearing it will be the last time, and that with my next tank, the windshield will be crystal clear. Yet, it never happens.

It's not merely the terrifying chronicity of my illness that drives me to the point of requesting aggressive psychiatric intervention, but also my realization that the episodes are escalating. I caress the Browning pistol I found in my father's closet upon his death, and while I want so desperately to execute Piscotel or Dinwiddie or St. Martin or Didion or Prudhomme or any of The Forty, I know the only reasonable alternative is to use it on myself. After all, in my screaming attacks when at home, I am always staring into the mirror, howling at someone else, but seeing only me.

Last week, in unexplainable desperation, I snuck into my grandfather's old church. Many years ago, my grandfather's life changed radically after a tornado tore through his home and drove a nail into his unused Bible. He placed the evidence in a glass case at the altar in his new church where it stayed protected for over 60 years – the twisting hand of God at work.

Feeling compelled, inexplicably, to break an imaginary curse, I took an old memento of my grandfather's that I'd kept as a good luck charm – a carved wooden shell that I found in his library after he died – and, in a midnight mass of desperation, in a fit of unbridled rage, I smashed the shell into the glass case freeing the Bible from its cage.

With the King James prize in hand, I looked to the page where the nail had supposedly pointed, to the verse he had circled so many years ago, prompting him to convert to Christianity and to build a church. Yet, to my surprise, on close inspection of the nail track, the point penetrated a few pages deeper, and I could trace an indentation in the page marking Ecclesiastes 4:5. The tiny point of the nail had, in fact, stopped at: "The fool foldeth his hands together, and eateth his own flesh."

I have grown to consider two possibilities, neither certain, but providing comfort in reducing chaos to dualism – after great study of my genealogy, it is possible that I am the thirteenth generation of a curse, and that the curse will end with my death. Or, the alternative view is that, quite simply, there is a neurologic aberration, a blemish in my brain, not unlike the fate of Ivy Pettibone. The neural tracts that were designed for normal maturation were groomed instead into rhythmic reverberations through the false neurotransmitters of alchemy I imposed upon myself years ago. New pathways were forged and lubricated after my recovery. Now, those aberrant tracts have been hijacked by the events of my life, and they require no stimulus to perpetuate, caught in a relentless cycle of rage, firing at will.

I favor the latter theory. My studies have taken me to the sub-stations of the amygdala, where I believe sits the heart of the problem. I have no desire for psychoanalysis or brain alchemy with serotonin reuptake inhibitors or cognitive therapy or any magic tricks with operant conditioning – we are nothing more than a boiling stew of chemicals and our souls are inborn clusters of neural connections that don't know how to talk directly to our prefrontal cortex.

Or else, if adopting the theory of a "curse," we are spirits, in the Platonic sense, the philosophy that Augustine of Hippo hijacked for Christianity in his neo-Platonic interpretation of what and how we believe. Thus, we are relieved of huge responsibility given that all is preordained, yet prisoners of our own free will, and the two shall never meet.

I have read and studied all your publications, including your PhD thesis from Harvard, and since my appeal to the spiritual theory has not worked, I am hereby volunteering to be a test patient for stereotactic interruptions of my hijacked neural pathways to stop the cycles. I have arrived at several possible sites in my brain for surgical interruption, and we can try them serially or all at once. I understand that your work heretofore has been restricted to the criminally insane, a diagnosis that escapes me only because I have not yet pulled a trigger.

I offer this manuscript to claim my candidacy for psychosurgery, saving us both a great deal of time. It would take many years of barren therapeutic sessions to reveal this much information, and I do not have that much time, even if you do. If I am not a candidate, I will add this manuscript to the volumes I currently crank out in my secluded asylum, then delude myself that someone will care. Someday.

End.

Editor's note: This is the conclusion of Dr. Callaway's first manuscript as presented to me (Ray Divine, MD, PhD), wherein Chase offers himself as a test subject for stereotactic psychosurgery, a promising new approach to mental illness (understanding that the forerunner – prefrontal lobotomy – has a checkered past). However, Chase Callaway was not finished. More of his writings follow, compiled from voluminous notes that were discovered later.

34
HAGIOGRAPHY

In my pre-operative sessions, I've crystallized the notion that my rabid outbursts, although easily triggered by external stimuli, are usually clocked internally by rooted memories. My first functional MRI revealed massive hypertrophy of the hippocampus, having stuffed those memory-laden neurons with vast bits of information, forcing new dendritic spines, perhaps new neurons, but clearly forging a muscle of memory beyond nature. Yet, this compensatory plasticity is, for now, a failure since the circuitry between the hard drive cortex and the software hippocampus remains locked in a deadly loop. Indeed, the hypertrophy is *contributing* to the regular excitation of the damning currents.

Although I left Matherville for a remote location some time ago to escape as many excitatory stimuli as possible, I can't help but believe that my madness would have been worse had I stayed to absorb the onslaught of ruinous stimuli. I am now in self-imposed exile.

I tried to live in my beloved hometown, but it eventually proved impossible once the cavalcade of corruption was sanctified. Immediately after the death of Darby Raven, Molly St. Martin became a media darling, appearing both in print and TV, as part of an incessant advertising blitz for the Breast Pavilion. During my tenure, in spite of my relentless pleading to publicize our multidisciplinary clinic that beat nearly all other major cancer centers to the punch, the university balked. The lack of PR made growth a bigger challenge, but in the end, it was word of mouth that saved the day anyway. Now, however, after partial collapse of Pavilion programs (and complete annihilation of my vision), the university was totally committed to creating a veneer that would not allow anyone to see what really happened.

In my new role at Permian, I had no drive, no energy, yet no other way to earn a living. During my university days, I had spoken to several *hundred* groups over the years, explaining the revolution that was taking place in breast care, and how we were leading the pack. Most of this was orchestrated by the Raven sisters, and it was a super-human effort. Now, although dead to the world, I was expected to do the same by Permian administrators.

However, few bought into the idea that Permian Medical Center was anything but loaded with cash. Fund-raising ideas simply fell flat. Then, I made the shocking discovery that I could no longer face a crowd of hopeful women. My voice would break, and I would choke on my words when, inevitably, it would strike me that some women in the crowd had to be familiar with certain aspects of the Breast Pavilion story, that is, the phony version so thoroughly promulgated, barren of truth. And, yes, occasionally one of The Forty would be in the crowd.

In my final public appearance, speaking to an intimate group luncheon about the MRI revolution about to take place in breast imaging, I listed my former credentials, including the "Founding Medical Director of the Far West Breast Pavilion." Immediately, I noticed a gray-haired woman rising out of her seat with an angry look on her face. I paused and offered her the floor.

Restraining her anger, she said, "I don't know how you can go around claiming to have started the Breast Pavilion. That's where I go for my mammograms, and everyone knows that Dr. Molly St. Martin established that facility."

I sighed. Inside, I cried. Finally, I spoke softly. "I began working to establish the Pavilion in 1989, and in spite of extreme adversity, we finally opened in September 1993. Dr. St. Martin joined us in 1995, six *years* after I began my work on the project."

Then I unplugged my 35mm projector and walked out. I would never speak to another group again.

A few weeks later, in the *Matherville Daily Texan*, I discovered a photograph of Molly St. Martin cheek-to-cheek with Porter Piscotel at a gala event, holding their champagne glasses, celebrating the successful Breast Pavilion. Amazing, in that Molly had initiated the crusade to get the Pavilion out from beneath Porter. In that single photograph, to the public eye, Molly validated every one of Porter's lies about me and the Pavilion. The Giant Blob of malignant institutional narcissism had completely engulfed her.

With Darby's death, there was no one left who was willing to stand up to the frightful majority and say, "This is wrong – no, it's worse than wrong – it's obscene. It is evil." The one exception might have been Jody Raven, but she was every bit as angry as I, and no matter how justified, a relentless rant is ignored. Jody had been devastated at the loss of her sister, and like me, never recovered.

Remarkably, I could not release these abominable newspaper photos from my hold. Like my father who had saved the newspaper clippings of the malpractice suit against him over all other happy memorabilia, I saved these photos and looked at them regularly, for reasons I still do not understand. I simply could not let go. This theme of intimately and awkwardly embracing tragedy has been studied by the psychologists and novelists for many years, without understanding its hold, so who am I to try now?

Editor's note: Interjecting my own opinions about this well-known phenomenon, many of us believe that, at a subconscious level, this powerful and persistent obsession is the sufferer's attempt to re-write history, and that the only way one can generate a different ending is to go back to that moment in time when neural pathways of memory were hijacked.

My daily conversations with Darby Raven in the weeks before she died still echo:

"They don't get it," she said. They just don't get it. I'm flabbergasted. For some reason, the Pavilion board members and their friends, *my* friends, are not seeing the stunt Molly pulled. And, they don't see that Piscotel is to blame one bit, given the Taylor family's spin on things where they support Porter all the way. I've tried every trick of gentle diplomacy I know. I've been reluctant to spell it out for them because they need to see it on their own. Jody isn't hesitant to spell it out, exactly as it happened, but no one is taking her seriously anymore because she's so angry. Uncontrollably angry. I need to be very cautious with how I describe what happened. People might recoil, knowing how much I think of you."

I was sick and tired of the high road by this time. "Darby, maybe you need to be blunt with these people."

"You might be right, Chase. I'm finally coming to that conclusion."

Aye, dead women tell no tales. Darby's stroke took her life less than a week after those words.

A ten-foot statute of Hardy Studebaker was erected in the center of the medical complex, lighted with an eternal beacon. President Skip Didion was immortalized with a statue on the main university campus. Dr. Dagmar won every award the medical school could deliver, including the prestigious Lifetime Teacher Award. Sam Dinwiddie was named Alumnus of the Year for the College of Medicine. Layton Prudhomme, the real estate magnate who made untold millions off the development of the medical center complex, personally endowed a chair in his own name. No fund-raising needed. Countless awards would follow for Prudhomme's relentless fight against all forms of cancer.

Porter Piscotel was selected as the Hardy Studebaker Master Teacher shortly after my departure, such that Porter made a clean sweep of the local awards and was now on his quest for national prominence. I couldn't help myself – I mailed Hardy Studebaker a letter, commenting on the "new level" to which the teaching award had gravitated. I knew I was about to crack and that I should leave Matherville before someone got hurt, namely me.

The portrait of me as a "paranoid" by the Piscotel-Dinwiddie team, while a sickening lie at the time, had turned out to be prophetic. The moment I saw a written list of The Forty, I embraced a new respect for the extremes people will take to preserve a lie, including the destruction of anyone bearing the truth. As a result, I did become paranoid, after the fact, and I no longer felt safe walking the streets of Matherville – not out of fear that I'd be assaulted verbally, but out of fear as to what I would say or do to a member of The Forty, or any of the other scoundrels. Had I run into one of them face-to-face, I would not have been able to control my rage, and my tongue would have split them down the middle.

Molly St. Martin had been prophetic as well with regard to my psychologic well-being. When cornered by those asking why she did not leave Far West and go with me to Permian Medical Center, she would reply that she had some concerns about my "mental health" (no explanation needed after dropping an atom bomb). She was premature in her diagnosis, but in the long run, she was spot on.

My "mental health" took another beating with the cover story in my alma mater's *Roadrunner*, the alumni outreach magazine for Far West Texas University. I had been asking for coverage of the Breast Pavilion in the *Roadrunner* for six years. Once, a reporter actually interviewed me, but no article appeared. After I left, however, the story of the Pavilion was put into print. The story of the "world class breast center," however, was unrecognizable to me. I had to search hard to identify a single true sentence. The bulk of credit was placed on the shoulders of the visionary Thatcher Nolan Taylor, M.D. who had built the log cabin with his own bare hands, with Molly St. Martin at his side. Cutting edge, labor intensive programs like genetic testing simply "happened." Prompting the article, in all likelihood, was the introduction of my eventual surgical replacement who was, of course, recruited from a world famous medical center. Later, I discovered that in coming to west Texas, he had received every perk I'd been heavily criticized for requesting a few years earlier, e.g., not attending on vascular surgery cases. Yet, I had sullied the name of T.N.T. and tried to destroy the discipline of general surgery with identical requests (*Editor's note: By my understanding, these "heretical" requests by Chase would become absolutely routine for dedicated breast cancer surgeons during the next 5 years.*) My name did not appear in the story, effectively wiping out my legacy in short order.

Those who make the claim in self-help books that insisting on credit, when credit is due, should be considered a vice, do not understand art. Credit-mongering might be a distraction in industry and technology. However, for the creator, the innovator, the artist, there is no other motivation. The artist will forsake money and fame before relinquishing credit. Imagine a novel with the wrong author's name on the cover. The matter would be settled in court. Imagine the same for a song. Indeed, I had once experienced thwarted credit in my brief music career. It's a sickening feeling. I never thought once about the money or the fame. My only desire with the Pavilion was credit, this being the measure of my redemption for the wasted years of my youth in California. How puny is the pain of that "stolen song" now, a mere inkling of grief compared to the story of the Breast Pavilion? My personal redemption had been denied by scoundrels simply by erasing my name and 10 years of my life (20 if one counts the foundational years in California, and 30 if one counts surgical education).

After I saw the *Roadrunner* article, I called the author, the editor, and the Chairman of the Board of Regents, and I chewed on them all, a madman out of control, confirming every derogatory word issued my direction. After all, the journalist had only written what she'd been told. Ugly is the only thing I can say about my behavior, and I knew I had to leave town.

When the biographers of the saints fictionalized their accounts of human lives, it was considered quite acceptable. When St. Francis of Assisi visited Rome with eleven followers, the biographer naturally changed the story to twelve followers with one traitor, just to make the saint more Christ-like. This was routine, old-fashioned hagiography, a practice that is alive and well as evidenced by the saints of the Breast Pavilion, as recorded for history.

My great-grandfather, as it turns out, was killed in the famous Storm of the Century, the Galveston hurricane. Few today are aware that a hurricane warning had been issued four days earlier by the U.S. Weather Bureau, but this information was withheld by the local government official who lived on the island. Because this individual had previously stated that a hurricane was impossible in Galveston, he refused to raise the warning flags. His stubbornness resulted in my great-grandfather's premature death, along with thousands of other innocents.

Fewer still are aware that, after the disaster, this same government official, in a classic act of malignant narcissism, generated a false textual history of the hurricane, including his own gallant efforts to warn residents of the impending disaster while riding horseback up and down the sandy beaches. This treatise was a wild and wonderful story, considered by all as the "the truth," but the man should have been hung from the gallows as a mass murderer instead.

Such was the behavior of so many characters involved in the Pavilion, culminating in the false text of the *Roadrunner* article. Be it hagiography for the saints, or re-written history for the sinners, mankind thrives on lies.

A good memory is a blessing, but a perfect memory is a curse. I could not shake from my mind the fabricated history in the *Roadrunner* and how it had officially defined an odious new truth built on a foundation of lies. The consequences for me were more profound and far-reaching than one would guess. If humans are so eager to re-write history while the players are still alive, then how could any holy text be reliable if written years after the events?

This forced me into a study of my own religious beliefs, which continues to this day, perhaps exacerbating my temporal lobe symptoms where religiosity proliferates in tandem with aggressive outbursts tied to the amygdala. Nevertheless, I chose to apply the same rigor we use in scientific scholarship to the ancient holy manuscripts and lack thereof. Just as the research team of Gunnar and Freya Pixley taught me to read and study the references in scientific publications (since quoted passages are frequently twisted or totally erroneous), so I sought to uncover the references of scriptural "authorities." It's a journey I do not advise.

The "original Greek" and "original Hebrew," for me, once assured purity and truth. Look closer, however, and there are multiple Greek versions, multiple Hebrew versions, Latin corruption, copies of copies of copies, then the stamp of humanity on them all. Countless manuscript fragments of the same text, often different, numerous languages, all tongue-tied. My faith dwindled and dwindled until I felt quite the fool. This angered me even more, for had I not been thrust in this direction, I would still find comfort in my faith. Thus, I came to believe that the characters in this Pavilion story had, in effect, killed my child, then robbed me of my soul.

Thus, of my dual theories to explain my circumstance – family curse or neuronal circuitry – I favor the scientific answer, the brutal mechanistic explanation of electrical wiring. I am ready for you to cut the renegade neural pathways of my limbic system that have left me a pitiable lump of clay. I have confidence that these hijacked circuits are both valid and culpable, since we have agreement between traditional functional MRI and your experimental technology of reflectance diffuse optical tomography. We know the hypergraphia bordering on graphomania, neophobia, loss of humor, loss of music, and religiosity are wired from the temporal lobe and its hippocampus to several cortical areas as well as the amygdala. We now have <u>three</u> targets that can be addressed sequentially.

I am ready.

Editor's note: During this time when Chase Callaway was actively writing this petition, asking for surgical intervention, I (the editor) was working on Institutional Review Board Approval for a multi-step, psychosurgical approach to achieve some measure of relief for Dr. Callaway and those patients similarly afflicted with intractable rage. Shortly before IRB approval, Dr. Callaway handed me yet another document (with letters, e-mails, and validating tidbits) addressing his remarkably disappointing experience at Permian Medical Center, something merely alluded to in his earlier writings.

His experience there bore uncanny similarities to the bizarre events at the Far West Breast Pavilion (almost enough to make one buy into Dr. Callaway's theory of a family curse). His personal humiliation by the Permian administration after establishing yet another Center of Excellence stood in sharp contradistinction to what should have been. He had sacrificed every aspect of his personal life in order to succeed professionally, not with "just another breast center," but with the breast center.

Since the coveted prize for Permian recruitment had originally been Molly St. Martin, when that failed, Chase Callaway was seen, in part, as a liability, siphoning cases from the existing surgical staff (without concomitant growth in overall numbers that Molly would have provided). To appease the surgeons, Darby Raven, shortly before her death, had an idea that was adopted by administration – Chase Callaway would voluntarily ration his case load to one new cancer every week. With income then augmented through a medical director's fee, his take-home would still be well below what it had been at Far West. But money was not the concern. Instead, Chase's concern was whether or not he would be able to rise above paralyzing depression mixed in a stew of anger, in order become *The Rainmaker* once again.

Dr. Callaway gave this new document a title – *"No Mercy in a Kakistocracy."* The manuscript was 719 pages, and I was certain I could carve away most of the excess, maintaining the gist of the story for inclusion here. However, I was not able to summarize the remarkable events to fewer than 50 pages without losing significant impact. Therefore, I will find another home for this particular document. Suffice it to say that Chase Callaway, while working at the Far West Breast Pavilion had been powerfully motivated by redemption, but at Permian, it was a matter of personal survival. That he was able to accomplish what he did there, in spite of his emotional baggage, and in spite of administrative indifference that sometimes bordered on malice, gives testimony to a human spirit that refused to be crushed. His decision for self-exile as the last step of his metamorphosis was due largely to a series of events at Permian that, once again, called for his phrase: "malignant institutional narcissism."

Even though the original 5,450-page treatise forming the basis for this book was presented to me as justification for enrollment in the psychosurgical program, Chase Callaway continued to write with vigor while his case was under institutional review, wrapped in red tape.

35
THAUMATOLOGY

When I pause to remember my former self as Chase Callaway, I can recall each of his steps, but not the thousand tears that pooled in each footprint.

Occasionally, recall was vivid. An earlier version of Chase had once been called to the home of "second mother" Sukie Spurlock to confirm the diagnosis of advanced breast cancer, whereupon he had prescribed a drug for last ditch amelioration of the disease. That prior version of Chase did not expect to see Sukie again as her death was surely imminent, plus he could not take any more heartache. I suspect, too, that he did not want to face – for the umpteenth time – the powerlessness of prayer in reversing advanced cancer.

But after the death of Darby Raven, after shedding the Third Exoskeleton, I was summoned to the home of Sukie Spurlock during an October storm, a night when lightning burrowed through the sky and thunder answered. Sukie had called me with perfect calm in her voice, an angelic tone, in fact. So I went, planning to say my final good-bye.

When I entered the house, a blast of stifling air met me head-on. Even though the temperature outside was comfortable, Sukie had fueled her furnace to the maximum. In a replay of my prior visit, the same dark faces of elderly men and women from Sukie's church encircled her bed. Each nodded in respect as my eyes greeted them one by one.

Silver-haired Sukie was smiling, lying in bed with her back propped up by a pillow. She looked at me with eyes that had loved a son for over fifty years. She sat up, then asked her friends to move toward the doorway, twisting a bit to turn her back to the crowd. She invited me (without words) to look at the large breast she hoisted above the loose elastic neck of her nightgown. The room brightened and dimmed with each flash of lightning, and the foundation of her wood frame house creaked in response to each clap of thunder.

Did she pull out the wrong side? This was impossible. The breast was perfectly normal! I touched the smooth brown skin, running my hand over its flawless surface. The cauliflower bumps that were ready to break through the skin had disappeared. The breast was soft. The skin was soft. Goosebumps covered my body, even in that fiery furnace of a room.

"You sir," said one of the voices. "We've been praying that you be the one."

"Yes, sir," said another. "We said the same when you came before."

"Faith, so be it," said another. "Sukie has never been a clanging cymbal. She quietly lives the truth. She had faith in you and faith in the Lord."

The crowd, each with clasped hands, murmured, "Praise God."

As had been recently described in the medical literature, advanced tumors could sometimes shrink with tamoxifen, but I had never seen a Stage III breast cancer disappear completely with a daily tablet. Miracle? Of course not. It was a drug, a triphenylethylene derivative that blocked residual circulating estrogens from entering malignant cells, resulting in cellular apoptosis...

My thoughts seemed absolutely foolish in light of the miracle that had occurred in the mind of Sukie and the church members assembled at her house. Using only her eyes to communicate, her gaze was riveted toward me in a manner she might have used in gentle reprimand so many years ago. My translation of the message in those eyes? *Oh, Chase, you will never see the miracles of God unless you acknowledge them for what they are. Yes, the Lord worked through your mind and your hands, but it's a miracle all the same. Don't stand there and tell me all that fancy stuff about the science of it all.*

Nearly hypnotized by her wordless message, I flipped through Sukie's many sayings that she had planted in my brain during the years of my youth, a period when Chase was a different life form. While so much else had changed, her back-porch aphorisms were eternal verities of life, and I could rattle off 10 of them, at least, that had survived the shedding of my exoskeletons.

In hushed tones at first, then swelling as each member of the crowd found their notes, the choir of Sukie's companions joined in song as they moved back into the bedroom, the site of a miracle and the miracle's instigator.

"Amazing Grace! How sweet the sound
That saved a wretch like me!

Lyrics, oh lyrics, I thought, as I listened to the black notes of the pentatonic scale. *Don't you wonderful folks know the origin of those lyrics? The words were written by a slave trader after his ship loaded with your ancestors nearly sunk during a monster storm. Once saved, don't you know that the "newly devout" slave trader continued to profit from slavery for years? So much for the conversion experience. And the music? No one knows. Yet, the black notes, common to the 'Negro spiritual', might well have percolated up from the African belly of a slave ship, then swept into the duplicitous mind of the slave trader.*

Thunder cracked around Sukie's house once again, this time rattling the dishes stacked in the kitchen sink nearby.

I once was lost, but now am found
Was blind, but now I see..."

Yet... instantaneous conversion might not be the experience for all. Recalling the story now, after the passage of years, your lyricist of this great hymn evolved into a clergyman and, after <u>decades</u>, *finally, a fervent abolitionist. Indeed, it took nearly a lifetime to wash away the hypocrisy.*

'Twas Grace that taught my heart to fear,
And Grace my fears relieved.

Rolling thunder continued to provide the harmony. I truly hoped that God would pick that exact moment to lift me off the Earth and give me a spot in Heaven. For in that brief time, I believed it was a miracle, and that I had been cured of my torment as well. I knew the miracle would be everlasting for Sukie, but for me, it was a mirage.

The African American choir saw me as a miraculous healer, the answer to their prayers, an odd feeling for one so estranged from my Maker. Then I recalled the epaulets being ripped from my shoulders and my sword broken, disgraced beyond eternity by my very own alma mater. Man without a mater. Man without a miracle. Yet, in those sweet moments of choral background and jarring thunder, I believed.

> How precious did that Grace appear
> The hour I first believed..."

36
A GOD UNKNOWN

I have had two stereotactic ablative procedures at the time of this writing. They are remarkably easy. With today's technology, one never need open the skull. Once the target is identified, the gamma knife destroys the offending circuitry through focused radiation, i.e., radiosurgery. Dr. Divine pleaded my case before the Institutional Review Board, and I had to appear in person before the ethics committee, and, of course, I had to sign my life away. But the joke was on them. My life was already away.

Recently, before the Society for Neuroscience, the Dalai Lama said, "If it was possible to become free of negative emotions by a riskless implementation of an electrode, without impairing intelligence and the critical mind, I would be the first patient."

Maybe his words are yet another online fiction, but to the best of my ability, I have confirmed this quote as true. Still, false attribution via cyberspace seems to be the norm, with few bothering to check their sources. What a disturbing sequence of mass manipulation unfolds when excitatory words are falsely attributed to respected persons in an attempt to embellish, while maintaining a semblance of credibility. "Disturbing" not because of any direct harm, but for the realization of the uncontrollable instinct of man to manufacture myth.

The world has never been the same since the science of philology emerged during the Renaissance to reveal false attribution. Lorenzo

Valla proved that *The Donation of Constantine*, shifting power from the East back to Rome, was a forgery, given that it was written in debased Latin, impossible for the time of Constantine, yet common usage in the Middle Ages. Paying attention to language was the key. Erasmus took the same approach to the Vulgate version of the Bible where the translation was so misleading as to often be the exact opposite of what was intended in the original manuscripts.

Editor's note: Deleted here is an extensive list of historical documents proven as forgeries, along with a scholarly look at the original manuscripts of the Abrahamic religions and the fragility therein. Dr. Callaway makes the point that intellectual supporters of religious practices today claim that historicity is no longer important, but rather the communal memory is what serves modernity (he leaves no evidence as to whether or not he agrees with this statement – his point revolves around the unseen force that prompts mankind to alter historical accounts).

After seeing how easily (and successfully) a rewritten history of the Breast Pavilion had flourished at Far West in *real time* accounts (no need to wait for my death), it was an easy jump to believe that the human compulsion of false attribution had thoroughly polluted any revelation God may have offered this planet. What a different world we would have if we insisted that all works granted canonical status be autographed.

Returning from my digression, with all the resources available today, I have not been able to disprove the fact that the Dalai Lama actually spoke those words. However, we no longer need implantable electrodes as he suggested. The hijacked circuitry can be corrected by painless destruction of the offending nests of neurons through radiosurgery. My doctors wanted to test the areas to be destroyed with electrodes before the actual destruction took place, but I declined. The "hot spots" on my functional MRI were quite clear, and the three danger zones (on each side) could be attacked one by one.

Behavioral therapy, as simplistic as it might seem, ranging from the saliva of dogs to the saliva of rabid man, has proven itself in outcome studies, passing all rigors of scientific scrutiny. It is, of course, the non-surgical method of re-wiring bad circuitry. In contrast, cognitive therapy has had only modest success in the long term. Does it not make perfect sense to extend that behavioral area of psychoneurology into more radical and definitive treatments in the direction of proven benefit, rather than let our bookshelves swarm with the pestilence of cognitive self-help books? Of course, this was, and is, my rationale to justify aggressive, probing intervention.

First, I underwent bilateral cingulotomy where a small bunker in the subgenual cingulate region (Brodmann area 25) was bombarded. With only mild improvement, if any, I took the next step with an anterior capsulotomy that qualified me as the solo subject of an article in *Psychosurgery Today* entitled, "MRI-guided stereotactic capsulotomy for intractable anger management and obsessive-compulsive disorder refractory to cingulotomy."

My anger was lessened by several degrees with the second procedure, and I would have been willing to stop at that point, had it not been for the voices. Auditory hallucinations, they say. Yet, they are real to me, and I wonder each time if I've not discovered a supernatural circuit, a portal to the other world.

It was just one woman at first. She said, "Take my hand." The instant I heard it, I knew it was Darby Raven, or her spirit, or an angel of likeness. When I closed my eyes, I could almost see her pale hand reaching out to me. Other voices have joined her, always women – women I've failed. Women whose cancer I might have cured had my energies been used in creative research rather than fighting scoundrel physicians, powermongers, back-stabbers, hopeless bureaucracies, third-party criminals, and in the end, at Permian – profiteering administrators who can sniff out a bonus hidden in a pile human suffering.

I failed these women by letting myself get bogged down in the sewer. My dead patients speak to me in voices that sound like chimes, ringing out as: "It's okay. It's okay. It's okay."

More recently, the voices have added admonitions to their compassion: "Forge on" or "Don't give up now." Sometimes, they sing the mystifying phrase, "let go," which seems incongruous to "forge on." So, I've been torn as to whether or not I am experiencing a miracle or madness. On one hand, the voices represent the most wondrous music

I've ever heard, and I don't want them to stop. On the other hand, I know there are boils in my brain still, which are located bilaterally in the basolateral nucleus of the amygdala, part of the mesolimbic dopamine system that can be permanently altered by addictions, long after the addictive activity has ceased.

I live far away from Matherville now, though still in the high desert near the Mexican border. Having withdrawn from all possible triggers to my obsessive and cyclic rage, it's difficult to evaluate the true effectiveness of my treatments so far. Perhaps, I'm only improved through my withdrawal from the world. Still, if it weren't for my augmented auditory perception, providing a channel either to Heaven or to Lunacy, I'd be finished with the gamma knife.

My sole remaining family member, my mother Ramona, does not even know how to contact me. Usually, in my trips to Dr. Divine's Department of Psychosurgery in Matherville, I drop her a post card, telling her that things are better, perhaps. I suspect she feels *saudade*, an emotion described only in the Portuguese language, akin to nostalgia. While nostalgia is a happy-sad mix that longs for something or someone when there is no possibility of return, *saudade*, on the other hand, is more of a wistful longing for something that probably doesn't exist, maybe never existed, but ushers the bearer toward the past or the future in this dreamy state. Saudade is what Ramona likely feels with my disappearance. I can only imagine.

I have no television and no newspapers, for these instruments are but reservoirs of dangerous stimuli where I might see the good fortune of those who triumphed in my ruin, or *because* of my ruin. So, I stay at home – just me and my cat, Tickery, an orange tabby with orange eyes and a tail stumped from trauma before I knew her.

My single-story house is small, shingled, and old. However, I spend little time there. Mostly, I work outside in my research garden or in my experimental sea, or I'm working to improve my laboratory in the Airstream trailer that was left on the property by the previous owner. I'm connected to the world via the Internet through expensive technology purchased from an obscure company in Israel. (***Editor's note***: *the author was writing in the era prior to Internet access via smart phones. His use of Wi-Max was one of the technologies being tested and* *introduced, along with WiFi, for the upcoming wireless world.)* Without land lines for online access, and out of the range of cellular towers, I rely on a transmitter I've placed in Matherville to provide high speed access through a private network, allowing me to live in cyberspace. Though alone, I am cosmopolitan in the truest sense of the word.

Then, in the evenings, I retreat to the world of yesterday by reading hard copy books in a small round barn converted to a library that I call the Panopticon.

My garden is circular in shape, outlined by a six-foot stockade fence to keep out the predators and other hungry animals that are focused entirely on survival. The fence has four gates that I designed, placed such that if I could stand in the center of the circle, I would view sunrise and sunset on the winter solstice through two of these narrow gates, and sunrise-sunset of the summer solstice through the other two. However, I cannot stand in the center, as I've placed a decorative windmill there, made of white pine turned gray brown by the elements, rising some 20 feet to the sky, and housing an irrigation system that sprays rain onto the rich, imported soil below in a most natural fashion. The water pipes course like arteries through the interior of the windmill, long ago covered by climbing vines. Morning Glories thrive in hanging pots on the lower rails of the windmill.

Beyond the western limit of the stockade fence is a saltwater pond with a sandy bottom, my experimental sea, created by equipping an old swimming pool with an elaborate mechanism to maintain salinity. I grow a variety of sea life, ranging from bizarre seaweeds to rare crustaceans, and I ship these specimens to the Natural Products Repository, a function of the National Cancer Institute, adding to their supply of 50,000 samples where many believe the cancer cure will be found.

In several cauldrons, positioned along the outer rim of the stockade fence, I grow stews of bacterial organisms, under extreme conditions of heat and acidity. Glass tops allow the sun's rays to generate superheated states where only extremophiles can live and thrive – microbes with whom I identify – "bugs" that thrive only under the worst possible conditions. I retrieve my distant kin from the stew and transport their colonies to scientists around the world who identify the by-products of these bacteria as potential cancer-killing toxins. Indeed, most everything from my biologic cookery is shipped somewhere, to someone, where research is performed in some way.

I do not restrict my work to cancer. My garden includes a variety of herbs, ferns, legumes, and miscellaneous plants that harbor untold secrets. As the transcendentalists used to say, "A weed is but a plant for which we've not found its use." The sections radiate from the windmill in pie-shaped wedges, divided by dusty gravel paths that, viewed from above, would look like the spokes of a giant wheel.

I've devoted one piece of the pie, for instance, to growing those plants that harbor chemicals akin to the exciting new class of drugs in the benzamide family that boost memory in the hippocampus. While we now realize that new neurons can form in the hippocampus, they must be trained. These chemicals boost naturally occurring glutamate, the most prevalent neurotransmitter in the brain, but they seem to do more – they might increase brain-derived neurotrophic factor, which locks in memory, meaning that their effects may continue long after the drug has been discontinued. Evidence is building that this spurring action might not only help in Alzheimer's, but also other disorders as well, ranging from schizophrenia to drug addiction to insomnia, and on and on. So, I grow and I ship. I grow and I ship. And, like all great scientists of antiquity and fiction, I experiment on myself.

My shipments to researchers (who dole out grant monies) cover my ongoing expenses, as well as food for Tickery and me. Yet, the initial investment was hefty. Since a quarter-century of medical practice coupled with belief in a "purpose" had left me with an anemic bank account, it is worth noting the odd way in which I established this new life. For many years, my dead precursor, Chase Callaway, had been sending family friend Sukie Spurlock a monthly tithe. Throughout the centuries, humans have squared themselves with God through generous donation, be it to an edifice or to indulgences or to actually feed the poor. Likewise, I paid for a horrible sin of my youth through a regular tithe to Sukie in which I never failed a payment. When Sukie Spurlock died of a heart attack in her sleep two years after my last memorable contact with her (breast cancer free, apparently), she willed everything to me. In fact, she had never spent one penny of the money I had been sending her for decades.

In my Garden of Science, my heart continues to believe in a God, while my head engages in relentless battle. I have emerged as a Deist, of sorts. A *saudade* Deist.

The miracles and majesty of DNA are so expansive, so mystifying, that I have to respect its Creator so much more than a god who allows revelation through sloppy manuscripts.

God created our planet with the answers to our problems here in nature. We have not yet tapped even a fraction of one percent of the biological benefits in the world. Taxols that kill cancer cells came first from pine needles, so multiply that discovery by a million to understand the high-hanging fruit that's still out there.

The departure from the God of my youth was difficult, and that's why I introduced the word *saudade*. After years of believing in Calvinistic predestination and names being written before time in the Book of Life, I was forced to the conclusion that my name wasn't written therein. I can understand why selfish prayers aren't answered. Yet, when viewed objectively, I couldn't see that the world was altered one iota by my empty pleadings. If one can conveniently ignore the mutually exclusive concepts of predestination and free will, as many do with great comfort when paradox becomes orthodox, then I should have been able to choose. The only conclusion I could reach was that my name was not in the Book of Life, no matter how much I longed for it to be.

In my new policy of searching for origins and correct attribution, I sought to know the man Calvin and his writings. Here was someone who created the first totalitarian regime in European history (a theocracy) and was, in fact, best I can tell, a borderline madman. He endorsed murder without remorse, and according to the rules of his own game, might be roasting in Hell. Only Calvin knew the truth, only he could interpret the Bible, and if you disagreed even on a single verse, he banished you even if you were his closest friend. If you took it one step further, as did Michael Servetus with his book, *On the Errors of the Trinity*, then Calvin called for the death penalty. Yes, Calvin was kinder and gentler than the other executioners in that he recommended "humane" decapitation (without trial) for Servatus. Others, however, overruled Calvin and strapped the book to Servetus' leg and burned man and book together as one. Even then, it was considered a horrific act, and many saw the ogre that Calvin had become. Calvin went to his grave quite proud of the burning flesh of Servetus which, to him, had helped purify the world.

Intrigued by the burning, I procured a copy and read *On the Errors of the Trinity* by the once-scorched Servetus. I thought it insightful, discerning, and genius for its time. This led me toward further study of the Evangelical Rationalist movement that was a tiny group of intellectuals spawned by the Reformation. My studies then took me to the Radical Spiritualists who also took a scholarly approach to the original manuscripts and came up with the conclusion that all the trappings of modern religion were external, none of which had originally been God's plan. From there, it was a short jump to Deism. I realize, too, that from Deism, it's a short jump to nowhere.

"It's chemistry, brother, chemistry," says one Karamazov to another, as he explains his 19th century revelation that nerves in the brain have quivering tails, and it is this, the quivering of the tails, which make us who we are, not because of a soul. Yet, he says, he is quite sorry to have lost God in the process of discovery.

Was the book's author prescient? A few short years ago, the Nobel Prize in Medicine was awarded for the discovery of synaptic remodeling, in essence, the same quivering tails of neurons. The skilled novelist, however, must direct his characters to make convincing arguments that are opposed to the author's own beliefs. As for Dostoyevsky, his tombstone is inscribed with *John 12:24* – Verily, verily, I say unto you, except a corn of wheat fall into the ground and die, it abideth alone: but if it dies, it bringeth forth much fruit.

. . . .

So, what do I do in my little world besides tend the garden and snorkel in my saltwater pool to harvest marine biologics? I study. Incessantly. All day and into the night. I work to expand my hippocampus, and I satisfy its cravings by eating those plants that might grow new dendritic spines in new neurons, remodeling foods that might increase the known and unknown neurotransmitters, foods that might cement those relationships into productive memory. I continue this endeavor now while I wait to see if we are going to proceed with the third and final gamma knife intervention.

I am fully aware that knowledge does not lead to wisdom. The Buddhists have been trying to tell us this for centuries – that wisdom comes instead from the contemplation of suffering, and in turn, all suffering comes from excess passion – all part of "extinguishing the flame." In fact, it has been noted that true wisdom diminishes knowledge. Yet, as I reflect, it's not really wisdom that I seek. Rather, it's illumination.

I read and I read until the early morning hours. Illumination might be a weak surrogate for wisdom, but I pursue it all the same for I'm not so sure that wisdom isn't a false god. The walk from my house to the Panopticon is almost holy. There, my library lives and breathes. The library began with my grandfather's books – novels, medicine, and theology – now expanded to anything I can consume.

I exercise, too. My body first, but only enough to provoke mobilization of my stem cells that will, hopefully, assist in the remodeling of my brain. Then, my work-out moves to speed-reading exercises to boost my ravenous cravings. I try to put in four hours of reading a night, culminating in the partaking of soporific herbs in a potion that I've created to induce not only sleep, but also pleasant dreams.

Sleep disorders have always haunted me, beginning in my youth with simple insomnia. Later, I experienced such oddities as sleep paralysis and, rarely, sleepwalking. Recently, however, I have experienced something new and frightening – a rare sleep disorder, perhaps a side effect of my herbal concoction, which has prompted me to change the formula.

The affliction has an unimaginative, rambling name – REM Behavioral Disorder (RBD) – but the reality is quite colorful, albeit macabre. "Sleep fighting" is the lay term, with many variations. Distinct from sleepwalking, and different than night terrors, it begins with a vivid dream that features one of my countless enemies who has harmed me or ruined me, prompting me to yell, kick and slug, fists flying as fast as possible from dream to blurriness to wakefulness where I am actively slugging away as hard as I can while fully awake. If only it were that simple. Sometimes, I am screaming with full force long after waking up. Once I squeezed the enemy's arm with intent to break it off, but after moving to consciousness, I was drawing blood from my own arm with my uncut fingernails. Another time I awoke with sore knuckles and a hole in the drywall. Sometimes, in the dream phase, I grab and choke the enemy, hoping to kill, only to wake and find my hands around my throat squeezing the life out of myself.

Coupled with sleepwalking, anything is possible. Recently, I began chasing a nameless enemy with intent to kill, but he turned on me and attacked. The next thing I felt was an iron skillet slammed against my forehead. Waking instantly, I found myself out of bed, in the living room, where I apparently tripped, landing forehead first, scraped and bleeding. I was lucky to escape without a broken neck. For the past week, upon retiring to bed, I have looped a string from my wrist to a bedside lamp, hoping to force wakefulness prior to my next assault.

My grandfather's novels still have an impact on me. They provide another candela or two as to how things happened like they did. Stated alternatively, I want to know how the original Chase died. He talks to me from the grave sometimes, in the highlighted sections of the Bible of his youth, or in my grandfather's books where a younger Chase once turned down page corners to mark something of presumed significance.

Many pages have their corners bent, especially Dante's *Divine Comedy*. Is it any surprise that so many great epics come from great men in exile, dating at least as far back as John of Patmos? Revelations seem to emerge from such exile. Dante Allegro had been banished from his hometown Florence. Had he returned, he would have been burned to death. In his magnificent work, he saw practical information, not allegory. In my grandfather's simplicity, he thought Dante had truly visited Hell.

Nevertheless, it is worth several candles to me to read in Dante's *Inferno* that the worst sin imaginable – the sin of betrayal – deserves more punishment than murder, rape, or incest. Indeed, in Dante's creative spirit (and my grandfather's alleged personal encounter), Satan is munching on the bodies of Judas, Cassius, and Brutus. Why are Cassius and Brutus being consumed along with Judas? Dante believed that had Julius Caesar lived, the world as we know it would have been Heaven on Earth, or more practically speaking, Dante would have never ended up in exile. Such is the process of illumination, as Chase, too, was killed by the betrayal of a friend more than any single event.

I still contemplate the unjust suffering in Arthur Miller's *The Crucible*, his treatment of the Salem Witch trials with the intent to show that the same dynamics persevere today. Tituba, a voodoo priestess leads a group of young girls in harmless ritual that expands into the nightmare we all know. Indeed, if anyone was practicing the black arts, it was these very girls who end up as the accusers in one of humanity's most embarrassing chapters. In the most chilling scene of Miller's work, one of the girls is finally committed to telling the truth and stopping the madness, but when Mary Warren tries to muster the honor to testify in truth, her co-conspirators unite against her by mocking her words in a group chant that brings her back to their united front. Mary Warren caves and returns to the hysteria. In turn, this hysteria kills innocent, righteous believers. This scene is, of course, played out over and over in the business space, in medicine, in church, in families – wherever two or more are gathered, the group will define a demon.

In Chase's case, Dr. Molly St. Martin caved. For one brief moment, on the day she was whisked away to the Colony Club, she had the opportunity to stop the madness. Even later, a second chance to stop it all, upon realizing she had been misled. Instead, she joined the co-conspirators, those dabbling in the black arts, the accusers, the guilty. At first, she had said, "This is wrong, wrong, wrong, and I won't work at a place without ethical standards," but later, like Mary Warren after a short lucid interval, Molly began to chant along with the other hysterics. History will go on repeating itself, expressed in novels, because true accounts simply can't be true.

Also in my readings, I see mistakes that Chase made. In *Heart of Darkness*, Kurtz the ivory king, forgets that he is but one man in service to a large company. He takes possession of something that isn't really his, and this possessiveness, this passion, leads him to madness. "It's mine" is the greatest predictor of misery. No matter how much Chase believed the Pavilion was his, it was not. Intellectual property does not apply to huge visions that are realized. Such legal property exists only for small, contained ideas that can generate patents and profits. When a truly massive vision unfolds, all believe themselves the original seers.

In Golding's *Lord of the Flies*, it was not enough for Jack to win power, he has to kill Ralph. In a subtlety at the end that I'd missed in my high school required reading, it was not Ralph's fire built as a signal for help that saved them in the end. No, it was Jack's fire built to kill Ralph that saved the boys. Fire, the great cleanser throughout history, saved them.

Recently, as I was studying by candlelight, an odd thing occurred.

Fireflies are increasingly scarce in this part of the country, but somehow one managed to enter the Panopticon where it flitted about my bookshelves. Having a strong interest in bioluminescence and the substrates called luciferins that interact with luciferase enzymes, resulting in photons of visible light, I followed the little gal – a Phontinus texanus in the Lampyridae beetle family, I believe – until it came to rest on the spine of an unread book. It was the novel given to me many years ago by Ivy Pettibone as a gift for repairing the deformity of her fused fingers. In that moment, as I stared at the firefly shining her light near the title of the novel, *To A God Unknown* by Steinbeck, I felt once again that Chase and I were one and that Ivy's spirit was in the tiny firefly.

Martin Luther, the Monk of Wittenberg, had it easy – a lightning strike that nearly killed him led to his trust in God instantaneously. Oh, how I'd longed for lightning strikes for so many years. Yet, I wondered as I recalled the origins of Steinbeck's thin little book back at the insane asylum – could the tiny light from a tiny bug create its own tiny strike? When I pulled the book from the shelf, the luminous creature crawled onto my finger, then I carried her to the door of the Panopticon where I let her fly. Her light disappeared into a crescent moon.

I read the book in a single sitting. Steinbeck's protagonist in the novel, as it turned out, was incomprehensible to the reading public. His editor had advised him in so many words, "Either give this character a functional Messiah complex or make him a raving paranoid, one or the other, but don't leave him like this. No one will understand what you are talking about."

Steinbeck did not make the change. His editor was right. No one understood. While the reader of the novel is not privy to the etiology of the protagonist's "syndrome," in brief, Joseph is a man of immeasurable passion, and he is willing to self-sacrifice to the point of self-destruction to stay on his parched land. It's as simple as that. In today's parlance, this Joseph might appear as having some sort of "mental health problem," but rarely has powerful change come from those who enjoy perfect harmony in their lives. Although the book bombed seventy years ago with sales being less than a thousand copies, and though Steinbeck's own father was disgusted by the ending, it touched me deeply. I understood the protagonist in all his simple complexity.

It does not bother me that there is no cliché, no diagnosis, no motivation, to saddle onto the back of Steinbeck's Joseph Wayne. Yes, his wife broke her neck and died after a fall from the mossy rock, so perhaps in his misplaced desire for rain to save his land (referred to with the pronoun 'she'), Joseph takes the horrific step of bloodletting on himself, perhaps spawned by an accidental cut from a saddle buckle, symbolic no less, but horrific just the same by the time the exsanguinating act is complete.

As I have one-eighth of my blood originating from my Zionist great-grandmother, I am reminded now that one of the possible origins of the unpronounceable YWHW, the tetragrammaton denoting the God of Israel, is "He who causes rain to fall." Just as YWHW cannot be pronounced, so anyone who tries to target and fire a label onto Steinbeck's Joseph, or me, will find themselves unarmed.

When I entered Dr. Divine's office a few days after the writings above, I had to confess that the voices were with me still, often at night as I was falling asleep, often in the morning as I awoke, rarely during the day while I was working in the Garden of Science. The voices no longer frighten me. In fact, I welcome the melodious appellations as they call me. So, I was prepared to forget all about the third procedure. However, supervisory psychosurgeon, Dr. Divine, had a very fine and revealing test that lay ahead, as he questioned whether or not my improvement was due to self-exile rather than my two psychosurgery procedures. Of course, he had IRB approval to ultimately destroy three distinct regions of the brain on both sides (6 total loci). But for the third procedure, he had saved the best for last – the direct injection of stem cells in addition to the final ablation.

While wearing the helmet of Reflectance Diffuse Optical Tomography, a device complementing my functional MRIs, I sat complacently in a hard-backed chair while Dr. Divine instructed me (from behind a one-way mirror) to read the front-page news from the Matherville morning paper:

"**Far West Texas University Names Dr. Molly St. Martin to the Darby Raven Endowed Chair of Breast Imaging.**"

Editor's note: In the accompanying photo, Molly is wedged in between President Skip Didion and the dean, with Porter Piscotel squeezing his face into view at one side.

In fury, I ripped off the helmet, wrestling with the snake-like wires that connected me to the mother machine, then smashed the helmet to the ground. I jumped from my chair and began pounding my fists on the mirror, screaming, sweating, panting, until the glass broke, and my right hand turned into ground beef. Sedation came only after I was willing to sign the operative permit for surgical repair of my hand. Before sedation, I knew in my heart that I was capable of murder, and that the offending nuclei in my amygdala had to be destroyed.

While recovering from my hand surgery in the hospital, Dr. Divine visited my room and told me that in the seconds before I ripped off the helmet, the basolateral nuclei on both sides of my brain lit up in living color like he'd never seen before, and in the identical configuration as he had seen on functional MRI.

The primitive amygdala, its origins identifiable when we were still sea creatures, preceding humans by many millions of years, learned fear as the key to survival. Yet, it's the rapid appearance and growth of the basolateral nuclei that serve as chief executive for the limbic system, thus distinguishing man from salamander. Importantly, as ode to Steinbeck, there is no other animal on the planet so prone to self-sacrifice to the point of self-destruction.

Before I left the hospital, after the repair of my hand lacerations and pinning of two fractures, I signed my next operative permit: "Bilateral ablation of the basolateral nuclei of the amygdala with micro-craniotomy and injection of harvested and cultured stem cells."

Yesterday, I underwent my final ablation, though more complex than a simple gamma knife radiation bomb. Tiny burr holes were made in my skull, no bigger than a pencil lead, and a special healing elixir was injected painlessly via long needle into the symmetrical areas that had been obliterated on both sides of my brain by the gamma knife. Dr. Divine says the circuits leading out of the amygdala were the key spots, rather than the bulk of the amygdala itself. Nonetheless, his target was defined by the areas of illumination on both scanning techniques.

As before, the insult of the procedure itself is minor. I only had to stay overnight to observe for any seizure activity (none), and the only thing to look for now is a headache if the swelling becomes too great. I drove myself home where I can rest, at peace, albeit nervous about what the future might bring. So nervous that I am hesitant to return to Far West for further testing. Matherville, it seems, has an unlimited supply of stimuli eager to twist peace into rage.

How peculiar it is that, in my seclusion, the entire world is available to me through invisible radio waves. While some would call me a hermit, I would reply that, quite simply, I was born with skin too thin, and would remind them that Sir Isaac Newton, in his genius, was also extremely sensitive to criticism. In fact, he became so disturbed by his critics that he suffered a nervous breakdown in 1693 and did some of his best work with the world locked outside his door. His obsession with theology is well-known (writing much more on this topic than physics), but he was also an alchemist at heart. Yes, theology tends to be a great fortress for self-preservation, no doubt, but I am comforted by the fact that the greatest minds ever to walk this planet have struggled with the same questions, often with the same reactions to the Silence.

I sit here typing my thoughts (using my left hand and the right index finger) in my Airstream laboratory, but I cannot stop wondering how my new wiring will work. In my post-operative neurologic exam, Dr. Divine could detect nothing wrong. My EEG was unremarkable as well. Then, with mixed feelings, I've heard no harps or chimes from Heaven in the past 48 hours.

The only thing I've noticed so far is that the book I devoured immediately prior to my outburst and subsequent burr holes, *To A God Unknown*, seems unshakeable from my thoughts. I cannot get the final scene of bloodletting out of my head. I am compelled to read the book again, something I've never done unless years have elapsed between readings. Yet, time seems to be telescoping in and out. In a way, it seems like decades since I read the book, yet in another way, the words are rolling through my head right now. I'll delay no further. It's the time of night I should be reading in the Panopticon anyway.

With any motion of my hands, so brutalized over the years, and now the right hand surgically repaired and bandaged, I should experience excruciating pain. Yet, remarkably, I feel nothing in my useable fingers as they dance over the keys of my laptop, which I'll take with me now to write more in the Panopticon. I invite Tickery to join me, but she is curled into an orange ball, asleep atop a shipping crate recently arrived, a box reinforced with wooden slats that houses the next phase of my research.

37
PANOPTICON TO GENIZAH

Ensconced in my chair at the center of the Panopticon, I record my thoughts. The side table supports the book I'll re-read tonight. Next to the book is a brass candlestick that provides the romantic experience (classical sense) of watching words flicker by the light. The table is also home to a weighty compass, which I will explain in a moment. My computer is wobbling in my lap as I hunt and peck. So many spelling errors, almost unreadable. Still, it works in lieu of my transcription method of choice – longhand. The prognosis for my right hand's utility, after years of crippling abuse, remains poor.

Let me share with you about the Panopticon.

French philosopher Michel Foucalt, author of *Madness and Civilization: A History of Insanity in the Age of Reason*, made quite a splash not too long ago by demonizing Jeremy Bentham's Panopticon as designed 150 years earlier. Nevertheless, I found Panopticon to be the perfect name for my library. Bentham was an English philosopher who designed a circular prison where the guards could see all the prisoners, but the prisoners couldn't see the guards. Foucalt used this uncomplicated design as a metaphor for unwanted institutional spying in our lives. "Visibility is a trap," he said, and he criticized the "invisible omniscience" of Bentham's Panopticon.

Jeremy Bentham would have been disgusted, I'm sure, at this attack on his highly practical blueprints of 1791. Still, the legitimate and thoughtful concept of the Panopticon became tarnished. Perhaps, I'm on Bentham's side since I once encountered him face-to-missing-face. Yes, at the time of this writing, Mr. Bentham's mummified body sits regally dressed in a glass case at University College London. (The exact whereabouts of his head remain highly speculative, presumably a student prank from long ago. A prosthetic head sits in its place, a miserable attempt at dignity.)

I had seen the blueprints for the Panopticon at the time I saw Bentham's headless mummy while in London nurturing a scientific collaboration, so it was quite natural for me to convert my round storage shed into my library of similar design. My books were stacked to a height of eight feet around the interior wall, and then I added bookshelves at right angles to the wall facing the hub where I keep my reading chair and candle. The footprint is much like the spokes of the wheel in my garden. A step ladder of no distinguishing quality, other than it is wooden and quite old, allows me to reach the top shelves. From the original diameter of thirty feet, the spokes converge at the inner circle, leaving me with a central reading space of fourteen feet diameter.

The books are catalogued directionally by my compass which waits patiently beside me, pointing to magnetic north. If my log says a certain book is WNW292°—S4P, then it is located West North West at 292 degrees, shelf number 4, peripheral wall. The subtle shifts in the magnetic pole are not enough to affect my navigating these tens of thousands of volumes (and I hardly ever worry about the bizarre flip-flop of the magnetic pole from north to south that takes place every two hundred thousand years, give or take).

Above the eight feet of books, the barn remains mostly as I found it, with rafters and beams and tools and things that contribute nothing to my purposes. With a new roof and air-conditioning fueled by my generator, the barn is a refuge from my refuge, so to speak.

Here I sit, in the middle of the Panopticon, viewing my prisoners while they are unable to see me. Petrarch anthropomorphized books in an ode that turned his volumes into companions. And why not? The eternal verities were established long ago in the classics, and as such, one can still hear the whispers of flesh and blood. Yet, I have abused my friends, these tomes, sucking their blood into mine and forbidding their escape from the Panopticon.

Something's wrong. Thoughts are flashing like shooting stars through my head. Today is April 4. I recall a childhood epiphany on April 4. Not truly an epiphany, for there was no enlightenment that day when I felt an overwhelming euphoria. It was more like a herald – something of immense importance would happen in the future on April 4. Herald then, aura now.

My face burns. Not my entire face, just the crescent around my right eye. It feels as though the hot wax of my candle is scalding my skin. Flashes of light, more shooting stars, comets, asteroids. Headache. Spinning. Penumbra, that's what it is – the ischemic zone around the loci of my destroyed brain, this rim of jelly, is fighting back to life, tails of neurons quivering to survive.

When I shut my eyes, I see a page of printed words. No, not one page. I'm looking at pages flipping through my mind's eye, while I hear the sound of a thousand pigeons flapping their wings as they take flight. Although the print is small and fleeting, somehow, I know what is on every page. I'm reading the book backwards, watching the page numbers in the corner go from 186 to 112 to 84 to 29 to the Introduction.

I open my eyes for relief, and the flipping pages disappear. I look at the book, *To A God Unknown,* on the table beside me. This is the book that just now appeared to me in a matter of seconds, backwards, in my mind. The candle is fresh, still eight inches tall and newly lit. The light flickers. Perhaps, the bizarre page-flipping was a short dream.

But as I stare into the hollow part of the fire surrounding the wick, the empty space trimmed in blue, I see printed pages flipping within the flame even though my eyes are open. Again, the pigeons sound their flight. Oddly, I know this second book, too. I'm watching the pages of Sartre's *Nausea,* flip backwards so that Antoine Roquentin's realization that there is no purpose to life reverses itself away from the miasma of self-analysis. Then, the pages of Nietzsche reverse from his madness to self-analysis to curiosity. It occurs to me now, it's not merely the pages I'm seeing in reverse order, *I am seeing books I have read, in the order they were read – backwards.* I finished Sartre just prior to Steinbeck, and it was Nietzsche before Sartre.

Then Tolstoy invades with the *Death of Ivan Ilych*, and since the actual story begins at the end, I see the end at the beginning. After tribulations rivaling Job, Ivan screams in anger before he sees a light.

I believe my eyes are still open, staring into the flame.

Samuel Coleridge Taylor follows with the "Rhyme of the Ancient Mariner," his compensatory poem as he tried to re-establish his respectability after heroin addiction. The words seem to talk aloud as they flash before my mind, "About, about in reel and rout, the death fires danced at night. The water like a witches oil burnt green and blue and white."

Then, the passage in *Winesburg, Ohio*, where I realized how much I grieved the emotional schism between me and Matherville: "One shudders at the thought of the meaninglessness of life while at the same instant, and if the people of the town are his people, one loves life so intensely that tears come to the eyes."

Ever so quickly, from *The Future of An Illusion*, Freud's words emerge on the primordial instincts of incest, homicide, and cannibalism, and how only the first two prevail in society today. Clearly, he must have been considering cannibalism only in its literal sense.

Michael Faraday's "Chemical History of a Candle" took its turn, confirming that the writings are appearing before me in an exact reverse order. I recall now that Faraday was a member of a now-extinct Christian sect, yet he maintained his faith, unwavering to the end, with no conflict whatsoever when placed in apposition to his brilliant scientific endeavors.

Then, my readings on mental illness, dating back to the original shock therapy in 1934 when Zoltan of Hungary, in a catatonic stupor for four years was startled back to normalcy after a series of treatments by his neuropsychiatrist who injected an extract of camphor into Zoltan's buttocks to induce seizures. The re-wiring of brain electricity was random and chaotic, yet it worked, ushering in a new world. Indeed, Zoltan could be considered my forefather.

The crescent burning around my right eye is worsening, headache throbbing, I cannot look at the flame any longer. I shut my eyes. The pages are flying now. The pigeons are still frantic to fly higher. My legs grow numb and wooden, and my arms grow weak...I can barely hold my hands to the computer. I feel as though paralysis has begun with my toes and will soon ascend and consume me.

Three days pass, it seems, and I open my eyes. During those three days, I've traveled through every page I have ever read. At least, it seemed that long. I am stunned to see that the candle at my side is burning still, a stoic inch left in its column.

My crescent no longer burns, my head no longer hurts, the paralysis is gone, and I cannot begin to relate the avalanche of words that befell me during what now appears to have been an hour or two of bizarre sleep. I am trying to collect my thoughts. I am convinced that my brain has serially projected snapshots of thousands upon thousands of pages, and their afterimages are still present, though starting to fade.

I saw pages dating back to childhood, including the classic illustrations in *The Water-Babies*. I recall an error in the drawing of a microscope in my *Great Men of Medicine*. I saw histology and pathology photographs from every text I've ever read. I even saw equations from undergraduate biochemistry. Passages, too, from the Bible to the Bhagavad-Gita to the writings of Confucius (more false attribution) to Greek tragedies to classic novels, modern novels. The experience was orgiastic – no – regurgitative.

"I am the warden of this prison," I say aloud to my books. "You are my prisoners." Yet, they, all of them, hold me in their center and mock. I hear their voices as they speak to me in the fading images of my dream, in a way where I cannot tell whether the language is visible or audible:

From Ellison's *Invisible Man*, I see or hear, "And now I realized I couldn't return to Mary's or to any part of my old life. I could only approach it from the outside...I would take up residence underground. The end was in the beginning." Had I not hurriedly typed these words, they would have already faded.

Thousands of words echo now, and I hasten to write them down as they grow softer and disappear.

From Hawthorne's *Scarlet Letter*, I see and hear, "She shuddered to believe that it gave her sympathetic knowledge of the hidden sin in other's hearts." I knew this feeling – that my trip into the locked seclusion room at Riverdell allowed me special insight, a perspective I wish I'd never had. My letter "A," too, was something I never wished to wear, but for a healthy while, I'd turned it into an Asset. As Hawthorne put it for Hester: "...so much power to do, and power to sympathize – that many refused to interpret the scarlet A by its original signification. They said it meant Able..."

Recalling the waning voice of Sinclair Lewis in *Arrowsmith*, I hear the excuses that Martin makes as a doctor who gradually withdraws into a selfish hermitage, devoid of all feeling, having allowed his marriage to evaporate. When he is reduced to nothing more than a research insect, he says, "This new quinine stuff may prove pretty good. We'll plug along on it for two or three years, and maybe we'll get something permanent – and probably we'll fail!"

As I witness and grope to remember the pages of *Paradise Lost*, I recall why I had chosen once to read it (as well as *Paradise Regained* and *Samson Agonistes)*. Mary Shelley drew so heavily from *Paradise Lost* that she scripted her Creature to study the book, whereupon the monster (a budding intellectual) draws his own parallels to Milton's work. Now, I can barely make out Dr. Frankenstein's last words in tired neon on its last flicker: "Seek happiness and tranquility and avoid ambition, even if be only the apparently innocent one of distinguishing yourself in science and discoveries." Finally, the monster's last words: "Soon these burning miseries will be extinct. I shall ascend my funeral pile triumphantly, and exult in the agony of the torturing flames. The light of that conflagration will fade away; my ashes will be swept into the sea by the winds. My spirit will sleep in peace; or if it thinks, it will not surely think thus. Farewell."

A new order to the universe sweeps through my brain uninvited. I consider the horrid past that brought me to this moment, but I see that if I'd been in the shoes of my colleagues, I might have thought the same about Chase Callaway. Piscotel, Dinwiddie, Molly, the dean, Skip Didion, Layton Prudhomme, The Forty...and who would have believed the experience of starting over at Permian Medical Center would only drive me lower and lower? As those lives were scripted, so was mine, and I had failed to rise above their authorship. A remarkable peace has settled over me, anger is gone.

The sound and vision of my hallucinatory excursion is slipping to a memory of a memory, but I type fading words from *Cuckoo's Nest* that I read as a neophyte orderly at Building 19, long before Hollywood tinkered with the story. I can hear the silent Chief say, as he was killing the body thought to be a mock-up of McMurphy, "The big, hard body had a tough grip on life. It fought a long time against having it taken away, flailing and thrashing around so much I finally had to lie full length on top of it and scissor the kicking legs with mine while I mashed the pillow into the face."

I had once thought long and hard about the malignant narcissist, be it man or woman or institution, who suffers not. Unable to self-reflect, the narcissist breathes fresh air and thrives peacefully during its march of destruction. Yet, I hear the words now by R. L. Stephenson, stating that Jekyll realized the horror of Hyde was "knit to him closer than a wife," and something has struck me deep. The awfulness of how Chase – no I – had treated Livvy came flooding back to haunt me. I had betrayed her in a way that, many times over, supersedes anything Molly St. Martin might have inflicted upon me. True, too, for the neglect of my own mother, my cold shoulder to my father, and my distancing from my terminal sister. Somehow, I had been blind to these simple facts. I, too, was a practitioner of a more subtle form of malignant narcissism.

I look at the candle beside me. It has burned down to the final half-inch, and the wax is overflowing onto the table. Moments ago, in my mind, I held hundreds of quotes from books I read backwards during my dream. I intended to record them all before they left me. Now the quotes are few.

I do still recall, however, Dr. Johann Georg Faust, not from Goethe's version, or the Marlowe treatment, or any of the other sources, but as a collective memory of having read, from many sources, about the *actual historical figure*, a contemporary (and apparent foil) of Martin Luther. Dr. Faust, the alchemist, the scholar, the necromancer, spoke to me, "My desire to encompass all knowledge left me so despondent, I had no other alternative to consume all known knowledge but to sign my pact in blood. Knowledge, indeed, is the path only to unhappiness."

I stop my typing now. I'll explain when (and if) I return.

Listening to Faust whisper in my ear prompted me, moments ago, to search for Goethe's version. Barely able to rise from my comfortable chair at first, I steadied my better hand on the side table, then made my way to the catalogue I keep nearby. This record told me that the book was located at SSE157.5°— S4SL (S4 indicating the fourth shelf from the bottom, with SL being "spoke" wall (S), left side (L) when facing the spoke from the hub. After locating Goethe and thumbing through its pages for several minutes, my eyes fell upon these closing words, "It's a mystery, we can never understand life; ...all we can say is that the eternal feminine raises us to Heaven."

I waited to hear words spoken from my female chorus Above.

Nothing. The angelic hallucinations are gone.

I am in my chair again, exhausted. I hear no more words. I recall no details. I do remember how the books flashed through my memory for three days, it seemed. Yet, I can tell now it was nothing more than a dream. A vigorous dream, for sure, launched by my earlier ablative psychosurgery. Now, I'm failing to remember any words from any page.

I look to the book still resting on my side table, *To A God Unknown*. Oh my, I have forgotten it, too. I don't recall the plot, much less the pages and their words. I shall take it with me tonight, back to the house, and try to read it again.

My unraveling is clear in its message. For years I have taken an omnivorous approach to reading, escalating to mania in recent times. But I have twisted and warped science and theology as represented by the characters in novels, sucking them all into my own private world.

When I learned that our old friend – alchemy – had returned to become a real science, achieved through extraordinary pressures and heat (for example, creating carbonia – the hardest amorphous material known – out of simple carbon dioxide), in my mind, it only impacted one person on the planet – me – as an extremophile, a survivor of pressure and heat in a radically different form. When I read of the ancient origins of the free will vs. preordained argument, preceding even the Sadducee-Essene extremes and the impossible compromise by the Pharisees who tried to believe both mutually exclusive positions, I saw only my personal, fruitless struggle. When I studied the many novelists who expectorated their best words through the tightened lips of exile, I considered only how their lessons applied to me.

In short, I became the ultimate monster, that is, a human being who so completely distorts the universe into singularity that all happenings are compressed into one infinitesimally tiny life.

Pride is the sneakiest sin of all – not dime-store self-esteem or even a job well done – no, dangerous pride, sinful pride, is the foundation of all evil in that it whispers in your ear: "You are the most important person in all of creation."

The Panopticon becomes darker now, the only light being the eerie glow from the screen of my laptop. The candle has burned out. I recall Faraday's classic treatise on the global scientific principles that are revealed by the burning of a candle. I recall the abundant metaphors of light in all religions and, especially, the extinguished candle. I recall Moliere's care to keep the acts of his plays "one candle long" so they can be replaced and lit before the next act. It is such recall of minutiae that must cease.

I will padlock the Panopticon. I will leave tonight, with one book in my hand, and I'll not revisit for a long while, if ever. It is forbidden for Hebrews who follow orthodoxy to throw away writings containing the name of God, so the tradition evolved to create book cemeteries for proper burial, and it is in these genizahs where such documents are stored until interment. This I know with one-eighth of the DNA in my hereditary heart. I close my eyes, and I hear the click of the lock that will entomb my library.

38
TICKERY

Last night, I wondered if I had felt the hand of God. Today, I learned of an alternative explanation. After driving to the nearest public telephone at a market near the Mexican border, needing to hear a voice more solid than e-mail, I telephoned my interventional psychosurgeon.

"No, Chase, it doesn't sound terribly unusual. It sounds like a classic case of hypnagogic or hypnopompic hallucinations, in association with sleep paralysis. Hypnopompics occur when waking up, while hypnagogic hallucinations occur while drifting off to asleep. These are frighteningly real dreams that are associated with a very deep sleep pattern."

"But it was so real. And so crazy. I saw every single page of everything I'd ever read in my life, all in the matter of a few hours."

"Studies indicate that what you experienced likely occurred in a matter of seconds, not hours. The rest of the time you were in a deep, dreamless sleep. And yes, these unique dreams are so incredibly real that it's what we think is happening when people describe alien abductions, and it might account for the visionary experiences described by prophets in all the religions. Very real indeed, at least to the person having them."

"Another thing, Ray, when I tried to download some music this morning, I heard it as a screeching sound, as if a thousand discordant notes were playing at once. I don't mind telling you, it was a bit frightening. So, I pulled out one of my old albums, the one that the New

Bloods did years ago. I thought something familiar might help. It was awful. Can't describe it really. A cacophony, to say the least. Couldn't turn the music off quick enough."

A brief silence followed.

"I can't be certain, Chase. However, one of the areas that lit up on both your MRI and the optical tomography was very close to the region we believe is responsible for music processing. I thought this spot might be causing your auditory hallucinations. It's very rare, as I've told you before, for hallucinations to occur in a female voice, or in your case, multiple voices. It's even more rare for hallucinations to encourage the affected person. Most voices mock the victim at a minimum, and more likely, direct the victim to self-harm. Perhaps – and I'm only thinking out loud here – perhaps, in the process of ridding you of the auditory hallucinations, we've caused some collateral damage to the centers for music. We know that male and female voices are processed in different parts of the brain, and the female voice is closer to the music zones. Other than that, Chase, I really don't know."

So that's how it ended. I'm back at home now, waiting to see what happens next. Whether my revelation of last night was a religious experience or a hypnopompic hallucination, I suppose I'll never know. Yet, a calm prevails. Perhaps it's only the equanimity that accompanies the monastic life, but I seem to have lost my angels and their music for good.

. . . .

Two weeks have passed, and I am increasingly convinced that my peace is permanent. The emotion I am most pleased to have exorcised is schadenfreude, for which there is no comparable word in English. Of all the horrible beasts and barnacles that latched themselves onto my essence at Far West and later Permian, this one was the worst addition.

Too, through the bizarre phenomenon of holding enemies close, as mentioned earlier, I have collected old newspaper clippings of the psychic marauders I've encountered, both old and new. I have also saved notices of the awards and honors that were bestowed on my former tormentors. I don't know why I've done this, other than a postmodern

Freudian theory that this ritual represents a mutated form of cannibalism.

I realize now that these tormentors are all "former," not in the chronologic sense, but in the sense that they torment me no longer. So, I retrieve my stash of flesh-eating memorabilia, and I throw all of these things into the incinerator that, in turn, provides some of the heat I need to grow my extremophiles in the cauldrons placed around my Garden of Science.

I no longer dwell on the great philosophers, for none could escape themselves, all being prisoners to their unique experience. None found joy, and most found quite the opposite. I certainly do not wallow in the bleak pessimism of the brilliant Schopenhauer; however, I must admit a derivative here as the springboard to my new endeavor. Schopenhauer believed that music circumvents the intellect, offering itself to us as a universal language.

But music has been erased now, so I recall the attempt in 1887 by a Polish ophthalmologist to introduce a new, constructed language – Esperanto – as the universal second language. Indeed, hundreds of thousands learned the language, and some still speak it today. However, something far more pragmatic has entered the world and will, indeed, establish a new melody for the macrocosm, not through a formal construct, but through software. We are in the pilot stages of instantaneous translation and communication among all the peoples of the world.

I have always loved languages, but ever since my last procedure and the experience in the Panopticon, I find myself not only studying current and ancient languages, but also creating new words. It started with neologisms for new emotions, trying to fish from the stream of consciousness. Much like the polytheists who created gods through the simple creation of a name, I perhaps created a new emotion with the first word in my neo-dictionary – "somasavage."

Unlike Huxley's artificial peace derived through the ingestion of "soma," my emotion – the best way to describe how I feel now – is the dark half of "soma," more like the *Brave New World's* Savage who finally retreats in gloom to attend his garden. It also carries with it a robotic connotation, such that abiding sadness is held in check, perhaps at the preconscious level, forever ready to spring and destroy, but of no major concern at the level of consciousness.

In spite of – or because of – "somasavage," I find myself particularly adept, supernaturally so, at re-learning the languages I studied in years past, as well as learning new languages. For some reason, too, I find agility in the language of science, and I am pleased that I can now recall dates, authors, and references of publications in seven languages with a wealth of discovery remaining throughout the rest of the world. My memory, freed of all the trappings, seems to be razor sharp now.

Editor's note: Chase continues this document by writing in nearly illegible longhand (presumably his left hand), using a pencil on tablet paper. Later, the narrative is maintained by tape recordings that Dr. Callaway made using a primitive analog device.

Three months have passed since my last procedure, and I continue a Franciscan existence of sorts, though my nurturing goes well beyond the animals and insects, even to plants. When I cut the withered limb of a failing nettle, I feel the sting in my own limb, in disbelief that these same hands once severed dead limbs from humans with impunity; and, as a pathology fellow, even toyed with fragmented limbs of aborted fetuses while I studied and described the anatomy with total aplomb, dictating "products of conception" into a microphone. Yet today, if so much as a fungus dies, I sense a loss.

All creatures are miracles, including the ones I used to abhor. The spider in the corner of my kitchen spins a creative web of such beauty, I cannot tamper with it. The scorpions that live beneath the woodpile near my saltwater pond are, like everyone else, just trying to get along. The wasps that built a nest outside my front door are simply carrying out their genetic commands. We respect each other, and we leave each other alone. A praying mantis lives in the hedge outside my bedroom window, and it crawls up the glass to greet me every morning. I have made friends with a wide variety of creatures since my arrival here.

But by far, the animal that entered my heart completely, reminding me of a vestigial humanity, was the orange tabby I mentioned earlier, the cat I call Tickery.

Like the greatest of pets, she simply showed up one day, hungry, emaciated, and so covered in ticks that she appeared to have some sort of pox. Realizing the stereotypical pathos of a hermit and his cat, I plead a different case, and I argue a new emotion that I call "misure," which I define as a type of joy found in the brotherhood or sisterhood of sadness.

That first day with my new orange cat, not wanting to destroy the miracle of even a single tick, I pulled each and every insect from Tickery, and placed them in a new home. Just as we have aquariums for fish and aviaries for birds, the official home for ticks, in the world of entomology, is called a tickery.

I keep the ticks and their progeny alive through a technique I learned online from those who make the study of ticks their life's work. One modification, though – I draw my own blood from a juicy vein, just 10ccs a week. I make a blood sausage by wrapping the congealing blood in a cellulose membrane. Then, the little bugs jump on board and lunch away. It's a marvel to watch. My supply of ticks has been quite the bounty.

Tickery the Cat and I have become the closest of friends, and she is my constant shadow. We can stare into each other's eyes, and she knows what I am thinking, and I her.

While Tickery has me to thank for saving her from malnutrition, she did the same for me. In my abrupt retreat from a world of pain, I had shrunk my diet to include only those things that do not prompt or require death – milk and honey, primarily. My skin sprouted rashes, I lost weight, and my vision was starting to blur.

But after Tickery arrived and we started eating at the table together, one day, she placed a freshly dead mouse on my plate, along with one on hers. I realized then that the laws of nature were cruel and unyielding, and that Deism never cloaked itself as a way to escape the fear of death. Indeed, with my mouse meal (I took only one bite), I deeply understood how life feasts on death. In our shared communion that day, a bond was formed, and I believe Trickery trusted me as her own blood thereafter.

Since that time, Tickery and I have shared from a mountain of canned tuna and other foods that are delivered to my door once a month, balanced in nutrition, often demanding death at the origins, sadly, be it plant or animal.

Tickery sits in a chair beside me as I work on my computer, but she rarely chooses my lap. Feral in part, understanding there are no homes near me from where she might have strayed, she lives with me, likely, because of my original saving grace from her tick-infested days. She never brushes against me to prompt a good, solid petting, but at the same time, she is never more than a few paces away. She runs to me like a dog when called, but stops short of my reach, then sits and strokes herself with her tongue, pretending I don't exist. Most impressively, Tickery believes she is the lady of our manor, and she is willing to hiss down any predator that approaches the property, be it coyote or rattlesnake.

When I work in my garden, which consumes much of the daylight hours, Tickery climbs the center windmill and watches me from her perch. The windmill is decorative, and I recently removed the spinning blades at the top as they interfered with the water geyser that shot out for irrigation. As such, the windmill is more of a derrick now. Tickery's perch is at the highest point, where she can rotate positions to keep an eye on me.

I do my best to recreate nature in my garden. Nature does not irrigate its plants with sideways rain, or with an oscillating beat of unnatural streams of water. Nature allows rain from above. So, in the center of my derrick is a pipe, fed by my groundwater well, which is fed by my generator, which is fed by hydrocarbons. This pipe emerges at the top through a sprinkler head that separates the water into millions of raindrops that fall back to earth in a circle, every morning at dawn. Tickery knows better than to make the climb before sunrise lest she get a shocking bath.

My latest endeavor is setting up a histology lab in the Airstream, so that I can make my own microscope slides using special stains as I see fit. Scientists never bothered to finish the work that needs to be done in cancer research using the ordinary microscope before they abandoned all things "old-fashioned" and embraced the grant-succulent world of molecular biology. If a researcher today were to apply for a grant using only the old-fashioned microscope, he or she would be laughed all the way back to the 1950s. Yet, we never answered the most basic of questions when it comes to cancer. That's why so many left the microscope to look elsewhere, analogous to interplanetary travel.

But I remain interested in lost continents of antiquity and in finishing the work that was never done. For instance, one of the most famous breast cancer surgeons and researchers of all time wrote about curious cells in our bodies called "mast cells," and how they impact cancer, but his writings on this topic never continued beyond 1960. He made his fame later by generating an entirely new theory concerning the biology of breast cancer that allowed the introduction of lumpectomies and, at the same time, a reduction in the extent of lymph node surgery. He won every major award that medicine has to offer, with the exception of the Nobel Prize. Yet, no one followed up on the mast cells and their role in precancer becoming cancer.

I say "no one," cognizant of the fact that we have no idea who was doing what in the pre-Internet era when scientists were largely isolated by both geography and language (and sometimes, by their own choosing).

But there's a second reason I decided to pursue mast cells. A classmate in medical school named Will Glendenning had an oddball father with a basement laboratory designed solely for unraveling the mysteries of the mast cell. Will's father, a local GP in Lost Mine, Texas, devoted his life to the cause, though an early death stopped it all. Having visited that makeshift lab many years ago, it occurred to me that, perhaps, this dropped ball should be rescued and pursued. In fact, the memory of that basement laboratory is what gave me the idea to convert the Airstream trailer to a laboratory these oh so many years later.

My microscope is poised and ready, the tissue lab is nearly assembled, and when I return from Matherville, I will unpack the crate that Tickery, often perched atop, has adopted as hers. This shipping crate houses the microtome device with its sharp blade used to make paper-thin slices through paraffin-embedded tissue to be stained and mounted on microscope slides.

My surreptitious trip to Matherville this Friday, hopefully my last, is to have the most recent bandage, a cast this time, removed from my right hand. A few weeks ago, I underwent yet another hand surgery in an effort to restore function to this weary appendage. Introduced to this hand surgeon earlier, when I broke the glass of the one-way mirror, I asked him this time to limber up the digits of my claw.

With Tickery nervously watching every move, I tried to unpack the microtome, but I must wait until the cast is off, when my right hand can help.

Death's kind door is nigh ajar
Tongues of fire lick from afar
The curse hath slumbered since heels did hang
The dog awaketh to feel the pain.

And the other one, from many years ago...

Hickory Tickery start the clock
Boughs will break; locusts flock
Bullets melt in the name of gunnery
Horror smokes after sex in the nunnery.

—Viola's maledictions, Building 19, Matherville State Mental Hospital (1974)

It was a new dawn today – Sunday – but the world is now forever gray. I awoke to a clear morning at daybreak, but in a rare event for this high desert, a flash fog enveloped my territory in its cloud. What follows, I suspect, will be my last entry.

After the morning irrigation, Tickery climbed the windmill while I weeded the herb section of the garden. The surgery on my right hand has offered minimal improvement at this point, thus the last-ditch prescription – "more physical therapy." Still, as the strange fog settled upon us, in a moment of tranquility, with no wind, no sun, no dust –

only gray – I felt such a peace in my steady state of "somasavage" that I gave thanks to a God I no longer know.

Consider that I had, years ago, given up on prayers of miraculous intervention after countless failings and outcomes opposite to what seemed good and right. Too, I had given up on prayers of humble supplication for the same reason, even though expectations had been lowered. Yet, what harm could come from thanksgiving, especially to the god of the philosophers who, by definition, gives mankind the cold shoulder?

I turned Heavenward to give thanks for life, my own and others, for my gardens, both land and sea, and for my peace of mind now possible after the amygdalectomy. Specifically, I gave thanks for the companionship of Tickery. From my vantage, I could see her legs dangling at the edge of the derrick platform, her stumpy tail swatting the air, and I considered how, even if she fell from twenty feet, a cat will likely be unharmed. The fog was now so dense that Tickery was only faintly visible in the haze, and the sky above her was gone.

Not two minutes later, I heard the most ghoulish wailing and screaming and squealing I've ever heard in my life. When I looked up, Tickery was disappearing into the fog, clutched by the talons of an enormous hawk. Or, perhaps, an eagle.

A blotch of orange was soon gone, but the squealing continued for several minutes, growing fainter and fainter and fainter, muffled by the dense cloud. I died a new death with each scream. Long after it should have stopped, I could still hear Tickery begging for my help. I could do nothing. Still, I jumped in my truck and drove country roads through the fog, listening, looking, but there was nothing. The echo of Tickery's distress was playing in my head alright, but I heard no new hints of torture. Tickery was gone.

Within twenty minutes, the fog disappeared, and the sky was clear. It was as though a monstrous gray whale had descended from the sky to open its mouth for the passive capture of plankton and had incidentally swallowed Tickery, along with the last remnants of my soul.

Back home now, my hands are palsied and erratic. I'm lost, disoriented. I race through the split-second sequence over and over, is if

I could design a different ending, but I know I'm stuck with the truth – this is the law of nature I have embraced. This is Deism.

No, this is a curse. My hand, and everything it touches, is cursed. My life has been cursed. My family has been cursed. I had dismissed this possibility as ridiculous superstition years ago, but now it seems clear. Where will the madness go from here to find its home? I have no children, but the curse seems to fall on any life I touch, including feline. It will follow me to the grave.

I race through various scenarios to create an ending. I walk around my property, from saltwater pool to the garden, to the Airstream laboratory, to the locked Panopticon, to my house, and then back to the Airstream. I race, but where?

My state-of-the-art microscope is here in the Airstream where I feel most at home. For some reason, in my left hand, I am clutching my dead father's Browning pistol. In the curled and scarred fingers of my right hand, I palm the souvenir from my grandfather's library, a sculpted wooden shell. What comfort I find in a wooden conch or a loaded Browning handgun, I don't know. Yet, I let go of these relics, pausing to dictate my thoughts to the tape recorder, clutching them once again, over and over.

For some reason, a metal key pops into my mind. A universal key. Upon my humiliating ouster from my alma mater, research director Gunnar Pixley had given me a universal key to the entire Far West medical center, one that would open all doors, including the Breast Pavilion. At the time he gave it to me, I considered it an act of nostalgia, as it certainly would never be used. Now, however, deep from within, I feel "saudade," the wistfulness that clings to what's left of love after that love is gone. My path takes shape now. The work of the light microscope must continue.

I gulp down my latest version of soporific, hypnotic herbal tea. Sleep of some sort apparently followed, but then hypnagogic hallucinations took command as I tried to waken, though held in check by paralysis. I cannot move. I am frozen solid. Rage. Cures denied. Women die. Those like me who try to alter the course are killed along with them.

I believe I'm awake now, and I can move my body once again. Yes, still inside the Airstream. The paralysis is gone. I place the microcassette recorder, still running, in my shirt pocket to free both hands. I must unpack the crate that houses the microtome. The research must continue, and I will destroy anyone who gets in the way. I will kill those who have robbed me of my soul. I don't need the Browning pistol. I will slice them to pieces with the razor-sharp blade of the microtome. Suddenly, I see my enemies standing before me, all of them products of conception. I must get to the knife first.

I rush for the wooden crate, untwisting the wires that secure the lid in place. It's open. Packed separately in Styrofoam is the ultra-sharp blade that fits onto the device. I clinch the blunt side of the knife as I lift it from the Styrofoam. "Kill you," I scream. "I will kill you." I strike repeatedly at my faceless enemies until I hear screams. A peculiar thought enters my head – why am I using only one hand, my left, to kill these evildoers? Why is my right hand softly throbbing?

Horror. I was not awake when the slashing began. Now I am. Sleep fights. Sleep fights have done it once more, bridging the chasm between dreams and reality. Instead of killing my enemies, I have attacked myself. More accurately, I have attacked my right hand with my left.

Oddly, there is no pain, the sharpness dulled in my cursed claw. I look at my wound, several tiny jets of blood pumping vigorously from a deep cut that leaves three fingers completely transected at the base but held together by a bridge of flesh and bone. The index finger and thumb remain on the right hand. I cut a thin attachment that keeps the three fingers holding on to me for dear life. They plop onto the wooden crate, dead.

The calm is more secure. I am cut off from the world. Blood oozes between the fingers of my left hand that tries to hold back the hemorrhage from the right hand, but the blood still cascades over the moss, quenching the drought. I taste the sweet blood, a starving man in the desert sucking blood out of his own body. No, not for me – I let the blood cascade for a God Unknown. The fog is gone now. My body grows huge and light. It reaches for the sky, to be swallowed. I whisper, "I should have known it all along. The grass will grow out of me in a little while."

As you read this now, be you from Athens or Bethlehem, inspect my notes, for I have scraped a graphite stick across the peaks of the pulp, leaving trails for you to follow if you must.

Hickory, Tickery, start the clock.

39
EPILOGUE

From the *Matherville Daily Texan*, front page, below the fold:

Blaze Kills Former University Professor
Self-immolation suspected

A former professor of surgery was found dead Monday morning, victim of a fire that investigators say the man probably started himself. The deceased, Dr. Chase Callaway, 55, was a 1975 distinguished graduate of Far West Texas University College of Medicine where he went on to hold the highly esteemed Thatcher Nolan Taylor Chair of Surgical Breast Oncology. He subsequently resigned from the university and had been pursuing other interests at Permian-Charity Medical Center when an undisclosed illness prompted his retirement.

Fire Chief Lanny Tillman stated, "With no accelerants found at the scene, we are still in the process of sorting through the puzzling evidence. At this point, it appears that the doctor took his own life." Elaborating, he said, "The body was charred beyond recognition, much of it reduced to a peculiar ash, with identification made through an unburned portion of his right hand, where a recent surgical procedure allowed recognition of unique, identifying Z-shaped scars, in addition to the limited prints on three fingers. It appears to be a case of self-immolation in that Dr. Callaway was seated in a chair at what I'm told was his former office at the Breast Pavilion, with no evidence that he tried to escape a fire. To confuse the picture, the unburned fingers of his right hand were touching a Browning pistol, and we currently believe there was a self-inflicted gunshot, quickly after the fire was started.

"However, it's going to be hard to confirm the exact sequence of events due to this odd conversion of most the body to ashes, as with cremation, rather than the usual mummification when death is by fire. Still, one bullet had been fired from the Browning, and we found the bullet itself, partially melted, among the ashes on the chair. Fire started. Then bullet fired, causing death. Bullet lodged internally and emerges from the ashes. That's how I see it.

"Oddly enough, on the other armrest, there was a wooden seashell surrounded by ashes that we presume were the left hand, yet the shell itself was barely burned. Makes no sense. Furthermore, the room did not catch fire to any great degree, other than a charred ceiling above the deceased. So, we have a confusing picture that will be sorted out over the course of several days. We will provide an update once we know more."

University officials stated that the body was discovered by former colleague, Dr. Nola Kastl, who recognized the unique features of Dr. Callaway's deformed right hand. Unconfirmed reports indicate that Dr. Kastl also identified the doctor's distinctive handwriting in a note by the deceased who had been forced recently to write with his left hand. Contents of the note were not revealed, but apparently support the suicide theory.

Speculation that the scene represented the rare and controversial entity of "spontaneous human combustion," supported by minimal surrounding fire damage, was dismissed as urban myth by Chief Tillman who reiterated the point that a gun had been fired and that the bullet had to have lodged in the body shortly after catching fire, although the reverse order of events was conceivable. "Murder would be a more likely explanation than spontaneous human combustion," said Chief Tillman, "so we'll be interested to see what shows up in the very limited autopsy. A few structures are mummified rather than ash, so these parts will be examined closely."

Friends of Dr. Callaway were not available for comment, but his former departmental chairman, Porter Piscotel, M.D., Holder the Gretchen Studebaker Taylor Chair of Surgery, said the following: "Clearly, this is a sad day for the university family. As many recall, Chase Callaway was one of the most outstanding graduates from our medical school. Sadly, in his later years, he became plagued by mental health issues for which there was no effective treatment. This should not detract from the work he did while he was in his prime. The university has, indeed, lost a great teacher and a great researcher today." Dr. Piscotel further commented that plans would begin immediately to honor Dr. Callaway through the establishment of an endowed chair within the university.

From the obituary...:

Survivors include Ramona Callaway, mother, resident of Matherville; and, former wife Olivia Callaway, also of Matherville. Memorials should be sent to the: Chase Callaway Endowment Fund, Department of Surgery, c/o Henry Rapier, P.O. 5308, FWTSU, Matherville, TX.

. . .

Dot Glenndenning of Lost Mine, Texas, called her son Will to tell him about the tragic death of his old classmate, Chase Callaway. Many years ago, Will had dropped out of medical school during the third year, later becoming a financial analyst in the biotech industry, a science writer, and an avid reader of detective novels. When Dot's phone call came, Will was attending a business dinner at a restaurant in La Jolla, California, where he had difficulty hearing his mother's voice above the noise.

"He what? *He what?* How'd he— ee-gad, I can't imagine...no, I simply don't believe it, mother. I cannot believe it. I *refuse* to believe it."

END

ABOUT THE AUTHOR

John Albedo is an award-winning novelist whose stories take place in the south-central United States, often colored by a decade spent in Los Angeles. His current plans include completion of the trilogy collectively referred to as *The Brainbow Chronicles*.

Author's note: For publishing updates on
The Brainbow Chronicles, visit:
www.johnalbedo.com

NOTE FROM THE PUBLISHER

Word-of-mouth is crucial for any author to succeed. If you enjoyed *Cannibal Club*, please leave a review online—anywhere you are able. Even if it's just a sentence or two. It would make all the difference and would be very much appreciated.

Thanks!
John Albedo

We hope you enjoyed reading this title from:

BLACK ROSE
writing™

www.blackrosewriting.com

Subscribe to our mailing list – *The Rosevine* – and receive **FREE** books, daily deals, and stay current with news about upcoming releases and our hottest authors.
Scan the QR code below to sign up.

Already a subscriber? Please accept a sincere thank you for being a fan of Black Rose Writing authors.

View other Black Rose Writing titles at www.blackrosewriting.com/books and use promo code **PRINT** to receive a **20% discount** when purchasing.